Praise for Tom Bradby's

The Master of Rain

"A satisfying feast for the mind and the senses."
—*Charleston Post & Courier*

"This well-conceived and -rendered novel is a brooding tale of lust, murder and corruption . . . just what you want in a thriller." —*Star Tribune* (Minneapolis)

"Tom Bradby's *The Master of Rain* certainly makes him a candidate for eventual superstardom."
—*Fort Worth Star-Telegram*

"Like a Russian nesting doll, the plot's layers split to reveal new layers." —*Portsmouth Herald*

"This is an immensely atmospheric, gripping detective story with just the right mixture of exoticism, violence and romance." —*The Times* (London)

"Beneath the surface of this clever book, a thrilling yarn of murder and mayhem, we find a wise, richly layered, and utterly convincing portrait of what was the most evil and fatally fascinating of all the modern world's cities. No one has managed to bring Shanghai so alive, in all its ghastly splendor." —Simon Winchester

TOM BRADBY

The Master of Rain

Tom Bradby, a foreign correspondent for the British television network ITN, is the author of *The Master of Rain* and *The White Russian*. He has spent the last nine years covering British and American politics, as well as conflicts in China, Ireland, Kosovo, and Indonesia. While living in Hong Kong and writing this novel, Bradby researched historical records and archives of 1920s Shanghai. He now lives in London with his wife and three children.

ALSO BY TOM BRADBY

The White Russian

The Master of Rain

The Master of Rain

TOM BRADBY

Anchor Books
A Division of Random House, Inc.
New York

FIRST ANCHOR BOOKS EDITION, APRIL 2003

Copyright © 2002 by Tom Bradby

All rights reserved under International and Pan-American Copyright Conventions.
Published in the United States by Anchor Books, a division of
Random House, Inc., New York. Originally published in hardcover
in the United States by Doubleday, a division of
Random House, Inc., New York, in 2002.

Anchor Books and colophon are registered trademarks
of Random House, Inc.

The Library of Congress has cataloged the Doubleday edition as follows:
Bradby, Tom.
The master of rain / Tom Bradby.
p. cm.
ISBN 0-385-50397-0
1. Police—China—Shanghai—Fiction. 2. British—China—Fiction.
3. Shanghai (China)—Fiction. I. Title.
PR6102.R33 M37 2002
823'.914—dc21
2001042199

Anchor ISBN: 0-375-71333-6

Map designed by Jeffrey L. Ward

www.anchorbooks.com

Printed in the United States of America
10 9 8 7 6 5 4 3 2 1

To Claudia, Jack, Louisa, and Sam.

And Mum and Dad.

Thanks to Mark Lucas, the world's greatest agent;

Bill Scott-Kerr and Jason Kaufman,

a supportive, clever, and extremely insightful editorial team;

and, most of all, to Claudia, my inspirational wife.

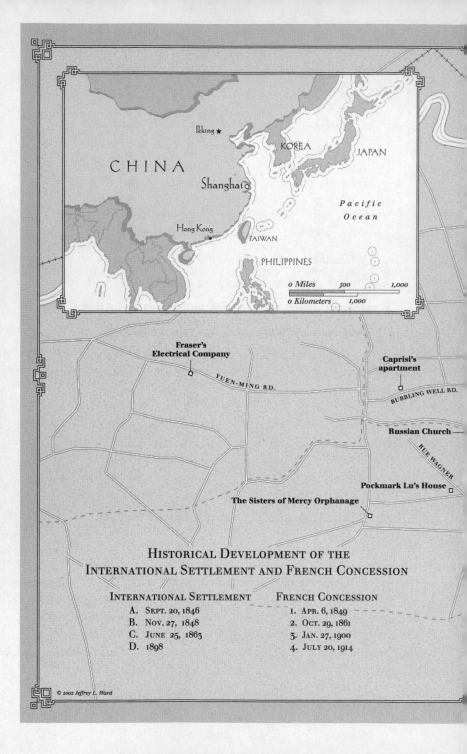

Peking ★

CHINA

KOREA

JAPAN

Shanghai

*Pacific
Ocean*

Hong Kong

TAIWAN

PHILIPPINES

0 Miles   500   1,000

0 Kilometers   1,000

Fraser's
Electrical Company

Caprisi's
apartment

YUEN-MING RD.

BUBBLING WELL RD.

Russian Church

RUE WAGNER

Pockmark Lu's House

The Sisters of Mercy Orphanage

HISTORICAL DEVELOPMENT OF THE
INTERNATIONAL SETTLEMENT AND FRENCH CONCESSION

INTERNATIONAL SETTLEMENT
A. SEPT. 20, 1846
B. NOV. 27, 1848
C. JUNE 25, 1863
D. 1898

FRENCH CONCESSION
1. APR. 6, 1849
2. OCT. 29, 1861
3. JAN. 27, 1900
4. JULY 20, 1914

© 2002 Jeffrey L. Ward

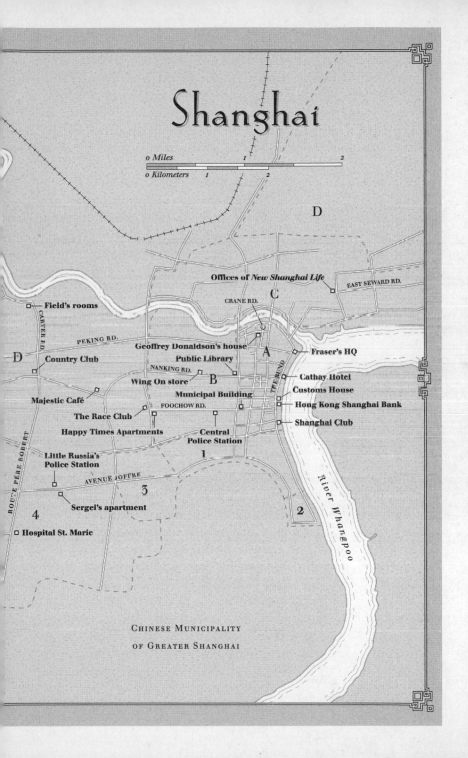

Shanghai

o Miles   1   2

o Kilometers   1   2

D

Offices of *New Shanghai Life*

EAST SEWARD RD.

CRANE RD.

C

Field's rooms

CARTER RD.

PEKING RD.

Geoffrey Donaldson's house

Fraser's HQ

A

D

Country Club

Public Library

NANKING RD.

B

Wing On store

Cathay Hotel

Customs House

Majestic Café

Municipal Building

FOOCHOW RD.

Hong Kong Shanghai Bank

The Race Club

Shanghai Club

Happy Times Apartments

Central Police Station

1

Little Russia's Police Station

ROUTE PÈRE ROBERT

AVENUE JOFFRE

3

Sergei's apartment

4

2

Hospital St. Marie

River Whangpoo

THE BUND

CHINESE MUNICIPALITY

OF GREATER SHANGHAI

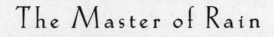

The Master of Rain

Shanghai
1926

———

ACCORDING TO CHINESE LEGEND,

AFFAIRS IN THE "OTHER WORLD"

ARE MANAGED BY BUREAUS OR MINISTRIES.

THE MOST SIGNIFICANT OF THESE IS

THE MINISTRY OF THUNDER AND STORM,

PRESIDED OVER BY THE MASTER OF RAIN.

IN THE CLOSE, INTENSE HEAT

OF THE SHANGHAI SUMMER,

THE MASTER OF RAIN STANDS ABOVE

THE DARK CLOUDS THAT HANG OVER THE CITY,

BROODING UPON ITS FATE. THE RAIN IS HIS GIFT,

AND THUS HE CONTROLS THE FERTILITY OF THE LAND

AND THE PROSPERITY OF ITS INHABITANTS.

HE IS AN OMNIPOTENT AND CAPRICIOUS

BENEFACTOR—OR TORMENTOR.

One

F ield felt like a lobster being brought slowly to the boil. For a moment he closed his eyes against the heat and the humidity and the still, heavy air. Only the clatter of typewriters hinted at energy and motion.

He wiped the sweat from his forehead with the sleeve of his jacket and looked again at the two figures gesticulating behind the frosted glass. They were still arguing, and he had the uncomfortable feeling that it might be about him.

Macleod's secretary had stopped typing and was appraising him with a steady gaze. "You're new," she said, pushing her half-moon glasses up from the end of her nose.

"Yes." Field nodded.

The woman wasn't showing any sign of discomfort, despite being three times his size and wearing a cardigan. "Take your jacket off if you're hot," she said.

Field smiled, glancing up at the fan. It turned lethargically, with no discernible effect on the air beneath it.

He put his hands in his pockets. Macleod's office door had the words *Superintendent Macleod, Head of Crime* engraved in the glass, and although it was not Field's position to say, the security of tenure this implied confirmed what he had already heard about the confidence of the man.

Field looked up at the fan again and the paint that was peeling off the ceiling above it. For a moment the sun broke through the thick blanket of cloud that had been loitering over the city for days, spilling light onto the desks at the far end of the room. Despite the dark wood paneling, the tall windows made the place seem less gloomy than the Special Branch office upstairs.

He tugged the corner of his collar away from his throat and wiped the sweat from his skin with his index finger. He'd never imagined heat like this.

Macleod's secretary was still staring at him. "How are you enjoying Shanghai?"

"Fine, thanks."

She started typing again, fat fingers pounding the big metal keys, then stopped and looked at him. "Slept with a Russian yet? Paid for a princess?"

Macleod's door opened and a small, lean man with dark, slicked-back hair walked past him. "Caprisi?" Field asked, but whatever had been going on in there, it had left Caprisi in no mood to talk. He headed for his desk, took his jacket from the back of the chair, pulled open a drawer, slipped a pistol into the leather holster that hung from his shoulder, and marched toward the lift.

Field turned to face Macleod, who stood at his office door, toying with the chain around his neck. He was a burly man, almost bald, with a thin crown of gray hair. "You're Field?" His voice was deep, with a broad Scottish accent.

"Yes, sir."

"Follow him down."

Field hesitated.

"Well, go on, man, what are you waiting for?"

Field got into the elevator after Caprisi and hit the button for the ground floor. It cranked into action with a jolt and a loud crack, and descended, as always, so hesitantly that it would have been quicker to crawl down the stairs on all fours.

Not that anyone wanted to take the stairs in this heat.

"You're new?" the American asked.

Field nodded. "Yes."

"Still a Griffin."

"No." Officially, he'd finished his training a month ago and had spent the intervening time being bored to death with routine office tasks. He was grateful to get out. Granger had told him that his job was to check that the murder was not politically motivated and keep an eye on the Crime Branch.

Caprisi shook his head dolefully before looking down at his shoes. Field noticed how carefully they'd been polished—just as his own had been ever since he'd come to the Far East and been relieved of the need to do anything like that for himself. He remembered his father's obsession with his lack of military discipline and allowed himself a smile.

The American moved quickly through the lobby, his leather soles slapping the stone floor. Outside, Field found himself squinting against the sun before it once again disappeared behind a bank of dark cloud.

A Buick with a long brown body and a bright yellow hood stood at the curb, its engine running. As he climbed into the near side, Field noticed there were three bullet holes in the panel by the door.

"Where's Chen?" Caprisi asked the driver, leaning forward against the scuffed leather seat.

The driver was an old man dressed in a white tunic. He turned and shook his toothless head.

Caprisi settled back and waited, looking out of his window, trying to contain his impatience, rapping the glass with his knuckles. Field saw that he had a large gold ring on the index finger of his right hand.

"Come on, Chen," he said under his breath. "What's he doing?" he asked the driver, although, so far as Field could tell, the man spoke no English.

Field turned to see a tall Chinese emerging from the entrance of the Central Police Station. He wore a full-length khaki mackintosh and carried a Thompson machine gun. He climbed onto the running board and ducked his head through the open window.

"This is a present from Granger," Caprisi explained, pointing at Field. "He's a Griffin," he said, ignoring Field's earlier intimation that his training was complete.

Chen seemed less put out by Field's apparent intrusion than Caprisi and reached across to shake his hand before barking an order at the driver and slapping the roof. He remained on the running board as they lurched forward, the gun banging against the bodywork. Field felt for his own pistol in his jacket pocket, suddenly aware of the rapid beating of his heart.

They moved a hundred yards down Foochow Road. Field looked out past Chen at the tide of humanity sweeping down the sidewalk beside them, until they were brought to a halt once more. Caprisi leaned forward to try to see what was causing the holdup, then sat back with a sigh.

"Granger told me you're from Chicago," Field said.

Caprisi turned to him, a thin smile playing across his lips. "Granger is the intelligence chief, so he should know."

Field didn't respond. As head of the Special Branch, and thus Field's boss, Granger was responsible for the suppression of communism in the city and the maintenance of order. He ran informers and conducted what American journalists called "Black Propaganda." Caprisi and Macleod worked in the CID—the Crime Branch, or C.1. Their responsibility was "ordinary decent crime." Murders. Armed robberies. The two branches were the most powerful departments in the force and they fought constantly.

"What brought you here?" Field asked.

Caprisi's face was impassive. "How long have you been in Shanghai, Field?"

"About three months."

"And you've not yet learned the golden rule?" Caprisi smiled again and Field realized he looked like a Caucasian version of Chen—thick dark hair, bushy eyebrows, a narrow nose, and an easy, sly smile. The sleeves of his dark jacket were pulled up above his elbows, revealing broad forearms, and bushy hair spilled out of his open-necked shirt. "Take my advice: never ask anyone in Shanghai about their past. Especially not a lady."

Field turned to the window as an old beggar woman thrust

a bundle of rags toward him. As Chen clubbed her aside with
the butt of his Thompson, he saw that the bundle contained a
baby.

"Take it easy, Chen," Caprisi said, almost to himself. He
leaned forward impatiently once more. "What's the holdup?"
he shouted. Chen leaned through the window and shook his
head.

"What's your name, Field?"

"Richard. But most people call me 'Field.'"

"Dick?"

Field grimaced.

"You don't like 'Dick'?"

"No one calls me that."

"What's wrong with it?"

Field looked at him, smiling. "There's nothing wrong with
it, Caprisi. It's just that no one calls me that. But if you want
to, be my guest."

"Spirit." The American smiled approvingly. "You'll need
that here."

"What's your name?"

"My name is Caprisi."

They had stopped again and could see now that a crowd
had gathered in the middle of the street. Caprisi opened his
door. Chen and Field followed as he shoved his way through.

The crowd parted reluctantly to reveal a scrawny man
lying flat on the road, a pool of congealed blood beneath his
head and neck. The upper part of his body was bare and still
glistening with sweat. The rickshaw, which had once been his
livelihood, had been crushed like a pile of matchsticks. For a
moment they all looked at him silently. Field knew enough
about the city to be certain that this random accident was
likely to plunge a large, extended family into destitution.
Caprisi was checking the man's neck for a pulse.

"What happened?" Caprisi demanded before switching to
Chinese. Field only understood the last instruction: "Move
aside, move aside."

On the way back to the car, Caprisi asked, "How's your Shanghainese?"

"I'm getting there," Field said, walking fast to keep up.

"Congratulations." Caprisi's mood had soured. "Hit by a car. Oldsmobile. Westerners, who didn't bother to stop."

Their driver edged through the crowd before hurtling down Foochow Road to an apartment building opposite the racecourse. There was another police car parked outside, with two uniformed officers standing guard by a sign saying *Happy Times*. They nodded as Caprisi and Chen headed into the ornate lobby. An elderly Chinese in a red uniform with gold brocade sat behind a marble desk. He smiled at them.

"Field, come down and talk to him later, will you?" Caprisi ordered.

"Top floor," one of the policemen said as they stepped into the lift.

Caprisi hit the button for the third floor and the lift began to move. It was swifter and smoother than their own, with polished wood panels and mirrors. Field tried not to look at himself, but Caprisi moved closer to the mirror, unselfconsciously removing something from his teeth. Chen caught Field's eye and smiled. He was holding the Thompson down by his side, its magazine resting against his knee.

The top landing was spacious, with two doors separated by a gold mirror. Another uniformed officer was standing guard by the door on the right.

Inside, the main room was not as big as Field had anticipated, but the flat was a far cry from his own quarters. The wooden floor had been recently polished. One wall was dominated by a long sofa covered in a white cotton sheet and silk cushions in a kaleidoscope of colors. There was a handsome Chinese chest beside it, upon which sat a gramophone. A rattan chair had been pushed up against the French windows, which opened onto a small balcony.

A bookcase in the corner was lined with embossed leather spines and framed photographs.

Field pulled at his collar again to ease the pressure on his neck before following Caprisi through to the bedroom at the far end of a short corridor.

He recoiled at the smell and then the sight of blood on white sheets, and tried to shield this reaction from Caprisi. A Chinese plainclothes detective he did not recognize was dusting the bedside table with fingerprint powder. A photographer was lining up a shot and there was the sudden thump of a flashgun.

"Jesus," Caprisi said quietly.

The woman lay in the middle of the big brass bed that occupied most of the room. Her wrists and ankles were handcuffed to each corner, her body half-turned, as if twisting to be free. She was wearing silk lingerie: a beige camisole and panties, a garter belt and stockings. She had been stabbed repeatedly in the stomach and vulva and had bled profusely. The blood was now dry; it had taken some time for her death to be discovered.

Caprisi made his way round to the far side of the bed, next to the wardrobe. He glanced through a separate door into the bathroom.

"Don't touch anything."

Field nodded, without moving or taking his eyes from the woman's face. She had short blond hair, and her lips were still pink with lipstick. Her mouth was half-open, giving the disconcerting impression that her face was distorted with pleasure.

"Jesus," Caprisi said again.

Field did not respond.

"Ever seen a dead body like this?"

Field shook his head.

Caprisi leaned forward, examining her. "Good-looking girl." He sat close to the woman's waist. Field tried not to look at the patch of dark hair, which became visible as Caprisi took hold of the top band of her panties and began to lower them, until they were around her knees. The corpse was stiff and he grimaced with the effort. "She's been dead some time," he said. Field felt the dryness in his throat as Caprisi leaned down to take a closer look, using his fingers to try to open the gap between her thighs. There was dried blood everywhere, most of the sheet a dark red.

Caprisi wiped his fingers on the lower part of her leg, then pulled the panties back up. He stood, looking down at the body, frowning. "Hard to tell," he said, more to himself than Field. "But I'm not sure . . ." He looked up. "What do you think?"

Field shook his head. "About what?"

"I don't think there's been an assault. A sexual one."

Field didn't answer.

"She's still got her underwear on," Caprisi said.

"That doesn't mean she wasn't assaulted."

"True, but there's no sign of any semen on the camisole, underwear, or stockings. None that I can see." He walked past Field toward the door. He looked angry. "We'd better get Maretsky down here," he said, stepping out into the corridor. "Chen, get Maretsky, will you, and tell him to get a move on."

Caprisi returned to the other side of the room. "So tell me about the woman, Field. Field?"

"Yes."

"Are you all right?"

"I'm fine."

"You're bunching your fists."

Field unclenched his hands.

"Tell me about her."

"In what way?"

"What's her name again?"

"Lena Orlov," Field said. "Granger asked Records whether the address rang a bell and Danny pulled out the file on Orlov straight away. The photograph matches. I can see it's her."

Caprisi frowned. "Tell me about her."

"I'm not sure if I know all that—"

"Then why has Granger given us the pleasure of your company?"

"The file is not extensive."

"Save me having to look at it."

Field took a deep breath. "Suspected Bolshevik sympathizer. Attended meetings at the *New Shanghai Life*. Lived here. But we don't have much more than that."

Caprisi had been eyeing the white photograph frame beside the bed. He picked it up, took a closer look, then threw it across to Field. Field noticed how he gritted his teeth when he was angry, making the muscles in his cheeks twitch. He could see the American suspected that Special Branch had a separate agenda.

The picture was of a family, seated formally on a lawn in front of a large country house. The mother was a thin, elegant woman; the father sat stiffly in military uniform. There were five children, three boys in white sailor suits, and two blond girls in pretty white dresses, leaning against their mother's knee. Lena had been the elder of the two girls. Field, suddenly somber, put the picture facedown on the bed. The body in front of him had been transformed suddenly by this glimpse of a past.

"Her father was a tsarist officer in Mother Russia, and you think she's a Bolshevik." Caprisi shook his head. "You guys should do your research."

The Chinese detective was still on his knees, brushing the bedside table. Caprisi put a hand on his shoulder. "How are we doing?"

"The cuffs are clean. Everywhere else is heavy."

"The cuffs could be evidence."

There was one window in the room, high and small. Caprisi stood on the bedside table to open it and stuck his head out. "Shares a balcony with the woman next door; the girl who found her. Go and talk to her, will you, Field? And everyone else in the building."

Two

Field didn't need any encouragement to get out of the bedroom, and he breathed a little more easily in the hallway. He tugged at his collar again and wiped the sweat from his forehead with the sleeve of his jacket. He wished he could afford a lightweight suit like the one Caprisi wore. He had been grateful to his father for the gift of his Sunday best, but it was warm enough to be comfortable in a Yorkshire winter and highly unsuitable for the stifling summer heat of the Far East.

Field knocked once on the door opposite and waited. In the few minutes they'd been inside, the bulb in the hallway light had blown.

He heard movement, but no one came, so he knocked again.

A shadow moved along the crack at the bottom of the door and it was suddenly pulled open.

The woman was standing with her weight on one leg, light from a window behind her caressing her thighs through the thin white cotton of her dressing gown. Field could not see her face clearly and took a step back.

She was frowning at him.

"I'm from the Shanghai police."

"You don't say."

She was tall—not quite as tall as he was, but still close to six feet. Luxuriant dark hair spilled over her shoulders and hung down to her breasts. Her gown was pulled tight, showing off the supple curves of her body.

Her nose was small, her cheeks curved in a manner that made her seem warm, even if her dark eyebrows were knotted together in a frown. But what struck Field most was her skin. Even in this light—and she had half turned now—he could see it was brown and smooth, making his own appear as white as alabaster.

"Can I come in?"

"Why?"

Field cleared his throat. He tried to smile, but wasn't sure if he'd managed it. "It would be easier than standing in the corridor."

"Easier for you or for me?" She spoke English well, her Russian accent faint.

"It will only take a few minutes of your time."

"I'm not dressed, Inspector."

"I won't look," he said, but she didn't smile and he quickly regretted it. "And I'm not an inspector."

A glimmer of amusement seemed to stir at the corners of her lips. "I can see that." She stepped back to allow him in.

The apartment was the same size as the one next door. The wooden floorboards had a rug over them, and, instead of a sofa, two old, threadbare chairs faced each other in front of a low Chinese table. There were pictures on the wall—crudely painted Russian landscapes in thick oil—a mirror, and, as in Lena Orlov's main room, a bookcase, although this one had at least twice the number of books and photographs.

Field stepped through the open doors to the balcony and looked down over the racecourse. A line of horses was being led along the track in the distance. A tram rattled noisily past as the clock on the tower above the clubhouse struck two, audible despite the wail of a police siren somewhere close.

He turned back. "Very nice," he said.

She was standing in the middle of the room, still appraising him frankly, although, he thought, with less hostility now. Or perhaps that was his imagination. He saw that she was a strong woman, the veins and muscles standing out in her forearms as she clasped her shoulders. For reasons that were not

entirely clear to him, the plight of this woman, how she'd
got here and how she could afford to live like this, was, for
Field, suddenly and confusingly a cause for concern. Everyone
always talked of the White Russians and the circumstances
into which they were forced, but their predicament had not,
until now, seemed real.

He was standing next to the bookcase and could see a col-
lection of Russian books behind a photograph that was similar
to the one in Lena Orlov's apartment. The father, also in military uniform, sat this time in front of a less grand house,
without a wife and with only two children, almost identical
girls in white dresses with long dark hair, smiling shyly at the
camera. They all held each other, displaying an easy warmth.
The elder of the two girls had draped an arm protectively
around the younger. Field thought again of the contrast
between Lena Orlov's squalid demise and the evidence of her
own happy past. He felt like a voyeur. He coughed. "You read
a lot?" he asked, gesturing at the books, which were all in
Cyrillic script.

The girl did not smile.

"My father once said every man should read *Anna Karen-
ina*," Field said.

"How wise."

He cleared his throat again. It seemed drier than ever.
"I'm sorry," he said. "You found the body?"

"Yes."

"How?"

Her eyes narrowed. "What do you mean how?"

"I mean you . . . went around to see Miss Orlov?"

She shook her head irritably. "I went to ask for some milk,
but there was no answer."

"So how did you get in?"

"The door was open."

Field looked at her. "Did she usually leave her door open?"

"I have no idea."

"You didn't know her well, then?"

"Not really."

"What does 'not really' mean?"

"It means no."

"You weren't friends?"

She was staring at him, her hands still clutching her shoulders. She straightened, shifting her weight. "We nodded at each other on the landing, that was all."

Field glanced at the books and photographs. "It seems odd," he said, "the two of you living next door to each other, similar backgrounds, strange city, but not knowing each other."

"If it seems odd to you, Officer," she said, "then how little you understand."

Field tried to hide his embarrassment by turning again to the family photograph. Of course, two women living here from similar, proud backgrounds might have had every reason to avoid each other.

He opened his notebook and took the old fountain pen his father had given him from the top pocket of his jacket. "I'm sorry," he said.

"Sorry for what?"

She'd sat down, her head bent, hands now clasped around her body.

"I don't wish to take up too much of your time. Could I just take your name?"

She looked up. "What's yours?"

The faint smile was back, her fragility evaporating.

"My name is Field."

"That's not much of a name." Her voice was husky, like a singer who has spent too much time performing in smoke-filled nightclubs.

"Richard. But most people call me 'Field.'"

"How unromantic."

Field gestured with his pen. "Can I take your name?"

"Medvedev."

He waited. "And your first name?"

"I don't think we're on first-name terms, do you?"

Field wasn't certain how to respond to her teasing, and couldn't tell whether it was gentle or barbed.

"Natasha," she said. "Natasha Medvedev. But most people call me Natasha."

"You found the body about an hour ago?"

"Yes." She removed her arms from her shoulders, and for a moment her dressing gown parted sufficiently to reveal the curve of her breasts. His face reddened as he realized she saw the direction of his gaze.

"You went around for milk?"

"I'd run out."

"So you knocked, but there was no answer?"

"That's right, Officer."

"There was no answer, so you went in?"

"We've just been through this."

Field looked at her. "I'm sorry. Perhaps I'm being stupid. You went around to get milk, you knocked, there was no response, so . . . then what?"

She didn't answer.

"It's just, if you hardly knew the woman, it would seem more logical to turn around and come back to your own flat."

Natasha was looking at him as if he were the stupidest man she'd ever met. "The door was open."

"So you went in to see if you could borrow some milk?"

She didn't bother to answer.

"Then what?"

"Then I found the body."

Field stopped writing. "How did you do that?"

"Inspector, I think this conversation has gone as far as—"

"I'm not an inspector."

She sighed. "No, well . . ."

"Was it the smell?"

She screwed up her face in disgust.

"It's just," Field said slowly, "that I don't see how you got to the bedroom when the kitchen is on the other side of the living room." He pointed. "The same layout as here."

Natasha Medvedev stared at him, and he held her gaze. He had no idea what he saw there. Contempt, perhaps. What he didn't understand was that it would have been very easy to make up a convincing lie, and she wasn't bothering to do so.

Field was still standing close to the photographs, and he took a step toward the bookshelf as one at the back caught his eye. Natasha was standing on what looked like the dance floor of a nightclub. She wore a figure-hugging dress with a plunging neckline, her unfashionably long hair tumbling over her shoulder just as it did now, her face impassive. By contrast, the woman next to her—not in the same league as her friend and with too much makeup, but an open, friendly face— was smiling.

Field held it up, pointing to the second woman. "Lena Orlov."

Natasha Medvedev shook her head. "No, another friend." As she said it, she was transformed again, clutching herself once more, dropping her head, so that her hair fell forward.

"Oh God," she muttered under her breath.

Field did not know what to do. He took a pace toward her, then another. He shut his notebook and slipped it back into the pocket of his jacket.

"I'm sorry, Miss Medvedev."

She did not respond.

"Is there anything I can get you?"

She shook her head, gathering her hair at the back of her neck with her hand.

"There's nothing I can do for you?"

She looked up. "You can go away."

Field hesitated again, wishing that her eyes betrayed something other than bored hostility.

"Of course. Thank you for your time."

"It's been my pleasure."

"I doubt that."

She shrugged.

Field stepped out into the corridor, pulling the door quietly shut. He breathed in deeply, allowing himself a moment's peace before returning to the savagery of the apartment next door.

He put his hands in his pockets.

Was it just that he couldn't fault her, that she was physically perfect? Is that all it was?

Caprisi was standing by the French windows in the living room, looking out toward the racecourse. He turned as Field came in. "Chen's already been downstairs," he said. "There are two couples below, both away in New York. We'll have a talk with the doorman in a minute. Chen says the flats on this floor belong to Lu Huang. Pockmark Huang."

Field nodded. "I see."

"Do you?"

"Yes."

"You understand?"

"Yes. So . . . both these women belong to Lu also." Field tried to dispel a sense of discomfort at the combination of this news and the recollection of Natasha Medvedev in her white dressing gown. Why wasn't she dressed when it was past lunchtime?

"There is no sign of the murder weapon," Caprisi said. "The handcuffs have been wiped clean, so . . ." He turned to Field, staring right through him. "Somebody has been cleaning up. Somebody has been in here after the murder and cleaned up." The American looked up. "What did the woman say?" he asked, but his demeanor suggested he already knew the answer.

"She was not helpful," Field said quietly.

Caprisi turned to the window and looked out toward the clock tower, wrestling with himself. "Fuck it."

Maretsky emerged from the bedroom, blinking through his small thick glasses. His hair was even longer and scruffier than it had been when he'd come down to lecture the new recruits. Once a professor of philosophy at St. Petersburg University, Maretsky had found a niche here as an expert in the methods of Shanghai's criminals. His official title was head of Modus Operandi and from his desk in the main police library and records office, he assisted both the Crime Branch and the Special Branch. He brought his philosophical and psychological training to his work and had somehow managed to command wide respect in an intensely macho force. His insightful lectures had been, Field thought, the highlight of the official police training.

Maretsky took a couple of paces toward the window. "She's in sexually appealing underwear." His Russian accent was as faint as Natasha Medvedev's. "She's handcuffed to the bed, so that she cannot move. There's no sign of a struggle, but nor is there any indication of assault, or even of consensual intercourse. As you say, no semen on her panties or on the bed." He shrugged. "Of course, there's a lot of blood."

"So what does that mean?"

"Is it what she liked?" Maretsky asked, glancing at the photographs on the bookshelf. "The handcuffs, I mean. And the underwear. Or is it a man's sexual fantasy? A man whom she is in love with, or serves in some way."

"They had an argument, lovers' quarrel?" Caprisi asked. "He ties her up, then they have a fight?"

"No." Maretsky shook his head emphatically. "This must be about a much deeper, more virulent rage. Look at the body. We are probably seeing rage against women in general, not Lena Orlov in particular."

Field thought of the woman lying on the bed and the disconcerting appearance of pleasure that death had left playing on her lips. He found himself imagining the terror on her face as the knife was plunged into her, again and again.

"Chen says," Caprisi went on, "that this flat and the one next door belong to Pockmark Lu. And therefore, presumably, the women in it."

Maretsky said, "She was obviously a . . . you know, high-class."

"She was his woman?"

"I'm sure he would have had her, but she may have had other uses."

"Hiring her out?"

Maretsky shrugged. "A gift, perhaps."

Field was struggling, and failing, to accept the idea of Natasha Medvedev submitting herself to a man against her will.

"It's certainly vicious," Maretsky said, almost to himself.

No one answered.

Maretsky was carrying a small leather briefcase—almost like a lady's handbag—and he tucked it under his arm and moved toward the door. "We'll talk later," he said.

"Has there been anything similar?" Caprisi asked.

Maretsky shook his head. "Nothing that springs to mind. I'll check with the French police."

For a few moments after Maretsky's departure, they stood in silence, Field reflecting on how quiet it was here—a far cry from his own quarters with the endless grunting and bellowing that went on at all times of the day and night.

He could not imagine what kind of man could have done this.

"Check this room," Caprisi said. "I'll do the others."

"Looking for anything in particular?"

"Use your head."

Caprisi went through to the kitchen and Field heard him opening and shutting the cupboards. He looked about before moving the gramophone and opening the Chinese chest beneath. It was empty. He stared out of the window, running his finger through the condensation that had gathered on the glass since their arrival. The panes were small, the narrow metal bars between them painted white. The building must have been completed recently, because the humidity and heat of the summer frayed the paintwork of most buildings very quickly.

He turned to the bookcase and pulled out a tall, thin, dark leather photograph album.

The pictures were similar to the ones in the frames—a testament not just to a lost era but to a vanquished world. This was the chronicle of Lena Orlov's life before the revolution had forced her from Russia, and Field could see immediately, much more vividly than from a thousand books or newspaper articles, how painful the loss of this past had been.

The photographs seemed to recall a pastoral idyll: a large country house, a lake, a summerhouse, a magnificent wooden yacht, a father who looked severe and a mother who smiled in every picture. Field had read that most of the Russian aristocrats with money had fled to Europe, but the Orlovs, too, had clearly been wealthy.

There was a photograph of a little girl whom Field assumed to be Lena, with a dog and a woman he thought must have been her nanny. It was the last picture in the book, taken by a sledge in the snow, in front of the house, a number of suitcases visible on the shaded, iron-framed veranda in the background. Had this been the end, the departure?

He closed the album and put it back, wondering what had become of the brothers and sister who would be called upon at a time like this to come around and sort through her effects.

He thought how hard it would be for any sibling to accept that their sister had died like this. Or were they dead, too?

There was a large leather-bound volume that looked like a Bible next to the photograph album, and thinking of his father, the religious fanatic, Field took it down and opened it, only to discover that a large hole had been carved inside, creating enough space to hide a small notebook.

Lena Orlov—he assumed it was Lena—had written in a neat, flowing hand, in ink, and each line contained a date, the name of a ship (he assumed), and a destination. The last entry was: *26th June. SS Saratoga—Liverpool.*

That was in just over a week's time.

Not all of the destinations were in the United Kingdom. Some of the ships had been bound for Amsterdam, Bordeaux, Antwerp, Calais, and Kiel. It did not say what they had been carrying, nor was there any indication as to why they had been listed.

At the bottom of the page, Lena had written: *All payments in ledger two.*

Caprisi came back in and Field handed him the leather volume and the notebook. He glanced down the list. "Where did you find this?"

"On the bookshelf."

"Shipments," Caprisi said.

"Yes, but of what?"

The American shrugged.

"Something to do with Lu?"

"She must have had a reason for hiding the notes. What is this . . . 'payments in ledger two'?"

Field heard the sound of someone running on the stairs. A second later Chen burst into the room. "The doorman—he's been taken."

Three

aprisi didn't hesitate, and Field followed as they crashed down the stairs, not certain what Chen had meant. The door at the bottom slammed so hard against the wall that one of the panes of glass shattered. They ran through the lobby and out into a burst of sunshine. Caprisi pushed Field into the back of the Buick, and Chen resumed his position on the running board, this time without the machine gun, which lay on the floor in front of them. Caprisi picked it up and put it on the seat, then pulled out his own pistol. Field did the same and found that his hand was shaking.

Chen shouted at the driver in Chinese, gesticulating at the black car in front. "Follow it," Field heard him say. They drove fast down Foochow Road in the direction of the Central Police Station. The driver swerved to the right in front of an oncoming tram, the heavy car tilting violently. Field found himself inches away from an advertisement on the front of the tram extolling the virtues of the Majestic Café at 254 Bubbling Well Road—*The largest cabaret in Shanghai.*

They were almost up on a sidewalk as they passed the police station, then once again returned to the center of the street, missing a dog that yelped and darted into the crowd and an old man carrying vegetables in baskets suspended at either end of a long pole.

Just before they reached the pale stone grandeur of the Municipal Building, the driver turned right into Kiangsi Road, pushing the Buick as fast as it would go and honking as he crossed Avenue Edward VII into the wider, quieter boulevards of the French Concession. The distinctive towers of the Russian church were visible in the distance.

The car's suspension was not all its makers promised, and Field struggled to get a clear view of who or what they were following. As they reached Boulevard des Deux Républiques and the boundary of the old Chinese city, the rising tide of oncoming humanity forced them to slow dramatically, until it was clear that they'd make better progress on foot.

"All right," Caprisi shouted, hammering the door, before clambering out, the Thompson in one hand, his pistol in the other. "Chen!" He held up the machine gun as the Chinese disappeared into the crowd.

There were hundreds of rickshaws, plowing through a milling, whirling throng, jostling and pushing toward the marketplace. Occasionally, Field would see a fedora or catch a glimpse of a long tunic and bright white shoes—the garb of the dandy—but he was trying not to lose Caprisi, who was concentrating on Chen.

The streets were narrow, the distinctive curved roofs blocking out the light, the lanterns hung beneath them below the level of their heads, so that they were forced now and then to weave and duck.

Field realized, to his surprise, that he was still clutching the gun. He put it by his side and tried to relax, but it was impossible to make easy headway, and he could feel his own aggression increasing, along with that of those around him.

He tripped over a dog and knocked into a woman who was carrying a basket of vegetables on her shoulder, and she cursed him until he swung around and she saw the barrel of his Smith & Wesson revolver.

For a moment he stared at her old, wizened, hostile face and the goods that were now all over the dusty road. He turned, feeling a moment of rising panic as he failed to locate Caprisi. Then he spotted the American detective's head bobbing from side to side ahead of him.

Field tried to speed up, losing Caprisi again as they entered a narrow, dark alley and then almost bumping into him and Chen as they emerged at the edge of a square. Field's height allowed him to get a clear view of what was happening ahead.

There was a crowd of hundreds, drawn back to the edges of the marketplace, watching as a man drew a long metal sword and put his foot on the neck of the doorman, who had been stripped, his red and gold tunic lying in the dust. Even above the hubbub, Field could hear his whimper and feel his fear. His own heart was pumping; sweat was stinging his eyes.

He wiped it away with his sleeve again, his hand still shaking. Caprisi lunged forward, but Chen stopped him, a strong hand on the American's shoulder. He was shaking his head.

There was a hush in the crowd now, the blade bright as it was raised above the man cowering in the dust.

And then, before Field could credit that any of this was happening, it swung down, and the images before him seemed suddenly disjointed and unreal. He heard the thud as the head hit the ground and rolled, sending a puff of dust into the air.

There was an animal grunt, full of suppressed rage, and it took Field a few moments to become aware that Chen was wrestling with Caprisi. Voices were raised in anger as they thrashed into others in the crowd.

Chen lunged and caught the American off guard, pushing him into a nearby alley. The American swung wildly, but Chen was bigger and stronger and had Caprisi pinned up against a mud wall.

"Not now," Chen said through gritted teeth. "Not now."

"It's never—"

"Leave it."

They held each other, highlighted by thin rays of sunshine that shone through the dust hanging in the air. Field stood a few feet away, the smell of human feces from a honey cart catching in his nostrils.

Chen released his colleague. Caprisi dusted himself down. "Welcome to Shanghai, Dick," he said.

. . . .

"You're not in England now," Caprisi said as they got into the lift.

Field had no idea what he was talking about.

"Take your jacket off. You won't be impressing Granger."

Field would have removed his jacket if his shirt hadn't been soaked in sweat. His tongue felt like rough stone and his head was pounding from exertion, heat, and shock.

"Your place or mine?" Caprisi hit the button for the third floor and leaned back against the side as the lift lurched into action. He'd barely broken sweat. "You might as well come up to Crime," he went on. "Or is it down to Crime?" He shrugged when it was clear he wasn't going to get a reaction. "You can take the prints to the bureau."

Field was trying to forget about the way the doorman's head had rolled forward through the dirt, blood from the severed artery in his neck spurting out into the crowd. "What are we going to do?"

"About what?"

"About what we just saw."

Caprisi frowned at him. They reached the third floor, but there was no one in evidence ahead and Caprisi made no move to leave, his hand pressed flat against the edge of the door. "What do you mean, what are we going to do?"

"The man was murdered."

"Was he, Field?"

"Of course he was."

"He was a communist."

"Why do you say that?"

The American smiled. "You don't have records on him?"

"We don't even know his name."

"But there's a war going on."

"A war?"

"Against the red tide. I thought that was your department."

"The suppression of—"

"He was taken by Lu's men. Tell me you understand."
Field didn't respond and Caprisi looked tired of the game.
"They will have melted away into the Chinese city or the hinterland. In the unlikely event that we had managed to find one
of them and persuaded him to testify, Lu, or whoever gave the
orders, would say that the murdered man was a communist
and that he was dealt with in the Chinese way. In the climate
of the times, his claim would be met by understanding and
sympathy."

"So we let him get away with it? We stand back and let—"

"Don't they teach you anything in training?"

"About what?"

Caprisi looked exasperated.

Field felt the flush in his cheeks. "The doorman was hardly
a communist."

"But threats to the grand capitalist hegemony are everywhere."

"You're sounding like a Bolshevik yourself now."

"Is that an accusation?"

"Don't be so fucking stupid."

Caprisi looked at him, his hostility not assuaged. "What do
you want to do, Field? Maybe we should apply to the French
authorities and go down to Lu's house in Rue Wagner and
arrest him, just like that. Arrest the most powerful man in the
city, a guy who makes Al Capone look like a social worker. You
think anyone is going to testify against him?"

"So that's it?"

"That's it for you."

"I was sent to help."

"And help you have."

"So, case closed. The woman, too." Field looked at his
watch. "An hour of our time and that's it. No immediate
answers, so . . ."

"It's a C.1 matter, Field."

"So that's it? That's how C.1 works?"

"For you, that is it."

"You were angry back there."

"No I wasn't, Field."

"Chen had to—"

"Of course, I was fucking angry."

"Then why—"

"Do me a favor." Caprisi was pointing at him. "Don't be so naive, all right?"

"So we bow to a gangster? They're Lu's apartments, so we just leave it?"

"Couldn't have the empire doing that."

"It's not about—"

"I know you've been bragging about your connections."

Field stared at him.

"Geoffrey Donaldson's your uncle, is he? Municipal secretary, member of the Shanghai Club, drinking right at the head of the bar, mixing with the taipans . . ."

"For Christ's sake." Field tried to control his annoyance.

Their voices had become loud and heated, and they both found themselves glancing around to see who might have heard, but only Macleod's secretary was looking at them and she now turned away.

Caprisi appeared suddenly chastened. "I'm sorry," he said, touching Field's arm. "I'm tired . . . you know?" He took his hands from his pockets and led Field down to his desk, which was pushed into a corner beneath one of the big windows at the far end of the room. He picked up a white form from the basket ahead of him. "Let's take this one step at a time. Have you done much crime work?"

Field shook his head.

"Okay, trust me, the doorman is an incidental, relevant only in that he was part of a cleanup operation. The girl . . ." He shrugged. "The prints will be in the lab. They'll look to see if there is any match on file. Even if the handcuffs are clean, other prints might tell us who has been to the apartment over the past few days, which is better than nothing. But you've got to fill this out and take it to the lab before they'll release the results. They'll bring them to my desk when they're ready, tomorrow or the next day, and stick them in the tray. You may have to keep on their back because they're always complaining about their workload. If they have a match, they'll do a memo and you go to Maretsky and he'll brief you about who the guy is. But if they've got a match, I'll come and see Maretsky with you, okay?"

Field nodded, turning away, assuming it would be better to return to his own desk on the fourth floor to fill this out.

"And, Field . . ."

He stopped and turned back.

"Please get yourself a new suit. It's painful to see you dressed like a polar bear in the desert."

Field looked at his new partner. "The doorman was killed because he saw the murderer entering the apartment block."

Caprisi nodded his head slowly. "Correct."

"The murderer was Lu, or someone else who had received Lena as a 'gift.'"

"Probably."

"Or someone with whom she had made a private arrangement."

"Lu looks after his goods, so she's unlikely to have taken that risk."

"A boyfriend, a . . . lover."

"It cannot be ruled out, but, as I said, she'd have to have been a brave woman."

Field turned around, got back into the lift, and went to his own office on the floor above. The only natural light up here was from a series of windows set high on the wall, all with frosted glass, as if the work of the department was best kept from prying eyes. Granger's office was exactly the same as Macleod's, though he'd resisted the temptation to engrave his name in the glass. There was no light on within, but as Field walked down past the bank of secretaries—all Chinese in his department—toward his tiny cubicle in the corner, Granger opened his door.

He was a huge man, even bigger than Field, six feet five or six, with a broken nose and a handsome, craggy face. His hair was unconventionally long and disheveled.

"What happened?" Granger still spoke with the thick accent of his native Cork.

Field stopped. "We saw the doorman of the building being bundled into a car and taken down into the Chinese city, so we followed and witnessed him being beheaded."

Granger frowned. "Outside the Settlement?"

"Yes. They took him out."

"Who?"

"Caprisi said it was Lu's men."

"Did you see them?"

Field shook his head. "Not really."

"What did Macleod say?" Granger asked.

"About the doorman?"

"Yes."

"Nothing. I haven't seen him since we got back."

"What about the woman?"

"It doesn't look political. Maretsky said he thought it was sexual, but I'll . . ."

Granger nodded, as if satisfied. "Stick with it."

"Yes, sir."

"And stop calling me 'sir.'" Granger was looking distracted. "What did Macleod say about the woman?"

"Nothing . . ." Field had to struggle to prevent adding "sir" again. "I haven't seen him."

"Stick with it," Granger said again. "It's Caprisi?"

"Yes."

"How did he handle himself?"

Field frowned.

"Forget it. Give me a shout if you have any trouble."

Granger turned and shut the door quietly behind him.

Four

ield's cubicle was as spartan as his life here. Apart from his telephone and Lena Orlov's file, which he'd taken out of Registry earlier, there was a huge pile of papers and journals that he was required to "keep an eye on" with "a view to censorship," as Granger had put it. Apart from the *China Weekly Review* and the *Voice of China*, Field was required to read *Shopping News* and the *Law Journal*. It was tedious work. Detective Sergeant Prokopiev, his neighbor here and in the housing complex, did most of the big newspapers and journals and all the ones that might conceivably be of any interest, leaving Field with the dross.

On top of the file was a letter that he'd written earlier to his sister and he decided to check through it before dropping it into the mail room on his way down to the registry and the fingerprint lab. He gazed into the middle distance for a moment, then shook his head and took out his fountain pen, ready to make corrections.

Dear Edith, he'd written, *I'm so sorry it has taken me all this time to put pen to paper. I have penned a note to Mother, but don't know whether she will have passed it on or if you'll have had time to get up to see her.*

In case you haven't, I'll give you as much of the story as I can manage. Apologies if I'm repeating myself.

I arrived here three months ago and went straight into basic instruction, which involves everything from weapons training (necessary) to the rudiments of the Chinese language (hard, but essential, as our pay is based, to a degree, on our proficiency) to the topography of the city and even the mysteries of street numbering.

I ought to tell you a bit about the journey out, but it was uneventful. I shared my cabin with an Indian and all his luggage(!) and I can't say it was the most comfortable voyage, but it was good to see Colombo, Penang, and Hong Kong.

I'm now working in the Special Branch, the "intelligence" department. I'm surprised to be here, but I'll come to that in a minute.

I want to tell you something of this city, but it is hard to know where to begin or what to say. It is like nowhere else I've ever been, a cross between the solid majesty of modern Europe or America and the worst kind of barbarism of the Middle Ages.

Field looked up, confronted again with an image of the doorman's head rolling in the dirt. The doorman, Lena, his father . . .

It is true to say that, though the city assaults your senses at every turn, it is what I'd expected. It is exciting in a way that is hard to do justice to in a letter. It pulses with life and a sense of the possible. I feel I should be more shocked than I am by the poverty and violence, but so far it only adds to a sense of the exotic.

I think of it as like Venice in its heyday, the source of all the art you so love, a mercantile metropolis—the city of the future in the land of the next century, as people here like to say.

My salary is, as yet, very poor, allowing me to survive, but no more. I will get on, though, and make some money here. I will send some to Mother as soon as I can, since I know you . . . well, I know how it is (please don't show this letter to her).

I will return to take you and Arthur to Venice.

The same foolish fantasy of our childhood, you may think, but I can tell you, Edith, that, out here, I feel you can dare to dream and anything seems within reach. The city has an energy that is hard to describe—don't they say the same of New York, that it is built on quartz? Nobody has done us any favors in life, but I intend to make my own luck.

I do my duty and I take pleasure in bringing justice to a land where it would be all too easy for there to be none, but more than that, I feel I belong. Maybe it is because no one really does belong here.

Am I making any sense?

I was trying to explain the city. The big groups here are the Americans and British and they've built the great houses and offices of the Bund—the waterfront—which makes the city feel like Paris or New York. Together, in the last century, they were awarded this concession of land, which is now called the International Settlement (I'd like you to tell me to stop if you know some of this, but since there are thousands of miles between us, I'll err on the side of caution) and which is effectively a piece of America and Britain run by the big business interests here and their chiefs. Geoffrey is the secretary to the Municipal Council, an important job that has prompted a lot of "chat" amongst uncharitable police colleagues (the police are low down the social order here, on the whole). I dropped Geoffrey a line when I arrived, but he said he's been very busy, so we're only getting to meet tonight.

Field wondered again why this meeting with his uncle had not come sooner, but he blamed his father, not Geoffrey.

Alongside the International Settlement is the French Concession, which is run by the French, so I'll leave you to draw your own conclusions. A lot of the White Russians who fled the Bolsheviks live there and have shops and small businesses. There are thousands of them here now, most in a desperate situation—all former army officers and their families, or professionals, or aristocrats. A lot of people like the idea they can take advantage of these people. I mean the women, especially. Well, you know what I mean. There seems nothing you can't buy here and there is so much for sale.

Field looked up, pulling his collar away from his neck and trying not to think of Natasha Medvedev, with her white gown and tumbling hair and the morning sun caressing her legs.

Foreigners living in the Settlement or French Concession have the right to live by the laws of their own countries—a unique situation in history—but Chinese people living in these areas and the foreigners who don't enjoy these rights (Russians, Bulgarians) are subject to the Chinese law of the "mixed courts" in the Settlement, which makes their position precarious. Sometimes, Chinese wrongdoers are just ejected to the Chinese city itself, where they are brutally dealt with by local warlords. This is especially true if their crime is "political." Anyone caught trying to sow Bolshevik ideas is in deep trouble.

The Chinese city is outside the International Settlement and French Concession. This is the beginning of the real China, where everyone lives under Chinese law, not that there is much. Ever since the fall of the imperial dynasty, the whole of China has been controlled by competing warlords, and Shanghai is no exception. Foreigners are mostly okay, but many of the local Chinese do have a rough time of it.

Field thought again of the sound of the doorman's head hitting the ground, echoing through the silence of the crowd.

I've found myself in the Special Branch, as I said. I'd like to report that this was because my superiors spotted a vein of natural genius, but actually it is because Mother is a Catholic and because of my rugby. I've already found this to be the most extraordinary force. It's made up primarily of Americans, Brits, and Russians (and the locals, of course), but it's controlled by two factions, the Scots and the Irish, and everyone—American, Russian, English—has to fall into one camp or other, like it or not. The commissioner is from New York but is too fond of the bottle and is rarely seen out of his office on the sixth floor. The real power rests with my boss, Patrick Granger, who is head of Special Branch, and with Macleod, head of Crime.

Granger is from Cork and fought with the IRA after 1916. They say he was a friend of Michael Collins and that the two fell out. I don't know. Like everyone else here, he doesn't talk about his past (it's a strange city like that—I'll tell you more next time). Macleod, by contrast, is a Protestant (Presbyterian, I

think) from Glasgow, who scowls a lot and gives the impression
he thinks the city is a mess and a discredit to all concerned. Both
men are rugby fanatics and where you end up is largely down to
religion and sport, though there are some exceptions. Granger
found out that I'd played flanker at school and my mother was a
Catholic and that was that. I have my first game for his team this
week against—yes, you guessed it, Crime Branch. The two men
seem to have a deep-seated enmity and rivalry that everyone has
a theory about, not always convincing. You are expected to show
loyalty to your faction and I suppose I'm Granger's man now.
He's a big fellow, in every sense, and gives the impression of
looking out for his men, though he also always talks to you as if
his mind is elsewhere and sometimes looks right through you. I
think you'd find him quite handsome—he certainly dresses well.
Hardly like a policeman at all. Macleod has been perfectly
friendly too, but it doesn't do to even contemplate loyalty outside
your faction.

I must go. I've endless journals to look through, which seems
to be my task (all publications in the Settlement are censored for
Bolshevik propaganda, which certain Russians living here are
secretly trying to export to the Chinese masses). I will try to tell
you more of this strange city next time. Sometimes I wish you
could see it and sometimes I'm glad you can't. Opium dens are
illegal and we sometimes raid them, but you can get heroin from
room service in all the best hotels. You can get anything on room
service. No one who has money wants for anything. Anyone who
hasn't money wants for something.

One last thing might interest you. A mythical Chinese gangster—I've not met him or seen him—but they say this man
called Lu, who lives in the French Concession, controls much in
the city and nothing happens without his knowledge and say-so.
I find it hard to believe and accept the level of influence ascribed
to him, but he appears to have taken the lead in fighting
Bolshevism. Whenever they suspect a local Chinese, even if he's in
the Settlement, of working for the Bolsheviks, they expel him to
the local warlords in the Chinese city, who cut his head off. This

is seen as a necessary expedient on behalf of the British and American authorities in order to persuade local Chinese not to spread Bolshevik propaganda—Lu is making too much money to want a Bolshevik revolution—but there is also a feeling I've picked up amongst police colleagues that Lu is getting too big for his boots and shouldn't be allowed—literally sometimes—to get away with murder. He's using the well-founded fear of Bolshevism amongst foreigners here to get away with doing anything that he wants and undermining (some feel) the authority of the big international powers.

Field looked up again, running his hand through his hair.

He picked up his pen and wrote, *This is a dangerous city, but I'll do my best to keep safe. Love to Arthur ... isn't it about time I was an uncle?*

He found he was smiling and was tempted to write that he'd "met" someone very beautiful today, but thinking of Natasha Medvedev and the misleading boast he'd been about to make suddenly brought down a familiar blanket of loneliness and depression.

He still did not believe that a woman like that could submit herself to a man against her will.

Field began to sweat again, the blood pounding in his head. He loosened his tie and unbuttoned his collar, fumbling around his throat until he found the silver cross. He took it off and held it in his palm, tightening his fist until it hurt.

He fought to contain the anger that still came upon him when his confusion was complete, knowing what his father would have made of the city and of Natasha and Lena and the women like them.

Field had a sudden, clear image of his father, with his trimmed mustache, neat hair, and carefully polished shoes. He could see the waistcoat and the shirt that his mother had starched, the chain of the silver cross just visible above the collar. For a moment he allowed himself to hate the man, for his unyielding, obstinate, puritanical priggishness, for his cane and the power with which he had wielded it.

He gripped the cross more tightly, thinking of his mother and the quiet shock with which she had met his decision to join the Shanghai police force.

Field breathed out and opened his eyes. He was here now and it was his life. He put the cross in his left hand and ran his right through his hair. He put the chain back around his neck, did up his collar, and tightened his tie.

It was all in the past now. That was the point of being here. It was why he'd made the journey.

Field wrote, *Your loving brother*, folded the letter and put it in the envelope, sealed the back, then wrote her address in his careful, flowing hand.

He turned and saw Yang looking at him. She was "his" secretary, his and Prokopiev's, a tiny, slim dark girl with a neat, pretty face and an upturned nose. Her gaze was steady, and for a moment he thought her mind must be elsewhere, but she shifted her head a little, without looking away, and he knew that she was still appraising him. She wore a short cream skirt, without stockings, the thin cotton hem rumpled halfway up her thigh.

Field found it hard to take his eyes from the smooth skin of her legs.

He turned back to his work, distracting himself by reading a memo pinned to the corkboard on the side of his cubicle, which was from Commissioner Biers's office and instructed them to *ensure all files removed from Registry are forwarded to other personnel complete, with cover correspondence detailing any removals. Anyone forwarding a file MUST inform Registry in writing who the file was forwarded to and upon which date.* It added: *All envelopes will now be opened in Registry, rather than the relevant sections, unless addressed directly to individuals.*

Field had never met Biers. He'd only ever seen him once, coming into the lobby, in uniform, his nose and cheeks red from, Prokopiev said, a night's hard drinking. Field thought he'd seen him stagger, but later decided it might have been his imagination.

He pulled forward the form in front of him. It was form number 6.3000–3.23, the number listed next to the logo of the Shanghai Municipal Police, a star with the words *Omnia Juncta in Uno* inside it. Field's Latin was shaky, but he assumed that meant "all acting in unison."

In the box marked *Made by* he wrote his own name, and in the one marked *Forwarded by* he crossed out the "by," wrote "to," and wrote Caprisi's name, before going on to fill out the address at which the fingerprints had been found and the nature of the crime—*murder.* He left the time blank, not certain whether this referred to the time of discovery or of the murder itself, which had not yet been determined. Caprisi hadn't mentioned the pathologist, but Field assumed they would go and see him together.

For a moment Field wished he'd ended up in Crime, which had always been his intention. He thought there was something vaguely disreputable about his own department.

He pictured Lena Orlov again, and the way her body had strained to avoid her assailant, then he thought about Natasha and her nonchalant disinterest. What did she really think? Hadn't the two of them been friends? Perhaps that had been the cause of the moments of fragility he'd witnessed.

Field flicked open the file in front of him and glanced at the small picture clipped to the single sheet of paper it contained. It was a poor photograph, which made Lena look like a convict, her blond hair flattened and her face gaunt. Field thought of the happy family scene in front of the country house in Russia.

He turned, feeling Yang's eyes on him, but she was staring in a different direction now, toward Granger's office.

Field wondered about Yang and Granger.

He stood, clutching Lena's file and the instructions for the fingerprint bureau, ignoring Yang's casually interested glance as he passed.

In the lift he opened the folder again. It listed where in Russia Lena was from—near Kazan—and detailed three meetings she had attended at the *New Shanghai Life,* a magazine funded by Bolshevik intelligence officers from Soviet Russia working undercover at the consulate, but most of the file entries had been written by Prokopiev, who was as gifted with written English as Field was with his Chinese, and even by their standards, this was thin. They had files on so many people and most gave few insights. He'd learned more in five minutes at the woman's flat.

Field wondered why she'd attended meetings at the *New Shanghai Life.* The family had certainly looked as if it was part of the old, decimated aristocratic class and were unlikely recruits to the Bolshevik cause.

The fingerprint bureau was on the fifth floor, *C.6* printed in the middle of its frosted glass door. Field knocked once, then entered.

The room was in darkness save for the light from two desk lamps, one of which pointed toward a sheet of paper hanging from a piece of string that ran from one side of the room to the other. A tall man with gray hair and glasses, wearing a white coat, was using the other to look at a brown leather ledger, like the ones that filled the bookshelves above him. He sat hunched over it, holding a magnifying glass. He did not bother to look up.

Field cleared his throat. "I've brought the paperwork on the Orlov case."

"The Russian prostitute?" The man was English.

"Yes."

"Fine. Put it in the tray by the door."

Field let it drop into the wire basket. "Have you got anywhere yet?"

The man looked up, staring at Field over his glasses. He had a long nose, with black hairs poking out of both nostrils, and poor teeth. "Do I look like a miracle worker?"

"Not really, no."

The man stared at him. "You're new, aren't you?"

"Yes."

"Where are you from?"

"Yorkshire."

"Bad luck." He exhaled heavily, turning back to his work. "Two days, minimum."

"*Two days?*"

"Minimum, I said." He straightened, gesturing at all the ledgers above him. "Do I look as if I have any assistance?" He muttered something to himself, then added audibly, "There were different prints in the apartment, so it might take longer."

"Have you found a match for Lu?"

The man hesitated. "Pockmark?"

"Yes."

"You may be disappointed to discover that I haven't looked at the Orlov prints and they're not next in line."

"It's a murder case."

"So tell me something new."

Field took a step closer, looking over the man's shoulder at the pages of prints in the ledger that he was using to try to find a match for the one on the piece of paper in front of him.

"I'm Field, by the way."

He didn't respond.

"You're Mr. Ellis."

"I'm Ellis."

"Is there any chance that, when you do come to the Orlov case, you might be able to check Lu's prints against those you took from the bedroom? It's just it would help to—"

"Field." The man did not look up. "Have you seen me in S.1 recently?"

"No."

"Well, when you do, telling you how to do your job, then you can come up here and help me out with mine."

Field retreated, shut the door quietly, and crossed the corridor to the registry, a stuffy, hot room without ventilation or light. It was run by Danny Black, a first-generation Irish immigrant from New York, who'd fled from the civil war in Ireland to the East Coast of America, only to have found his way mysteriously thereafter to Shanghai. Without ever having talked about it, Field knew that he was Granger's man, toiling away in the undergrowth for reasons unknown. He worked alongside Maretsky, who had a glass cubicle at the far end; both fat men with glasses and curly hair, they could have been twins. They were assisted by a Russian woman of similar physique who sorted through the files, occasionally filling in at the front desk whenever Danny or Maretsky was involved in Modus Operandi briefings or research. Maretsky also had an office up on the sixth floor.

There was no one in evidence, so Field filled out one of the white forms. He wrote: *Natasha Medvedev, Happy Times block, Foochow Road.*

He hesitated a second before taking another sheet, writing *Lu Huang* on it and hitting the brass bell on the front desk beside him.

After a minute Danny emerged from behind one of the iron shelves at the far end of the room. "Mr. Field," he said. Everyone liked Danny. His face exuded good-humored bonhomie. "What have you been up to?"

"A Russian woman," Field said.

Danny looked up from the forms. He appeared worried. "Lu?"

Field waited for him to expand, and when he didn't, said, "Yes, Lu."

Danny looked shifty. "We've not got a file for Lu."

Field frowned.

"There's a background file," Danny added hastily.

"Then I'll take that."

Danny turned around, disappearing behind the shelves and reemerging a few moments later with one bulging folder and a slim one.

"Can I get the current file on Lu?"

"There isn't one."

"There must be one."

"We don't have it." Danny was flustered.

"Where is it?"

"I don't know."

Field hesitated. "I thought all files have to be signed out and a memo put through to you if forwarded anywhere different."

"Yes."

"So you have a note of who the file's signed out to?"

"No."

"But—"

"I mean yes. Granger has it."

"Well, I'll get it from him, then."

"Sure." Danny looked down. He was filling in the book in front of him, writing the file numbers and subjects alongside Field's name. He turned it around for him to sign before shutting it and retreating behind the shelves once more, without looking back.

Field took the stairs to the third floor, where Caprisi was on the phone, his jacket over the back of the chair, along with his leather holster. Watching him, Field noticed how well groomed he was, his hair neatly trimmed at the back and sides. A leather wallet was open on the desk, and Field saw that there was a photograph inside of a young woman with short dark hair, holding a young boy.

Caprisi put down the phone and swung around. He saw the direction of Field's gaze and snatched the wallet up, slipping it into his trouser pocket. "Come on, Krauss has got the body."

Five

Caprisi led Field down the stairs to the basement and through the swing doors of Pathology to the darkened lab at the end. There was a single, bright light in the ceiling and the room was heavy with the smell of formaldehyde. Krauss, in his long white coat, was standing next to Maretsky.

Lena Orlov lay flat on her back on a metal trolley in front of them. A white sheet covered her from the swell of her breasts to below her knees. Somehow she looked more peaceful here.

"No assault," Maretsky said, shaking his head.

"No sexual assault," Caprisi corrected.

"Time of death," Krauss said, with only the faintest hint of a German accent. "I would say around one o'clock in the morning. If the Russian neighbor found her at one o'clock in the afternoon, then I think she'd already been dead almost twelve hours."

"No consensual sex?" Caprisi asked.

"Not as far as I can tell."

"Then why the fancy underwear and the handcuffs?"

Krauss shrugged. Field didn't know if it was the light, but Lena Orlov's skin looked even whiter than it had in the flat.

"Some kind of fantasy," Maretsky said. "Was she a prostitute?"

"We're not sure of her circumstances yet," Caprisi said. He turned and it was a second or two before Field realized that he was required to expand.

"Her file is thin," he said.

"There's a surprise," Caprisi said.

"She used to be a tea dancer," Field went on. "She attended meetings with known Bolsheviks, but I agree with Caprisi, that needs further investigation, because it looks like she was from an aristocratic background in Russia."

"All right," Maretsky said firmly, as if not wanting to dwell on this. "So it's the usual gray area. A tea dancer makes an arrangement with a man for a sexual meeting, either through her association with Lu or some other avenue. She lets him into the flat . . . Did anyone see him come in?"

"I just sent Chen back down," Caprisi said, "but Lu owned the building, so you can be reasonably sure that no one will have heard or seen anything."

"The man comes in," Maretsky went on. "He makes sure she is in these panties . . ." Maretsky thought for a moment, a chubby fist to his mouth, staring at Lena Orlov's face through his dirty, round, steel-framed glasses. "I think this is a precise fantasy. Everything must be right. He gets her to wear these particular underclothes. Perhaps they have had a relationship or . . . arrangement, and she knows this is his exact fantasy. He handcuffs her to the bed." Maretsky's accent seemed to get thicker, Field noticed, the more he had to think, as if the process of drawing on a mental filing cabinet compiled during a different era automatically transported him back there. "Then he . . . This is the point." He shrugged. "One could say it is a convenient way of ensuring that she cannot resist or fight. Perhaps it even allows him to put a hand over her mouth. But, of course, it's more than that. This is part of the fantasy. She must be helpless. Supine. Entirely under his control."

They were silent again.

"So they'd met before?" Caprisi asked. "Whoever it was, it was definitely not a first assignation?"

"Possibly." Maretsky shrugged again. "Probably. I would guess there was a pattern that led up to this: same setting, with the underwear and the handcuffs, but not going to this point. Perhaps culminating in some form of violence, but not murder."

Field looked at Lena Orlov's face. There was no sign of any bruising there, nor on her neck or shoulders, but she seemed nonetheless to bear the hallmarks of a victim. Perhaps it was because of what he knew, or thought he did, of her circumstances, but he could imagine her allowing herself to be beaten.

He saw Natasha Medvedev again in his mind's eye, strong hands clutching at her shoulders until the knuckles whitened. Would she have submitted herself to violence in this manner?

"So it couldn't be the result of an argument?" Caprisi asked. "Jealousy? Lovers' quarrel?"

"It's possible, but it is better to begin with what is likely."

Maretsky displayed a disarming modesty. Field thought it was the deliberate act of a clever man to tailor his manner to his audience.

"But you think not?" Caprisi asked.

Maretsky turned to the pathologist.

"Savage stabbing. Eighteen in all," Krauss said, nicotine-stained fingers pressed to his lips. He dropped a hand and pulled back the sheet, revealing Lena's naked, punctured body. The blood had been cleaned from her skin, which made the livid bruising around the stab wounds even more visible. There were so many holes that in some places the skin looked as though it had been stretched too thin and hung like thread. In others—around the top of her vagina—incisions grouped close together had created deep craters. Field blanched and turned away. Caprisi eyed him curiously, as if surprised at his squeamishness.

"See," Krauss went on as Field forced himself to turn back. "Frenzied. Again and again, in her stomach and in the upper part of her sexual organs." He reached down and put one long, slim, bony finger on the dark mound of hair at the base of Lena Orlov's stomach. "Here, and on her breasts also."

"This is not sudden anger," Maretsky went on, no longer prepared to invite conflicting views. "Not the anger that stems from a disagreement or jealousy: that would be done in a flash, then instantly recoiled from. One incision, or a couple at most, instantly regretted as the perpetrator senses this will result in death and that he has gone too far. No, this stems from a deep-seated rage. It is perhaps sexual in nature. It has been building for a long time. The relationship . . . arrangement . . . has been leading up to this point, though poor Lena has not known it. It has exploded here."

"He's done this before?" Caprisi asked.

"Perhaps."

"Perhaps, or he has?"

"He has, I would say."

"But we haven't seen anything like it?"

"I'm checking the records. And we're talking to the French gendarmerie. We've even contacted the Chinese police, not that that will do any good."

Once again, they all stared silently at Lena Orlov's body, until Field cleared his throat and took a step back.

They left Maretsky and Krauss together in the basement—both, Field thought, in their own way, creatures of the darkness—and got back into the lift. Caprisi pulled across the metal cage door with unnecessary aggression and leaned back heavily on the wall behind him.

"I'm sorry to be ignorant," Field said, "but are all tea dancers prostitutes?"

"Try one for size and you'll see."

Caprisi hit the buttons for the third and fourth floors, then leaned back again with a sigh, his face softening. He seemed suddenly less hostile. "You know," he went on, "they say these Russian women commit suicide at the rate of one a week. They come here with nothing . . ." Caprisi turned to him. "You imagine, you grow up in a beautiful house, with a large staff

and the belief that the world is there to serve you and then"—
he flicked his fingers—"all gone. Months if not years of terror
as you escape across the vast wilderness of your country, and
then you wind up here, penniless, your father and mother
probably dead. How do you support your siblings? What do you
do to stay alive? If you do nothing, then you live on the streets
and slowly starve to death."

The lift seemed to be moving more slowly than ever. Field
thought of the big house his own mother had been brought up
in and the shame of his father's bankruptcy.

"Some teach English, or music, or French or Russian. Many
of them go to the cabarets and offer themselves for a dance at a
dollar a time. You want more? Maybe, maybe not. Depends on
their mood, on you, on the money."

They'd reached the third floor. Caprisi jammed his foot in
the door.

"That's the demimonde. *Les entraîneuses,* they call them.
The entertainers. Beautiful, sad women, reduced to a life
nothing could have prepared them for, and which many cannot manage."

Caprisi was staring at Field with intense, dark eyes. "Try
one, Field, and see how much you hate yourself." Then he
stepped out and walked away.

Field now put his foot against the door. "I didn't know you
were married."

Caprisi turned. "Who says I'm married?"

"The photograph . . . I thought . . ."

"Don't pry, Field. I told you that."

"Why did Chen have to restrain you today?"

"Don't make me repeat myself."

They stared at each other.

"What do you want me to do?" Field asked.

"Whatever you were sent here to do. Write up your file.
Tell Granger."

"I was sent to help."

Caprisi smiled thinly. "Tell Granger you've helped."

"What about Lena Orlov?"

"What about her?"

"Shouldn't we find out where she worked, what her life was like, who she mixed with, whether anyone saw the man in her apartment?"

"*I* should."

Field frowned. "Shouldn't this go a little beyond internal politics?"

"Tell Granger that."

Field felt the sweat breaking out on his forehead again. "You don't trust me, do you?"

Caprisi shook his head. "No."

"Why not?"

"I don't trust anyone from Granger's mob."

"That doesn't make sense. We're from the same force."

"You think so? Then good luck to you, Dickie."

"I'd appreciate it if you didn't patronize me."

Caprisi frowned. "Why would I want to do that?"

"I may be new, but I'm not stupid."

"I'll have to take your word for that, Dickie."

Caprisi held his stare. Field tried hard to see what was behind the American's dark eyes. He suddenly felt as if everyone in this city were a total, unfathomable stranger, and would remain so.

"All right," Caprisi said, his face softening again. He took a pace toward him. "All right, Field. I've got some paperwork to do, but come down in a couple of hours and we'll go from there."

Field looked at his watch, embarrassed.

"You have a social engagement. Drinks at the Shanghai Club?"

"He's my uncle."

Caprisi looked as if he was going to say something else, then thought better of it. "Tomorrow morning, then. Nine o'clock, if that's not too early for you. We'll meet and then go to the ten o'clock briefing."

"What about Lu?"

"Easy, polar bear." Caprisi smiled. "As I said, welcome to Shanghai. It's one slow step at a time, if we manage to take any steps at all."

Granger was on the phone when Field knocked on the glass door of his office a few minutes later, but shouted, "Come in."

Field stood awkwardly in front of him, trying to pretend he wasn't listening to the call. Granger was discussing arrangements to go to the cinema with his wife. He smiled at Field as he suggested they see *Trifling Women*.

The office was small. A bookcase behind him was lined with leather-bound volumes. There was a black-and-white photograph of an attractive dark-haired woman.

Granger said, "I love you, too," and put down the phone. He leaned back on his chair, taking a cigarette from the silver case on the table and a box of matches from the pocket of his waistcoat. "Have a seat." He pointed at the leather chair in the corner.

Field shook his head. "I don't want to bother you, sir. I just need the current file on Lu Huang."

Granger frowned. "Why are you asking me?"

"They seemed to think you had it."

"Danny told you that?"

Field hesitated. "He said he thought you had it."

"Shit. I don't think I have." Granger sucked in the smoke and blew it out slowly, still leaning back on his chair, his big head resting on the bookshelf behind him. "Biers is so bloody anal about all that stuff."

Field watched the thick smoke being dissipated by the ceiling fan. He decided Granger was one of those people it was almost impossible not to like. Doubts that crept into your mind when you were away from him were almost instantly quashed upon return to his orbit by the warmth and force of his personality. "Sorry to bother you, sir."

Granger stood, throwing his cigarette into the metal bin in the corner. He moved around the desk and placed a large arm around Field's shoulders. "Anytime. Like to keep in touch." They were at the door. "Must get you round for dinner. Caroline always wants to meet my new boys."

"Yes, sir."

Granger reached again for his cigarettes and lit another, inhaling the smoke and blowing it noisily toward the ceiling before offering one to Field. "How are you finding the city?"

"Exciting." Field hesitated. "Overwhelming, on occasions."

"You'll get used to it." Granger waved his arm expansively. "Greatest city on earth."

"Better than Dublin?"

"Jesus!" Granger laughed derisively as he returned to his side of the desk and sat himself down once more. "The work's a bit dull for you, but we'll get you doing something more interesting . . . Ready for the match on Saturday?"

"Yes."

Granger pointed his cigarette. "You know, you want to watch that little shit Caprisi. He's their scrum half. He might be a Yank, but he's learned fast and he can play."

"I'll watch him."

"Good. See if you can break his leg before Saturday. How's your diary? For dinner, I mean."

Granger was smiling and Field found that he was, too. "I'm busy, but I think I'll be able to fit in with whatever your wife suggests."

Granger nodded and Field took a pace toward the door. "What did you want with the Lu file, anyway?"

Field turned. "Just . . . background."

Granger's eyes narrowed fractionally. "Sure."

Field closed the door quietly and returned to his cubicle in the corner. It was almost six o'clock. The office was empty, Yang's chair pushed neatly up against her desk. He thought he'd walk down to the Bund, despite the heat, which gave him fifteen or twenty minutes to kill before he was due to meet

Geoffrey. His dinner jacket—his father's—was on a hanger on the hat stand in the corner.

Field sat at his desk, still clutching the brown files he'd taken out of Registry earlier and the envelope he'd forgotten to drop into the mail room. Lu Huang's name was written in pencil on the outside of the top file, faded with age. There was a typed summary on the front of this background file, and above it, Granger had written in pencil: *For MI6. Copy to State Department, Washington, P.G. Jan 12th 1926.*

Lu Huang is the head of Shanghai's notorious Green Gang, the most powerful triad, whose influence is pervasive across both the International Settlement and the French Concession, particularly the latter. He currently resides at 3 Rue Wagner, in a house full of bodyguards and concubines. We estimate he has around twenty thousand men at his beck and call, armed and loyal to his every whim. This is more than double the number of soldiers and police officers at the Settlement's disposal, even if one includes administrative members of the force. We have expressed our views on this situation before and do not need to repeat them here.

Lu originally hails from the township of Gaoqiao in Pudong. His early life is shrouded in mystery and myth, but there is a general consensus that his family was poor. They drifted to Shanghai, like so many others, to try to make their fortune, but found only squalor and disease. Lu's mother died in the first year here, when he was a small boy (aged five or six, we estimate). His father remarried the following year, another woman from their township, only to die himself shortly afterwards. The stepmother then returned to the village but was kidnapped by brigands. Lu, now about seven or eight, was left to fend for himself.

He returned to Shanghai, drifted into a life of petty crime and then into the welcoming arms of the Green Gang, rising to prominence and then ultimate power through a combination of cunning and ruthlessness unique even for one of the most vicious organizations in the world. During 1923 he effectively oversaw the destruction of the Red Gang and is now undisputed master of crime in the Shanghai metropolitan area. He is probably the most powerful man in all China.

The primary source of the Green Gang's income is opium illegally imported from India, an operation we believe is worth millions of dollars a year. Lu controls every aspect of its distribution and sale, as well as having a grip on prostitution across the city. He has a close relationship with the authorities in the French Concession (diplomatic discretion should perhaps prevent us from indicating how close).

In the past year, Lu has made great efforts to present himself as a legitimate and respectable member of the community, buying a series of "front" companies, donating money to charity, and making regular appearances in the social columns of the North China Daily News. The changing perception of him in normally conservative high society is partly due to the increasing sense of insecurity of the International Settlement as a result of the anarchy that continues to tear the country apart. There is great fear, as I have already documented, that the communists, who now hold sway in the south, will soon conquer the whole of the country. It is felt by some that Lu may be an important figure in ensuring that the Settlement and the French Concession are not in any way violated (the Alabama and Sheffield arrived today, serving as a reminder of the consequences to any Chinese force of attempting such an action).

As recorded in previous dispatches, we have ourselves made contact with Lu, whilst in no way, as a force, weakening our attempts to stifle and close down his criminal activities. It is clear, though, that he is as committed as we are to the total resistance of Bolshevism. He has, on occasion, provided useful intelligence on Michael Borodin and other Comintern agents who are trying to foment revolution in the Settlement, funding the communist army in the south and operating under the cover of the Soviet consulate (see summary on activities of Sov. cons. and Comintern 11th Dec 1925).

At the bottom, Granger had written, again in pencil: Borodin. Communists on move. Unifying China? Pact with devil?

The rest of the file was full of newspaper clippings, many detailing Lu's charitable and legitimate business activities. One had a photograph of him handing over a check to a middle-aged woman at the Horticultural Society of Shanghai charity tea. He was a portly man in a long silk top, a chubby hand holding his end of the check up toward the camera lens. Another showed him doing the same for the Sisters of Mercy Orphanage.

Field shut the file and tapped his fingers on its cover. This was only a summary, so he wondered what was in the "current" file that was still in Granger's possession.

Field opened Natasha Medvedev's folder with a mixture of nervousness and excitement. A passport photograph of her, of poor quality, was attached to a single sheet. Her summary was as sparse as Lena Orlov's.

Natasha Medvedev resides at the Happy Times block on Foochow Road, on the top floor. She is a native of Kazan on the Volga and arrived in Shanghai via Vladivostok on the 21st January 1922. She is an associate of Michael Borodin.

Beneath that, Field could only see a series of dates and times, listing meetings she had attended at the offices of the *New Shanghai Life.* This information had obviously come from an informant, because alongside each entry, someone—Prokopiev, probably—had written: *said nothing of note.* There was also a list of the seven occasions upon which she had been seen entering the Soviet consulate. Two of these were late at night.

Field picked up his pencil and tapped it gently alongside each entry, going down the page. Natasha Medvedev was, he thought, just as vulnerable as Lena Orlov had been. Russians did not enjoy the rights of extraterritoriality here—the right to be governed by the laws of their own country—so anyone caught "fomenting revolution" was liable to be tried by the mixed courts and then expelled to the Chinese city and the merciless hands of the local warlord. This had happened a month ago to a Hungarian. He'd been tried, found guilty, and "put in prison," but his family was still trying to locate him.

Field returned to Lena Orlov's file and placed the two summaries next to each other.

The two women were from the same town and they'd attended the same meetings at the *New Shanghai Life* on the same days.

He stood, looking at his watch, suddenly worried he would be late.

Six

Field emerged onto the street, relieved to feel a breeze on his face, even if it did carry with it the smell of dead fish and stagnant water from the wharves and the sulfurous pollution of factories over in Pudong, on the far side of the Whangpoo River.

He had changed into his father's dinner jacket, but it was just as thick and hot.

Once it became clear he wasn't getting into a car, he was besieged by a group of rickshaw pullers—every one scrawny and shabbily dressed—imploring him to use their services. He shook his head and waved them away, but without discernible effect. He walked purposefully the other way, passing the open doors of a packed restaurant and a billboard advertising "Money Exchange." The signs along the street ahead were mostly in Chinese, competing for the attention of the hordes rushing to their destinations. Long cotton banners twisted in the breeze.

An old man with no legs thrust a flat cap in Field's direction and tugged at his trousers as he passed. Field fended him off and careered into a smart, handsome Eurasian wearing a white fedora and a long gray cotton tunic, with a silver watch pinned to his chest and bright, white shoes. Behind him was a woman in a long, figure-hugging white dress, her hair pulled back in a tight bun to reveal a pretty, oval face. Perhaps it was his imagination, but he thought she smiled at him.

Ahead, a thousand telegraph wires crisscrossed a dark,

brooding sky, heavy with monsoon rain. The first drops landed
on his face. Field wondered if he should feel homesick, but he
didn't. He missed nothing at all about Yorkshire.

Outside the white portico entrance to the tall red brick
building that housed the American Club, Field stopped to light
a cigarette. He looked up at the Stars and Stripes fluttering
above the entrance. He was opposite the Municipal Adminis-
tration Building and wondered if Geoffrey, too, would be
walking. He couldn't really remember what his uncle looked
like. Field realized he was nervous, and recalled Edith accusing
him, in a rare moment of disagreement, of "hero-worshiping a
man who has played no part in our lives."

Field stepped off the sidewalk and waited for a tram to rattle past before crossing the road and turning onto the Bund,
the city's business heart, the Wall Street of Asia. The wind was
strong here, so that the Chinese walking next to him lost his
hat and had to scrabble on the sidewalk to catch it. Field
stopped and ran his hand through his hair, then put both
hands in his pockets and watched the new Buicks and Oldsmo-
biles rolling past. A black Chevrolet moved slowly among
them, with burly bodyguards—White Russians—standing on
each running board, machine guns resting casually over their
shoulders.

The Shanghai Club at number 2 the Bund was an ornate,
classical stone building, with a red iron-framed awning shielding its entrance, Italianate cupolas capping a colonnaded facade
of Ningpo granite. The street outside was quieter than usual, a
group of chauffeurs kicking their heels, talking and smoking
next to their sleek black cars. The rickshaw pullers stood discreetly about twenty yards down the street.

On the Whangpoo, Field could see two dragon boats pulling
away from the shore, their sides and bows decked out with
bright-colored silk hangers and paper lamps. He waited again
for a tram to come past, then crossed the road, walking
between the line of cars parked down its center. He headed for
the war memorial—a bronze angel standing above a square

stone pillar. Some children were playing tag around it while their parents watched the dragon boats.

Field looked at his watch. He did not want to be either early or late.

He waited for a few minutes. A steamer, loaded to the gills with people bent low beneath a canvas awning, made its way downriver. It was towing three cargo barges, but still moving faster than a similarly overloaded sampan struggling to get out of its way. Both were making for the wooden jetty that jutted out ahead of him.

Field leaned over the wall, looking down into the muddy waters. The lights along the shore came on suddenly. They were electric here.

He looked at his watch again and turned to survey the solid majesty of the Bund. It was like the Strand, or any of London's other classical streets; every building along it, he thought, a projection of European and American power. He pushed himself away from the wall and walked back across the road and through the iron gates. The glass doors at the top of the steps swung back as he reached them.

"Good evening, sir," the doorman said, bowing, next to a pair of Greek goddesses that guarded the entrance. He spoke with a thick Russian accent and wore a bright blue and gold uniform. Behind him, a broad staircase of white Sicilian marble climbed toward the first floor.

"I'm here to meet Geoffrey Donaldson."

The man pointed toward the lobby. "Mr. Donaldson is not in yet, but if you'd like to wait through there . . ."

Field walked through to the colonnaded hall across a black and white marble floor. The opulence of his surroundings was testament enough, he thought, to confidence in the permanence of the European presence here. He looked up at the ceiling with its ornate plasterwork and the enormous light that hung from a chain thick enough to hold a ship's anchor. There was a balcony above and, on the walls behind, pictures of Shanghai life—hunting out in the fields beyond the city limits, men standing at the Long Bar of the club, and a panorama of the Bund.

Field moved to a glass cabinet full of silver trophies at the edge of the lobby. Beyond it was a bulletin board covered in the latest Reuters reports, pulled from a telex machine. He read one that detailed further intercommunal riots in Rawalpindi and was grateful again that he'd not chosen to join the Indian police instead.

Field turned to see a tall, sandy-haired, pleasant-looking man limping toward him.

"Richard." He was smiling. Field tried to wipe the sweat from his hand in his pocket before offering it. "I'm sorry to be late," Geoffrey said.

"No, I was early."

"Did you see the dragon boats?"

"Yes, in the distance."

"You should take a closer look. It's quite a spectacle."

Field was suddenly embarrassed and searched for something to say. "How often do they have them?"

"Once a year. They are to celebrate a hero's death. A faithful minister of state was dismissed by his prince, or so the legend goes, and threw himself into a small river in Hunan to show his humiliation. His friends gathered to throw rice across the water so that his spirit wouldn't starve, and since then, on the anniversary of his death, they race boats on the river, presumably looking for his body." Geoffrey smiled. "Let's go through."

He led the way down the corridor toward a set of glass doors that Field guessed must have been twenty-five feet high, with brass handles the size of a medium-size dog. As they approached, the doors were opened by Chinese waiters in newly pressed white linen uniforms.

The room he found himself in was the size of a tennis court, perhaps larger, furnished with sumptuously upholstered golden sofas and high-backed leather armchairs, dim lamps, and potted plants. A series of ceiling fans turned in unison.

A long, L-shaped bar made of old, unpolished mahogany stretched all the way from one end of the room to the other.

"The longest bar in the world," Geoffrey said as he led Field to the bay window at the far end, overlooking the Bund, the preserve of taipans and other members of the city's elite. "Thought we'd have a quick drink, then meet up with Penelope at the country club. Been there?"

Field shook his head.

"Have you come here?"

"No."

Field thought it would have been so easy for Geoffrey to patronize him—just a brief raise of the eyebrows, perhaps to remind him, as the family back home so often did, of their reduced circumstances—but his warm face was without any hint of prejudice. He was exactly how Field remembered him from their last meeting almost ten years ago, and he liked this man instantly again.

"Gin and tonic times two," Geoffrey instructed the waiter, turning to Field to see if that was all right. He leaned against the bar to take the weight off his wooden leg. "How is your mother? I got the letter you posted for her."

"She's all right, thank you. You know how things are."

He nodded. "I keep trying to send her money, but . . ."

"She won't take it. It's good of you to try." Field sipped his gin. "I'm so sorry about . . . I know it's a long time ago now, but Mother told me . . ." Field pointed to his uncle's leg.

"Can't be helped." Geoffrey's smile became somber. "I miss your mother. I've never held with all this nonsense from the rest of the family. I'm rather sorry I've been so far away." His face was full of the compassion of a man who understands suffering. "I was, of course, sorry to hear about your father. Is your mother . . . is she all right—financially, I mean?"

Field did not know what he should say, or what his mother would want him to.

"Don't worry," Geoffrey said, touching Field's shoulder. "I'll have another go at her." He took out a packet of ciga-

rettes. Field didn't feel like smoking, but wanted to be socia-
ble, so accepted one when it was offered. "I never quite gathered," Geoffrey went on, "and it's difficult to write to your
mother about it. But the final verdict was suicide?"

"Yes." Field nodded, taking a drag of his cigarette.

"It was the business . . . the bankruptcy?"

Field hesitated. "Yes, I suppose so."

"It was you who found him?"

"Yes. It was."

"Sorry. Probably crass of me to talk about it."

"No, really . . ."

Geoffrey was staring at his hand. "He was a good man, your
father."

Field didn't answer.

"Quite tough, I suppose, but his heart was in the right
place."

Field sensed some reaction was expected of him. He
shrugged.

"Sorry, not my business, Richard."

"It's the family's business."

"Jolly tough if luck goes against you. That's all life is,
Richard, the merry-go-round of fate. I believe they loved each
other, and in better circumstances, things might have been
very different."

"But we have to live with the circumstances we are pre-
sented with."

Geoffrey looked embarrassed. "He was tough on you, I
know. Or so it's been said. But not for want of affection, I'm
sure."

Field felt his face reddening.

"I'm sorry, truly. None of my business. It's just . . . so easy
to get out of touch. That is the one trouble of being away. It's
hard to bridge the miles that separate us." He cleared his
throat. "The letter from your mother was a little odd, in fact."

Field frowned.

"Said she was worried you would take advantage of our

position and . . . you know, I'm only mentioning it because it's a load of bloody nonsense. You're family, so of course, we'll help you in any way we can."

"I can assure you . . ."

"Don't be silly, man." Field could see there was steel in his uncle's eyes. "You're thousands of miles from home in a strange city. Of course, it's an absolute pleasure for us to have a link . . . I only mention it because it worried me. I've never held, as I said, with this marrying-beneath-yourself business—your father was a fine man and I'm just concerned it may have got to her in a way I'd not envisaged."

"There's no need to worry. She's fine."

Geoffrey patted his shoulder, smiling again. "Said they'd wanted you to be a missionary."

Field smiled back. "I don't think there was much danger of that."

"Thank God we've got you out here."

A man in a white linen suit appeared through the swinging doors and made his way toward them. He moved with an easy, athletic gait. He ran a hand through his blond hair.

"Geoffrey."

Field saw that his uncle's smile of welcome was wary. "Charles. This is Richard Field, my sister's boy. Richard, Charles Lewis, taipan of Fraser's, Shanghai's biggest trading company."

Lewis's handshake was firm, a smile breaking the handsome solemnity of his face. He was about Field's height, but there the similarities ended. Lewis, from his slicked-back hair to his finely polished leather shoes, was every inch the son of privilege, confidently shouldered.

"Richard's just come out, joined the police force."

"The police," Lewis said with gentle, mocking admiration. "Excellent. Not in the Traffic Branch, I hope."

Field hesitated. Granger was always warning them not to tell anyone in the city what they did, but as members of the Municipal Council, both of these men were responsible for governing and overseeing the municipal police force. "No," he said.

"One of Macleod's men?"

"I work with Patrick Granger."

"Ah." Charles Lewis raised his eyebrows. "You look like you've been pounding the streets all day."

Field smiled thinly. "There was a murder," he said. He realized immediately he'd been trying to show off, and regretted it.

"The Russian woman," Lewis said. "I was just reading about her in the *Evening Post.*"

"Lena Orlov."

Perhaps it was Field's imagination, but he got the impression Lewis had known Lena Orlov, or at least recognized the name.

"Handcuffed to the bed. Kinky." Lewis took his hands from his pockets. "What are we doing?"

Geoffrey Donaldson looked at his watch and turned to Field. "We had better get along to meet Penelope." He put his glass down on the bar, facing Lewis again. "You're very welcome to come along," he said without enthusiasm.

Lewis smiled. "Never say no to dinner with Penelope."

Charles Lewis led the way out. Field held back to wait for Geoffrey. In the lobby Lewis took his trilby from the porter and walked straight through the doors. Geoffrey grabbed Field's arm. "He's all right," he said. "Charlie's all right."

"Yes," Field said. "Of course."

Outside, Lewis's chauffeur had already brought up his new black Buick and they climbed into the back before setting off down the Bund, past the brightly lit monoliths. The dome of the Hong Kong Shanghai Bank was ghostly against the night sky. They turned left into Nanking Road and Field looked out of the window in silence at the streets and shops still bustling with life.

The country club on Bubbling Well Road was similarly grand, a wide circular stone entrance giving way to an airy stone-floored lobby with plants in large silver pots. There was a reception area on the left, but Lewis led them straight through to a veranda that overlooked a small fountain and several acres of flat, well-tended lawn. A group dressed in white was playing bowls in the corner, close to the wall; another group, nearer, croquet.

It was growing dark. An Indian waiter in a starched white and gold uniform was hanging lanterns all along the terrace and placing joss sticks and spraying paraffin beneath each table to ward off mosquitoes.

Penelope Donaldson was waiting for them at the far end, one long leg crossed over the other, both resting on a wicker and glass coffee table. As she turned toward them, Field saw immediately that she was pretty, with bobbed, jet-black hair. Her skirt was short, her mouth small. She wore, Field thought, a lot of makeup.

"Charlie!" she said, standing and putting her arms around his neck, kissing him on the mouth. "What a treat."

"Penelope," Geoffrey said a little stiffly, "this is Richard Field, my—I suppose our—nephew."

She stepped forward and offered a slender hand, her smile warmer and more engaging than Field was for some reason expecting. "We'll get along fine," she said, "just as long as you don't call me 'Auntie.' "

Field smiled back at her.

"The boy's in the police force," Lewis said.

"Good Lord," she responded with the same mock admiration.

"Working on that Russian woman found handcuffed to the bed."

"How exciting," she said, ignoring Geoffrey's frown. "It's sexual?"

They were all looking at Field, who was wondering what the *Evening Post* had written about the story—sensational nonsense, probably—or from where they had received such detailed information. "In a sense, yes."

"What do you mean?" Penelope asked.

Field wasn't sure it was a good idea to get into this. "The consensus seems to be that it is a crime of a broadly sexual nature."

"Perhaps he couldn't find keys to the handcuffs," Lewis said. Penelope laughed. Geoffrey looked embarrassed.

Lewis turned his hat in his hand as he contemplated Field. Field thought him the most supremely arrogant man he'd ever met. He was handsome, and he knew it, and was clearly totally comfortable at the apex of Shanghai society. Slowly, he turned away, toward Penelope. "You weren't at the Claymores last night."

Geoffrey interrupted by signaling for a waiter, another Indian, this time all in white, without any brocade. The three men opted for gin, Penelope for "a slow comfortable screw."

She laughed as she said it, embarrassing her husband. Field could see from the menu in front of him that the cocktail was called simply "The Screw."

"How are you finding Shanghai?" she asked him when the waiter had gone.

Field sat up straight. "Hot."

"Got yourself a girl?"

"Penelope . . ."

"What?"

"Give the chap a break. He's only been here five minutes."

"I'm sure he has. Probably found a Russian already. They're a bargain. Grateful, too, I gather, unlike us lot."

The waiter arrived with a large silver tray, the drinks, and two bowls of peanuts. He set them down carefully, bowed once stiffly, and retreated.

"Come on, then, Richard . . . is that what we should call you?"

"Most people just know me as 'Field.'"

"We can't call you that! It's far too impersonal."

"Delusions of grandeur," Lewis said.

"Richard," Geoffrey instructed his wife.

"All right—Richard. You must have a girl. Handsome chap like you."

Field blushed. She was smiling at him. She leaned forward, the strap of her black dress falling off her shoulder to reveal a small, firm breast and nipple, only just visible in the half-light. She followed the direction of his gaze but made no move to pick the strap up.

"It's been all-consuming since I got here."

"You've been training?"

"Yes."

"With guns?"

"Amongst other things," Field said.

"How very brave. I'm sure your mother told us you were a fighter. Didn't she, Geoffrey?"

"Richard is an accomplished boxer."

"And she said you have a temper . . ."

"Penelope," Geoffrey said sternly.

"No, I like a bit of spirit," she said.

"Better watch our step," Charlie Lewis added.

"Have you learned Chinese?" Penelope went on.

"I wouldn't claim to be fluent."

"Neither would I, but then I don't speak a word. Geoffrey and Charlie do, of course."

"Ignorance," Charles Lewis said languidly, "is the preserve of the taitai."

Field was frowning.

"Consort of a taipan," Geoffrey explained, "but in more general usage, expatriate lady."

"So you've not sampled the exotic delights of the city?" Penelope asked again, raising her eyebrow but still not lifting the strap of her dress.

"Penelope." Geoffrey was smiling benignly as he eased back in his chair, stretching out his false leg. "Do give the chap a break."

"No, it's a serious issue," Lewis said. "A man, whatever his station, must live here."

"Or a woman," Penelope said. She took a sip of her cocktail, which was yellow in color, with a cut strawberry resting on top. "I think he should have a Russian." She leaned forward again. "They're so beautiful and sexy, don't you think, Richard?"

Penelope smiled and touched his leg, the front of her dress dropping still further. "I'm sorry, we're teasing you." She sat back, taking a cigarette from the silver case on the table in front of her. "Everyone expects Shanghai to be decadent, so we like to give the impression of debauchery, but you're too nice to be teased, and you're family."

Field had drunk both the first and now this gin and tonic quickly, and was beginning to feel the effects.

"Another one, Richard?" Geoffrey asked.

Field shook his head.

Geoffrey leaned forward and stubbed out his cigarette in the silver ashtray. "I think we should go through to dinner."

To Field's dismay, Penelope Donaldson put her arm through his and led him along the veranda to the French doors, leaning against him a little, so the smell of Parisian perfume caught in his nostrils.

"How is your mother, Richard?" she asked.

"She's fine."

"I keep telling Geoffrey he should send money."

"She won't accept it."

"I'm sorry about your father."

Field had been trying not to look at her, but he turned and found himself flushing. Her brown eyes were soft, her gaze solemn now; only the corner of her mouth betrayed her amusement. He shrugged, not certain what he should say.

They had reached the dining room, which was again huge, the walls covered in floor-to-ceiling mirrors, in between which hung dark paintings of English country landscapes.

There were only a few groups eating, and another Indian waiter led them to a table by the window. It looked out onto the veranda where they'd just been sitting and the lawns beyond.

As his chair was pulled back, Field glanced up at the giant chandelier and wondered if he should offer to pay for his own dinner. He suspected that it would be bad form, but did not want to be seen as another poor cousin intent on sponging off the wealthy branch of the family.

Geoffrey ordered a bottle of champagne and lit another cigarette, offering the case around the table, so that, as the waiters filled their glasses, they were all smoking.

Field had never had champagne and had often wondered whether he would like it. He took to it so quickly that it was hard not to gulp it down.

"So who do you think is your man?" Geoffrey said when the waiter had placed the bottle in the silver wine bucket next to him.

"For the murder?" Field said, beginning to feel quite drunk.

"Yes."

"We've hardly begun—"

"Initial theories. A Jack the Ripper?" He turned to Lewis. "An Eastern Jack the Ripper?"

"The woman's flat belongs to Lu Huang."

Both the men opposite him frowned. "He's your suspect?" Geoffrey asked.

"Difficult to say at this stage. It's just that it was his apartment, and my colleagues think it was his men who bundled the doorman down to the Chinese city and presided over his execution."

"Doesn't seem Lu's style, stabbing a woman," Geoffrey said.

"I get the impression he's more or less above the law."

Geoffrey Donaldson shook his head vigorously. "No, no. We'd love to get him for something if we could, but . . . you know." He sighed, leaning back in his chair. "He has the French in his pocket and he's careful what he does and doesn't do in our jurisdiction, but . . ."

"Isn't the abduction of the doorman a crime in our jurisdiction?" Field had begun to sound truculent, so he took another large sip of champagne. "As well as the murder of the girl, of course."

"Yes, absolutely," Geoffrey said, nodding. "If you boys could get him on this, it would be marvelous, send a signal . . . you know. Don't you think, Charlie?"

"Absolutely," Lewis said without enthusiasm.

"The municipal authorities keep open contacts with Lu," Geoffrey said, "for reasons I'm sure you appreciate, but that doesn't mean he's above the law." He took another drag of his cigarette. "Anything you can do to teach everyone in this city a lesson on that score would earn you a lot of plaudits."

"That's enough politics, boys," Penelope said. "It's only a Russian girl, after all . . . Let's order, and then I want to know everything about Dickie's life here."

She looked down at her menu and then stood to excuse herself. As she passed her husband, she draped her arm over his shoulder affectionately and he placed a hand over her own. They both smiled.

By the time they'd finished dessert, Field was drunk and had said considerably more than he'd intended to. He'd talked about the rivalry between Macleod and Granger and told them about Prokopiev and his habit of leaping out of bed in the middle of the night and beating on the walls all the way down the corridor outside, shouting something incomprehensible in Russian.

They had smiled while he told this story, but Field thought he'd talked too much. Lewis's eyes had begun to glaze over.

"I propose," Lewis said, "that I take our boy here on a tour of the city's 'exotica.' " He stood, then they all did.

"Excellent idea. I'll take Mrs. Donaldson home," Geoffrey said.

"Now hang on a minute . . ." Penelope interjected.

Geoffrey cleared his throat noisily.

"Well," Penelope said petulantly, "a girl knows when she's not wanted." She leaned over and kissed Field on the cheek, her skin warm and her hair soft. As she did so, she touched his hip with her hand, leaving it there as she pulled her head back, before slipping it into the pocket of his jacket. "I hope you'll be virtuous tonight."

"Actually, I really ought to be getting home."

"Nonsense," Lewis said, adjusting his jacket and glancing at himself in the mirror.

Field's face was reddening. "I'm not actually sure I can afford . . ."

"Don't be ridiculous," Geoffrey said, looking at him with astonishment. "You're a policeman. Fraser's will pay."

Penelope's hand was still in his pocket and she scratched his side, then leaned forward to give him another kiss.

She picked up her shawl from the back of the chair and walked toward the door. Geoffrey edged around the table, smiling at him. "Good to see you, old chap." He shook Field's hand. "Let's stay in touch."

"I'd like that."

"Let's see to it, then." He nodded at Charles, then set off after his wife, who'd already gone through the big wooden doors.

Seven

ewis looked at Field. "You need a new dinner jacket, old man."

"This one will be fine in the winter."

Lewis smiled as he led the way out to the reception area and the stone steps beyond. Field had not realized how drunk he was and half wished that he'd had the good sense to say no to this excursion.

Charles Lewis leaned through the window when his chauffeur-driven Buick came to a halt. "Delancey's," he said before climbing into the back, Field following him. As they drove off, they saw Geoffrey and Penelope Donaldson getting into rickshaws. "He's a good man, Geoffrey," Lewis said. "One of the very best."

"Yes."

"Doesn't even seem to mind about Penelope."

"What do you mean?"

Lewis smiled at him, leaning back into the far corner of the rear seat. "You must have seen she's a bit of a goer."

Field frowned.

"You should give her a try. Goes like a belter. Geoffrey doesn't mind."

"I'm not sure what you mean."

"Handsome chap like you could use a bit of experience."

"Geoffrey is my uncle."

"So what? She's no blood relation, is she?"

Field's moral dismay was only offset by the image of Penelope's nipple that had somehow contrived to stay with him. "I'm sure she's not at all like that."

"He won the Victoria Cross in the war, you know," Lewis went on.

"Yes, my mother is very proud of him."

"And so she should be. He's a bloody good sort."

Field found that this reflection of his own judgment on his uncle made him warm to Lewis a little, but they were both silent until the car pulled up outside a dimly lit building that showed no sign of being anything other than a warehouse. He began to wonder if this was some sort of joke until he saw a bouncer standing a few feet away, hidden in the shadows. The door was opened immediately to reveal what looked like a seedier version of the club they'd just been to, with a bar to their left and tables in front of a stage bathed in red light. A Chinese waitress in a skimpy, figure-hugging cream dress led them through to a table at the front. On the stage, two women were kissing each other. One was naked, the other wore a garter belt and stockings.

The one who was naked had blond hair—both were Caucasian—and she broke off the embrace and began to run her tongue over the other girl's nipples until they were erect and proud, the girl arching her back in feigned, or possibly, Field supposed, real pleasure, as the blond sank lower, sitting her partner on a chair and raising her stockinged legs over each arm, parting the dark hair at the base of her belly and moving her tongue slowly toward the pink lips beneath. Field and Lewis were only about two yards from the seated woman as she moaned with pleasure, pushing her hips up and her head back.

The blond pushed her buttocks back and her legs out.

Field was sweating. A glass of beer was placed in front of him by the waitress and he turned and looked first at her, then at Lewis, who was smiling at him. Lewis leaned forward. "For Christ's sake, man, will you take off your jacket?"

After a moment's hesitation, Field did so, swinging it over

the back of the chair and immediately feeling better, even though he could smell the stale sweat.

"And the holster. Guns make the girls nervous."

Field took off his leather holster, which he'd forgotten he was wearing, and hung it underneath his jacket. He took a large sip of the beer. A middle-aged man with a gray beard and glasses sitting by himself on the other side of the room was staring at him.

The women on the stage were a writhing, groaning mass now, the blond-haired one thrusting her buttocks out toward them, legs apart, while the woman in the chair had wrapped her own around her partner's neck.

The Chinese waitress came back and, without any prompting, sat on Field's lap. "Oh," she said, laughing at him, moving to his knees and stroking his groin with her hand. Field took hold of her wrist to make her stop, but he did not push her away. She was pretty, with an oval face and dark eyes, her body slim and light. Her skirt was pulled up so that Field could see that she was not wearing any underwear. She reminded him of Yang, Granger's secretary.

"You want another drink?" she asked in good English.

"No," he said, his voice hoarse. He saw that another girl had gone to sit on Lewis's lap. Beyond that, at the next table, a group of expat men seemed to have their wives with them, or girlfriends, and were just watching the show. The man with the beard was still staring in their direction.

"You want upstairs room?"

"No." He shook his head.

"You have hotel. Fifty dollar, one night."

Field could see that he had been brought to a place that catered to taipans, since fifty dollars was almost as much as he earned in a week.

Lewis got up and led his girl toward a set of stairs in the corner.

"Your friend go."

"Yes."

Field felt a sense of inexplicable drunken fury and wanted

to leave, but was prevented from doing so, he knew, by his mother's obsession with adhering to social protocol.

"Come on," the girl said, reaching for his crotch once more, so quickly that Field was unable to get his hand on her wrist until she had taken a hold of him.

"Stop it," he said.

"I show you happy time."

"I don't doubt it . . ."

"We go upstairs . . ."

"I have no money," he said in exasperation.

She took her hand away, looking at him in amazement. "Your friend. On account."

She stood, taking his hand gently now, and, despite every bone in his body screaming at him to remain where he was, Field found that he was following her, forgetting about his jacket and pistol and oblivious to everything but the swaying of her hips and buttocks as they moved inside her silk dress.

The room was at the top of the building, down a long corridor, and it was less seedy than he'd imagined: a brass bed like the one he'd found Lena Orlov on this afternoon, covered in a white sheet. Before he'd had time to change his mind, she'd let her dress fall, revealing small dark nipples and slim hips.

She sank to her knees in front of him, skillfully unzipping his trousers as he tried to prevent her, and taking him into her mouth.

Overcome with shame and revulsion, he tried to reject her, but she held his balls in one hand and gripped both them and his buttocks when he tried to pull away.

She took her mouth from him and pulled him hard onto the bed. Field closed his eyes as he felt the roughness of her hair against his groin and the wetness inside her.

He pulled away, standing, head pounding, face red, fighting for breath. "No," he said. "I'm sorry, no."

He stumbled out into the corridor, shoving himself back into his trousers as the girl shouted something at him in Chinese. She was standing naked in the door to the room.

There was a scream from somewhere close, the cry of a

woman in pain, and Field instinctively moved toward the
source of the noise before checking himself. His girl shouted
abuse again.

There was another scream, high-pitched and piercing. It
died down to a quiet sob. Field finished doing up his trousers,
hating himself, and walked slowly along the corridor, listening
to the sound of the girl crying.

It had come from a room close to the stairs, and the door
was ajar, the two bodies inside illuminated by a candle flickering high on a shelf.

The girl's arms were tied to the top of the bed, her legs visible on either side of Lewis's back.

For a moment Field stood still. He saw Lewis move, then
turn around. Their eyes met.

Field moved quickly down the stairs. He retrieved his
jacket and pistol from the chair and walked to the door.

Outside, without saying anything, the doorman offered
him a cigarette. Field took it in the hope that it would relax his
nerves, but it had the opposite effect.

He closed his eyes. Christ, he was drunk.

He waited, pacing one way and then another, wondering
what he should do. He couldn't see any rickshaws and they
seemed to be down some kind of back alley.

The door opened and Lewis was standing there, his hat on,
unruffled and cool. "What was that all about?"

Field stared at him. "I don't fuck prostitutes."

"Suit yourself." Lewis shrugged. "They're pretty top-end,
you know. Good-time girls."

Field didn't respond, taking another deep drag on his cigarette.

"They're only Chinese girls." Lewis saw the look on Field's
face and frowned. "All right, we'll take it down a step." Somehow the Buick had appeared from nowhere and Lewis bent
over to speak to his driver once more. "Majestic Café." He
turned to Field. "Come on, Russian girls. They sometimes do
it for free."

Field shook his head. "No. Thanks, but no thanks."

Lewis was laughing at him again. "Come on."

"No, I've an early start."

"Haven't we all."

Field shrugged. "Maybe I just haven't adjusted yet."

"Don't you want to see where Lena Orlov worked?"

Through the haze of his drunkenness, Field tried to identify what kind of look had crossed Lewis's face, but he couldn't
be sure. "What do you mean?"

"I mean, don't you want to see where Lena Orlov
worked?"

"You knew her?"

"Hardly. Of her. She danced at the Majestic. We took a
turn once, but she was too tarty for me."

Field found himself thinking not of Lena but Natasha. "All
right," he said.

On the way to the club, Field had barely registered where
they were going, but he saw now that they'd been in the Outside Roads Area, a part of Shanghai that was not quite under
either international or Chinese jurisdiction—the road belonged
to the international community, but the houses off it were a
gray area—and it took a few minutes to return to the better-lit
streets of the Settlement. They didn't talk on the way.

The Majestic Café was on the first floor, and Field recognized her voice as they walked up the newly carpeted staircase.
"Best Russian girls in town," Lewis said, but Field ignored
him.

Her voice was low, husky, languid, as if the song could go
on all night. As he came to the top of the stairs and saw her,
she was almost caressing the microphone, her hips swaying
gently from side to side with the mesmeric rhythm of a
metronome, her unfashionably long brown hair tumbling
down the front of a close-cut, regally elegant white dress.

Ahead of them, couples twirled slowly on an enormous
dance floor, but on both sides, those still seated watched the
stage, held by the power of her voice.

"I think you'd better shut your mouth, old boy, in case you catch a fly," Lewis said, smirking at him. "Jacket on," he whispered.

Lewis walked forward to the iron balcony overlooking the dance floor, and for a moment Field thought that Natasha was looking at him, but her eyes returned slowly to the middle of the room, her hips still swaying as she threw her head back and smiled.

The song came to an end and she put the microphone down. For a moment there was a hushed silence, as if they wanted to be sure she had finished, and then the room was filled with thunderous applause, some of the men close to the stage on their feet and shouting, "Encore! Encore!"

She waved them away, almost contemptuously, before climbing down the small wooden steps at the end of the stage. As a large man stood and walked up to take her place, she tried to make her way down the side of the dance floor, past well-wishers and admirers who impeded her progress. She bent her head to kiss an elderly, balding man who was seated in front of her, and he held her arm, whispering in her ear. Field noticed how low her dress was cut. She had a string of pearls around her neck that reached almost to the floor when she was bending down, and her hair obscured her face.

She laughed and the man stood, taking her hand and leading her through to the dance floor, smiling smugly, Field thought, as they took their place among the twirling couples.

He forced himself to turn away, only to find Lewis still smiling at him. "In love, eh?" He shook his head. "Beyond your price range, old man."

"She was a friend of Lena Orlov's."

"She was, but then, I think you'll find Natasha has quite a few friends, if you know what I mean."

Field turned to face the dance floor again, to avoid saying something he would regret. His eyes were drawn back to her even though he tried to focus on almost anyone else.

She towered over the old man, but he was clutching her—pawing her—his hand on her buttocks.

Was that what she did? She danced and fucked men like that for money?

Field looked up across her head, to the tables beyond. This room had formed the backdrop for the photograph he'd seen of Natasha and Lena together.

"Does she work here?" he asked Lewis.

"Who?"

"Natasha . . . Miss Medvedev."

"Not anymore."

"She used to?"

"Not so very long ago, she was the star attraction, but she only takes a turn now if she wants to. She sings when the mood takes her. Great voice."

"What has caused the change in her position?"

Lewis shrugged. He was playing the indolent, ignorant playboy, but Field had already judged him a man of shrewd intelligence, much sharper than he liked to make out.

Field was suddenly certain that Lewis had slept with Natasha.

The band temporarily halted, the white man at this end of the stage lowering his trombone and wiping the sweat from his brow with a cloth. Lewis turned around, descended the steps to the dance floor, and walked to the other side. He followed Natasha as she glided elegantly to her place on the plinth above and waited as the elderly man she had danced with kissed her hand.

Natasha smiled as she saw Charles Lewis, and Field watched him kiss her on the cheek and lead her back to the floor as the band started up again.

Field found it impossible to take his eyes off them.

They were a handsome couple, the same height, his face square and handsome, save for a broken nose, hers so perfectly formed it was uncomfortable to look at.

Field tore himself away and turned around.

He needed to have a piss, so he walked to the set of swinging doors beside him and pushed his way through to the corridor beyond, smacking the doors loudly into the walls.

He washed his hands, looking at his face in the mirror and seeing his anger reflected back at him. He breathed in deeply and bent his head.

Back in the lobby, he bought a packet of cigarettes from the attendant. He smoked one, looking out through a small window at the end at the rooftops behind the Bund. It was time to go home now. Lewis would probably not even notice he'd gone.

He was leaning against the wall, thinking he was smoking too much, when Natasha Medvedev came through. Her smile faded as she saw him. He straightened, holding the cigarette down by his side.

"I'm not one of your schoolmasters," she said.

Field tried to laugh, but wasn't certain he even got as far as a smile. Self-consciously, he took another drag.

"Are you going to offer me one?"

He dug the packet from his pocket and chucked it at her. She caught it and took one, waiting until he leaned forward to light it.

"You're not much of a gentleman, are you, Officer?"

"And you're not much of a lady."

She inhaled, blowing the smoke out of the side of her mouth, before moving over to the wall opposite him and leaning back against it.

Field threw his cigarette, which he wasn't enjoying, out of the window and put his hands in his pockets.

"I saw you arriving with Charlie Lewis. You're a friend of his?"

"I hardly know him."

"Well, you should get to—"

"You danced here with Lena Orlov." Field had taken his hands from his pockets again and spoken with unexpected ferocity. "You were friends."

"So?"

"Everything you told me this afternoon was a pack of lies."

"And you're hurt?"

"That's an offense, do you know that?"

"Is that a threat?"

"You can laugh at us all you want, but you're vulnerable here, Miss Medvedev, no matter how much you sleep with the likes of Charlie Lewis or Lu."

She was staring at him. "Is that what you think I am? You think I'm a prostitute?"

From a standing start, he'd insulted and perhaps—this couldn't be true, but somehow seemed to be—hurt her. He wished he were less drunk. The conversation had developed a momentum that their brief acquaintance hardly merited.

"I'm sorry," he said. "I didn't mean to offend you. The ways of the city are strange."

She was still looking at him, her hostility not assuaged. "They are strange, and perhaps it is you who should be careful."

"Is that a threat?"

"It's a warning."

"You were good friends with Lena Orlov."

"Yes I was." Now she threw her own cigarette through the window.

"Then why did you lie to me?"

"Because I didn't want to answer a lot of questions."

"Why did you go around to her apartment?"

She sighed. "To get some milk."

"But—"

"I went in because it was unusual for her door to be unlocked. That was the only lie." She sighed. "Lena was a Russian girl, Detective."

"Like you."

"Yes, like me."

"So it doesn't matter."

She looked at him, then came forward and took the lapel of his jacket, flicking it with one long, thin finger. "You need a new suit, or you'll boil to death. The summer has only just begun."

Charles Lewis walked in through the doors and stopped.
"Conspiracy," he said. "He's not rich enough for you." He took
Natasha Medvedev's hand. "Come on, I want one more
dance."

Field left and took a rickshaw back to his dingy room in the
Carter Road quarters. The steward was asleep in his chair
when he got to the top floor and the corridor quiet. Prokopiev's
door was, thankfully, shut.

Field closed his own door carefully, lest Prokopiev hear,
and took off his jacket, switching on the fan on the wall beside
him.

The room was tiny. Yellow paint peeled in large strips off
the walls and ceiling on account of the damp. There was a
small window, but Field had learned never to open it in the
summer because of the mosquitoes.

He sat down at his desk, put his holster on the starched
white sheet beside him, and opened the leather-bound diary.
He returned to his jacket to remove his father's fountain pen.

Underneath the date and still feeling drunk, he wrote: *Met
a girl—a woman—and can't stop thinking about whether or not
she is compromised and . . . honest. Don't know why it matters,
but it does.*

He stared at the page for a few moments more—this was
the first thing he'd written for weeks—then slipped off his
shoes, trousers, and shirt and slumped down onto the bed. He
leaned forward again to flick the light switch and clumsily
knocked the copy of *The Great Gatsby* he had bought last
week onto the floor. He didn't bother to pick it up.

There were no curtains, so the streetlamps created dappled
pools of light and shadow on the walls and ceiling.

Field closed his eyes. His head and heart pounded as he
imagined Natasha doing what the Chinese girl had done, his
hands entwined in her long hair. His whole body was covered
in sweat.

Eight

e have made the assumption," Caprisi said, looking around the C.1 office, "that the doorman was killed because he could definitively identify the murderer. Chen has been through the building and the surrounding area, and everyone insists they saw no one arrive or leave. But the murderer must have come in sometime during the evening."

They were in a small group outside Macleod's office. It was not yet nine and Field was glad he'd come in early, though his awakening several hours ago was the result of a night's drunken, dehydrated sleep and Prokopiev berating the steward on their landing for bringing him tea rather than coffee.

"Where does Lu come into it?" Macleod asked.

"Lu owned the flats," Caprisi said. "We believe his men were responsible for the abduction of the doorman."

"Says who?"

"Chen."

They all looked at the Chinese detective, who smiled.

"All right," Macleod went on, "his men were cleaning up, so he might have killed the girl, but why?"

"His flat," Caprisi said, "his girl. His pleasure."

"Wouldn't he take the precaution of getting her over to the French Concession first?"

"Perhaps he lost his temper, although"—Caprisi looked at Field—"Maretsky says it is more premeditated than that." He shrugged. "Maybe Lu is arrogant enough now to think he can get away with anything, anywhere."

Macleod nodded.

"We should apply to the French authorities for permission to interview him formally."

"Yes." Macleod's voice was hard and confident, but he fiddled with the chain around his neck as he talked. He looked at Field—which all of them kept on doing, he noticed, as if eyeing an enemy in their midst. It was clear that none of them trusted him or felt comfortable with his presence. "So you think it could have been Lu himself?" Macleod went on.

"It could have been," Caprisi said. "But if it isn't, then he knows who it is and is protecting him. That's why they disposed of the doorman. There was certainly a cleanup operation. There was no murder weapon, no prints on the cuffs."

Macleod was staring at the floor, still fiddling with the chain. In some ways, he reminded Field of his father; he seemed to have the same sense of moral and practical certainty.

Caprisi had a notebook open in his hand. "So we talk to Lu when permission comes through from the French. We try the apartment block again and talk to Natasha, the unhelpful neighbor."

"Natasha and Lena were close friends," Field said. "They danced together at the Majestic Café."

All three detectives looked at him in silence for a moment. "Okay," Caprisi said, "since we are short of direct evidence, we should work on tracing through Orlov's life. Was she a prostitute? Did she have a regular man? Did she exclusively belong to Lu, and did he lend her to anyone else? And there's this." Caprisi produced the leather volume with the hole cut in it and handed it, open, to Macleod, who took out the notebook and glanced through it.

"Names of ships, departure dates, and destinations," Caprisi explained.

"I can see that."

"We don't know its relevance, but if Lena was one of Lu's girls, it may have something to do with him, or with the man who killed her."

Macleod shut the book and handed it back to Caprisi. "Right. Keep me briefed. The municipal authorities wish to be kept closely informed on this investigation, and the commissioner wants regular updates."

They all frowned, including Field.

Caprisi turned away. Field followed Chen toward the American detective's desk.

"Field," Macleod said. Field stopped and turned. "You playing rugby tomorrow?"

"Yes, I believe so, sir."

"Granger has been telling everyone you're a find."

"He's never seen me play."

"You're fit?"

"Yes."

"You're sure?" Macleod was smiling.

"I'm sure."

"Caprisi, make sure you break this boy's leg." Macleod took a step toward Field and stretched his arms above his head. "He's good, you know, for a Yank."

"So everyone says."

Field sensed the tension as soon as he entered the ten o'clock briefing. It was held in a large, gloomy room behind the duty sergeant's counter on the first floor. Field took a seat at the back behind Caprisi, at a desk almost identical to the ones they'd had at school, even down to the graffiti. Someone had carved in big letters: *Smith for fucking Pope.* There was graffiti etched into the dark wooden panels beside him, too, paint on the walls above peeling off in large chunks. There were no pictures or adornments of any kind and the two fans hanging down on long metal poles from the ceiling stood idle. Field had never seen them work. Whatever the police budget was being spent on, it wasn't building maintenance. The whole building had an aura of decay about it.

The old clock between the frosted glass windows at the end

of the room was tilted to the side, but still showed that the briefing was late again.

Field leaned against the wooden panel and closed his eyes, losing himself in the hubbub around him.

He was jostled and turned to see a group of officers in full protective gear coming through the door. Sorenson, a small, surly, dark-haired man from Ohio, took off his heavy metal jacket and let it drop to the floor with a loud thud, then stacked it and the helmet against the back wall along with his machine gun. He had been unfriendly during Field's attachment to the incident room here in Central, and didn't bother to acknowledge him as he shoved his way into a seat next to one of the Chinese officers on the far wall.

Caprisi lit a cigarette and then, without looking around, threw the packet over his shoulder onto Field's lap.

Captain Smith walked in. He clipped Caprisi over the head playfully with a buff-colored folder on his way to the lectern. He was tall—six feet two or three—with a narrow face and white hair. Like most of the men in the room, he was in blue summer uniform, the silver badge on his lapel above his name tag highly polished. He ran his fingers along his nose. "All right, gentlemen." He was looking at the file in front of him. "I'm going to let Mr. Granger begin today."

Granger had been standing quietly in the doorway and now ambled forward, a cigarette in the corner of his mouth. As he took Smith's place at the lectern, he half closed his eyes against the smoke, which drifted up toward the ceiling.

"Borodin is back in town," he said with an obvious distaste for the communist agitator. "He's been in the south to organize the Reds down there and make sure the funding is getting through, but he arrived back at Central Station last night." He cleared his throat. "There is only one strike at the moment, over in Pudong, but be on the lookout for any information you can pick up. I will be doing the rounds of the other stations, but we believe they will be targeting Central for leaflet handouts and quick impromptu rallies. He'll be using students to do

the dirty work. We want to respond swiftly and I hardly need
remind you what happens when the mob gets out of hand." He
looked around the room. "So make it a priority. Of course, the
Municipal Council is very anxious that we keep up last year's
tough line." Granger took another drag of his cigarette. "Any
questions?"

Apart from a couple of coughs and feet scuffing the floor,
the room was silent.

"All right," Smith said, stepping forward. "Sorenson led a
team out on the armed robbery this morning at a jeweler's
shop on Boone Road that you will probably have heard about.
It looks like our friends in the Green Gang again, but they're
improving their speed; they were long gone by the time we got
there. They wore masks, so no IDs from the old couple in the
shop, but we did get a license plate, B4563. Please make a note
of that."

Field watched the uniformed officers around him writing
the number down in their books.

"We've also got a kidnapping this morning. Bubbling Well
Road, next to the Italian consulate. Young boy, about eleven,
dark hair. Father's quite high up in Fraser's. Chinese, obviously. Not sure why they've reported it. I'm sure they'll pay up
in the end. No message in the paper yet, but probably the
Green Gang again. There's a picture of the boy pinned to the
back wall there, so take a look at it on the way out. Now . . .
there was a Russian girl murdered yesterday in the Happy
Times block on Foochow Road." Captain Smith was smiling as
he said this and there was a jeer from the men. Sorenson whistled at the back. "I give you Detective Caprisi."

Caprisi got up and walked to the front as the men continued to cheer and whistle. He wasn't smiling when he turned
and faced them.

"The Russian girl's name," Caprisi said, having waited for
them to stop, "was Lena Orlov. She was tied up, stabbed
almost twenty times. There does not appear to have been a
sexual assault."

"He couldn't get the handcuffs undone," Sorenson said. There was a guffaw of laughter.

Caprisi ignored it. "Has anyone ever heard of anything similar . . . not murder, but violence against Russian girls . . ."

"I've got a thousand," Sorenson said. "A thousand cases."

"I've got two," someone else added, and there was another guffaw of laughter.

"The flats belong to Lu," Caprisi said, his mood souring further. "So do the women in it. The doorman was taken away and executed yesterday, and everyone else in the neighborhood claims not to have seen a thing."

Field noticed that Maretsky had come in and was leaning against the back wall, also scowling. Field assumed he'd heard the laughter.

"Chen and I are dealing with any direct leads," Caprisi went on. "Along with Richard Field from S.1. But we want to hear about anyone who could give us a sense of this falling into a pattern."

"I'll raise you two thousand," Sorenson said. "Two thousand Russian tarts being slapped about . . . two thousand cases . . . no, three thousand . . ." There was more laughter, and Field watched Maretsky turn and walk out, his face a picture of disgust.

"Try not to be an Ohio boy all your life, Sorenson," Caprisi said easily as he thrust his hands in his pockets and walked back from the lectern.

"That's it," Smith said. Chairs and desks scraped across the floor as everyone got to their feet and began talking. Sorenson stood and picked up his jacket and helmet. He hadn't shaved this morning, his short hair and bullet head making him look like a convict. "You've never used handcuffs?" he asked Caprisi.

"Sure, Caprisi was fucking her," Prokopiev said, standing up next to Sorenson. "Little Russian girl, little bit of pain . . ."

"You should keep a hold of the keys, old man," Sorenson taunted.

"I was fucking her, too, of course," Prokopiev went on.

"She danced at the Majestic, right? The spoiled little princess screamed."

Caprisi stood still, his head tilted to one side, staring at the floor. Prokopiev took a step closer, towering over the American. He was a huge man, with the body of a wrestler, short, spiky hair, and a bulbous nose above big lips.

"Back off, Prokopiev," Field said quietly.

The Russian turned to stare at him. "Ah, the new boy." Everyone was looking at Field now. "You couldn't even find your dick in a storm, or maybe . . . I see now . . . Good for you, Caprisi, just like Slugger, just like old—"

Caprisi launched himself into Prokopiev's stomach, so that the Russian was caught off guard and spun back over a desk, smashing into the officers who'd gathered behind him. Field took a step forward, saw Sorenson turn, and watched the punch coming. He ducked easily and struck him with a powerful left on the side of the jaw, so that he fell onto Prokopiev.

"Enough!" Granger shoved the men aside and yanked Sorenson roughly to his feet. "You should know fucking better. All of you. Get up, Prokopiev." He waited as the Russian got up and dusted himself down, glowering at both of them. Field wondered if Granger would discipline them, but he said simply, "As if there isn't enough trouble out there." He turned and pushed Caprisi out of the door, glancing at Field and indicating that he should follow. The two of them walked past the desk sergeant and climbed the stairs beside the lift, not stopping until they had almost reached Crime on the third floor.

Caprisi bent over, as if trying to catch his breath. "Give me a minute, would you?" he asked. "In fact, make that an hour."

"Sure."

The American straightened and looked out of the small, slitted window at the smoke drifting across the rooftops. "I'll be in here if you need me."

Field took out his cigarettes and offered Caprisi one, but the American shook his head. "What did Prokopiev mean?" Field asked. "About Slugger."

"Forget it, Field."

"Sure." He took a pace back. "I'll . . . I'll meet you in an hour." Field turned away and began to climb the stairs.

"Dick."

Field stopped.

"Where did you learn to punch like that?"

"My father taught me."

"Thanks."

"It's hard," Field said, "not knowing . . ."

"You don't understand, do you?"

"Understand what?"

Caprisi shook his head, bemused. "You really don't know?"

"Know what?"

"We'll get there, Field." Caprisi raised his hand and walked away. He was smiling.

Nine

ield didn't want to go into the Special Branch offices to face Prokopiev's hostility and Granger's wrath, so he went on up to the sixth floor. It was dark up here. The door at the end of the corridor was blue, with paint peeling around a small pane of frosted glass. Field knocked once and then entered without bothering to wait for an answer. He dropped his cigarette and felt the heat as he stubbed it out under the sole of his shoe.

Maretsky was seated at his desk. He was reading the newspaper with his back to the door, his feet not touching the ground.

"I thought I might find you here," Field said. Maretsky did not reply, turning back to his newspaper.

It was a tiny room, the desk occupying most of it. Field had to step to the left and shut the door before he had anywhere to stand. There was a bookcase behind him, full of newspapers, and the wall opposite was covered with yellowing clippings in fading newsprint pinned to a corkboard. Every one of them referred to Lu Huang.

"There was a fight after you left," Field said.

"Sorenson is an animal." Maretsky did not raise his eyes from the newspaper. Field leaned back, crossing his legs. The article in the center of the corkboard opposite had a picture of a smiling Lu underneath the headline "Another Generous Donation to Sisters of Mercy Orphanage."

Maretsky swung around, looking at Field over the top of

his glasses. He followed Field's gaze to the clippings on the wall. "Sometimes he prefers them younger."

Field stared at him.

"Eleven or twelve."

"From that orphanage?"

Maretsky shrugged. "From wherever takes his fancy and whoever is willing to be bought, which means most people in this city."

"The donations are for procuring . . ."

"Oh, I don't know the specifics of individual donations, but it's a nice irony, don't you think?"

Field shook his head slowly. "No."

"I usually deal with visitors in the registry."

"I know."

"Then do me the courtesy of calling when you wish to see me."

"I need to keep out of the office until tempers cool."

"Well, this is not a rest room."

"Who was Slugger?"

Maretsky frowned. "Slugger?"

"Prokopiev taunted Caprisi by referring to a Slugger . . ."

"Slugger Davis. Alan Davis. A detective from London. Caprisi's partner until the end of last year."

"What happened to him?"

Maretsky turned back to the newspaper. "Ask Caprisi."

"He won't say."

"Then I won't, either."

"I think I should know if I'm working with him."

"You think you are."

"What does that mean?"

Maretsky frowned. "What do you want, Field?"

"Can I smoke in here?"

"No you can't."

Field crossed his arms. "Why did you walk out of the briefing?"

"Don't you have work to do?"

"You know I'm on the Orlov case."

"The Orlov *case,*" Maretsky said, raising his eyebrows. "I see. When is it a case, not an incident, I wonder?"

"What do you mean?"

"A little Russian princess. A whore. Bit of a playful end. Why would anyone care about that?" He looked at Field, his piggy eyes burning with angry intensity. "You care about it, Field, why is that?"

"She was murdered."

"She was a Russian prostitute."

"So it doesn't matter?"

Maretsky hesitated. "Is that a philosophical question or a practical one?"

"It's just about doing a job . . ."

"Oh, is it? Of course. How foolish of me." He turned back to his desk. "We work within our limitations here, Mr. Field, and if you haven't learned that, you soon will."

"You mean *you* do."

"I mean *I* do, yes. I can see you're not a member of the club, but a bright young man . . ." He smiled. "It won't last, so I wouldn't worry about it."

Field tried not to betray his confusion. "Tell me about this case, Maretsky."

"You're the detective."

"So Lu can do whatever he likes?"

Maretsky faced him again. "Please, I have work to do."

"Tell me about him."

"You really don't understand, do you?"

"Don't patronize me."

"Don't patronize you?" Maretsky sighed deeply. "All right, I'm sorry, I'm just not used to idealism." He breathed out again. "Or perhaps I should say ignorance. You seem to be . . . energetic, but what will happen if you *pursue* this case with any vigor is that you will make a certain amount of headway and then you won't get any further. If you get somewhere close to the truth, it will become very dangerous for you. As to evidence, forget it. Witnesses will be too frightened to speak, and will be eliminated if they are foolish enough to do so." He rolled his eyes. "This is Lu's girl. He killed her himself, or gave her to someone else for the purpose—it doesn't much matter."

"But we can still establish the truth, can't we? Or do you consider that naive, too? We can still determine whether the murder was carried out by Lu himself, and if not, who it is he is protecting and why."

Maretsky didn't answer.

"Will he do it again?"

"Probably."

"Has he done it before?"

Maretsky hesitated. "Possibly. I can't be sure. We have no record of anything like . . . specifically like this, and the French say they have none . . . but . . ."

Field could tell that, despite himself, Maretsky was interested. "But what?"

He shrugged. "There is a confidence to it."

"What do you mean?"

Maretsky was silent. "It's a developed fantasy," he said.

"You mean he's done similar things before?"

"I mean there is a history leading up to this. You would have a pattern of violence against women. To begin with, beating, sexually abusing . . . the abuse becomes steadily more violent. Then, one day, it gets out of hand and he actually kills a girl. He enjoys it. So now he goes about achieving the same satisfaction with greater confidence. He knows what he wants. The kind of attire he likes, tied up, under control."

"So there might be a pattern?"

"There *is* a pattern. One *might* be able to find it."

"And now it will accelerate?"

"I would say he has done this before. It will certainly continue now, and it might accelerate."

"Other girls in Lu's possession?"

"I don't know."

"So we do nothing?"

Maretsky shrugged.

"So you won't help me?"

"I wish you good luck."

"Tell me about Lu."

"What about him?"

"He's your private obsession." Field looked at the clippings on the wall.

"Only in an academic sense."

"Then tell me about him in an academic way. Whatever has happened, he is at the center of it."

Maretsky closed his newspaper. He took off his glasses and placed them carefully on the desk. "There are many files," he said quietly.

"And most of them are not in the system."

Maretsky stared at his hands for a long time.

"Lu is restless. In ten years he has accrued to himself absolute power. You won't believe me, of course, won't accept the true nature of the word 'absolute,' or the influence I ascribe to him. Only those who know the city completely do. But it is true nevertheless. However, his power is never enough. Never. There is always someone not quite under control . . . something that is irritating, like a fly."

Field wiped away the sweat that had gathered on his forehead. "Money? In the French Concession, I mean. He's bribing people. Is that it?"

Maretsky smiled. "In the *French* Concession. Oh yes. Don't they say every man has his price?" He straightened. "It's true, of course. Every man does have his price."

"So he buys people."

"You misunderstand me. Every man has his *price*, but that does not mean every man can be *bought*."

"Try to be less obtuse."

"You're an intelligent man, Mr. Field." He nodded. "I can appreciate that, though perhaps not why you ended up here. I don't doubt you are flushed with idealism and an optimistic and perhaps even opportunistic sense of the possible."

"So it's not always about money? He finds other ways of controlling people. Blackmail?"

"It is *not* always money. He likes the feeling of absolute control and has developed a taste for more, shall we say, persuasive measures. He is a gangster, a nobody from nowhere who had terrible bad luck as a child in a country where bad luck usually means destitution and death. He survived. With a cunning and ruthlessness and skill we can only imagine, he has dragged himself up through the underbelly of this city to a position he could never have dreamed would ever be his. He has power and money beyond the imagination of most Chinese, let alone those who began life in such desperate circumstances. His position is an obsession. He will leave nothing to chance and do anything to protect it. He has systematically set out to buy everyone and everything in this city so that he can never go back to the world he has fought so hard to get away from. The fear of a return to poverty keeps him awake at night, still. In this city it is the survival of the fittest, and believe me, he has done everything in his power to ensure no one can touch him. He is unassailable. If he is behind these murders, then you cannot win and you may as well not try."

"So what other measures does he use?"

Maretsky frowned, as if frustrated that his message was not getting through. "Ask Caprisi to tell you about Slugger, Field." Maretsky shook his head. "But why do you, a bright ambitious young man with the right social connections—or so I have heard—why do you care about a poor Russian princess who fell by the wayside?"

Field straightened. He felt his face reddening.

"You are a knight in shining armor, is that it?"

"No one is unassailable, Maretsky."

"Then how little you really know."

Ten

s Field and Caprisi stepped out of the car in front of the Happy Times block, a few rays of sunshine broke through the clouds, giving the yellow stone a mellow glow. The building had wide, circular stone steps at its entrance, with a small area of garden on either side, the trees now in bloom, the pink petals of their flowers thick on the ground, where they'd been swept up by the winds that sometimes accompanied the summer monsoons.

In the lift Caprisi checked his hair and turned to Field as they reached the top floor. It was just the two of them. According to the American, Chen had gone off before the briefing to try to establish the identities of the men who'd seized the door man.

Field thought that Natasha Medvedev had been expecting them, because she was already dressed—in a long, floral skirt, with a simple white blouse—and they were ushered in without any resistance. Natasha ignored him and focused her attentions on Caprisi. She seemed different—quieter, shorn again of the air of sophistication and weary cynicism. All Field could remember was his anger at the sight of the old man clawing her buttocks the previous evening, light from the chandeliers reflecting off the sheen of sweat on his forehead.

"Can I get you something to drink?"

"Some water, please."

She turned to Field, without expression, but he shook his head.

Natasha came back with a glass of water and handed it to Caprisi.

"You were a friend of Lena Orlov?" Caprisi asked.

"Yes."

"How close?"

She shrugged. "What do you mean?"

"I mean you're both Russian girls. Did you know each other before you came to Shanghai?"

"Yes, we were at school together in Kazan, on the Volga. Our fathers were friends."

Caprisi got out his notebook, taking the stub of a pencil from the top pocket of his jacket. "Does Lena have any relatives here in Shanghai?"

Natasha shook her head. "No. Most of her close family perished." She looked at her feet, which were in open sandals. She moved them to and fro, before crossing one long, slim leg over the other, the skirt riding up the smooth skin of her calf.

"Did you see or hear anyone coming to the apartment the night before last?"

She looked up again. "I was out."

"All night?"

"More or less."

"What time did you leave?"

She thought for a moment. "About eleven."

"And you didn't hear anyone coming up the lift?"

"No."

"You didn't drop around before going out?"

Natasha shook her head.

"You went out . . . where?"

"The Majestic."

"So when was the last time you saw her?"

Natasha hesitated. "In the afternoon." She sat up straight, flicking her hair from her eyes. "I went for a walk on the recreation ground and, as I returned, Lena was coming in below. She'd been shopping on Nanking Road."

"How was she?"

"She was . . ." Natasha shrugged. "She was okay."

"Only okay?"

"What do you want, Detective? Her life wasn't a picnic."

Natasha was staring at both of them now, her brown eyes angry.

"She went into her flat," Caprisi went on, unruffled, "and you into your own, and you heard nothing more until you went out again in the evening?"

"Yes."

"And what about after your return that night? What time did you come in?"

"Between three and four. I don't recall exactly."

"On your own?"

She stared at him. "Yes."

Field took out a cigarette and lit it. The others ignored him.

"And you . . . There was nothing unusual?" Caprisi asked.

"I was tired, Officer. I went straight to sleep."

"Did you see anyone arriving or leaving her apartment?"

"No."

"Did you hear anyone inside?"

She shook her head.

"And, when you awoke, you went over to borrow some milk?"

"Yes."

Field had been watching Caprisi taking notes. The pencil stub was so thick that it would have been impossible to write neatly, even if that had been his natural disposition. Caprisi's handwriting was the worst he'd ever seen.

The American looked up, putting the pencil between his lips, as if it were a cigarette. He leaned back in the chair. "Did Lena have a regular man, Miss Medvedev?"

Natasha stared at her feet again. "Yes, there was a boy in the band at the Majestic . . . Sergei . . . but it was not—"

"There were other men?"

"I don't know."

"Men who paid for her favors?"

"She has a sister . . . in Harbin." Natasha looked up, face burning with righteous anger. "She's only seventeen. Lena did it so that her sister didn't have to."

They were silent.

"This sister," Caprisi said quietly. "She is the only other survivor from the family we saw in a photo next door?"

"Yes."

"How many men . . . I mean was Lena a—"

"No." Natasha shrugged. "When she felt she had to."

"One consistent man?"

"Sometimes."

"What about the last few months? Was there anyone—"

"I don't know. We . . . never talked about it." She shook her head.

"What work do you do, Miss Medvedev?" Caprisi asked.

There was a long silence.

"If you think it should be obvious to us, then you're wrong."

"I sing at the Majestic."

"Just sing?"

She didn't dignify this with an answer.

"That was where Lena worked."

"Well done, Detective."

"So you would have known . . . would have seen which men she was . . . making an arrangement with."

"That's not how it works."

"How does it work?"

"Some of the men are married . . ." She sighed. "A girl may dance with a hundred in an evening, hints exchanged in whispers. The arrangements you are referring to are not made on the dance floor of the Majestic."

"How are they made?"

"Lena had a telephone. A man might call on her."

"But you didn't see any particular man calling?"

Natasha shook her head.

Caprisi had the pencil in his mouth again. "These flats are owned by Lu Huang."

She didn't react.

"So what brings you, or Lena, to live here?"

"We pay rent. To a company on Bubbling Well Road. If they're connected to Lu, then I'm not aware of it."

Field did not think Natasha was a good liar. Caprisi must have agreed, because he was looking around the flat, clearly wondering how she could afford to live in such surroundings.

"You must be aware of what happened to the doorman."

She nodded, again dropping her gaze.

"We believe that Lu's men were responsible."

Field looked at her right hand, which was pointing at the ground, her wrist limp. She was wearing a gold bracelet.

"Can you think of any reason," Caprisi went on, "for such drastic action?"

Natasha shrugged. "They say he was a communist."

"Like you," Field said.

She stared at him.

"How does the daughter of a tsarist officer," he went on, gesturing at the photograph on the bookshelf, "come to attend meetings at the *New Shanghai Life?*"

"My father is dead."

Field felt his face reddening. "So you have decided . . ."

"So it's none of your business."

"On the contrary," Caprisi said slowly. "It's very much Mr. Field's business. The Settlement takes a very . . . strong view of émigrés who abuse its hospitality by using this as a base to export political ideas to the Chinese. That's right, isn't it, Mr. Field?"

"Yes."

Caprisi turned back to face her. "So what does Pockmark Lu get in return for allowing you to live here?"

"I told you. We pay rent."

"I can check that."

"Well, check it, then."

"Was Lena his girl . . . I mean his exclusively? Did he let her go with others?"

She shook her head in anger and frustration.

"Did he give her to someone as a favor, or a reward?"

She stared at both of them. "Have you finished?"

Caprisi hesitated. "Lena Orlov was stabbed. You saw the body. You were—"

"Friends, yes, but life has to go on." The hostility disappeared and Field saw again in her eyes the same deep hurt and fragility that he'd witnessed the day before. "Lena did what she had to do, that's all."

Natasha dropped her head again, her long hair tumbling down and obscuring her face.

Caprisi stood, but instead of moving to the door, he went to the window and looked out toward the racecourse. "Lena was stabbed almost twenty times." He put his hands in his pockets and turned toward her. "In the stomach and in the vagina. It looked worse after they'd cleaned off all the blood."

Caprisi looked at Field.

"You know, some of the wounds . . . Around the top of the vagina, for example, there were so many, so close together, that they created deep craters, right down to the bone."

Natasha appeared transfixed by a point on the wall opposite.

"Lena was Lu's girl, Miss Medvedev, as you certainly know. Can you be sure you or one of your colleagues won't be next? With that level of anger . . ."

She shook her head, then turned to look at Field. Her eyes glistened with unshed tears. Perhaps Caprisi was moved by this, too, because he appeared thoughtful and suddenly more sympathetic. He pulled out Lena Orlov's notebook and walked over to hand it to her. "We found this hidden inside one of the leather-bound volumes in her bookcase."

Natasha took it and glanced over the entries, wiping her eyes. She did not look at Field again.

"It's a list of ships, departure dates, and destinations,"

Caprisi explained. "There's one leaving at the end of this month."

She handed the notebook back to him.

"You've no idea why Lena would have been hiding this?"

She shook her head again.

"There is a note at the bottom: 'All payments in ledger two.' What could that mean?"

Natasha shrugged.

"What is ledger two?"

"I don't know."

"You never heard Lena talk about any shipments?"

"No."

"Was she involved in any way in any kind of activity that you think this might refer to?"

"I don't know."

"You never talked about anything like this?"

Natasha shook her head.

"What do you think 'ledger two' might be a reference to?"

"I've no idea."

"Speculate."

She shrugged.

"It just seems odd, doesn't it? Notes that were sensitive enough to be hidden, Shipments of something that obviously suggests some kind of criminal activity, and a reference to 'payments.' You must be able to make a guess."

Natasha looked straight at Caprisi. "You can go on asking all day, but I've already told you. I've no idea what you're talking about."

Caprisi stared at her. "We'll leave you, Miss Medvedev," he said quietly, walking to the door. "I can understand your distress, but . . . I've been doing this a long time." He sighed. "And I sense you could help us more than you're letting on."

Eleven

ownstairs, Field almost choked on the thick, sulfurous air. The wind had changed direction again and strengthened, bringing thick fumes from the factories across the river.

They climbed straight into the car and wound up the windows. Caprisi took out a white handkerchief and put it across his mouth. "This city is a cesspit," he said as the driver turned the car around. "Can't you tell your uncle?"

"What do you mean?"

Caprisi sighed and looked out of the window. "It's not exactly a democracy, is it? A small group of men who own the big businesses run the council, with your uncle at their head . . . No wonder the air is poisonous. It's poisoned by money, money, and more money."

"Isn't New York polluted? Or Chicago?"

"No. Anyways, not like this."

Caprisi crossed his legs, placing his notebook on his knee and flicking back through it. "What did you think?"

"About what?"

"About her. Natasha."

"I think she's frightened."

"I'd say so." He looked down at his notes again. "What's Lu's interest in these girls? Why is he paying for them?"

"The obvious interest."

"Natasha maybe, but there are hundreds of girls like Lena, and boys, of all ages." Field blanched again at this thought, but Caprisi didn't appear to notice. "Lena was nothing special, was she? He could have screwed her if he'd wanted. He didn't have to go installing her in a penthouse apartment. Natasha— now, there's a different story. That I can see. She's got class. She's special, a trophy, but not Lena."

"Perhaps Lena was a useful gift."

"Perhaps that was it."

"Or had useful information."

"On what?"

"On the communists."

Caprisi turned toward him.

"I don't think," Field went on, "that there is any doubt Lena Orlov was attending meetings at the *New Shanghai Life* and at the Soviet consulate. So was Natasha."

"So they're Lu's *agents*?"

"It's possible."

"But it can hardly be a secret that they live in his apartments. So what use are they?"

"Go-betweens."

Caprisi nodded.

"The communists are gaining power in the south," Field said. "Quite soon they're expected to advance north. Lu likes to have as many fingers in the pie as he can get. He's not going to be attending meetings himself, and these girls could provide information on what is discussed and planned amongst the Bolshevik underground here. Or perhaps the ownership of these apartments is *not* as commonly known as you suppose. We are only aware of it because of Chen, and he seems to know everything."

Caprisi nodded slowly again, staring out of the window. "Natasha Medvedev is frightened, but she's making no attempt to help herself."

"She doesn't trust us."

"She's lying about those notes."

Field nodded.

"How much do you think she knows about the shipments?"

"I'm not sure."

"It must be opium."

Field shrugged.

"Lu controls the supply line into the city from central China. He gets together with others to export the drugs to Europe. It's a whole new market. That's a departure for the Green Gang, but it would be incredibly profitable, wouldn't it?"

"I imagine so."

"Lu has a brilliant mind and total control of the underworld here, but he's going to need expat help to build a European operation. So . . . somebody else is involved. A syndicate, perhaps. Lena gets to hear of this, perhaps from Lu. She sees that it's explosive and begins to make secret notes. Dates, shipments." Caprisi looked down, deep in thought. "Lena and Natasha are friends. Does Lena talk to her, do you think? Are they close?"

Field thought about the pictures of the two women's families at home in Russia.

"Do you believe Natasha's account of how she found the body?" Caprisi went on.

"Yes."

"Why?"

"Because, if she heard or witnessed or was party to the murder, why would she wait so long before calling the police?"

"To allow the cleanup operation to be completed."

This opened up an area Field did not want to consider. "I don't know how close they could have been. Perhaps their past drives them apart, rather than bringing them together. Are they ashamed to be reminded of how life used to be? Or is the nostalgia what keeps them alive?"

"Both," Caprisi said as he watched the crowds hustling down the street. "There's something wrong with this." He swung around toward his companion. "Lu's men abducted the doorman, under our noses, a full twelve hours after Lena had been murdered. Does that make any sense to you?"

"What do you mean?"

"If Lu was behind the murder, why not remove the door-man at once, in the middle of the night?"

Field couldn't think of a simple answer and found himself instead thinking about what Maretsky had told him—or not told him—about Slugger Davis.

"Are you married, Caprisi?"

The American's intense, dark eyes rested on Field. "You're persistent, Dickie."

"I was once told it was my only attribute." Field tried to smile. "It's hard to know someone if you know nothing about them."

Caprisi turned back to the window and the street outside.

"You don't have to mistrust me," Field went on.

"I never trust Brits."

"Why not?"

"I just don't."

"Macleod is a Brit."

"He's a Scot."

"So it's the English?"

Caprisi didn't respond.

"How come you ended up with Macleod?"

Caprisi frowned at him.

"You're an Italian American Catholic. By rights, you should be with Granger."

"Some things transcend the small-minded . . ."

"Like what?"

"I was in crime. In Chicago. Macleod is a detective."

"You mean it was decided on a professional basis."

A thin smile tugged at the corner of the American's lips.

"So you came out here for a bit of adventure?" Field asked.

"There was enough adventure at home."

"Al Capone?"

Caprisi smiled again, a gesture that brought deep creases to his cheeks.

"So what brought you out here? I mean . . ."

"Jesus, you don't give up, do you?"

"I'm curious."

"Well, that's how you're going to stay."

"How old are you?" Field asked.

"What's it to you?"

"I just had a bet with myself, that's all."

"And what did you put your money on?"

"Thirty-five."

Caprisi's smile grew broader, his body breaking into a momentary chuckle. "Then you'd better stick to policing, Dickie Field, because my mother tells me I'm twenty-seven."

"Twenty-seven?"

Caprisi was looking out of the window on his side. "Yes, my friend, twenty-seven. Too much experience of the dark side, that's what it is." He turned back to Field, his expression suddenly serious. "We call them the cabal."

Field frowned.

"You don't understand, so I'm offering you an explanation."

Field waited until he realized the American wasn't going to expand. "Those who . . ."

"Belong to Lu. He buys influence any way he can and it's spread like a cancer. In the force we call them the cabal."

Field tried to decipher exactly what Caprisi was saying. "Who is we? You said *we* call them the cabal."

"Macleod, Chen."

"That's it?"

"One or two others. Most in our department are clean."

"But the rest of the force is dirty?"

Caprisi was staring at him. "Not all, Field, but more than you might imagine."

"How does it work?" Field asked.

"Someone runs the group from the inside. The commissioner is a joke, but is probably paid for his silence."

"You don't know who runs them?"

"We don't know for certain."

"Is it Granger?"

"He's your boss, Field."

"You think Granger heads this group...the cabal. He orchestrates..."

"He's your boss, Field."

"I'm asking you."

Caprisi shrugged. "Have you seen the way he dresses?"

Field stared out of the window.

"Last year it came to a head. We were closing down opium dens on Foochow Road. Lu didn't like it and neither did the cabal. For each raid, we needed uniform support, and every time we went out, even if we'd planned it at short notice, they were expecting us. We started to find we were being followed after work—all of us. By Lu's men, mostly, but they always seemed to know where we were going and what we were doing. And then they struck without warning. We were ambushed on our way out to a raid. Two of our detectives were killed, and Macleod ordered a tactical retreat, but he's not forgotten and neither have I."

"Is that when Slugger..."

Caprisi shook his head. "That's enough."

Field sighed and returned to looking out of the window. "It would be easier if you trusted me," he said.

There was a long silence, until Caprisi said, "I do."

"Why?"

"I don't know. Instinct."

Field took out his cigarettes and offered one to Caprisi, who shook his head.

"Macleod hates Granger," Field said.

Caprisi didn't answer.

"Because he thinks Granger is head of the cabal."

"Yes, but it's more than that. Macleod was brought up by his mother, in one of the roughest parts of Glasgow. He has a pathological hatred of disorder and decay and greed. His father was a womanizer and gambler, who ran off with a prostitute and left them in poverty. So if you take a look at Granger, I think you'll get the picture."

"Is Macleod married?"

"Yes."

"Yes . . . but?"

"He married a Chinese girl, but the council disapproves, so he never talks about it, or allows anyone to meet her."

Field turned back to the window.

"He seems rough, Field, but he's loyal to those he cares about."

Field faced his colleague again. He sensed he was expected to give an answer. "I can see that," he said.

The Majestic was empty, save for two elderly Chinese women who were scrubbing the floor on their hands and knees, lonely figures in front of the big mirrors at the far end of this cavernous room. The porter led Field and Caprisi through a wooden door in the far wall and up a steep, narrow staircase.

At the top was a tiny balcony, with an empty hat stand.

The porter knocked once on the door and a woman answered, "Come."

It was an attic room, painted red, with long sloping ceilings and a single small casement window, both sides of which were open. The woman sat at her desk, dressed elegantly in black, a silver chain around her neck, her white hair—long, like Natasha's—tied up at the back of her head.

"You've come about Lena," she said.

"Yes, but . . ."

"I've been expecting you."

She turned her chair, her big, bony nose less prominent face-on, and gestured for them both to sit. All around the walls, Field saw pictures and posters of theatrical productions, mostly from Moscow and St. Petersburg.

"You knew her, obviously."

"Poor Lena." She sighed. "Yes, Lena was one of my girls."

Caprisi took out his notebook and pencil. "Could I take your name, Miss . . ."

"Mrs. I'm Mrs. Orlov." Caprisi looked up at her. "No relation."

"What kind of work did Lena do here?" the American asked.

She sighed again. "Would you like some tea . . . coffee?"

They both shook their heads. Mrs. Orlov took her time, as if not wanting to be rushed. "Lena was . . . what can I say?" She was staring at the floor. "Lena was a dreamer. She dreamed of escape, a new beginning. New York, Paris, London, Rome. A life beyond the circumstances she found for herself here."

"She was a prostitute?"

The woman wrinkled her nose, but expressed no surprise or disgust. "She was a dancer, Officer. I don't know what arrangements were made beyond these walls."

"But you know arrangements were made?"

"Each girl is different. Some do, some don't."

"Down to money."

"Down to character. All the girls have impaired circumstances, or they wouldn't be here."

This was said, Field thought, as a matter of fact, without any hint of disapproval at those girls who used the opportunities the Majestic offered to take matters further.

"But Lena did make arrangements," Caprisi persisted.

"I believe so, yes."

"Why? Were her circumstances—"

"I believe she had a sister to support. But, as I said, each girl makes her own choice. Life is easier if you succumb, harder if you don't."

Field found this an uncomfortable line of thought.

"Whom did Lena make arrangements with?" Caprisi asked.

The woman shook her head. "I don't know precisely, but—"

"She lived—"

"Hold on, I was coming to that." The woman looked at Caprisi reprovingly for a moment. "About three months ago she moved into a new flat on Foochow Road."

"Owned by Lu Huang."

"Yes."

"So she was his girl?"

"Yes. And no."

Caprisi frowned.

"Lu Huang has many girls, but I'm not sure they all serve the same purpose."

"You mean he doesn't sleep with them all?"

She shook her head again. "I don't know, but I don't think Lena was his girl in that sense. She was not a concubine. I don't doubt that he basically owned her, and paid for her life, but I'm not sure what his purpose was."

Caprisi was sucking the end of his pencil.

"Lu has an intelligence network," Field said, assuming this was what the woman was driving at.

She turned to him. "Yes."

"Lena gave him intelligence on the activities of Bolsheviks like Borodin?"

"Yes."

"Didn't the Bolsheviks find her suspect because of her past?"

"Everyone can be anyone in Shanghai, Detective."

Field looked at Caprisi, who produced Lena's notebook. "Ships, dates, and destinations," Caprisi said.

She looked at it and handed it back. "It means nothing to me."

"Opium, possibly."

She shook her head curtly.

Caprisi folded it and put it into his pocket. "So if she was Lu's girl, she wasn't sleeping around. I mean—"

"Not unless he instructed her to."

"Unless he gave her to someone?"

"Yes."

"And did he?"

"I believe so. I don't know who, but I never saw her so happy."

Caprisi leaned back in his chair again, looking around the room. Field thought the woman probably knew more than she was letting on.

"How was her . . . mood . . . since she moved into Lu's apartment?" Caprisi asked. "Three months ago, you say?"

"She still came, still danced, but there was something different."

"To do with Lu, or this new man?"

"I do not know, but she talked of escape more often, with more conviction and . . . a sense of confidence. I think she felt she'd found some . . . some route to a new beginning, to whatever it was she sought. One of the last things she said to me, the day before yesterday, was that she had written to her sister and asked her to come to Shanghai."

"What's the relevance of that?"

"She would never have wanted her sister to know about her life here. It could only have been because she was planning that they both leave."

"Did she have any close friends—a boyfriend, perhaps? Outside of these . . . business arrangements."

"Sergei, yes."

"Sergei?"

"He plays in the band here."

Caprisi looked at his notepad. "He didn't mind . . . didn't object to what Lena was up to?"

"He understood."

"Understanding doesn't mean forgiving," Caprisi said, leaning forward. "There cannot be many men who could tolerate the idea of their girl selling herself."

"I'm not sure that was the basis of their relationship. I think it was more . . . fraternal." Mrs. Orlov looked down, crossing her hands on her lap. "Anyway, if you're thinking of him as a suspect, I think I can save you the time. He was here all night."

"From when until when?" Caprisi asked.

"From around seven until about six in the morning."

"Onstage all the time?"

"Yes, or sitting at the band's table to the side of the stage."

"Where would we find him?"

The woman turned to her wooden desk and rifled through the papers until she found a small black leather book, which she opened. She put on her glasses and wrote the name and address in a smooth, flowing hand. She turned and handed the piece of paper to Field, holding it between two long fingers, looking at him through hooded eyes. "Sergei Stanislevich. He lives in Little Russia, on Avenue Joffre."

Field thought she was much older than he'd first guessed.

"Good luck, gentlemen."

They both stood. Caprisi thanked her and they walked down the stairs to the ballroom. As they reached it, Field muttered that he'd forgotten something and darted back before Caprisi had a chance to ask him what.

The woman had not moved and did not seem surprised to see him. He was a little breathless from the heat and the sudden exertion. "Natasha Medvedev. They were friends. What are her circumstances?"

The woman stared at him, as if instantly divining his purpose and motivation, though he wasn't sure he understood these himself.

"Her circumstances?"

"Yes, she lives opposite Lena. Her flat is also owned by—"

"Her circumstances are the most . . . Of all the girls here, Natasha's are the most impaired," she said, half in sorrow, it seemed to him, and half in warning.

Field heard Caprisi call up from below.

"What do you mean impaired?" Field asked.

She shook her head. "Your friend is calling you."

Field turned around and came to the top of the stairs. "Dropped my pen," he said, but Caprisi's look told him he knew differently.

Twelve

hen they got back into the car, Caprisi was looking at his notes.

"So we know that Lu gave Lena to someone,"
Field said. "This man murdered her and Lu covered it up."

Caprisi stared out of the window. "You're jumping too far
ahead. It's still possible that Lu murdered her himself, or one
of his men did."

"But what about Maretsky saying that it was sexual, motivated by extreme anger?"

"Well . . ." Caprisi sighed, pulling up the band of his
trousers. They still hadn't moved anywhere. The driver waited
patiently for directions. "If Lu is covering up for someone,
then he must have a damned good reason."

"Should we go and see him now?"

"We can't. Macleod is talking to the French. There will be
hell to pay if we go to Lu in the Concession without applying
through the proper channels. Customs," Caprisi said, tapping
the back of the driver's seat. He looked at Field. "I want to talk
to this man Sergei as well."

Field settled back, trying to suppress the nausea that had
been threatening to overwhelm him all morning. He wound
down the window to allow some air in, though it was fetid
rather than fresh.

They turned onto the Bund and Field looked out at the
sampans, junks, and steamers that plowed the choppy waters.
As they rounded the last bend in the river, he recalled the

thrill of his first sight of the Bund—its giant buildings rising above a sea of patchwork sails.

A liner coming in toward the shore hooted loudly, a thick plume of smoke from its central funnel twisting up into the clear sky.

"We ought to talk to Borodin," Field said.

"Yes."

The wharf in front of the Customs House was teeming with life, a sea of white straw and dark felt trilbies.

A ship had just arrived from Europe or America, its passengers standing in groups on the dock, fanning themselves against the heat and trying to prevent overenthusiastic coolies making off with their luggage. It was noisy and chaotic, and as they got out of the car, Field found himself smiling at the expectant, hurried stride of residents and the anxious faces of those they were coming to meet.

The floor beneath them was filthy with rotten fruit and vegetables. He bumped into an American woman as she rushed headlong into the arms of a man with a cry of "Anthony!"

Caprisi led the way through the gate and up a long iron staircase. A small Chinese stood at the top, his long queue hanging down over the back of a green silk jacket. He did not turn around as they passed.

The office they entered was a flimsy wooden structure, which looked as though it wouldn't survive a light breeze, let alone the ferocity of a typhoon. Two more Chinese in long tunics were locked in a heated argument with a corpulent European who sat behind a desk. He waved his hand at them imperiously, concluding the argument, and after some hesitation, they turned and left, their faces impassive.

"CID," Caprisi said. The man's face softened. He picked up a white towel on the desk beside him and wiped his face. He had, Field noticed, very poor skin.

"Inspector Jenkins," he said, offering them each a chubby hand. Standing, he ushered them through to an airless office at the back, where an electric desk fan was riffling a pile of papers held down by a glass weight.

Jenkins was wearing a dirty khaki uniform, with thin cotton shorts and a leather holster on his belt.

"A Russian girl has been murdered," Caprisi said, taking out Lena's notebook.

"A Russian girl," Jenkins said in a manner that seemed to suggest that Russian girls being murdered was the natural order of things. He looked at the entries for a few moments, occasionally turning back a page, before looking up.

"This notebook was found hidden in the dead girl's bookcase," Caprisi said. "We don't see the relevance of the entries."

Jenkins looked back at the notes, then heaved himself from his chair and moved to a cupboard, reaching into his pocket for a key. Inside, there were four or five ledgers, and he took out the top one, placing it on a desk with a thump that raised a small cloud of dust.

He sat and looked through the notebook again, mulling over each entry, grunting as he did so.

It was a tedious process and Caprisi began to fidget, drumming his fingers against his knee and fanning himself with his notebook.

"They're all . . ." Jenkins trailed off. "All the same. The Electrical Company."

"What is the Electrical Company?" Caprisi asked.

"Subsidiary of Fraser's. Makes electrical goods here, ships them back to Europe. All these . . ." He looked down again. "They're consignments of sewing machines, mainly. There are some other goods as well, of course, from the same company, but sewing machines provide the bulk—I would say eighty percent—of these ships' cargo."

"Sewing machines?"

"Yes."

Caprisi looked at Field, but he could think of no explanation and shook his head.

"Why would a Russian tea dancer want to make secret notes about shipments of sewing machines?"

Jenkins shrugged.

"Speculate."

"I've no idea."

Field could see he was as mystified as the pair of them. "What about the last entry?" he said. "The *Saratoga* on the twenty-sixth."

Jenkins returned to his study of the ledger, running his finger down the pages until he found what he was looking for. "Ah, thought so. The *Saratoga* came in yesterday, from India. Empty."

"Empty?" Caprisi asked.

"I thought ships generally took goods both ways," Field added.

"Generally. Not always. Maybe she took cargo from Europe to India, had a contract out of here. Didn't want to wait for something out of Bombay."

"Must be a lucrative contract here to make it worth the rush," Caprisi said.

"Fraser's is a big company. The lure of regular work, I should think."

"If the *Saratoga* is in," Field said, "can we inspect her?"

"Of course." Jenkins stood and opened his drawer, pulling out a Smith & Wesson revolver and putting it in his holster before leading the way down the staircase and through the throng that was still emerging from the exit.

It was less busy on the wharf inside, though there were small groups of passengers waiting in the shade of the customs inspection area as coolies hauled their baggage onto carts, or, in some cases, their backs.

Jenkins walked briskly out into the sunshine. Field squinted until they reached the shadow of an iron-framed shelter. There were fewer people here: some coolies squatting, a small group loading sacks onto a river steamer. The farther they went, the larger the ships became. The *Saratoga* was moored about halfway along the wharf.

It was a white ship with two yellow funnels. A dirty blue lifeboat hung above a gangplank with a rickety handrail covered in white canvas. Jenkins led the way.

They stepped onto the wooden deck and looked about, sheltered by an awning. There were two circular portholes ahead of them on either side of a wooden door. Jenkins walked down to a big cargo deck in front of the accommodation area, below the bridge. As they rounded the corner, a young Indian, who had been lying out in the sun, leaped to his feet and eyed them warily. His shorts were scruffy and his vest stained.

"Where's the captain?" Jenkins demanded imperiously, but the man shook his head.

Jenkins led them back through the wooden door and up some steep iron steps to the bridge. The inside of the ship smelled of ingrained grease and the corridors were dark, like the lower decks of the vessel in which Field had set out from London earlier in the year.

There was no one on the bridge, which was small. "Only just got in," Jenkins said. "I suppose they'll be down Blood Alley."

"What about searching below deck, in the bow?" Field asked.

Jenkins grunted and retraced his steps once more. He pulled open a wooden hatch in the middle of the deck, watched nervously by the Indian, who made no attempt to help or intervene, and descended into the darkness below.

The three of them looked around the cavernous hold, but there was little to see. They were standing on an iron floor, ropes and winches and disused tools strewn around them, along with the other detritus of a working ship. It smelled of grease and salt.

"It would be a good cover for smuggling, wouldn't it?" Caprisi said.

"What would?" Jenkins asked.

Caprisi took a step forward. "What could be more harmless than a batch of sewing machines shipped by a subsidiary of Fraser's?"

"I'm not following you," Jenkins said irritably.

"If you wanted to smuggle something into Europe, you'd

choose a shipment of goods that customs officials were unlikely to be in a hurry to check thoroughly. You could hardly find anything more harmless than a bunch of sewing machines."

Jenkins frowned. It occurred to Field, as it had perhaps to Caprisi, that any operation of the kind they were talking about would be unlikely to leave the activities of customs officials to chance.

"I think we'd better find the captain," Jenkins said. "Come back to my office and give me a number—I'll contact you when he turns up."

Field was the last to come down the gangplank and he hesitated for a moment at the bottom. The sky was still a clear, bright blue. A huge Union Jack above the dome of the Hong Kong Shanghai Bank was slack in the still air. A flock of seagulls circled "Big Ching," the clock tower of the Customs House, before breaking out across the river, as if something had startled them.

Field looked back. The deckhand was still watching him.

Thirteen

ergei lived above the Siberian Fur Shop in the heart of Little Russia, in a tiny apartment with paint peeling from its walls.

He was the image of a radical student intellectual, with long, unwashed hair, a narrow face coated with stubble, and small, round glasses.

"Have you got a minute?" Field asked.

"Who are you?"

Field reached into his pocket and flicked open his wallet.

"Which branch?"

"It's on there."

"It doesn't say."

"S.1."

"Special Branch."

"Correct. My colleague here is from Crime. Can we come in?"

Sergei's eyes darted between them, but Field could not tell whether it was because he had something to hide or because he was nervous of visitors. He stepped back and allowed them to enter.

Inside, it was even smaller than Field had first guessed, and filthy. An unmade bed alongside the far wall jutted out into a sea of discarded clothes and dirty plates, glasses, and coffee cups. There was an abstract oil painting above the bed of St. Basil's Cathedral just south of Red Square. On a small table an overflowing ashtray rested against the base of a shabby lamp.

The flat stank. A violin and trumpet were propped up in the far corner.

Sergei sat down on the bed. Field and Caprisi declined his invitation to take the ragged sofa opposite. Caprisi walked over to the window and, without asking, opened it. He turned back to see if there was any reaction, but Sergei was examining his long, manicured nails.

Sergei looked at Caprisi, then back at Field. "You're from the Settlement."

"This is a murder investigation, Sergei," Field said.

"I don't want to get into trouble with the French authorities."

After appraising it distastefully, Caprisi sat down on the sofa. "I wouldn't worry about that."

Sergei flexed his fingers.

"When did you last see Lena Orlov?" Caprisi asked.

Sergei thought for a moment. "The night before . . ." He shrugged. "You know."

"The night before she was murdered?"

"Yes." He nodded for emphasis.

"Where?"

"At the Majestic. I play—"

"You play there, we know." Caprisi leaned forward. "I'd like you to take this opportunity to tell us anything that you know about Lena that might be relevant."

Sergei shrugged.

"You were her—"

"No." He shook his head. "No."

"What, then?"

"Friends."

"Where did you meet her?"

"At the Majestic." He nodded again.

"How long ago?"

"Two months, three, four. I don't know."

"Which?"

"Four, maybe."

"So you didn't know her in Russia?"

"No." He shook his head. "No."

"You met her at the Majestic?"

"Yes."

"You didn't know her before then?"

"No."

"You'd never seen her before?"

He hesitated. "I don't think so, no."

"You don't think so, or no for sure?"

"No."

"So you came here . . . how many years ago?"

"Four."

"Four years ago. Nineteen twenty-two. You've lived here in Little Russia all that time?"

"Yes." Sergei looked uncertain. "Not always in this apartment."

"Where else?"

"Farther down, with some others."

"Also musicians?"

"Yes."

"So why did you move here?"

"I had more money since the Majestic."

"Where did you play before?"

"The Excelsior." He shrugged again. "Other places."

"So when did you join the band at the Majestic?"

"Four months ago."

"And you'd not met Lena or seen her before then?"

Sergei shook his head. Field was certain he was lying.

"Did you know she was working for Lu Huang and living in one of his flats?"

Sergei sensed danger. "You must understand, we did not talk about her . . . work. We didn't talk about anything like that. The ground was always kept neutral."

"Did you go to her apartment?"

"No."

"So what was your interest in her?"

He shrugged. "She was not a bad-looking girl . . . You know, from Kazan. I mean . . ."

"Did you fuck her?" Caprisi asked.

Sergei smiled, a tight weasel grin, revealing a mouthful of decaying teeth. "Sometimes, you know . . ."

"No, I don't know."

"She liked a bit of Russian meat." He smiled again. "Liked a man to speak Russian to her."

"So she never talked about Lu Huang?"

He shook his head.

"She never talked about any other boyfriends or other men that she slept with?"

"No."

"You knew she was a prostitute?"

He grinned again. "I fuck her sometimes. She likes a Russian who doesn't pay, then she doesn't feel like a whore."

"So you weren't friends?"

"Sometimes she comes here and cries and I let her, then I fuck her some more."

Caprisi stood, sensing Field's anger. "Easy, man," he whispered, "we're out of bounds."

Field breathed out, unclenched his fists, and tried to force himself to relax.

"So," Caprisi went on, "when you slept together, it was here, in this apartment."

"Yes."

"You never went down to Foochow Road?"

The Russian shook his head.

"But you knew that was where she lived?"

Sergei hesitated again. "She may have mentioned it."

"She may have, or she did?"

"She did."

"But you never went there?"

"She didn't want me to."

"Was she in love with you?"

Sergei smirked again but didn't answer. "Cigarette?" he asked, offering the packet. They both declined.

Sergei was not wearing socks or shoes, and Field noticed his feet were as long and bony as his hands. Like his forearms, his legs appeared to be hairless.

"Did you know she slept with Lu?"

He shrugged.

"She moved into one of his apartments a few months ago. You knew where she lived, but she never mentioned that she was his woman?"

"I said we never talked about it."

"You didn't know she slept with him?"

"I didn't ask."

"The question was: did you know?"

Sergei shrugged again. "She liked to talk about Russia. I fucked her sometimes. That was it."

"So she never mentioned Lu?"

"No."

"Or any other man she was sleeping with?"

He shook his head.

"So you slept with her, but you knew nothing about her life and weren't curious?"

"No."

"Did you know about her family?"

"She mentioned a sister in Harbin. The rest, I don't know."

"Do any of them live in Shanghai?"

"She didn't say."

"Who were her other friends?"

"I don't know."

"What about Natasha Medvedev?"

He began to smirk again.

"What's so funny?" Caprisi asked.

"Nothing."

"Do you know her?"

"Sure."

"Were they friends?"

Sergei sucked heavily on his cigarette. "Sure."

"Who else?"

"No one else."

"So." Caprisi sighed. "Let's get this straight. You were her boyfriend, but you never went to her apartment, you know nothing about her life in Shanghai."

"She was a whore."

Caprisi stared at Sergei for a long time, forcing the Russian to lower his head and study the floor. "What did you talk about, then?"

"We only fucked."

"Where are you from in Russia, Sergei?"

"Moscow."

"Your father was an army officer or . . ."

"A doctor."

"Did you and Lena ever talk about the revolution?"

He shook his head.

"What do you think of the new Soviet Union?" Field asked.

Sergei looked from Field to Caprisi and back again, suspecting a trap. "Bolshevism is not the answer."

"And what is?" Field smiled encouragingly at him.

"My views are my views."

"Were they the same as Lena's?"

The Russian didn't answer.

Field smiled again. "You surely don't believe the current situation here is tolerable."

Sergei regarded him warily.

"I mean, if there has ever been a case for the redistribution of wealth, this is it, isn't it? Here, in this city, with so many families sleeping—dying, even—on the streets."

"I see inequality, but I'm not a Bolshevik."

"A reformer, then?"

Sergei nodded.

"You'd like better conditions for the workers. Shorter hours, better pay."

Sergei sucked his teeth nervously.

"Do you think the system can be reformed, or does it have to be changed entirely?"

"I don't live in the Settlement."

"Have you attended meetings at the *New Shanghai Life?*"

The Russian frowned. "No."

"Can you explain why Lena was doing so? After all, her father was an army officer."

"I'm not a Bolshevik."

Field paused. "I never said that you were."

"Their hearts were not in it."

"Their hearts?"

"Lena . . . Natasha."

"Why were they doing it?"

He shook his head.

"Presumably they were gathering intelligence for Lu?"

Sergei sneered. "No one would ever tell them anything."

"Then why was Lu paying for their apartments?"

He smiled again. "They are women "

"So it's about sex?" Caprisi asked.

"Isn't everything?"

Caprisi stood. "We'll want to speak to you again." He walked toward the door. "And next time, you're coming down to the Settlement."

Outside, Caprisi lit up first, inhaling deeply and running his hand through his hair. He paced to and fro by the car, occasionally glancing up at the window above the Siberian Fur Shop. Field scanned the signs in Russian script outside the shops that stretched away down Avenue Joffre. They were all small concerns—one selling Shanghai borscht, another a hairdressing salon, a third specializing in wedding dresses.

"Jesus, you get yourself worked up," Caprisi said.

Field didn't answer.

"I thought you were going to hit him."

Field put his cigarette to his lips. He couldn't see Sergei in the shadows behind his window, but he knew the Russian was there. "I don't like it when women aren't treated right."

"Then maybe you should go someplace else."

Field sighed. "My father hit my mother, all right? I don't like the way Sergei talks." He tried to change the subject to cover his embarrassment. "Did Lu not know she was coming down here? Is that why Sergei is so nervous?"

Caprisi resumed his pacing, then leaned back against the side of the car. "I can't see Lena taking that sort of risk."

"Unless she was desperate to have something—anything— that stopped her feeling like a whore."

The American looked up at Field. He flicked his cigarette away into the street.

"Is that why Lu killed her?" Field asked.

Caprisi shrugged, then shook his head. "I doubt it."

Fourteen

aprisi instructed the driver to take a detour down the Nanking Road and wait for him alongside the Wing On store.

Field opened the window an inch or two as the American got out. He took off his jacket, loosened his tie, and undid the top button of his shirt, holding it away from his body to try and dry the large patches of sweat. He took off his holster and placed it on the seat beside him, then pulled out a handkerchief and wiped his brow.

"Hot," the driver said, smiling.

"Yes." Field wondered how old he was. It was hard to tell. The average life expectancy for a Chinese was only twenty-seven, and many of them looked old before their time.

"Summer . . . hot!"

Field nodded and grinned, fanning his face theatrically. Then he reached for his cigarettes and got out.

The banners above him swayed gently as two trams passed each other in the center of the street, but the air was still. A buxom, middle-aged woman walked out of the Wing On with an armful of boxes and headed for a gleaming Buick. Her driver leaped out of his seat to open the back door for her, and a small Pekingese escaped, yapping around her feet as she settled herself on the cream buckskin seat.

A Chinese woman thrust a baby toward the open door. The driver pushed her to the ground, swearing loudly, then spitting on the pavement.

Field made to intervene, but thought better of it. He lit up as he watched the beggar retreat to the side of the store.

Unusually, she appeared to be on her own, so he reached into his pocket, walked over, and pushed a one-dollar piece into her hand. She was young, her eyes expressionless. It was a moment or two before he realized that the baby she was holding was dead.

Field turned back to the car. His breathing had quickened. The driver was shaking his head. Field threw away his cigarette and took refuge in the car again. He leaned against the side window and closed his eyes.

Caprisi pulled the door open and clambered in. He was carrying a brown paper bag. "Central," he said, tapping the driver on the shoulder.

"Get what you wanted?" Field asked.

"Sure." Caprisi paused. "When we get back, you'll go and see if there is a file on Sergei, right?" The American looked at him, his gaze level. "You know, about back there. I hear what you say, and I understand about your father and I'm sorry, but Lena was a prostitute, you know."

"So it doesn't matter?"

"I didn't say that. I just don't think it is a good idea to get so worked up about it."

Field looked out of the window again. "You care about it."

"But I'm looking at you all hunched up in there, with bunched fists, looking like you're going to kill that little fucker."

Field didn't answer.

"You won't survive in this city if you make everything personal."

Field looked at him but didn't respond.

There was a file on Sergei Stanislevich. Like Lena and Natasha, he was from Kazan on the Volga and had attended meetings at the *New Shanghai Life*.

Field was flicking through the contents when Prokopiev came in. The Russian nodded at him. "The Lentov file," he told Danny. Field noticed he hadn't bothered to fill out any paperwork.

Prokopiev leaned back against the desk, crossing his legs. He was wearing long black leather riding boots that looked to have been standard issue for the Cossack officer he said he'd once been. Field realized he was no longer prepared to take anything at face value.

"Where did you learn to punch like that?" the Russian asked.

"School."

"You punch like a boxer."

"I was a boxer."

Prokopiev smiled. "I would stay away from Sorenson. He's not happy about his jaw."

Field didn't answer.

"How is the prostitute?"

"Still dead."

The Russian shook his head. "Grow up, Field. That's what happens to little Russian princesses. They get fucked, and then they get dead."

"You don't talk like a Cossack officer."

Prokopiev didn't react.

Field stood and put the file back down on the desk. "Stanislevich." Prokopiev clicked his tongue. "Mr. Nobody. You think it was him?"

"No."

"Put it down to an angry client."

"Because she was a prostitute, or because she was a Russian?"

Prokopiev looked at Field sourly. "Because she doesn't matter."

"And what if there have been others ... if there will be others?"

The Russian leaned forward, and Field could smell the

alcohol on his breath. "It's an English expression: you make your bed, you lie in it." He laughed. "You fuck in your bed, you get fucked in it."

Field knew that Prokopiev was trying to provoke him, but it was still a struggle to tear himself away. He walked to the door and closed it quietly, resisting the temptation to slam it. He took control of himself with each step down to the first floor, where Caprisi had said they would find Chen.

As Field passed, two scantily dressed Chinese girls were being booked by the duty sergeant.

Caprisi was talking to Chen by the entrance to the toilet on the far side of the room, and they both nodded as Field approached. The bench beside them had civilian clothes hanging along it, and the floor was covered with wooden truncheons, which a clerk had obviously been sorting through. Each one had a leather strap, though most had been broken. Four machine guns and a couple of steel helmets had been stacked on top of the iron lockers in the corner.

The place smelled and felt like the changing rooms at the spartan boarding school Field had attended in Yorkshire.

Chen beckoned them both into the toilet, shutting the door behind them and checking that each cubicle was vacant before retreating to the sinks at the far end. The sun streamed through the window, illuminating the side of Chen's face.

Field thought that most people would probably consider the Chinese detective handsome. He had a square jaw, short dark hair, and steady eyes. He exuded a quiet strength.

Chen touched his ears to indicate why they had come in here. "One of the neighbors," he said quietly. "A building opposite. An old Chinese, lives on his own. Says he never sleeps. He saw a black car, probably Chevrolet, come up about four A.M. Bodyguards get out street side, but he can't see who goes in—it's dark and the car blocks his view. One hour, then whoever it is leaves, car goes off. He sees the girl Natasha come in before this—about three."

"As she said," Caprisi added.

"But not Lena. She is inside all night."

"No other visitors?"

"He cannot say. He's not always watching. When he is bored, he watches the street. Especially Happy Times. He knows the girls are Lu's."

"He didn't see anyone else?"

"He didn't say he saw anyone."

Caprisi frowned and shook his head. "But *four* o'clock. Krauss said she died at one, if not before."

"Maybe Krauss is wrong."

Caprisi slammed his fist down on one of the washbasins.

"Prokopiev tailed me there," Chen said. "How fucking stupid does he think I am?"

Caprisi's frown deepened. "He tailed you?"

"From here. I went on foot, down Foochow, and he was there . . . sticking out . . ."

"Did he want you to see him?"

Chen shrugged.

"All right," Caprisi said. "This feels to me like we're going down the same road that led us into trouble before with the opium dens. Wherever possible, we have to work together. If we leave this building to do anything, we should try always to be together, and armed."

The door opened and a uniformed Chinese officer walked in. He was young—just a constable—and he nodded at Chen respectfully.

Caprisi took Field down to the car but wouldn't tell him where they were going. They drove through the French Concession and out toward the edge of the old Chinese town before going on foot. The day had lost its heat, but not yet its light. Dust kicked up by the human traffic hung beneath the curved rooftops of the buildings that lined the narrow lane along which they walked.

They turned into a still-narrower alley, passing tiny shops

with carved, inlaid wooden shutters, beneath paper lanterns that had not yet been lit. They could hear the sound of a flute, and ahead of them a group of small boys was playing in the dirt. The smell of human excrement made Field gag.

They turned into a tailor's shop. Every inch of space had been used to the full. A dummy stood in the middle of a square cutting table. There was a mirror on the far wall and only just enough room to stand. Caprisi was smiling. "The best tailor in Shanghai. We're going to get you out of that suit."

"I . . ."

"You can pay me back."

The old man smiled and held up his tape measure. A young boy stood beside him, his face expectant, and Field felt it was churlish to complain. He allowed himself to be measured while Caprisi talked to the man in rapid Shanghainese. As he watched and listened, he realized how little experience he had with the local people, beyond his day-to-day police work or his living quarters at Carter Road. He admired the ease with which Caprisi slipped into conversation with them.

"He asks if all my friends are this tall," Caprisi said.

"I got that bit."

"He's asking about Lu."

"I heard his name mentioned."

"Says Lu's men boast they control all of the police in Shanghai."

Field didn't respond.

"I told him Lu's men were in for a surprise."

The old man thrust the tape measure roughly into Field's groin and pushed him irritably when he did not turn quickly enough. Then he pulled out a book of cloth samples and flicked through it before pointing at the one he thought most suitable.

"I explained that it was for summer use."

"That's fine."

Uneasy about Caprisi's generosity, and uncomfortable with the tailor's brusqueness, Field couldn't wait to get out. He stood in the alley as the American continued to talk to the old man.

"Ready in two days," Caprisi said when he emerged.

"Thanks."

"Don't mention it."

"No really, it was—"

"One good deed deserves another."

Field looked blank.

"I like having a partner who knows how to fight."

Field smiled.

"There's a teahouse around the corner," Caprisi said. They stepped over a prostrate beggar and walked up to a building with a low entrance and dark wooden panels along its hall.

The tearoom overlooked a small but pretty oriental garden, the delicate sound of its fountain still audible above the hubbub. They were shown to a table and Caprisi ordered.

"You've been here before," Field said when the waiter disappeared.

"A few times."

"You have Chinese friends here. In the city, I mean."

"Some." Caprisi looked at him. "You'll get there, Field. It's not just about language." The American touched his forehead. "You have to want to understand the people, and most foreigners don't."

Field lit a cigarette and leaned back in his chair. "Doesn't the poverty bother you?"

"Of course."

"I worry that it doesn't bother me enough."

"There's poverty everywhere."

"Yes, but it's so extreme here." Field leaned forward again. "And yet, it doesn't put me off the city. It doesn't stop me being excited about being here. It doesn't repel me. I feel guilty about that."

"You'll get over it."

Field looked at the American. "So why do you stay?"

Caprisi sucked on his cigarette. "It feels like home now."

"I'm not sure what that means anymore."

The American didn't answer.

"You won't go back to Chicago?"

Caprisi shook his head.

"Never?"

"Probably not."

"You don't have family there?"

Caprisi's jaw tightened.

"I'm sorry, I didn't mean . . ."

"It's all right. I don't much like talking about the past, that's all."

Field nodded and the American's face softened again. "I understand." After a few moments Field added, "I feel the same."

The waiter returned with a tray. He placed a red and gold china teapot in the center of the table and a cup and saucer grudgingly in front of each of them.

"You see?" Caprisi said as he moved away. "We're foreigners. We'll always be foreigners."

Field watched him pour the tea. "It seems to me sometimes," he said, "that everyone here is escaping, in one way or another."

"Except for the ones who can't."

Field frowned.

"Look at the Russians. The girl I saw you mooning at." Caprisi smiled as Field's face reddened. "It's a gilded cage, but that doesn't stop it being a cage."

"I suppose . . ."

"Where can they go? No visas. No passport. They don't belong anywhere anymore, and yet they once inhabited a world they had every reason to believe would last forever." Caprisi fell silent. "You say you feel the same, polar bear, but I don't think we can begin to understand."

Fifteen

y the time Field came out of the station, the day was fading fast. A rich red shroud had settled upon the buildings around him, the banners silhouetted against a darkening sky.

He walked quickly, gripping his holster, his jacket draped over his arm. He still had his tie undone and was grateful for the faint breeze.

Field hesitated at the entrance to the Carter Road quarters. He didn't relish spending the evening in a ringside seat at Prokopiev's circus.

But the Russian was out, and Field found, as he entered his own room, that a letter had been pushed under the door.

The envelope boasted the crest of the Municipal Council, and his name had been written in blue ink in a flowing hand.

My dear Richard, Geoffrey had written. *It was good to see you again after all these years and to welcome you to Shanghai, albeit belatedly, for which, again, many apologies. I'm afraid the workload of a municipal secretary is rather a burdensome one.*

We would be delighted if you could join us for a late supper tonight at home, however. I believe you have the address. About ten should do it, though alternatively you could join me earlier at a function at the headquarters of the Hong Kong Shanghai Bank, and we might manage a drink before dinner. I have a talk to give at eight—some local worthy women—but should be free by nine. It's in the conference room on the first floor. Mention my name at the door and explain who you are.

Penelope and I would be delighted if you would treat our home as your own during your time here. We know how lonely it can be to be so far away. I'm rarely in during the early evening, but Penelope usually is and would be very pleased to see you whenever you wish.

Fond regards, Geoffrey.

Field looked at his watch and then at the dinner jacket that hung from a line of cord he'd strung in the window. It didn't sound like the kind of occasion at which a dinner jacket would be required, but he put it on to be on the safe side, then walked out and hailed a rickshaw.

If anything, the dinner jacket was hotter than his suit, but the wind had risen again, and as he turned onto the Bund, it was strong enough to keep him cool for the first time that day.

The waterfront was still busy. A crowd milled about on the sidewalk in the semidarkness beneath the trees on the far side by the wharf. A bright moon now shone above the well-lit buildings, which were decorated in honor of the king's impending birthday. The Union Jack on the dome above the Hong Kong Shanghai Bank twisted and snapped in the breeze. Field paid the rickshaw man and walked through a line of parked cars. A group of Chinese children was patting one of the bronze lions guarding the bank's entrance. Local superstition encouraged them to believe that it would give them strength.

Inside, the huge wooden doors through to the main hall were padlocked, so Field turned back and walked to the rear entrance. A wide stone staircase led up to the first floor and, at the top, a sign announced that Geoffrey Donaldson, secretary of the Shanghai Municipal Council, would be giving a talk entitled "The New Jerusalem."

Two stout women in dark jackets sat behind a trestle table, next to a uniformed bank security guard.

"I'm Richard Field, Geoffrey Donaldson's—"

"Yes, of course. He said you might be coming." The woman smiled and wrote down his name, then handed him a leaflet. The doors to the room had been thrown open and he could see Geoffrey already at the lectern.

It looked like a ballroom. The carpet was crimson, and huge gilt-edged mirrors lined the walls.

"Here," he heard his uncle say as he moved closer, "we are privileged to have an eyewitness view of the future. And this is the future, let no one be under any illusions about that. China is a developing market, on a scale undreamed-of in the history of commerce. And which nation leads the charge into this land of promise? As the secretary of the Municipal Council, I should perhaps not be partisan, but I hope you'll forgive me a little native pride." He smiled, surveying his audience. "British companies are leading this charge. Thirty-eight percent of all foreign holdings in China are British, and three-quarters of our 600-million-pound investment is here in this great city.

"But let me put back 'my secretary of the Municipal Council' hat. We are not technically part of the British Empire here, as you know all too well. And I know you share my frustration that we do not always get the support from Washington and London that we feel is our due.

"Anglo-Saxon values have built the greatest empires the world has ever known: decency, honesty, integrity, justice, a sense of fair play. A society based on all of these principles is what we are building so successfully here."

Geoffrey shifted his weight from his good leg for a moment. He touched his mouth with his hand before smoothing the hair around one of his temples. "All of us are, I know, offended at times"——he had changed his tone and was speaking more quietly——"by the poverty we see on the streets every day, and may I say again, I am not alone in admiring the Volunteer Corps of Shanghai for the tireless work it does—you all do—in alleviating some of the suffering, but this, let me tell you is the rub . . ." He leaned forward onto the lectern, a finger pointing toward the ceiling. "Every man jack out there in this city knows that if he works hard and is honest, then he can pull himself up by his bootstraps and secure his family a better future. That is what we are about here. That is why there is no city that has a future as golden as Shanghai's. That's why, I believe, we have every right to say that this is the New Jerusalem. A profitable city, of whose values we can be justly proud."

There was a momentary pause and then the applause was thunderous, almost everyone—perhaps three or four hundred people—getting to his feet. Geoffrey raised his hand modestly. "I'm afraid . . ." He waited for the noise to die down. "I'm afraid I was intending to take questions, but have inevitably run on and . . ." He waited again. "I'm sorry to say I have some council business to attend to upstairs, so if you'll forgive me . . ."

Geoffrey walked as swiftly as he could down the side of the room. Field found it almost painful to watch him. He followed him out of the room and into the lift. As he pulled the door shut, Geoffrey breathed a sigh of relief. "Sorry, a bit jingoistic, but got to fire up the audience, if you know what I mean."

Field looked at the leaflet. There was a picture of Geoffrey in uniform and details of his career: Cambridge, service in the trenches, his Victoria Cross and beyond.

Geoffrey chuckled. "The Shanghai Volunteer Corps. Christ! Not a woman in there under forty . . ." The lift still hadn't moved, so he hit the button for the sixth floor. "Don't get Penelope started on that lot."

The lift jolted into action and Field leaned back against one of the wood panels. It was the only lift he could recall having been in that had a carpet on the floor.

"I won't be long," Geoffrey said. "I'm sure the chaps won't mind if you sit in." He brushed a loose thread from the sleeve of his tailored gray suit. Field was already having second thoughts about his dinner jacket.

The lift stopped and they stepped out into the bank's dining room. It was not big, but it was at the corner of the building and the windows were tall, so that it afforded magnificent views of the river and the bright lights of the city.

Geoffrey joined a group of men around a big oak table. A sideboard behind them was covered with silverware. Huge oil portraits adorned the walls. Field saw Lewis sitting at the far end in a round-backed leather chair with a cigarette in one hand and a drink in the other. Commissioner Biers was next to him, and Patrick Granger stood behind them with his hands in his pockets.

Geoffrey ran his hand through his hair, which was shot through with flecks of white. Field thought his face seemed older than it had the night before. "Some of you already know Richard, my nephew, new to the city. Just thought it would interest him to sit in, and since this is not a formal meeting of the council, I didn't think you would have any objections." A few of the men shook their heads. "Gin," Geoffrey said, turning to a Sikh waiter in a red and gold tunic.

Geoffrey sat forward in his chair. Field moved to one of the windows. "Right," Geoffrey said. "I've just had the pleasure of addressing the Volunteer Corps of Shanghai, women's division!" He lit up. "So forgive me if I'm a little incoherent."

"Never before you've had a drink, old boy," Lewis said.

All the men wore dark suits. Field could see immediately that Lewis and his uncle were the driving forces among the group.

"I intend this to be a brief meeting," Geoffrey said, "so that you all get an intelligence update and have the chance to give me some feedback. Patrick is here to fill us in."

Granger took his hands out of his pockets, crossed them over his chest, and stepped forward from the shadows. "As Richard here and some of the rest of you will know, Michael Borodin returned from the south last night. Our intelligence is that he will now focus his attentions again on trying to re-create the atmosphere of last summer, but with greater intensity. He has formed a core unit of activists, mostly Chinese students, operating in various premises around the city. But we have intelligence that Borodin and his colleagues at the Soviet consulate have received considerable new funds from Moscow. Some of the propaganda outlets, like the *New Shanghai Life,* have received further subsidies, but we believe most of the money is going into street activity—producing leaflets and posters, obviously, but most seriously, buying action."

"Buying action?" Lewis asked.

Granger turned to him. "Last summer they were funding the strike committees. This time we believe they may have enough money to pay the strikers directly."

The room was silent.

"Thank you, Patrick," Geoffrey said. "My own view is that further funds may be needed to counter this new initiative."

A bearded man next to Lewis groaned.

"You may not like it, Simon, but if the Soviets are pumping more money in, then so, too, must we. The Branch and Patrick are doing a fine job, but we can't allow them to slip behind in any way."

"We should shoot a few more of them."

Geoffrey cleared his throat. "I was the first to propose resolute action last year, but pictures of piles of bodies on the front page of the *New York Times* would be counterproductive to say the least." Geoffrey looked around the room, as if daring them to disagree.

"Why don't we just shut down rags like the *New Shanghai Life?*" Lewis asked. "Apart from anything else, it's an interminable read."

"They are putting the positive case for the new Bolshevik government, which we cannot in all conscience prevent them doing, or at least not without the risk of creating the kind of headlines that would prompt a stream of anxious telegrams from Washington."

"Since he keeps feeding all this material back to New York, perhaps we should just shoot Stirling Blackman."

One or two of the men laughed. Granger smiled. "We keep a careful eye on the *New Shanghai Life*, especially when Borodin is around," Granger said, "but the rags are careful and always stop short of incitement. However, we suspect them of leaflet printing in secret, and, of course, if we catch them doing that, we'll shut them straight down."

There was a long silence.

"What's Lu got to say about all this?" Lewis asked. He

turned toward Granger, whose face was half in shadow. "Come on, Granger, you're supposed to be the one with the contacts."

Granger cleared his throat, ignoring the barb. "We are led to believe he opposes Bolshevism as forcefully as ever, but we ... obviously we are doing our best to close down his criminal operations, so our intelligence may not be as good as it ought to be."

"Perhaps," Lewis said, looking slowly around the room, "we should consider reaching an accommodation with him until we're sure there is no chance of Bolshevism making any kind of advance." He pushed back his chair and crossed his legs. "Then we can turn up the heat again."

"That's out of the question," Geoffrey said. "He is at least as much of a threat to this city as the Bolsheviks. Perhaps more so." He, too, pushed his chair back. "Any other questions?" He stood. "I wanted you to be kept informed, that's all."

The Sikh waiter pushed open a pair of double doors built into the wood panels to reveal another room beyond, similarly furnished, with leather armchairs gathered around an empty fireplace. A long sideboard was covered in food, and as they entered, another Sikh waiter took a bottle of champagne from the ice bucket and popped the cork. Two strikingly pretty and scantily clad Chinese waitresses in silver dresses handed around food on silver trays.

Field looked out over the rooftops behind the Cathay Hotel, uneasy about his presence here. He turned back to find Biers alongside him, already with a glass of champagne in his hand. "We met before, I'm sure."

Field took his hand. "We did, commissioner, but I was still a Griffin ..."

"Never forget a face."

Field doubted this was true. Biers's nose was red, a tracery of capillaries covered his cheeks, and he looked unsteady on his feet. Granger handed Field a glass. "Good evening, soldier."

"Good evening, sir."

Biers gulped down his champagne. "I'd better go, or Mary will kill me." He smiled at Field and walked toward the door, stopping to shake Geoffrey's hand.

For a moment Granger and Field stood in awkward silence. "I hadn't realized Borodin's return was quite so significant," Field said.

Granger shrugged. "They like to be kept informed." He leaned closer, smiling. "Geoffrey plays them beautifully."

Granger moved around so that his back was to the others. He looked Field up and down. "You need some new clothes. A bit of a supplement might be in order."

Field opened his mouth to speak, but Granger cut him short. "Bright, ambitious chap like yourself . . . right social connections." He looked at Field's dinner jacket, then at the sober-suited taipans in the room. "Can't have you trying to get by on a detective's wage."

"A supplement?"

Granger held up the lapel of his jacket. "Not bad, eh, for a poor boy from Cork?" He leaned closer, his eyes on the naked back of one of the Chinese waitresses who was offering food to a group beside them. "We don't like to see bright officers disadvantaged in this city of wealth, if you understand my meaning."

Field didn't respond, uncertain what Granger was driving at.

"And, as a result, we have a discretionary fund. Check your wages. You might be pleasantly surprised." He cleared his throat. Field saw that Geoffrey looked as if he was approaching. "Anyhow, you can come and help me out tomorrow with the ten o'clock briefing in Hongkew."

"That's . . . I'm still working on this case with Caprisi."

Granger shook his head. "You don't want to get too closely involved. Just keep in with Caprisi and keep me informed."

"You don't want me to be involved?"

"Informed but not involved. You're in the Branch, Richard. We just need to keep an eye on what the opposition is up to . . . unless you'd rather be in Crime?" Granger was smiling at him.

"I'm fine where I am, thank you, sir."

There was another awkward silence.

Lewis stopped chatting to one of the waitresses and ambled over. "All right, old man," he said quietly. "One of your men, Granger?"

"New stock."

"Good stock. Had him out last night." Lewis smiled at him. "Slightly blotted his copybook at Delancey's, but picked himself up when I said I'd show him where this Russian girl worked."

Granger said, "Which Russian girl?"

"The Orlov woman."

"The prostitute?"

Lewis was smirking. "Not one of your tarts, was she, Granger?" Field found himself smiling, until he recalled the screams of the Chinese prostitute in the darkened corridor of the club.

"You don't want to dig too deep, old man," Lewis told Field. "You never know what you might find."

Granger sighed. "He's just keeping his eye on Macleod's lot."

Lewis eyed him dispassionately. "I thought it must be something like that."

Sixteen

The breeze had brought in bad weather from the East China Sea. A light drizzle cooled their cheeks as they stepped onto the Bund. There was a thin sheen of water on the sidewalk and Field's feet were instantly damp from the unseen holes in the soles of his highly polished shoes.

Geoffrey had a car and driver waiting for him. On the very short journey to Crane Road, Field wanted to ask him about what Granger had said tonight, but thought better of it.

He had not understood whom Granger had meant by "we." What was the discretionary fund?

Field tried not to dwell on the idea of more money.

If it was a legitimate payment—though perhaps even to consider that as a possibility might be naive—then he would be able to pay Caprisi for the new suit and even get a decent pair of shoes.

The house in Crane Road was down a quiet cul-de-sac, a single bright light on the wall illuminating a long wooden veranda. At the sound of the car doors shutting, Penelope came first to the window and then the door. She stood at the top of the steps, beneath the bougainvillea, a hand on her hip. "Your dinner would be in the dog," she said. "If we had a dog."

She wore a closely cut, yellow silk dress, with a low neck beneath a thick string of dark pearls. Geoffrey shuffled forward and she bent to kiss him.

"He won't let me have a dog," she said to Field as she put

her cheek to his, the smell of her scent as strong as it had been last night. The floor of the veranda was old and worn, and the planks creaked beneath their feet.

"Good evening, Chang," Geoffrey said as he handed the servant his jacket. Field took off his own, hesitating a moment before also removing his holster.

"Straight to the table," Penelope said. "I'm sure you boys have managed to find time for a drink."

The dining room was smaller than he'd imagined, the silverware on the square, polished table bright in the candlelight.

"Richard, on the far side, beneath Christopher of York— one of our most distinguished ancestors."

Field glimpsed a large dark portrait of a man in full military uniform. He sat down, taking the linen napkin from the glass in front of him.

"Red wine, Richard?" Geoffrey asked. "It's—"

"Lamb," Penelope said.

"Whatever is . . . Yes, please, red."

Geoffrey stood again and left the room.

"You survived the Volunteers." Penelope leaned forward as she took out her own napkin. The dress was just as revealing as the one she'd worn at the country club.

"It was a good speech."

"He can charm." She sighed. "Which is, of course, why I married him." She leaned forward again. "You have no idea how handsome and dashing he was in uniform." She smiled, a gesture that was at once both weary and almost bashful. "Do you know, Richard, you're a big man, and yet I don't think there is an ounce of fat on you."

Field looked toward the door to hide his embarrassment.

"You really must get yourself a girl. It's a terrible waste." She sighed, smiling at him. "You always look so hunched up and angry, like you're about to hit someone." She smiled again, imitating his posture. "You're not about to hit someone, are you?"

"I try not to, most of the time."

"See. You look lovely when you smile."

Field frowned.

"And now you're scowling again."

"So one can't win, really."

"Of course not. That's a woman's prerogative." She looked suddenly more serious. "What are you angry about?"

"I wasn't aware of being angry about anything."

"Everyone is angry about something."

"Perhaps you're right."

"Do you ever talk about your father?"

"No."

"Is that wise?"

"Probably not," Field said, irritated by this unwarranted intimacy.

"Is that why you're so angry?"

Geoffrey reentered the room, carrying a decanter. Two servants followed, the old man and a shy young girl with a wide, flat face and hair pulled back from her forehead. "A Bordeaux, I thought. Do the trick?"

Field realized his uncle was talking to him. "Yes, of course . . . I'm sorry, we don't often have wine in the mess."

"Then we must get you into more civilized accommodation."

"He could come and live here," Penelope said.

Geoffrey filled their glasses. "Can you imagine being in a city as exhilarating as this and being stuck with your uncle and aunt?"

"Speak for yourself, darling!"

Geoffrey sat down, pulling his chair in, before reaching for the salt and grinding it over his plate. The window was open, the cicadas noisy. The candle flames flickered in the faint breeze that carried with it the damp, musty aroma of the street. Field ate a mouthful of lamb. It had been cooked with apple and was served with thickly cut, creamy potatoes. It was by far the best food he'd had since arriving in Shanghai.

"This is very good," he said.

"I slaved all day over it," Penelope said. "Didn't I, dear?"

Geoffrey smiled at Field. "You begin to see why we can never come back and live in England."

Field took a sip of his wine. He heard the low rumble of a foghorn on the river. It seemed to be answered by others.

"Who is Stirling Blackman?"

Geoffrey replenished their wineglasses before answering. Field noticed Penelope's was already empty.

"Blackman is not . . . how should one say? Not always a friend of the city." Geoffrey looked at Field. "The thing about the *New York Times,* Richard, is that it thinks it invented the notion of integrity. The difficulty is that it sometimes provokes a response from Washington, which in turn causes problems in London."

"How is the Russian girl?" Penelope asked.

For a moment Field assumed she was asking about Natasha. "She's like a ghost," he said eventually. "Her friends are either too frightened or too disinterested to want to talk about her." He put down his knife and fork and took another sip of wine. "Her fate does not seem to elicit much sympathy . . . not in the force, anyway. She did not keep good company. She began life in such gilded circumstances and her end was so squalid. It seems . . . tragic, in its own way."

"You're a romantic, Richard," Penelope said.

"No—"

"She was a whore, you know." Penelope's mouth had tightened and her eyes narrowed. "I wouldn't get yourself too worked up about it."

There was a momentary silence.

Geoffrey cleared his throat again. "Richard is right, I fear. We cannot get into the business of ignoring cases on the basis of who the victim was, tempting as it may be at times."

"Our concern," Field said, "is that it may be part of a pattern. That the perpetrator may strike again."

Penelope looked up with an emollient smile, as if regretting her earlier harshness. "Thank God for the boys in blue."

"The difficulty with the Russians," Geoffrey went on, "is that none of us like to ponder their fate too closely. It won't happen to us, of course, but we've all seen the photographs: the big houses, the servants, the military schools, and holidays in the Crimea. It's uncomfortable, particularly for those lower down the European social order here, who've never had any of those things."

"They're unreliable," Penelope said.

"Perhaps that's no surprise," Geoffrey said, "under the circumstances."

"It's no surprise that it happened to them. If they'd been . . ." Penelope looked at her husband, her face harsh again. "Well, you know what they're like. No wonder there was a revolution."

Geoffrey looked at Field. "Better to give them a wide berth. That much is certainly true."

By the time Field stepped back out into Crane Road it was past midnight and a thick blanket of fog had descended. The smell of damp streets—from the dirt and dust that settled in dry weather—swelling drains, and the pollution caught in his nose and mouth. He was tempted to put a handkerchief to his face and breathe through it as he had seen others do. Instead, he put on the dark felt trilby that his uncle had pressed upon him and lit a cigarette. At least it tasted better than the air around him.

Field began walking, his footsteps noisy, his feet again quickly damp. Another foghorn sounded on the river and he heard the rattle of a tram on the Nanking Road ahead, a Chinese banner on the corner highlighted through the gloom by a gas streetlamp—as in so many areas of the city, they had not got around to installing electric lights.

Field crossed the main road and carried on, pacing out the silence, his metal-capped heels creating a steady staccato. He passed somebody hidden beneath a blanket, then realized that it was an entire family as they receded into the fog once more.

He felt driven.

Perhaps, he thought, it might have been wiser to have stayed with his uncle.

He turned left into Nanking Road. Chinese men and women appeared suddenly through the fog and disappeared back into it just as quickly.

Field thrust his hands deep into his pockets. He saw the sign for the Majestic ahead, and his pace quickened.

He handed the doorman his hat and climbed the shabby red and gray staircase, emerging into the refurbished splendor of the ballroom on the first floor as she began singing. It was as if she had been waiting for him.

Natasha stood in front of the microphone, and for a moment he lost himself in the sight and sound of her, his eyes locked on her long legs and narrow hips as they swayed with the rhythm of the music. Her voice drifted lazily around the hall. She had her eyes shut, and as she opened them, it seemed to him that she was smiling at him.

He stepped forward a couple of paces, then saw Charles Lewis sitting close to the edge of the iron-framed balcony, staring at her.

Field moved quickly down the staircase and around the back of the dance floor. He climbed up to the balcony opposite where he thought he would be able to stand unseen in the darkness.

Even up here, away from the stage, few people talked among themselves. It wasn't difficult to be captivated by the power of her voice.

Natasha wore a black dress. A short, thick string of white pearls, held in the center by a gold clasp, hung down to her breasts. Her hair was glossy and unkempt.

She had opened her eyes, and, however absurdly, Field still could not shake the notion that she was singing to him.

As she finished and acknowledged the applause, Field realized he was attracting a few curious glances, mostly from the women at the large table next to him. Looking around him, he could see that, while the groups close to the balcony were

small, intimate, back here it was ten or twelve to the table.
Everyone was sumptuously dressed, the men with gold watch
chains to match their companions' jewelry.

He turned back to the scene below him and his heart
missed a beat. Charlie Lewis turned her slowly around the
center of the dance floor, his cheek close to her own, his hand
resting just above her hips, in the small of her back. She
looked as though she was pressing herself against him, and he
was smiling, whispering in her ear. Field saw that she was
laughing. He stepped back, imagined the two of them naked
together, on the bed, the candle flickering above them, her
hands tied to the bedstead, her legs raised . . .

Field breathed out heavily and forced himself to move
toward the door. He did not look at the dance floor as he passed
it and walked slowly up the stairs opposite. A girl in a silver
dress was selling cigarettes by one of the tables, and he killed
a few moments by buying a packet of Capstan and wondering
what it would feel like to be rich. He could not imagine being
like Lewis and never having to think about the price of anything.

"You're back."

He spun around. She was two or three feet away from him,
her brown eyes resting steadily upon his face.

"Yes."

Although the band was loud, this corner seemed quiet.

"A professional or social visit?"

"Just a visit."

"You were watching me."

"Yes."

"Is that part of the job?"

Field swallowed. "Not unless I want it to be."

"And do you?"

"I don't know."

"Why don't you know?"

Field offered her a cigarette and when she declined, put
them in his jacket pocket without taking one. "May I buy you
a drink?"

"I doubt you could afford it."

"Why do you say that?"

She shook her head, her face still expressionless. "It's not an accusation." She looked him up and down. "Most policemen could afford . . . but I think you are the one who cannot."

"I've never been ashamed to be poor."

She stared at him, shaking her head. "Oh, I don't think that is true."

He felt his face reddening. "Do you always mean to provoke?"

Natasha did not answer. Field looked down at the floor below. Lewis was bending over a table on the balcony, in animated conversation. Field heard himself say, "Do you want to dance?"

She laughed, then looked around her. "No," she said, shaking her head. "No."

"Am I that funny?"

She smiled again, but this time it was not at his expense. "You have an honest face." She looked up at him. "Do you think I have an honest face?"

Field almost said, "I don't know," but something in her eyes made him hesitate. "Yes," he said eventually.

This time her smile was one of resignation. "Perhaps I will see you again."

"Was Lena a friend?"

Natasha hesitated. She came closer to him, glancing around to check that they were not overheard. "I cannot help you."

"He must have put a hand over her mouth, so that her screams were silent."

She did not look at him. A muscle twitched in her cheek. She tucked a strand of hair behind her ear.

"Perhaps he was plunging the knife into her just a few feet from where you were sleeping."

"I was not there."

"We don't know for sure when she was killed, so—"

"I was not there."

Field took a pace toward her. "Lena is like a ghost. No one wants to talk about her. Don't you think, after all that she went through, she deserves better?"

Natasha stared at the floor, as if in another world.

"Do you imagine Lena will be the last victim?"

Natasha had raised her head, her face suddenly fearful, and Field turned to see a man whom he knew instantly to be Lu Huang reaching the top of the stairs. He was smaller than he'd appeared in the photographs, his hands hidden in front of him, in the folds of a long silk robe. His face was round, coarse, and ugly, his hair in a long pigtail. Even in this light, Field could see evidence of the poor skin that had earned him his nickname. He was accompanied by two Russian bodyguards, with closely cropped hair and black suits, who moved confidently, drawing the attention of the other customers but making no acknowledgment of their presence.

Natasha had half turned toward him, as if drawn by some magnetic force. Her face, now coldly beautiful and brittle, seemed drained of all spirit. She followed him, not bothering to excuse or explain herself to Field, and as Lu sat down at a corner table that was obviously reserved for him, she took a chair a few feet away. They did not even glance at each other or exchange a word, and it was a few moments before Field understood what was happening.

She was sitting straight and stiff, like a doll. She was there for Lu to look at, to be seen with. She was his trophy.

People had turned discreetly to look in their direction. Lu now acknowledged one or two with a curt nod.

Charles Lewis walked toward the table, a waiter scurrying forward to pull back a chair. Lu turned to face him, suddenly animated, his bullet head level with Lewis's shoulder. They looked familiar with each other's presence, as if from long acquaintance. They both ignored Natasha, who stared vacantly down at the dance floor.

Field could not move, could not think clearly. His stomach turned over so fast that he felt like vomiting.

Lewis was gesticulating with his right hand, as if emphasizing a point. Lu's head was motionless as he listened, then he nodded, raising his head and looking around the room. Lewis lit up a cigarette and leaned back in his chair, crossing his legs.

Lu stood and moved around the table. Natasha stood, too, her elegance somehow diminished as he came level with her. She allowed him to place a hand on her arm.

He led her down the stairs to the dance floor and then they were locked together, Lu's head only just above her breasts, so that, when they turned away from him, Field could not see the Chinese at all.

Field searched Natasha's face for some acknowledgment, but received none, her gaze and smile frozen. The other dancers had quietly made space for them, but were careful not to look too closely, and at the tables people had turned away and resumed their conversations.

Lu and Natasha turned again and Field could see his chubby hand placed firmly against the base of her spine, pushing her hips toward him.

Field watched in a daze until the music stopped and Lu Huang returned to his seat, without touching or acknowledging his dance partner. She sat down and stared again into the middle distance.

Field turned, forcing his feet forward. He walked toward the two bodyguards, who had retreated to the door, and knocked into the one with blond hair. The man pushed him back, swearing in Russian.

Field moved fast. The man ducked, but Field was too quick, his right hand catching the bottom of the man's jaw and spinning him into the cigarette girl.

Field turned and drew his revolver as the other bodyguard was still struggling for his gun. As he fumbled for his badge, Lewis appeared. "All right, boys..." He lowered Field's weapon and turned to the Russians. "Police," he said. "Let's forget it, shall we?"

Before they could answer, Lewis gripped Field hard on the

arm and marched him toward the stairs, not letting go until they reached the street. Field noticed that both Lu and Natasha had affected not to notice the scuffle.

Lewis exhaled, facing him in the shadowy gloom of a gas streetlamp still cradled by the fog. It was cool here, after the sweaty heat of the Majestic. "Jesus."

Field stared at him.

"Wait here."

Lewis walked back into the nightclub and Field was about to leave when he returned. "You walk in, you apologize, you bow your head once, you wait until he speaks. If he does not, you leave."

"I'm not—"

"You'll do as you're fucking told or you'll be on the next boat home."

Field pulled his mouth back, furious at being treated like a child. "So we have to kowtow to a gangster."

"*We* don't, Field. *You* do. You're a junior detective and you've just insulted one of the most powerful businessmen in the city in one of its most public places. It is now a question of face."

"So he's a businessman now."

"He is as far as you're concerned."

"I'm not going to go in there and crawl—"

"Then you're an arrogant fool." Lewis shook his head contemptuously. "I'm only standing here because I'm fond of your uncle, so don't insult your own intelligence and mine any longer."

Field stared at Lewis. He breathed in deeply and walked back into the Majestic. The band still played, but at the top of the stairs, a flustered Chinese man in a dark suit—the manager of the nightclub, Field assumed—guided him through a heavy red velvet curtain and into what appeared to be a private dining room. As he entered, a door was slammed shut behind him.

Lu was flanked by his two glowering bodyguards. Natasha sat in the corner, head bowed. Lu had his hands tucked into

the wide sleeves of his gown, and his eyes, too, radiated a cold
fury. Field had never before been in the presence of someone
who appeared to exist solely to damage and destroy.

Field could not look at Natasha, but he was overwhelmed
by her presence. His heart was thumping, his palms sweaty,
his mind confused.

"Your name?" the blond Russian asked.

"Field."

"First name?"

"Richard."

"You are a police officer."

"Yes."

"Which department?"

"S.1."

"Special Branch."

"Yes."

"You believe my men are communists?" Lu spoke in a low
monotone, his anger barely restrained.

"No. Of course not. I apologize."

They were silent.

"It was an accident," Field said.

"No, Mr. Field, it was a mistake?" Lu shook his head once,
curtly, his anger not soothed by Field's apology. "The good
reputation of the police is important to Shanghai. You cannot
afford mistakes." He sighed. "You are a friend of Mr. Lewis?"

"In a manner of speaking."

Lu frowned.

"Yes."

Lu suddenly pulled his hands from his sleeves, clenched
his right into a fist, then opened it again, as if demonstrating
the ease with which he could crush whatever came within his
grasp. "You are fortunate to have such friends."

"Yes."

Field tried not to meet Lu's eye. He caught sight of his own
reflection in a large gold-framed mirror that hung behind a
small bar at the far end of the room.

"These are troubled times," Lu said.

Field did not answer.

"Mistakes . . ." He tipped his head to one side. "Mistakes can be costly." Perhaps it was Field's imagination, but he thought Lu glanced at Natasha's bowed head as he spoke. "You are foolish to have done this."

Field forced himself to say yes.

"We should not meet again," Lu said quietly. "No, we should definitely not meet again." He dismissed Field curtly with his hand.

As Field turned, he saw Natasha, her head bowed in supplication, her hair shielding her face.

The blond bodyguard ushered him, none too gently, to the door.

Lewis was waiting for him. He didn't ask what had happened. "This is Shanghai, Richard, not Twickenham."

"So he can do as he wants?" Field asked, his anger returning.

Lewis looked at him, still bemused. He took a silver cigarette case from his jacket pocket, lighting up himself, then offering one to Field. "Listen, old man, all good things come to those that wait, if you understand what I mean."

Field did not respond. A doorman emerged from the club and handed him his trilby, before quickly retreating.

"Bright young man." Lewis smiled. "You'll be all right." He laughed, the cigarette still in his mouth. "Perhaps, one day, you'll even be able to afford old Natasha, if he's got tired of her and she's worth having by then." Lewis was still smiling. "It's a joke, old man."

"You seem to get on just fine with Lu."

Lewis's face darkened. "I hope you're not implying what you seem to be, Field. I want you to be in no doubt that I'd like it very much if Lu didn't exist, but until we find a way to bring that about, needless friction would serve neither of us. You'd do well not to fight what you can't change."

"That may be your philosophy, but it's not mine."

"Then you're going to find life here rather tough going, old man."

. . .

Field didn't sleep. It was a cooler night, but in the tiny box that was his room in the Carter Road quarters, that made little difference. He lay still, staring at the ceiling, his whole body covered in a thin sheen of sweat. The mosquitoes had no respect for the nets or spray and he watched them gathering in the corners of the ceiling in the half-darkness.

He turned on his side, trying once again to shut out the sounds from next door.

They grew louder, something—Prokopiev's head perhaps—banging against the wall. There was a low grunt, then a muffled scream, followed by the too-familiar sound of a beating, so that Field was on his feet, his fists clenched tight.

He pressed his knuckles against his forehead, then tried to block his ears, but Prokopiev's companion was crying loudly now and Prokopiev was hitting her harder.

Field jumped onto the bed and thumped the wall with the flat of his hand. "Shut the fuck up!"

The beating stopped, the girl's crying dropping to a strangled whimper. "Shut the fuck up, Prokopiev," Field repeated, breathing heavily before slumping back onto the bed and once again staring at the ceiling.

Prokopiev began talking to the woman roughly in Russian, and after a few minutes Field heard her getting dressed. Prokopiev, he knew, was paying her.

She walked away, her heels clicking loudly in the corridor.

"Get fucked, English boy," Prokopiev said, but Field didn't answer.

He closed his eyes and tried to relax, but his heart was thumping.

He thought of the fear in Natasha's eyes tonight and recalled what Maretsky had told him about Lena not being the first victim, nor, probably, the last. Why hadn't he told Caprisi about that already? They should have been working with a much greater sense of urgency.

Field wanted the new day to begin immediately.

Seventeen

ield was waiting next to Caprisi's desk when the American arrived for work. Caprisi put down his leather case and hung his raincoat from the hat stand in the corner. "All right," he said, "*I* get in early, but this is . . . How long have you been waiting?"

"I couldn't sleep."

"No shit?" The American shook his head. "And you couldn't shave, either?"

"I forgot."

Caprisi sucked his teeth. "You're anxious to get to work?"

"I was just thinking . . ."

"Hold your horses." Caprisi lifted a finger. "Let me stop you. In the spirit of the overworked and underpaid Criminal Investigation Division, unlike your own department, Chen and I now have to deal with this armed robbery yesterday and—"

"That can wait."

"Says who?" Caprisi shook his head. "We'll get back to the Orlov case, but—"

"No, we can't do that."

"We *can't*?" Caprisi cleared his throat before turning to pour himself a glass of water from the purified jug in the corner.

Field took his hands out of his pockets. "Lena wasn't the first and she won't be the last."

"Is that so?"

"Maretsky doesn't believe this was the first case, and he is sure the perpetrator will now have a taste for it."

"A taste for roughing up Russian girls narrows it down."

"You sound like Sorenson and Prokopiev."

Caprisi's mouth tightened. "Be careful, polar bear. We've a heavy workload and this can wait."

"It can't."

"Now . . ."

"I saw your face in Lena Orlov's flat and down in the Chinese city. Why was Chen restraining you?"

"Back off, polar bear."

"What happened to Slugger?"

"I said back off."

"Was he a homosexual?"

Field held Caprisi's stare. The American suddenly took a pace closer. "Slugger was twice the man you'll ever be."

"And Lu had something to do with his death?"

"Slugger liked men, Field, you're right." He shook his head. "You want to know, I'll tell you. Slugger liked men. I didn't know, his wife didn't know, his kids didn't know, but Lu found out. As I said, we were closing down a lot of opium dens on the Foochow Road, angering Lu and upsetting the cabal, and Slugger wouldn't be bought, so they set him up. There were pictures, just for fun. Slugger wouldn't bend to the blackmail and decided to leave. He told us what had happened, put his wife and family on the boat to England, and some men in raincoats met them as they came down the gangplank in Hong Kong and handed his teenage son a photograph of Slugger fucking another man. So Slugger walked up to the top of the Peak and blew the back of his head off."

"I'm sorry."

"No you're not. You didn't know him."

"That doesn't stop me being sorry."

Caprisi turned back to refill his glass, and it was a few moments before Field noticed that Chen had come into the room and was leaning against one of the cubicles. "Field wants to concentrate on the Orlov case," Caprisi said.

Chen shrugged.

"Maretsky says he doesn't think there are any cases here, but what about in the French Concession?" Field asked.

"He's asked them," Caprisi said.

"Yes, but if they're as corrupt as everyone says, then they will probably have lied to him, or lied about the details."

Caprisi frowned.

"A death would still have been reported in the newspaper. The gendarmerie might not have given all the details, but they would have to provide some."

Caprisi looked far from convinced.

"If we could find any deaths that seemed even vaguely similar, then a little investigation might show a connection. It's a long shot, I know, but if we could establish that there was even a single other case, then a pattern might emerge."

Caprisi took out his pad and the short stub of pencil and made a note of this underneath one saying "fingerprints." He looked up. "What about the factory that was referenced in Lena's notes, and the shipments of sewing machines?"

Field looked at Chen. "Is that a red herring? Are we sure there is a connection between that notebook and the girl's death?"

"Why did she want to keep it secret?" Caprisi asked.

Chen moved closer. "Lena was Lu's girl. The factory has some kind of criminal activity associated with him. When I went down yesterday, they were nervous . . . the manager was not there."

"I saw Lu and Charles Lewis together last night. They seemed very at ease in each other's company."

"Where?" Caprisi asked.

"The Majestic."

"What were you doing there?"

Field felt his face reddening.

"Ground research, I see." Caprisi shook his head. "The fish don't come bigger than Lewis, do they, Chen?"

The Chinese detective shook his head.

"Lewis doesn't have any connection with Lu, does he?" Field asked.

"Not that we know of."

"Is it possible that Lewis could be involved—that whatever is going on at the factory could be at that level?"

"Anything is possible," Chen said. "But whoever is behind these shipments, if they are as significant as we think, is more likely to be someone lower down in Fraser's."

"Lena was Lu's girl," Caprisi repeated. "So, really, it has to have been him."

Chen shrugged again. "He likes girls, boys. He has her, for sure, but if she is not a favorite, perhaps there are other uses. She is a spy, a conduit to the Bolsheviks and agitators, part of his intelligence network, or maybe he lets an associate use her."

"I'm not expert on Shanghai real estate," Field said, "but isn't a penthouse in the Happy Times block, with a balcony overlooking the racecourse . . . that's serious money. There must be many cheaper ways of gathering intelligence on Borodin."

They both nodded.

"And if we think about it from the killer's point of view . . . whoever it is cannot fail to know that this woman is an asset of Lu's. To murder her in this way shows a supreme confidence that there will be no repercussions."

Caprisi clicked his tongue against the top of his mouth. "Chen. Would Lu, as a point of culture, let anyone else sleep with one of his women? I mean, have we got this wrong? Would he even consider lending her to someone?"

"Probably. A concubine, certainly not, but this woman is not a concubine, so it is less clear. It is . . . He is Chinese. Easy for me to understand, hard to explain."

"Try."

Chen sighed. "Russian girls, they . . . Lu is Chinese, so if he has a Chinese concubine, then another man who has even looked at her is dead. No question. That is face. Chinese to Chinese. But Russian girls will be different . . . This is more complicated. Russian girls are a category to themselves. He keeps them, he fucks them, but there is not so much . . . face. Control is a little looser. He requires them to carry out other tasks.

They are perhaps business gift, now to one man, now to another. Sometimes, if they are very beautiful, they are for show. He would keep them, but the money is nothing to him, small. He might go to apartment, but more likely to have them come to him when required. The face is different, that is what. If they humiliate him in public; if they are disloyal, or give information to enemy; if they fail to do what he asks, then they will be executed."

Chen frowned, as if unsure of whether he had adequately communicated his interpretation of Lena's precarious position.

"But he is," Caprisi said, "not in the business of letting other people fuck his women for free? This Russian boyfriend, for example, what is his position?"

"If she chooses to do this, it is very dangerous. Perhaps Lu will tolerate—what is it to him? Only Russians. Or perhaps he will be annoyed. If the woman is beautiful, favored above others, it is very dangerous. He may execute immediately. If less important, perhaps he will ignore once—no point in wasting assets. Each case different. But, of course, it could be he like to murder. This is different. Russian girls are good, then. Inferior."

"Maybe Krauss is wrong," Caprisi went on. "The man opposite says Lu arrives at four—perhaps he murders her then. She dies at four, not earlier."

Field recalled his exchange with Natasha the previous evening and his suggestion that she might have been in the building while Lena was being murdered. He thought about her hasty denials.

"Krauss was wrong about that Chinese boy last year," Caprisi said. Field frowned, but the American waved his hand to indicate it was too complicated to explain. "But if it was Lu, he was quick."

"It does not take long," Chen said.

"To tie her up?"

"A minute. Two."

"So he's angry. He's learned she's been fucking Sergei?"

"Sergei is still alive." Chen smiled, raising his eyebrows. "Besides, Maretsky is right. So many wounds." Chen mimed the stabbing. "Anger."

"He likes doing it. He enjoys it."

"Then why here?" Field asked. "Why not in the French Concession? Isn't that safer for him?"

Caprisi and Chen looked at him. There was a long silence.

Caprisi said, "Don't discuss this, Field. Not with anyone. If there is physical evidence—if any useful prints come back, or any other documentation—we do not keep it in the office. You give it to me. I'll hold it at my apartment. Is that clear?"

Chen was looking at Field as though he were an idiot.

They heard the lift stop. Macleod pulled the metal cage back and walked slowly down the room toward them. He was wearing a long gray raincoat and a brown trilby. He carried a black leather briefcase with dull brass buckles. He went straight to the corner and poured himself a glass of water, as Caprisi had done.

"That's better," he said, taking off his hat and wiping the sweat from the dome of his head with his hand. "Good morning, gentlemen."

Caprisi was sitting on his desk. He pulled up a chair to rest his legs on. "Field wants us to concentrate on the murdered Russian girl."

Macleod looked at him without smiling. "When he gets to manage his own department, then that's what he can do."

"Maretsky says there will be more."

Macleod walked into his office, taking off his raincoat and placing it on the stand, along with his hat, before coming back to the doorway. "More what?"

"More victims. More deaths."

"And what makes him so bloody sure of that?"

"He thinks it is part of a pattern. Some deaths already, perhaps in the French Concession, more to come."

Macleod sighed. He sipped his water. "Well, you can give it priority, but we've got too much going on to clear the shelf."

"It could be an avenue into Lu. Perhaps he's overreaching himself."

Macleod thought about this. "All right, you can clear the decks for a few days, see where it takes you. Field, have you got a minute?"

Field followed Macleod into his office. The Scotsman closed the glass door behind him and his manner instantly softened. He was no longer frowning—he even smiled once as he encouraged Field to sit opposite him. "How are you settling in . . . It's Richard, isn't it?"

"Yes."

"You seem to have come far, for a Griffin."

"Well, I'm not sure . . ."

"You have a confidence about you and I like that."

Field did not know how to respond.

"Caprisi thinks you're a good man."

"That's . . ."

"He has good judgment." Macleod was not meeting Field's eye. "It's been a while since I got really involved in training." He turned to Field now, smiling again. "Used to be my beat before CID."

"A lot less interesting."

"Yes." Macleod nodded. "But it had its uses. The training department is the future, of course."

"Then God help us."

"Yes." Macleod didn't bother to smile. He was staring into the middle distance, over Field's shoulder. "I'm sure there is a great deal of excellent instruction, but I'm not sure they really tell . . ." Macleod cleared his throat. "I'm not sure that they equip Griffins with what they really need to know, if you see what I mean."

"I think so," Field said, not seeing at all.

"You're a good man. Good family and all the rest of it."

Field wasn't sure if this called for a response.

"I wanted you to be clear about what is going on—what we face, if you understand my meaning."

"Yes, sir."

"Granger and I don't always see eye-to-eye on this and . . . You're a member of his department, so it's perhaps unfair of me to talk to you like this, but I think it's important . . . I feel it's important that I get my view across to anyone who seems to be reliable and trustworthy."

Field nodded.

"Granger views Lu as a fact of life that must be dealt with in an adult way; as he would see it, lived with, even compromised with. That's his view and I suppose he's entitled to it. I'm afraid I view Lu Huang as an evil that must be eradicated. Whilst he continues to exist, we are doing no more than trying to stem the tide of violent crime." Macleod looked at him again. "Lu's tentacles are long."

"Yes."

"They stretch even inside this building."

"Caprisi said."

"He has explained?"

"Yes."

"It takes time to understand, of course."

"I think I understand now."

Macleod was fidgeting with the cross around his neck. He reminded Field again of his father, though, oddly, Field did not feel resentment, but a quiet respect.

"Good," Macleod said, bringing their meeting to an end. "I suppose, in theory, you have been detailed to my department, or at least working out of it, so I thought it important to have a chat."

Eighteen

iscussing Lena's murder made Field feel like a caged animal, but despite his own sense of urgency, and Macleod's approval, Caprisi and Chen said they had other things to attend to first.

While he was waiting for them, Granger's secretary called down to the department to find out where he was. Field had forgotten that he was supposed to be accompanying him to the Hongkew district.

Granger was in a sullen mood. "Morning, son," he said as Field climbed into the new yellow and gray Chevrolet and settled into the backseat. The leather was smooth to the touch, the walnut trim highly polished. Granger sat easily, his big legs stretched out in front of him. As Field tried to free a small stone that had become lodged in a hole in the sole of his shoe, he couldn't help noticing the quality of Granger's clothes.

As they raced along the Bund, past the Hong Kong Shanghai Bank and the Customs House, Granger took a small bottle of whiskey from a compartment built into the walnut dash. Field declined his offer and turned to look out of the window at the neatly laid-out gardens next to the imposing building that housed the British consulate.

They crossed Garden Bridge, the water beneath the iron structure teeming with sampans. The fog had lifted, but it was still warm and overcast and close.

The driver hooted loudly at another car as they passed the Soviet consulate, before entering the narrower streets around the Hongkew market. The signs and banners here were in Japanese, though the difference to the foreign eye, Field thought, was not marked.

Field had never been into the Hongkew station before; it was a cramped but well-organized building. The constables were mostly either Japanese or Chinese, and they all stopped talking, respectfully, in the corridors as Granger strode past.

The briefing was the same as the one Field had heard the day before, and afterward there were no questions, so they had saki with the Japanese S.1 officer who was attached to the station. Granger talked more about Borodin, becoming personal and abusive, still furious that the Russian's diplomatic status allowed him to send his children to the American school and keep mistresses in different apartments around the city.

In the car on the way back, Granger said quietly, "Charlie tells me there was some trouble last night at the Majestic."

"It was an accident."

"Well, don't do anything stupid, eh?" Granger smiled. "Can't have you getting damaged before the match this afternoon."

Field had completely forgotten about it. "You don't play?" he asked.

Granger shook his head. "Not anymore."

"But you did?"

"Might have for Ireland." He lowered his voice, the laughter still in his eyes. "If there had not been a war on."

"The Great War or . . ."

"The war of independence. The Irish war. Rebellion, to you. Now, I'm the worst kind of coach . . ."

"Were you and Michael Collins friends?"

Granger looked at him, as if weighing him up. "Yes."

"How did you end up here if you were fighting the English?"

"New York for guns, then a girl."

"Your wife?"

Granger smiled. "No."

"They say the commissioner is about to retire."

"Within the month."

"Do you think . . ."

"If it's Macleod, we're all finished."

"But the Municipal Council must favor you overwhelmingly."

"Don't be so sure." They had stopped outside the Cathay Hotel, and Granger was looking at him steadily, his hand on the door handle. "I've a meeting."

"I'll get out here as well."

"I'll get the driver to—"

"No, it's fine. I said I'd meet Caprisi at the library." Granger narrowed his eyes. Field shook his head. "Nothing important."

They got out of the car. Granger adjusted his clothes. Field wondered when his light suit would be ready.

"Don't make the mistake of underestimating Macleod, Field. He may not mix with the council socially, but he's been on a private sales job for years." Granger lit a cigarette. "I'm sure he's given you one of his little chats . . ."

"Yes."

"Policemen shouldn't act like missionaries, and I get tired of him lecturing us all like joyless schoolboys."

Field hesitated. "He seems sincere in what he believes."

"You think so?" Granger frowned. "So you bought the speech?"

Field shook his head. "No, I just said I thought he was sincere in what he said."

Granger looked agitated. He dropped his cigarette and stubbed it out with his foot. "I don't like Macleod. If he becomes commissioner, it will be a disaster for the force, the city, and me personally. We'll be forced into a head-on confrontation we cannot yet win. Think about it. Look around you. Containing Lu, trying to keep his influence at bay in the Settlement. Maybe. Eradicating organized crime? Forget it." Granger shook his head. "This is China. We have to accept that building some kind of civilization here is going to take longer than people would like. And I'm tired of being made to feel like a criminal for not signing up to the whole puritan sermon. It's a time for knowing who your friends are."

Field thought about his confrontation with Lu last night, recalling the discomfort and unease he'd felt during the meeting itself and the anger that had returned shortly afterward. "Loyalty is one of my few qualities."

"I like that, Field." Granger put an arm around his shoulder. "You're a good man. You've got plenty of qualities, believe me." He turned toward the hotel. "We can go far if we work together."

As he watched a doorman jump forward, Field wondered again what it must be like to be rich enough to arrive in Shanghai and climb into the liveried cream Cathay Hotel Chevrolet that he'd seen waiting on the quayside when his own liner had docked. He imagined the rooms as a more modern version of the Shanghai Club, full of leather and glass. It was said that the taps were gold-plated. It was common knowledge you could get almost any drug from room service.

He looked up at the narrow, conical roof and the balcony that surrounded it. He could see some guests leaning over, gazing out toward the river. Another sedan pulled up behind Granger's and a woman in a cream skirt made her way toward the entrance, her chauffeur following with a hatbox.

Field nodded at the doorman, half expecting to be refused entry, not yet used to the idea of belonging in such surroundings. Inside, it was cooler, the white marble floor spotlessly clean. He walked slowly down the long corridor between rows of potted plants, then turned into the reception area.

It was as fashionable as he'd imagined, an iron-framed balcony above the swinging doors giving way to a gilt-edged ceiling. There were new designer clocks all along the wall behind the reception desk with the local times in different cities.

Field's eyes were drawn to an attractive blond-haired woman sitting in the tea lounge. She had an infectious laugh and reminded him of Lena Orlov. Then he noticed that her companion—the man she was laughing with—was Granger.

"Can I help you, sir?" One of the bellboys smiled at him.

"Er . . ." Field took two swift paces backward, so that he was out of view. "No. Just looking for someone, not here. Thanks."

He turned around.

"Would you like to leave a message?"

"No . . . no thanks."

Outside, Field crossed the road and walked in front of the Customs House.

The girl must have been another of Granger's women.

Field needed cash, but had to wait in a long queue in the central hall of the Hong Kong Shanghai Bank. The ceiling was made of elaborate colored glass.

He looked at the Roman figures surrounding the dome at the entrance, representing Sapienta, Fides, and Prudentia, among others.

To his left, small groups of men and women huddled together beneath two huge chalkboards. The one on the left listed the closing prices on Wall Street, headed by Reading and Baldwin Locomotive, a plus sign next to the final price showing that both had seen small rises on the day. The other listed Shanghai prices, and two men in long tunics stood in front of it, one of them reaching up to rub out and replace the figures as a colleague farther back shouted out instructions.

Field looked at his watch, thinking that he would probably be early for the meeting he'd arranged with Caprisi and Chen at the central library. It would give him time to get started.

He shuffled closer to the front of the line. A tiny Chinese, his head only just above the counter, was arguing with the teller. Field examined the boards behind the counter that listed currency rates in English and Chinese.

When he was the next in line and confident of not losing his place, Field filled out a slip for a withdrawal of thirty Shanghai dollars. He looked up through the brass grille to try to calculate what his salary was worth in pounds this month.

He finally stepped up to the counter and smiled at the young girl behind it as he pushed the form across. "An account balance also, please."

The girl checked the slip he had filled out, then got up and walked back to the huge filing cabinets that stretched all the way from one end of the room to the other. She checked the number and disappeared around the corner.

She returned a few moments later with a buff-colored file and ran her finger down the page before taking a sheet of paper from the box in front of her, writing down an amount, and handing it to him. She began to count out the cash for the withdrawal he had requested. Field looked at it for a moment and frowned. He showed it to her. "Are you sure you have the right account?"

She looked at the file. "Mr. Field, yes?"

"Yes."

She nodded.

Field frowned again. "Has there been a credit?"

She checked it once more. "Credit today, two hundred; credit today, two hundred."

"Two credits?"

"Yes."

"Both for two hundred?"

"Yes."

"Four hundred in total?"

"Yes." She was looking at him now as if he were the stupidest man she'd ever met.

"The first one for two hundred—my salary, the same source?"

"Police force."

"Yes. What about the other? Who . . ."

"Cash."

"Cash?"

"Yes, pay in cash."

Field found it hard to control the excitement in his stomach as he walked out of the bank into the light drizzle and subdued bustle of the Bund. It seemed clear that the supplement

Granger had talked of—which had to be the source of the extra money—was effectively doubling his salary, and, for the first time in his life, it would leave him with something to spare. It would mean a decent pair of shoes, nights out—he would be able to afford to drink at the Majestic. He could put some aside, send some home to his mother. This winter she'd be able to pay for coal.

His first thought had been that the supplement was generous and even of questionable honesty, but his qualms faded quickly. The fact was his salary was poor, even mean, and if Granger wanted to make sure his men got extra from department funds to reflect the nature of their work, then that made sense.

A few minutes later he sprinted up the wide stone steps of the public library on Nanking Road and entered a room that was almost as cavernous as the bank he'd just left.

The bookcases were two or three times his height. One of the librarians was retrieving a book from the top shelf with the aid of a small stepladder. The reference counter was directly ahead. A sign in English and Chinese hung from the ceiling above it.

Field took out his identification as a timid-looking Chinese girl approached him. "From the Special Branch." She looked as if she might faint, so he smiled encouragingly. "I need the last six months of the following." He smiled again. "Got a pen?" She scurried back to her desk to get a pen and a piece of paper. "The *North China Daily News,* the *Shanghai Times,* the *Evening Post and Echo,* the *Evening Mercury,* and the *Journal de Shanghai.*"

Field took a seat at one of the long wooden tables and waited.

It was about twenty minutes before she wheeled them in on a trolley with the help of a porter dressed in a dirty gray tunic. Field thanked her and looked over the leather-bound volumes, their titles etched in gold.

He began with the most recent copies of the *North China*

Daily News, which had not yet been bound and were kept loose in a box. He went back to a week before the Orlov murder.

Most of the front page of the first edition he looked at was covered in advertisements for everything from flytraps to shaving balm. *Never mind the swarms of mosquitoes in your neighbourhood,* one said. *They will not pester you when you are protected by XEX. For sale; $4 per bottle at leading dispensaries.* Only for the rich, he thought.

Field's eyes were drawn to a private notice beneath the advertisements on the left-hand side. *Cool and comfortable, well-furnished, detached three bed house to let for three months. Garden, tennis, garage, centrally located in French Concession, near French Club.*

He sat back. It did not give a price, but how much could something like that be? If the monthly supplement went up a bit, he'd be able to afford it comfortably and still send money home to his mother. There would be funds for a car, a driver, and a couple of servants.

Field shook his head, trying to suppress the pleasure that knowledge of the money sitting in his bank account was giving him.

He turned to the headlines: "War in Hunan" and "Comrades Bickering Up North." His eyes were drawn to an article below: "Kuomintang and Communism." *Canton, June 17. General Chiang Kai-shek has announced he is not in sympathy with the "reds." The strongest of all the Kuomintang leaders has openly and vigorously announced that he is not in sympathy with the communists.*

The paper did not yet seem to have picked up on Borodin's return.

He began to scan the pages methodically, but there were so many small items that it took time. His hands were covered in black ink almost immediately, so that he smudged each new page that he touched.

He found an item headed "Russian Suicides Drop." *The*

Central Coroner has reported a drop in the number of Russian suicides in the Settlement in the first half of this year from 12 to 9. The French Concession has reported a similar drop, from 25 to 22.

Field looked at the item for a long time.

He worked backward methodically, soon lost in what he was doing. He was looking at a picture of the Duchess of York's new baby girl, Elizabeth, born in April, when Caprisi came and sat in the chair opposite him, Chen beside him. "Progress?"

"I'm guessing they might simply have been passed off as suicides."

Caprisi shook his head confidently. "If there is a pattern, then the other girls will probably have been stabbed. Even the French police wouldn't try to pass that off as suicide."

"Why not?"

"What's the point? You might get an angry relative causing trouble. Simpler to let an investigation run into the sand." He cleared his throat. "It will be down as a murder, but the details will have been obscured or changed. Have you got the Chinese papers?"

Field shook his head and Caprisi nodded at Chen.

"Do you speak French?" Field asked Caprisi.

"Italian."

Field got up and lifted over one of the piles, a cloud of dust rising as he dropped them in the middle of the big oak table. "Take the *Mercury.*"

They read on in silence. Field found another piece about Lu Huang. There was a picture of him directly above one of the new Shah of Iran with his son, but while the one from Iran was of reasonable quality, Lu's was dark and shadowy. The feature covered "the Shanghai society figure's largest donation to charity yet."

Field felt his anger rising as he read it. The donation had been to the Sisters of Mercy Orphanage and had been made because he "loved children" and wanted young orphans to be

given the kind of care he had never received. The lady inter-
viewer had obviously been overawed by Lu's wealth and power.
Field was about to stop reading when his eyes were drawn to a
comment at the conclusion. "I am a Chinese!" he had said.
"Always keep good records. Always records of everything.
Guarded at safest place—home. Always know who owes
money! Who already paid!"

Field looked up at Caprisi, then went back to scanning the
pages, the thoughts he'd been about to voice not yet clearly
formed in his mind.

Nineteen

They worked patiently and in silence, the hours ticking by. Each time Field looked up, more time had passed than he'd imagined. He'd expected Caprisi, in particular, to have grown bored and gone off to do something else, but the American continued to scan the articles methodically, pencil in hand. Chen sat next to him, head bent, doing the same with the Chinese newspapers.

In the end, Field was left with the *Journal de Shanghai* and Caprisi with the *Shanghai Times*. Field did not trust his schoolboy French, but he had no option but to try. He opened the first volume.

"Cigarette?" Caprisi asked, and Field nodded.

The three of them smoked in silence on the steps of the library.

"There would have to be a record of it, wouldn't there?" Field asked. "The level of crime cannot have reached the stage where the murder of a woman goes completely unrecorded?"

Caprisi took a long drag of his cigarette. "There will be a record, if there was a murder."

"You're indulging me."

Caprisi shook his head. "No, it was a good idea."

The American looked at Chen, who shrugged to indicate that nothing was lost by trying.

"If you were a criminal," Field said, "would you keep a record of everything?"

Both Caprisi and Chen looked puzzled.

"Would you record bribes, drug shipments, whatever it is that you are into?"

"Record what?" Caprisi asked.

"Transactions. Such and such a payment to someone in the French police, this amount of drugs arriving from India or from inland China on this day, distributed in these quantities to these locations."

They were still frowning at him.

"Crime is a business like any other."

"Sure," Caprisi said.

"You would still want to keep accounts. I mean especially here, where they're so meticulous."

Chen nodded. Caprisi shrugged. "You thinking of becoming an accountant?"

Field looked down the street. "I used to be, in a way."

"In what way?"

"I used to do my father's books."

Caprisi snorted. "You want to bust Lu for not paying his taxes?"

Field smiled. "Lena's notes suggest that payments were recorded in 'ledger two.'"

"Correct."

"I've just read an interview with Lu. He boasts about what good records he keeps of all those who owe him money."

Caprisi nodded. "Getting to the point . . ."

"He obviously has to record all details of shipments and so on. He must also keep track of whom he bribes and for how much. Lena must have seen those records. The interview says that he keeps these records at home. He wouldn't need to lock them in a safe all day; entries are being made all the time, and no one is going to steal them. The French are no threat and the house is like a fortress. It's better guarded than a bank. The only people who have access are his women."

They didn't answer him.

"If most of his actions are criminal, then most of those records will provide *proof* of criminal action."

"As you know, Field, he lives in the Concession."

"Yes, but supposing we could get hold of them? Supposing there was the political will to mount a prosecution? It shouldn't take much for the Municipal Council to decide he's got too big for his boots."

"Who says there is the political will?"

Field decided to drop it, but he could see he'd got Caprisi thinking.

"You should talk to Macleod," the American said. "But you answered your own question. How would we ever get a look at them in the first place?"

They finished their cigarettes. "Is Macleod as dour as he sometimes appears?" Field asked.

"He's Scottish."

Field smiled. "I know, but that's not necessarily——"

"He wants to clean up Shanghai, then go home and be a minister of the Kirk."

"Do you think he'll succeed?"

"I'm sure the church will have him."

"No, I mean——"

"I know what you meant, Field." Caprisi smiled. "What do you think?"

Field didn't answer immediately. "Nothing is impossible."

"Quite right," Caprisi said, mocking him. "This is almost part of the empire, after all."

Field grinned. "Fuck off, Caprisi."

They worked for another twenty minutes before Field found what he was looking for. It was a brief paragraph on page two of the *Journal* of May 2. He kept his finger on it as he tried to translate. "The body of an...*entraîneuse*...entertainer was discovered last night by gendarmes in Little Russia. She is believed to have been stabbed to death at home." Field looked up.

Caprisi pulled the newspaper across the table. He pinched his nose between his fingers as he glanced at the print, leaving a smear of black ink.

"They don't even give her name," Field said.

"Make a note of the date," Caprisi said. "There's a station in Little Russia which would have received the first call. You should go down there tomorrow. Forget the French CID, they'll tell us nothing. See if you can find out more details—how many times she was stabbed, was she handcuffed?" Caprisi looked at him. "I don't need to tell you what to ask. Better that you go alone. Think up some excuse to have a quick look through the report cards for that period."

Caprisi's driver pulled up opposite the Soviet consulate, and they crossed the road, light drizzle drifting into their faces as they walked alongside the tall wire fence. The building looked deserted.

Beyond the perimeter were two Chinese shops, one selling spices, the other hardware, a narrow staircase in between providing access to the cramped, damp offices of the *New Shanghai Life*.

A corridor, with piles of the magazine stacked all along one wall, led into a small room with five or six desks. Two typists sat in one corner, hammering away.

Everyone turned to look at them. Two men cut short an animated discussion behind a wood and glass partition. Field recognized Borodin immediately. He was a tall, lean, well-built man with a hawkish face and closely cut dark hair.

"Can I help you?" he asked from the doorway, his English spoken with a faint American accent.

Field, who was closest, led the way down between the desks. He produced his identification. "Richard Field, S.1. My colleagues, Detectives Caprisi and Chen, are from the Crime Branch."

Borodin was as tall as Field but leaner. He reminded Field a little of Granger, with his well-cut three-piece suit and polished shoes, but he was an aggressively angular man, his face hostile and suspicious. "No crime has been committed here.

This is a legitimate magazine to try to counter the propaganda your newspapers put out about the new Soviet regime."

"I don't doubt it," Field said easily.

"I must ask you to leave, or we will have no choice but to register a diplomatic protest."

"I wasn't aware this was diplomatic territory."

"I must ask you . . ."

"Please, Mr. Borodin."

The Russian stopped.

"A Russian girl has been murdered. We believe she worked here from time to time."

Borodin stepped back to allow them through the partition, his face still suspicious. A thin, intellectual-looking man with round glasses stood from behind the desk and proffered his hand, but not his name. He was the spitting image of Sergei.

Chen moved to the back of the room. Caprisi and Field leaned against the glass, opposite Borodin. The walls were lined with more copies of the magazine, except the section behind the editor's desk, which was covered with pictures of Russian leaders. Field noticed there was not one of Trotsky— just Stalin, in the center, surrounded by Kamenev, Zinoviev, and Lenin.

"Do you recall Lena Orlov?" Field asked.

The editor was staring at his desk, and Borodin, who was clearly going to be the spokesman, tilted his head thoughtfully to one side. Field was beginning to see why Granger detested this bespoke revolutionary. "Orlov?"

"Medium height, blond, quite pretty," Caprisi said.

"From Kazan," Field added.

Borodin shrugged. "Perhaps she came to a meeting."

"Just one?"

"Many people attend. There are many people who do not accept the version of the new Russia put forward by your newspapers."

"So she came once?"

"Sure."

"What about Natasha Medvedev?"

Borodin shrugged again, as if not recalling the name.

"You would remember her," Caprisi said. "Tall, thin, strikingly beautiful."

"There are many beautiful Russian girls here, Officer."

"So we understand," Field said. Borodin stared at him. "What about Sergei Stanislevich?"

Borodin shook his head. Field turned to the editor. "What about you?"

"I'm always at the meetings," Borodin said.

"You've just been in the south."

"I am happy to speak for the staff."

"Then you didn't know Stanislevich?"

Borodin shook his head.

"You must keep details of those who attend your meetings, names, addresses—"

"Of course we do not." Borodin looked horrified. "So that you can harass anyone who wishes to counter the propaganda that you—"

"Yes," Caprisi said. "I think we get the message."

"Stanislevich, Medvedev, and Orlov all come from Kazan on the Volga," Field said. "They attended meetings here—and yet they claim not to have known each other well."

Borodin was frowning.

"Stanislevich says he didn't know either of the women in Russia."

"Do you know everyone in London, Officer?"

"No, but—"

"Nor do I in Moscow."

"Emigrés spend time together," Chen said, his voice quietly menacing. "These people knew each other well, and you remember them."

Borodin stared at the Chinese detective, trying to intimidate him and failing.

Caprisi sighed and straightened. There was no point in continuing this interview. "Thank you for your time, Mr. Borodin," he said.

As they reached the bottom of the stairs and emerged into

the drizzle again, Caprisi said, "This *fucking* city." He took out his cigarettes, looking across at the consulate. "No one is going to say a fucking thing."

Field was silent. The image of Natasha Medvedev hugging her sister and father in front of their home was imprinted on his mind. He recalled the easy warmth that showed in their faces and body language—perhaps, he thought, because it was so at odds with his own experience of family life. He could not match the woman in the picture with the one who could put up with the dour extremism of the office they had just left.

After they had got back into the car, Field leaned his head against the window and closed his eyes, recalling his father's face with complete clarity and then his mother's—the two of them kneeling in church on Sunday.

Instead of anger, Field felt only a deep, painful sorrow that life had not somehow turned out differently. It was true, he thought, that they were not bad people, just fallible beings, bowed down by the weight of expectation; his father ashamed of his business and social position, expecting and demanding more of himself than had ever really been possible; his mother wanting more from the love she had sacrificed so much for than he had been able to give.

For a moment Field felt at peace, but the anger at his father soon returned. Expectation was not a burden placed upon you by others; it was a choice you made for yourself. His mother had not made excessive demands; she'd just wanted some sign of the love she'd sacrificed her relationship with her own parents for, because otherwise what was the point in her life?

Expectation was a choice you made. If Albert David Field had demanded less of himself and put less pressure on all of them, then happiness would have been within reach. They had all been punished because he viewed himself as a failure, a judgment based on criteria that mattered to no one but himself.

By the time Field had finished with this train of thought, he hated his father all over again.

. . .

Rugby was usually a game for the winter in Shanghai, as it was in Europe. Field had not really considered this until he arrived in the changing room at the police academy. As he pulled on his black shorts and thick woolen socks, he remembered Caprisi saying that it was supposed to be an endurance test, a trial of strength between the two competing branches of the force. Last year an overweight Italian had collapsed in the heat and been carried from the field unconscious.

Field didn't recognize at least half the men in this room, and realized most of them had been drafted in from outside the force, to improve the odds. He introduced himself to a burly Irishman from Belfast who turned out to be one of the managers of the Cathay Hotel and, Field assumed, a friend or acquaintance of Granger's.

He laced his boots, then walked through to the shower area and poured himself some water from the purified jug in the corner. He washed his hands and looked in the mirror, grateful that he'd had his dark hair cut very short the previous week. The clean-cut face that stared back at him hadn't changed much, though he felt he'd aged more in the last few months than in the previous five years.

He wondered what was going through Natasha's mind as she attended Borodin's meetings. What he hated most about the Bolsheviks, and about extremists in general, was their overwhelming certainty.

The tunnel emerged at the bottom of a wooden stand and Field turned to see Granger sitting with his wife about three rows up, wearing a trilby and a dark brown trench coat. Granger beckoned him over and Field turned, his boot studs making him unstable on the stone steps.

"Caroline, this is one of my new boys," Granger said, standing and taking off his hat. "Field, this is my wife."

The woman smiled. She reminded him of Penelope Donaldson, but was broader and plumper, her face and smile warmer. She had black bobbed hair and wore vivid lipstick and a bright red dress. She was a vibrant and, judging by the gold bracelet on her wrist, wealthy woman. Field wondered who the blond girl in the Cathay Hotel had been.

"Good luck," Granger said, his voice low as he turned and saw Macleod rounding the far corner of the stand. "And watch the Yank."

Field walked back down the steps and out onto the pitch. He nodded to Macleod as he passed, without any visible sign of response. The grass was thin, the earth beneath it hard.

The man from Belfast was throwing the ball to one of his colleagues, and Field jogged over to join them in the far corner. No one from the opposing team had yet emerged.

"David," the man said, "this is Field, our open side flanker."

Field was thrown the heavy leather ball and caught it, then kicked it into the air.

After a few minutes they jogged down the pitch, passing the ball along the line and back again.

At the end, Field found he was perspiring gently. He was grateful that the white-and-black-striped shirt he'd been given was made of cotton. He caught the Irishman's eye. "Too much time on the boat and not enough exercise since."

"When did you get here?"

"Three months ago."

"You're the picture of bloody health compared to the rest of us. We'll watch you do the running."

Some of the opposition emerged, Caprisi among them. The American was tying the knot on his shorts as he approached. "Ready for this, Field?" he asked quietly.

"I suppose so." He hesitated. "The prints are in. They came up to me for some reason. They're in my tray. No obvious match from the bedroom, Ellis says, and he's still working through the living room, but at least we have them if we can find a suspect."

Caprisi didn't answer. He was looking at the referee, who had just ambled out of the tunnel. Field watched, too, as the man put his whistle slowly to his lips and blew loudly.

"The search begins," Caprisi said.

"The search?"

"The search for knives." Caprisi's expression was a mixture of weary cynicism and amusement. "An Italian team got razors onto the pitch a couple of years ago, so now everyone gets frisked."

Field's captain was Eccles, the fly half, an Irish inspector from the Hongkew district with a fearsome reputation for drink and a nose to prove it. He exhorted them to "show the fuckers who's in charge of this force." His breath reeked of whiskey.

There was no discussion of tactics. Everyone automatically assumed his position as the whistle went and the ball was kicked high into the air in Field's direction. He called "mine" loudly, caught it, and looked up to see the oncoming wall. He dodged an enormous lock forward and ran back toward the center of the pitch, only to see Caprisi sprinting toward him, his ears pinned back and his mouth open, like a predator closing in for the kill.

Field attempted to prevent the tackle, but Caprisi caught him around the middle and he lost his balance, hitting the earth hard. Both sides piled on top of them.

Field tried to free the ball but couldn't. Caprisi tugged at it with one hand and pushed hard into his face with the other. Field was kicked in the leg, the knee, the groin, the stomach, and then the head. Someone grabbed his hair, someone else had an arm around his neck.

He waited for the whistle, but it didn't come, and the ball was wrenched from his grasp. The figures on top stood and ran off one by one, leaving him facedown in the dirt in more pain than he could remember.

He felt a hand on his shoulder and was hauled to his feet. He turned to see Caprisi.

The American smiled and patted him on the back.

Two hours later Field was sitting in a chair in the corner of a tavern, clutching a full tankard of beer and feeling dizzy from exhaustion and alcohol.

Patrick Granger was standing on a table in another corner of the room, reciting, in full, Yeats's "Easter 1916." His melodic voice was resonant with emotion, as the last of the evening sun filtered through the frosted glass window, touching the side of his face.

"Now and in time to be," he said, his eyes scouring the room, "Wherever green is worn, Are changed, changed utterly: A terrible beauty is born."

He raised his tankard. "To the martyrs!" He drained the contents and then burped loudly. "And to *grudging* forgiveness of English bastards!"

As Granger stepped down from the table, the team captain broke into another rendition of a rebel song. It was quickly taken up by those around him.

"Drink up, Field," Granger shouted as he stumbled toward him. He placed a protective arm around Field's shoulder and waited for him to finish his tankard. "You may be English," he said, slumping down on the seat beside him, "but you know, I forgive you."

"You were there in 1916, weren't you?"

"I was indeed. Michael and I were not important enough, thank the good Lord . . . a short spell in North Wales . . ." Granger was looking at him. Field could see how drunk he was. "But that's enough about me." He grabbed Field in a rough embrace. "Glad you're one of us, Dickie. You should be one of us. You are one of us, aren't you?" Granger was looking at him oddly.

"Of course," Field said.

"Right! Fine player. Waiter!" Granger stood, holding up his tankard in the direction of the bar. He crossed back to the other side of the room and joined in the singing.

Field pushed his own tankard away and reached for his cigarettes. He looked up to see Caprisi smiling at him.

The American was leaning against the wood paneling on the far side of the room, on the periphery of the gathering, a long glass in his hand. When the singing died back down, he came over and took one of Field's cigarettes.

"Well played," Field said.

The American shrugged.

"You're not drunk, I see. I thought it was mandatory."

Caprisi didn't answer.

"How come you're here, anyway?"

"I'm a Catholic. It's allowed."

"Let me get you a drink."

"No thanks."

Field stood. "Come on, you can't drink water all night."

"I said no thanks."

There was steel in Caprisi's voice and Field sat back down. On the other side of the room, Granger was building a pyramid on the table with full tankards. "You don't drink."

"No."

"There's no prohibition here, Caprisi."

"Back off, Field."

Field paused. "You are a man of mystery . . ."

"Mysteries are not always interesting."

"To the curious, they are." Field smiled. "I'm still not sure I understand."

"All you need to understand here is who your friends are, Dickie." He glanced across at Granger's group. "Macleod thinks you have an honest face. He doesn't want you to join the cabal and neither do I. Unless it's already too late, of course."

Before Field could answer, Caprisi got up and walked swiftly away.

Twenty

ater that evening Field moved very slowly into the darkened Special Branch office, trying to determine whether there was any bit of him that wasn't in pain.

He flicked on the light in his booth and sat down. He stretched his legs, straightened his back, and put his hands behind his head, then slumped forward and fiddled with the light switch.

The buff-colored fingerprint file lay in his in-tray and he flicked the corner of it, ignoring the pile of publications to be censored that had been placed in the middle of his desk. He decided to splash a basinful of cold water over his face before giving the file a closer look.

On the way back from the washroom, Field poured himself a drink, then returned to his desk.

For a moment the significance of the empty tray did not register. The folder had been taken, no note left in its place.

Field stood and took the stairs to the fingerprint bureau two at a time, forgetting his bruises.

Ellis wasn't there. An elderly Sikh frowned at Field's inquiry. "No, sahib," he said. "They have not come back here."

"Check the originals, will you?"

The man walked over to a row of cabinets. "What's the name again?"

"Orlov, Lena."

Field waited, drumming his fingers. Eventually, the man turned. "No," he said bluntly. "There's no record of prints for a case under that name."

"Where is Ellis?"

"Ellis is on leave."

"On leave?"

"Yes."

"Where?"

"I believe he has gone to San Francisco. He will be back in three to four months."

Field took the stairs down to Crime, but the office was as dark and deserted as his own, thin shards of light from the street cutting across the empty desks. He walked to Macleod's office and back, but there was no one there.

He returned to his own office and stood in the middle of the room, his hands in his pockets.

After a few minutes he headed down the stairs to the ground floor. In front of the reception desk, he waited for Albert, the doorman, to finish his telephone call. Albert was in his seventies and had been wounded in the Boer War.

"Albert, who has been in tonight?"

The old man's brow creased in concentration.

"It's quiet up there. Has anyone from my department, or from Crime, been in? I mean in the last few hours, since the match."

"Mr. Granger made an appearance."

"Granger?"

"Yes."

"How long ago?"

Albert shrugged. "Twenty minutes."

"Are you absolutely sure?"

Albert nodded. "And Macleod."

"Macleod?"

"And Caprisi. They came in together."

"When was that?"

"About forty minutes ago."

Field turned and ran back upstairs, first to Crime, where the office was still dark and empty, and then to the Branch, where his desk lamp was still the only sign of life. He stopped again in the middle of the room. "Sir?" he said.

He walked slowly down to Granger's room, knocked, and waited.

Field glanced over his shoulder, then slipped through Granger's door. He peered through the blinds, back down toward the lift, then walked around and sat behind the desk, his heart thumping. The in-tray was full of sheets of paper. He lifted the top one and held it up to the light. It was a memo from Commissioner Biers to "Heads of Department," about the "ordering, use, and abuse of stationery."

Field put it down, glancing toward the lift again before opening the drawer to his right. An embossed invitation to a function at Fraser's lay alongside a leather pistol holster. It was four months out of date.

The shrill ring of a telephone made Field start, and it was a moment before he realized that it was coming from his own desk. He shut the drawer and walked out, closing the door quietly behind him.

Field sat and wiped the sweat from his forehead, hoping the ringing would stop, but it didn't.

He picked it up. "Richard Field."

"Dickie."

"Hello . . . Penelope."

"I've been trying to get you all evening, but there's been no answer."

"I'm sorry, there was a—"

"You've been busy, I know."

"I haven't yet written a note to thank you both for dinner, both dinners. It was a marvelous—"

"Don't be silly. Don't mention it. Geoffrey thinks you're terrific and is very proud to have you as a nephew. And so am I."

Field felt his face flushing with pleasure. "Well, I—"

"Are you free tonight?"

He looked at his watch. It was eight-thirty.

"I don't have any plans, but—"

"Then you shall come out with us. There is a dance at the race club and—look, I know it's last-minute, but Geoffrey wants to show you off to everyone. You won't disappoint us, will you? Surely Crime can spare you at this time of night?"

Field noticed that Penelope rarely drew breath.

"I'm not busy. But are you sure?"

"Geoffrey is insistent. He instructed me not to take no for an answer, so I shall meet you at the entrance at ten."

Field put down the phone and stared at it.

"Granger," he whispered to himself. "Fuck." He felt the resentment rising inside him, tasting the bile in his mouth. Was it his fault? Hadn't Caprisi told him enough? Shouldn't he have been more careful and hidden the fingerprint file? He felt stupid and naive.

He wondered where Granger had gone, and he stood up intending to go and look for him. He stopped. Of course, the building was huge. He could be anywhere.

Field stood outside the race club, looking up at the clock tower, then back across to the Happy Times block, where a light was on in Natasha Medvedev's apartment.

So far, he'd seen no sign of her through the windows.

He watched the guests arriving, wondering why he hadn't found an excuse not to come. It was not just that he was incorrectly dressed—all the men were wearing white ties and tails, which he did not possess—but that the others, with their well-cut coats and dresses, jewelry and finely polished shoes, belonged to a world in which he increasingly wanted to be included.

He looked at his watch and then walked in through the tall glass doors. He waited at the bottom of a marble staircase, beneath a magnificent crystal chandelier.

"Dickie!"

Penelope was wearing a white dress, a circle of diamonds sparkling brightly around her neck. She kissed him, brushing a white-gloved hand on his arm, her body pressed briefly against his. Her skin was soft, a hint of French perfume catching in his nostrils. She was wearing red lipstick, generously applied, and as she stepped back, she laughed and began to wipe it off his cheek, ignoring the fact that it was staining her glove. He noticed for the first time how long her eyelashes were.

"Come."

She slipped a hand into the crook of his arm and began to lead him up the marble staircase.

"I'm sorry," he said. "I seem to be improperly dressed. I didn't—"

"Don't worry," she said, and smiled at him.

For the first time, Field liked her, because, of course, his dress *was* an issue and people *would* notice.

At the top of the stairs, she led him into a room that was even bigger than the Long Bar at the Shanghai Club. The floor-to-ceiling windows overlooking the track were all open in a fruitless attempt to air the room. In the center stood a table with a silver bowl big enough to bathe in, filled with flowers. At the far end was the biggest brick fireplace he'd ever seen.

The room was packed, so that most people were forced to shout to be heard, and she led him in the direction of the fireplace, clutching his hand and occasionally looking back at him and smiling.

Geoffrey was surrounded by a small group—all men—at the far end of the room. One was Charles Lewis, another a tall, thin man of Middle Eastern appearance with dark hair and a beard.

"Richard!" Geoffrey stepped forward to greet him, the circle widening a fraction. "Charlie you know."

"Good evening," Lewis said.

"And this is Simon Hayek, you may remember from the other night at the council meeting."

They shook hands, the man's dark eyes scrutinizing his face.

"You're in the Crime Branch?" Hayek asked.

"No . . . not normally."

"You're a detective . . . political?"

"We were just discussing," Geoffrey said, "whether General Chiang Kai-shek was secretly a Red. You probably have views on that."

They were looking at him.

"It's not really an area I've been working on." Seeing the disapproval in their faces, Field changed tack. "But I would say that the department's view is that he is cynical. He will use whomever he can to advance himself, disposing of them later. The Reds have support and money in the south and he will use that to try and unify the country under his rule. What happens then may be a different matter."

"Or may not," Hayek said. "Any more sign of protests?"

"I don't think we are aware of any."

They nodded vigorously.

"We've broken them," Hayek said. "We said a bit of steel would sort them out and we were right, Borodin or not."

Field was not so certain that the unrest was over for good or that the decision to open fire on protesters last year had been a good one.

"And that's what we need now," Hayek went on, "to show Chiang and the Reds and anyone else with designs on China that they're not going to get their bloody hands on the Settlement and that is final." Hayek looked to Geoffrey for approval, but appeared to get no reaction. "Lu Huang runs around the city like he damned well owns the place, and no one says boo to him."

This time Geoffrey nodded.

"If anyone thinks he's an insurance policy, then forget it."

"He's close to Chiang," Lewis said. "We know that. He has links with the Reds."

"He's a bloody gangster."

"He's getting too big for his boots," Geoffrey said. "That's certainly true. It's sending the wrong signals."

Penelope Donaldson straightened. "Communism will come to China, as surely as it came to Russia. And if you don't believe that, then you've learned nothing."

There was silence in their small circle.

"Penelope," Lewis said, turning slowly toward her, "you know, I never saw you as a Bolshevik."

She melted immediately. "Look, are you boys going to talk politics all night?"

At that moment the band struck up. Lewis, who had begun to look bored, slipped away.

"Dickie?" Penelope asked.

She took his arm.

"I can't . . ."

"Come on. I'll teach you."

She dragged him away as the band seemed to gather steam, settling into a frantic beat.

"Richard." It was Geoffrey. Field paused, watching Penelope disappear into the crowd on the dance floor. "I've got some work to do—tedious stuff. Would you mind looking after her for me, see she doesn't get into any trouble?"

"Yes. Of course."

"She hates it when I desert her and, anyway, I can't dance."

"Yes. Of course."

He laughed. "Make sure she doesn't damned well drink too much."

"Yes."

Penelope came back and grabbed his hand. "Come on," she said. "Or I shall assume you're standing me up."

When Field looked back a second later, he saw Geoffrey moving in the direction of the door.

Penelope paused by a Chinese waiter in a white linen jacket holding a silver tray. She took one of the champagne glasses and drank its contents in one swift movement before placing it back in the same position, all the time keeping a firm grip on Field's hand.

Then they were on the dance floor, and some—though not all—of the people around them were doing the Charleston. As he watched Penelope step back and begin to dance, he thought of the letter he had read in the *North China Daily News* at lunchtime exhorting Shanghai's socialites to give up "this ridiculous dance that has young things who should know better flapping and kicking in a manner that shows no consideration for fellow dancers."

Field did not know how to do the Charleston. It was not as simple as it looked and Penelope was laughing at him.

"Come on," she said, leaning forward and putting a hand on his shoulder. "You've got to put your heart into it."

She moved her arms and her legs and he tried to follow, slowly understanding its jerky ritual, before being bumped from behind by a corpulent man with slicked-back hair.

Penelope moved closer. "You're getting the hang of it brilliantly."

Ten yards away, Charles Lewis was looking at him and smiling. He was dancing with a Chinese girl not much more than half his size. She reminded Field of the prostitute he had almost slept with the other night and he could hear again the screams from the other end of the corridor.

The rich, he thought, could get away with anything here.

Twenty-one

ield wanted to stop now. "I need a drink," he said, smiling thinly and wiping the sweat from his forehead. He turned his back on Lewis.

"In a minute."

Penelope danced more manically than ever, shutting her eyes, as if wishing to lose herself in the music and the movement of her own body. Her bangs swung across her forehead, like a pendulum, and her lips were pursed, as if offering a kiss. Her dress, like the one she'd worn last night, was loose, and with each movement, her small breasts thrust against the silk. Field found it hard to take his eyes off her and he wanted to stop dancing.

"All right," she said, laughing. "All right." She took his hand. Field felt uncomfortable again at the intimacy of this gesture and tried to free himself, but she would not let go, leading him to the big doors along the side of the room and out onto the balcony. "You know," she said as they reached the rail and looked down over the track, "you're too young and handsome to be a stick in the mud."

"I don't intend to be."

"You could dance if you tried. You're athletic enough."

Field did not know how to respond.

Penelope clicked her fingers and a waiter he'd not seen appeared from the corner behind the door. Despite the throng inside, they were alone out here, save for a few small groups at the far end of the balcony, the racetrack illuminated like a frontier post beneath them.

Penelope took two glasses and filled them both with ice from the silver bucket on the edge of the tray. "Do you drink whiskey?" she asked, handing him one.

"Not often."

"Do you have *any* vices?"

"A few."

"Hold on," she instructed the waiter before he could move away. "Your health, Mr. Field." She upended her glass and, as she had with the champagne, drank it in one go. He hesitated for a moment and then, before she could reprimand him, followed suit. "That's better," she said.

Penelope replaced the glasses on the tray and took two more.

"How long does this go on?"

She shrugged. "As long as we feel like."

"We?"

Her glass dropped a fraction. "You don't like me, do you, Richard?"

"You've both been charming to me—more than I could have expected."

"Why more than you could have expected?"

"I'm sure you know the answer to that."

"Oh, all that stuff about your mother marrying beneath herself . . . it doesn't mean a thing."

"It matters at home."

"Not to me it doesn't." She lifted her glass and again drained its contents.

He followed suit again. "Geoffrey said I should persuade you not to drink too much."

"So you're my keeper?"

"No, of course—"

"There could be worse keepers."

He flushed. She took his glass, summoned the waiter back, and took two more. "So what *are* your vices, Richard?"

Field hadn't eaten tonight and he was starting to feel the effects of the alcohol again. He sighed. "My vices?"

"You don't have any."

"I have vices."

"So what are they?"

"Self-doubt. Is that a vice?"

"No. In moderation, it's a virtue."

"Well—"

"Hold on." She raised her glass.

"You know—"

"No. You've got to keep me company, that's your job."

He frowned. "My job?"

"You're my keeper."

"Penelope . . ."

"Drink." She tossed back another and Field did the same, shaking his head afterward. It was burning his stomach now. She gave the glasses back to the waiter and took two more.

"That's enough."

"Now, Dickie, you mustn't—"

"I'll—"

"No you won't."

"Just give me a few minutes. Can we slow down at least?"

She smiled, her face softening. "All right, Mr. Field. Let's start with the traditional sins. Greed?"

He shrugged. "Would I like to be rich, never to have to worry, to afford . . ." He gestured with his hand at the men and women inside the ballroom. "If that is greed, then yes."

"Envy?"

He hesitated. "Envy, yes. Sometimes, yes."

"Sloth?"

"No."

"Avarice?"

"I think I answered that with greed."

She took a sip of her whiskey and looked at him, a hint of amusement at the corners of her mouth. "Lust?" she asked quietly.

Field didn't answer, but she drained her glass and exhorted him to follow with her hand. "One more," she said when he hesitated. He drank.

"I've never met a woman who drank whiskey."

"How sheltered your life has been."

"In some ways."

"In what ways has it not been sheltered?"

Field smiled. "What about you?" he asked.

"Have I been sheltered?"

He shook his head. "Which of the sins do you fall prey to?"

"All of them, probably. Most people seem to think I'm wicked."

"Greed?"

She sighed. "For happiness, yes."

"That doesn't count as greed."

"Some people think it does."

"Penelope . . ," A man stood at her shoulder. He wore thick glasses and had wavy hair and a neatly trimmed beard, both shot through with gray.

"Stirling," she said, her voice starting to sound slurred. "Stirling Blackman, may I introduce Dickie Field, my . . . cousin, or . . ."

"Nephew," Field corrected.

Blackman offered his hand and they shook. "Richard," Field said.

"Stirling."

"You two should talk. Stirling is a reporter for the *New York Times.* We were talking about you, Stirling, only last night, or was it the night before? I can't remember."

"Not taking my name in vain, I hope."

"Oh, Geoffrey was, but you know how hard he finds it when people won't see the big picture. Dickie is in the Special Branch."

Blackman tilted his head to one side. "Always interested to—"

"You should talk, but not now. I need to go home. Come on, Dickie."

"I'm not sure . . ."

"Please. Be a gentleman."

Field nodded at the reporter and followed Penelope. "Perhaps we could have lunch," Blackman said.

Field wanted to tell the reporter to back off, but Penelope had already gone through the doors into the ballroom and was weaving her way through the crowd inside.

He followed her, skirting the edge of the dance floor. A drunken woman lost her balance and crashed into him. Field picked her up and took her arms from around his neck. He lifted his head and froze.

They were standing at the top of the staircase.

Lu had the same bodyguards in tow. Charlie Lewis and Hayek were part of the group that surrounded them. So was Natasha, though she managed to remain remote, staring into the middle distance.

Field took a pace toward them as she turned. Her eyes locked on his for a split second. Her face was frightened and hostile and her eyes flashed a warning. Charlie Lewis raised his head and gazed idly in Field's direction. Field thought he was laughing at him, and had been all along.

Lu gesticulated slowly with his hand. Hayek listened intently. Lewis straightened, put his hands in his pockets, and turned to talk to Natasha, almost obscuring Field's view of her.

Field knew he had to move. The Chinese had not acknowledged him, but Field sensed that was deliberate.

Lu edged forward, and the group moved with him. Natasha was now directly in front of Field. She wore a long silver dress, and as he watched, she raised her arm and pulled her hair back from her neck, gathering it to one side and letting it fall again. She shifted her weight from one foot to the other and then back again. Her shoes were thin and elegant, a single strap above the ankle.

Lu shook his head curtly, as if dismissing something that Hayek had said, and broke away. Natasha stayed by his side. Field watched as Lu raised his arm to allow her to place her own within it. She was so much taller than him that the effect was both ridiculous and grotesque.

Field fought back a wave of revulsion. He wiped his forehead and forced himself to walk slowly down the stairs.

Penelope waited at the bottom, fumbling in her purse for some cigarettes. She took one out and offered him the lighter. "You want one?" she asked as he lit it for her.

"No thanks."

She was drunk now, but so was he. Drunk and disoriented and angry.

A car pulled up and she led the way out to it. As he climbed in after her, Field could not help looking up toward the Happy Times block. There was still a light on in Natasha's apartment. Would Lu go up there later?

Penelope placed a hand on his leg. "Be a dear and open your window."

Field sat up straighter, trying to prompt her to take away her hand, before leaning forward to do as she had asked.

She slipped off her shoes, swept her feet around and placed them on his lap. She smiled at him. "Be a love. They get so sore dancing."

Field found himself taking two of her toes between his fingers and massaging them gently before moving down to the base of her foot. The skin was soft, her nails neatly painted. She leaned back and groaned. "Dancing in those shoes is bloody agony."

Penelope's head was on the armrest beneath the window, her eyes shut, as she slid her other foot against his groin. Field tried to push himself farther back into the seat.

As they pulled up outside the house in Crane Road, Penelope picked up her shoes. "Come on."

"I'm bushed. I think I'll—"

"Don't be silly. Geoffrey will be very disappointed not to see you."

Field hesitated for a second before stepping out after her. The number one boy opened the door as they climbed the steps of the veranda.

"Let me take your jacket," she said.

"No, I'm . . ."

"Come on, Richard. You've been boiling all night."

Field handed it to Penelope, who gave it to the servant. "Is the master in?" she asked, but he shook his head.

Penelope was already walking through to the sitting room, but Field hesitated again, looking first at the front door, which had been shut, and then at his jacket, which was being taken through to the cloakroom.

"Penelope."

She didn't answer. He followed her obediently through to the living room. He stood between a grandfather clock and an antique teak desk, beneath thick oil paintings of the English countryside, not dissimilar to those at the country club.

She had poured him a drink.

"You know, I don't want to be a bore . . ."

"You are being a bore."

"I have a very early start."

"But you're young and fit and Geoffrey will be furious with me if you are not here when he gets back."

Field looked down at his glass. She drank, but he couldn't face any more whiskey. Through the haze of his own inebriation, he had the feeling that she was nervous.

"Come." She took his glass and placed it with her own on a low Chinese table before grabbing his hand and leading him toward the door to the hallway. "You've got to see our greatest treasure." He resisted at first, then once again found himself following her, this time out into the hall and up the stairs. "It's a giant gold Buddha," she said, and as soon as he entered the room, he saw it beside the bed.

She turned to him. "What do you think?"

"It's magnificent," he said without enthusiasm.

"Would you hold on a minute?"

She stepped into the bathroom, slipped her dress from her shoulders, and stepped out of it as it fell to the floor.

She was wearing a white garter belt and stockings, but no underwear, the patch of dark hair at the base of her belly smaller and neater than he'd imagined, her breasts rounder and more upright than they'd seemed when she'd leaned toward him at the club.

She reached behind the door for a long silk dressing gown. She wrapped it around herself and looked up, catching his eye. He realized she had known he was watching.

"Richard . . ."

"I'm going to go now."

"Of course."

"Thank you for a pleasant evening."

"Richard, you can kiss me good night."

He didn't move.

"I'm not that unappealing, am I?"

She walked over to him, flicking his lapel with one long finger, as Natasha had done two nights before. She leaned forward and kissed him on the cheek.

"Are you in love, Richard?"

He didn't answer, his face burning.

"I sense a man in love, Richard. Isn't that so?"

He stepped back. "I don't know," he said, turning to go.

"Richard?"

"Yes."

"Do I disgust you?"

"Of course not."

"Then your haste does you a disservice."

"You are my uncle's wife."

"And you're ashamed of me?"

Field sighed deeply.

"Your uncle hasn't fucked me for years. Did you know that?"

Field turned away again and walked down the stairs.

"Good night, Richard."

Twenty-two

he car pulled up in front of the station in Little Russia. Field watched through the window for a moment as three priests, with long black beards and metal crucifixes, crossed Avenue Joffre and walked slowly in the direction of the Russian church. They passed a small group of Chinese children begging, without a glance.

He asked the driver to wait and got out of the car. He stretched, every muscle in his body aching after his exertions on the rugby pitch the previous afternoon.

The police station stood between, but twenty yards back from, two rows of shops. On one side was a tailor's, on the other another fur shop. Sergei's apartment was not more than a hundred yards away.

Inside, the station felt almost like a gentleman's club. A wide hallway was filled with tropical plants, their leaves swaying gently under the ceiling fans. A Vietnamese constable in a clean, freshly pressed uniform stood behind the front desk. Field introduced himself, produced his identification, and waited while the constable went to find the officer in charge.

He tried to control his impatience.

The lieutenant was like a caricature of the colonial Frenchman. He was almost as tall as Field and wore jodhpurs, riding boots, and an open-necked, loose-fitting white cotton shirt, which emphasized the depth of his suntan. His hair was dark, his nose big and broken. His posture and easy manner reminded Field of Lewis. "I am Givreaux," he said, his handshake firm.

"Field, S.1."

"How can I help you, Mr. Field?"

"I'm trying to trace the whereabouts of an Igor Mentov, whom we believe used to live on Avenue Joffre."

Givreaux shrugged. "I don't know him." He spoke with only a slight accent, but "him" was still clipped.

"We think he was here for only a short period, but our understanding is that he was arrested for an offense, possibly a minor one, at this station on or around May 1."

Givreaux shook his head and exhaled noisily. "More than a month ago . . . I don't know. Maybe."

"Would it be possible to look through the incident reports for that day?"

"It is necessary for you to liaise with our intelligence section. They will fill out the papers, come down with you."

"My secretary has prepared the paperwork. I understand it will be on its way today, but our intelligence is that this man is going to board the train for Harbin tonight. Time is running out for us."

Givreaux looked less sure. "How will it help to look at an old—"

"It's about being sure of who he is and what he's been up to before we close in. He is part of a conspiracy."

Givreaux pursed his lips. "I will have to call them."

"Of course."

"Please have a seat."

Field sat in the rattan chair beneath one of the fans, enjoying the flow of cool air. He crossed his legs and lit a cigarette, glad to be out of the office. The question of the fingerprint file gnawed away at him. He heard Granger's voice in his head: "It's a time for knowing who your friends are."

Givreaux came back into the room, his leather boots echoing on the old wooden floorboards. "All the officers are out," he said. "I should make you wait, but . . ." He seemed to make a decision. "It is not such a big deal," he said, mostly to himself. "The constable will go down with you. Put your head around the door when you are finished."

The constable was a young man with an open, friendly face. He led Field down a corridor behind the counter to a big airy room at the end of the building. Every available inch of wall space was filled with wooden box files.

"What date?" the constable asked.

"Let's start with May 1."

The man fetched a stepladder from the far end of the room and placed it in the middle of the section directly ahead of them. He climbed up and removed one of the file boxes, which he placed on a low wooden desk.

Field sat down. For a few moments the man stood uneasily beside him, then he walked quietly away to the window. Field began to leaf through the cards. He found May 1 and worked quickly through it, but the incident reports were restricted to assault, robbery, and lesser offenses. There was no reference to the murder he had read about in the newspaper.

Field went back and looked through the cards again. Most of the reports had been filled out by a Detective Constable Ngoc and countersigned by a Detective Sergeant Pudowski. There had been two armed robberies on May 1, one in the morning at a fur shop on Avenue Joffre, another at a jeweler's on Rue des Colonies, both by two masked men carrying machine guns. There was an assault on a Vietnamese driver in the French Park and an incident in which a woman's handbag had been snatched. Field counted the cards. There were fourteen in all. Not one even hinted at what he was looking for.

He began to work backward. There were only five incidents on April 30, all written up by Ngoc, none of them serious.

"Would you like some tea, sir?" The constable was smiling at him. He did not appear suspicious.

"Yes, please. Lemon, no sugar." Field listened to his retreating footsteps. "Constable . . ." He waited until the man had turned. "If an incident occurred within this area, there would always be a report?"

"Yes, sir."

"Even if it were, for the sake of argument, a serious crime, say a murder, and the call had gone first to headquarters on Rue Wagner, you would file a report, because it occurred in your area."

"Yes, sir."

"In all circumstances?"

"Yes, sir."

Field smiled and turned back to the box, suddenly less confident that this process was going to lead anywhere. If the headquarters staff wanted something hushed up, he thought it likely they would instruct Givreaux's men not to attend the scene of the crime, in which case it would be well nigh impossible to file a report, even if they had wished to.

He worked back all the way to April 4, which was where the box started. Most days, there were only a few incidents. May 1 turned out to have been exceptionally busy.

The constable brought him tea and he sipped it slowly and ate the biscuits that had come with it.

There didn't seem much else that he could usefully do.

He leaned forward to look through the cards for May 1 one more time, going extremely slowly, so as to pick up anything he might have missed. After flicking through five or six, he noticed that there was one missing.

Each card was coded, the serial number written in black ink at the top left-hand corner. Here the cards jumped from F6714 to F6716.

He looked carefully through the whole box to be sure that it had not been filed wrongly, somewhere else.

"Constable . . ." Field leaned back and put his hands in his pockets. "In the Settlement, all incidents have to be first noted in the incident book, usually by the duty sergeant, before an incident report is written up and filed."

"Yes, sir."

"It's the same here?"

"Yes, sir."

"Would you mind showing me the incident book for May 1?"

The constable nodded and left the room, walking briskly down the corridor. He was gone for perhaps ten minutes and Field began to think he might have consulted Givreaux about this new request, but when he returned, he apologized for the delay and explained that one of the detectives had been noting down the details of a domestic dispute he'd attended.

Field took the book.

He flicked through the pages, his pulse quickening.

It was there, in Ngoc's neat flowing hand: *Incident number F6715. Body of woman found stabbed, Avenue Joffre. Anna Simonov.*

There were no further details, nor was there a house or apartment number. Avenue Joffre stretched the entire length of the French Concession, so door-to-door inquiries were likely to prove time-consuming and possibly fruitless. Field assumed that, somewhere, there must be a file on the case.

He turned around again. "You would keep files here on important cases or individuals?"

"No, sir. Rue Wagner."

"They're all kept at headquarters?"

"Yes, sir."

"There are none here at all?"

"No, sir."

"So what happens if you want to look at a file? Do you have to go down to Rue Wagner?"

"A car delivers the file in the morning and takes it back in the evening, sir. Or we can go down if there is a hurry."

Field nodded and smiled, turning something over in his mind. He held out the incident book. "Do you remember this case—Simonov? Do you remember the address or section of . . ."

The constable looked at the entry and shook his head, but his smile vanished.

Field turned the book around and began to leaf through its pages. He worked forward but nothing caught his eye, so he went to the Simonov entry and worked back to the beginning.

He reached March 31, where the book began.

F6222, an entry read. *Body of a woman found stabbed. Avenue Joffre. Ignatiev, Irina.* Field closed the book carefully and put it on top of the box. "Thank you."

He walked briskly down the corridor and was about to continue through the hall, but he changed his mind at the last minute and turned right, into Givreaux's office.

"Success?" the Frenchman asked. He stood and moved to the side of his big teak desk. It was covered in paperwork, held in place by a series of crocodile-skin weights.

"In a sense, yes." Field cleared his throat. His instincts were to leave it at that, but he could not resist pushing further. "Do you remember the Simonov case?"

The lieutenant was unfazed, responding with an indolent shake of the head.

Field persisted. "Anna Simonov, Russian girl stabbed more than a month ago."

"I don't recall."

"It was dealt with by CID at Rue Wagner?"

"Probably."

"I imagine it is quiet here, relatively speaking."

"Depends on what you mean by quiet."

"You get a lot of murders?"

Givreaux was staring at him, now understanding the drift of his questions. "Not a lot, no." He moved closer. "I forgot your name. You are Richard . . ."

"Field."

"Field, yes." Givreaux's gaze was level.

"What about Irina Ignatiev?"

Givreaux's brow creased, as if he were trying to recall the name.

"Her body was also found on Avenue Joffre, on March 31—two and a half months ago."

Givreaux shrugged.

"Also dealt with by Rue Wagner?"

"Sure. It was . . . I remember now. It turned out to be a domestic, I think. Why, are you—"

"Is Constable Ngoc around?"

"Ngoc?" He shook his head. "No, I don't think so."

"He made a note of the incident here."

Givreaux nodded. "It was CID who attended."

"Is there any chance I could have a word with Constable Ngoc?"

"He will not be in today." Givreaux showed Field to the door. "I'm sorry not to have been more help."

Twenty-three

Field instructed his driver to take him down to the Customs House on the Bund. It was still overcast and the light drizzle left him again with wet feet, so he took the stairs to the seventh floor in an attempt to stamp out the water. As he climbed, he looked down toward the neat public gardens next to Garden Bridge.

The immigration room was small and crowded. It smelled of damp from too many raincoats and umbrellas. Field strode over to the counter in the far corner and interrupted the woman behind the grille as he produced his card. "I'm afraid I need some assistance."

An older woman in a black cardigan turned around and stepped forward to examine his ID before moving to unlock the partition door. She ushered Field into a back room.

"I'm correct in thinking that everyone who arrives in the city has to register with you here?" Field shook his foot to try and get rid of the last of the water.

"In theory, yes. As you know, not everyone does."

"But Russians have never been refused entry, so there would be no point in trying to come in illegally."

"Less bureaucracy."

"But life is difficult without identification papers," Field persisted, thinking of the hours he'd spent here filling out the necessary forms.

"That is true."

"And if a Russian, a noncitizen, changes his address, he is supposed to inform you?"

"In theory, yes."

"And most do?"

She shrugged. "There is no reason not to. The majority do."

"Okay, I have two names and I urgently need an address for both of them."

The woman put on her glasses and looked at his notebook. "Do you know in what month of what year the women originally came here?"

"No."

"You don't know what year?"

"I'm sorry, but I can't be sure."

She sighed. "It will take two to three days, Mr. Field."

"Three days?"

"Do you know how many people arrive here every year?"

"Thousands."

"Sometimes more than a hundred thousand." She looked down at the names again. "I can assume they arrived after 1918?"

"Yes. Probably after 1920, but 1918 to be on the safe side."

"May I take this page?" She ripped it out. "Please give me your telephone number."

Field wrote it down. "You can't do it sooner? These two women have both been murdered and their cases are a crucial part of a bigger picture."

"I will do my best. But it will still be two to three days."

Outside, Field gripped the wooden banister of the staircase and placed his forehead against the window, gazing down at the traffic moving slowly along the Bund, far below. He felt the anger and frustration swelling within him.

It found its expression twenty minutes later, back on Avenue Joffre, when Sergei Stanislevich opened the door a fraction and then, upon seeing Field's face, tried to close it again.

Field thumped it with both hands, sending Sergei tumbling back into his bed, the towel around his waist falling down. There was a squeal as a small, naked Chinese girl leaped off the bed and tried to cover herself. Field thought she could not be more than fourteen or fifteen.

He turned away instinctively and did not turn back until they had both hastily dressed themselves. The Chinese girl fled down the stairs.

"Right, Sergei," Field said, shutting the door behind her. "I'm going to ask you some more questions, and if I don't think you're telling me the truth, you're going to regret it. Is that clear?"

The Russian nodded, his Adam's apple moving violently as he swallowed. Field picked up a violin and put it carefully on the floor before seating himself on the arm of the sofa and crossing his legs. There was a tray beside him, a syringe and two long metal spikes alongside a simple opium pipe.

Field sighed. "Irina Ignatiev and Anna Simonov."

Sergei clearly recognized the names.

"Who are they?" Field stood.

He shook his head. "I don't know."

"You do."

"No . . . no."

Field took a step toward him.

"Anna . . . the second one, no, but Irina . . ."

"You knew her?"

"No, but . . ."

"But what?"

"Lena mentioned her once."

Sergei had pushed himself back to the far side of the bed and leaned over to take out a cigarette.

"In what context?" Field asked.

"In what—"

"How did the conversation go?"

Sergei looked confused.

"Why did Lena mention her?"

"She was another of Lu's girls."

"Irina?"

"Yes."

"Irina Ignatiev?"

"Yes."

Field thought about this. "What did Lena say about her?"

"She'd heard he had another Russian girl over here in the French Concession. She wanted to know what the girl was like, whether I had met her."

"And had you?"

"No."

"Where did Irina live?"

He shook his head. "I don't know. I'd never heard of her before."

"What else did Lena say about her?"

"That was it. She wanted information from me, but I'd never heard of her."

"She lived somewhere on this street. Which house?"

He shook his head so vigorously Field thought it might fall off.

"Lu has other Russian girls?"

"Probably."

"Who?"

"I don't know."

"Natasha Medvedev?"

"Yes."

"You know her."

"Only through Lena."

"And from the Majestic."

He shrugged. "Yes."

"Did Lena mention any others?"

His head shook as he sucked heavily on his cigarette.

"So you know only about Irina and Lena and Natasha. You've never heard of Anna Simonov?"

Sergei shook his head, and this time Field thought he was telling the truth.

"Lena and Irina have been killed, but not Natasha."

Sergei smirked. "She fucks better."

Field stood, his fists bunched, then, watching the puzzled reaction in Sergei's face, he fought to bring himself under control. "What do you know about Natasha?"

"I don't know anything."

"You must know something."

"She thinks she is superior." He snorted.

Field hesitated. "Lena is dead, so is Irina. Let's say Anna Simonov was also one of Lu's girls. Who else does he keep, apart from Natasha?"

Sergei was recovering his self-confidence fast. "How should I know?"

"Think."

"I only knew through Lena and, like I said before, we didn't talk about it."

"You've never talked about it with Natasha?"

Sergei crossed his legs. He examined his feet carefully, smoke from his cigarette spiraling slowly toward the ceiling.

"You've seen Lu at the Majestic."

Sergei looked up. "Of course."

"Apart from Natasha, whom else have you seen him with?"

"I've seen you with Natasha."

Field stared at him. "Whom else have you seen Lu with?"

The Russian shrugged.

"No one, or too many to list?"

"Natasha usually sits close to him."

"Why is that?"

Sergei looked at him. Eventually, he said with a leer, "You've seen it."

There was a long silence.

Field felt a burning need to get out of this room. He put his hands in his pockets. "I'll be back, Sergei," he said.

Field returned to his quarters in Carter Road.

The common room was empty, so he went to the phone and dialed the exchange, asking to be put through to Maretsky. It rang and rang, and he was just about to cut the connection when Maretsky picked up the receiver.

"It's Field."

The Russian was out of breath.

"I need your help."

Maretsky still did not answer.

"Another Russian girl was murdered on May 1, and a third at the end of March. Both women lived on Avenue Joffre."

"I'm busy."

"Irina Ignatiev and Anna Simonov. I think they were both Lu's girls."

"I really don't have time."

"Maretsky." Field breathed out heavily, his heart still beating fast. "Come on, give me a break. It's like fighting with a blanket over your head. Caprisi says you have a contact in the gendarmerie. All I need is an address for both women, so we can establish a pattern."

"Caprisi is familiar with the procedures for applying for information from the gendarmerie."

There was a long silence.

"Irina Ignatiev was murdered at the end of March, Anna Simonov on May 1, Lena Orlov three nights ago. As you said, there is a pattern."

"Thank you for keeping me informed, Detective."

"Someone is going to be his next victim."

"Someone will be, yes."

"And that fact leaves you cold? It was you who predicted that there *would* be more victims."

Maretsky sighed. "What is fueling this, Field? An admirable philanthropic concern for Russian women in general, or for one in particular?"

"Maretsky . . ."

"I ran into Caprisi today."

Field was silent.

"I hope she hasn't been foolish enough to give you any encouragement."

"I don't know who you are—"

"I'm not an idiot."

"I want to prevent it happening again," Field said.

"Before it happens to her."

"Please, Maretsky."

"I really do hope Natasha hasn't given you any encouragement, Field, because if she has, she's a fool and so are you. And if she hasn't, then you're just victim to an unjustifiable obsession and you should develop a sense of reality before you lead a lot of other people into trouble."

"I wish you could hear yourself."

"I've seen it before, Field, and it never ends well."

"I just need your help."

"I have to survive, Field, and so does she. And so, probably, do you. So follow the advice of those around you and desist."

There was a note from Caprisi in his room: *Where the fuck are you? French agree to interview with Lu, scheduled tomorrow. Be in my office nine sharp.*

Field tore the note up and put it in the bin, then lay down on his narrow bed, but couldn't sleep. He was haunted by the image of Natasha, twisting desperately to avoid the slashing of the knife.

Twenty-four

ield finally slept for a couple of hours but was still at his desk long before nine. He pulled over the tray that had contained the fingerprint results, then looked at the pile of journals to be censored.

He pushed his chair back and took the stairs down to the registry. His still-damp soles slapped loudly on the stone steps as he moved through the pools of light cast by the narrow window slits. The place was open, but Danny did not smile at him and there was none of the usual banter.

"Everything all right, Danny?" Field asked as the Irish American went to check whether or not there was a file on Irina Ignatiev or Anna Simonov.

"Sure. Early morning."

After a few minutes Danny came back with a single buff-colored folder. "Only Ignatiev," he said quietly. He examined Field's paperwork with exaggerated care before handing the folder over.

Field leaned against the wall outside and opened the file. It contained a single sheet, which read: *Irina Ignatiev has been seen attending a meeting at the* New Shanghai Life. *She is a native of Kazan on the Volga and arrived here via Vladivostok. She resides in the French Concession.*

Field sighed, flipped the folder shut, and went to return it. "Have we got any surveillance reports on Lu?"

"Surveillance reports?"

"Yes."

"I believe not."

"We've never mounted any kind of operation against him?" Danny cleared his throat.

"What about around the time of his takeover of the Green Gang? We must have kept a watch on him then. Will you look, please?"

Field waited until Danny had disappeared behind one of the iron cabinets, then stepped past the counter and followed him.

Danny was startled. Field could see that he knew exactly where the file was. He handed it over reluctantly.

Field returned to the front desk. He pulled over a form and filled it out. He signed his name at the bottom. Danny did not catch his eye.

This time Field walked into the stairwell before opening the file. He turned so that a thin stream of light from one of the windows fell directly upon it. There were two sheets tied together in the corner by a piece of string. The file had been written up by D.S. Prokopiev and was dated December 12, 1923:

Routine like clockwork. Business conducted primarily from house at Rue Wagner. No bodyguards visible from street, but three to four always in hall, plus others in servants' quarters at back. Fifteen to twenty bodyguards in total, operating in shifts.

Each day, leaves the house at one exactly. Just before one, car pulls up. Driver remains inside. Door of house opens and four bodyguards come swiftly down steps. Armed with Thompsons. Surround car and complete visual surveillance of street. Chief bodyguard, Ivan Grigoriev, always closest to door. When Grigoriev satisfied, he returns inside and one minute later escorts Lu down to car. Lu walks slowly. Drive off in direction of Nantao.

Go to Willow tearooms in Yaofeng Road, where Lu worked as kitchen hand when first came to Shanghai. Further business conducted, visitors searched by two bodyguards at door. A further two at end of corridor by entrance to room. Grigoriev stays inside, but emerges about forty minutes later to complete visual

surveillance of street once more. At two exactly, Lu leaves tea-
rooms. Car door no more than ten feet from entrance.

Return to house is between five minutes and ten minutes past
two. Lu goes in and stays until evening, when he leaves the house
three to four times a week. He goes to the Majestic or another
nightclub. Or one of his private clubs or residences. He usually
returns between three and four in the morning.

Field folded the report and slipped it into his pocket.

"It's the social butterfly," Caprisi said easily as Field went into
the Crime Branch. "You've been spotted leaving the race club
with the wife of the municipal secretary."

"She's my aunt."

"Of course she is."

Macleod smiled indulgently, fiddling with the chain around
his neck. Field heard a rustle behind him and turned. Chen stood
there, his hands in his raincoat pockets, wearing an expression
that could have indicated anything from warmth to outright
hostility.

"The prints are missing," Field said.

Caprisi's brow furrowed.

"I told you that the results were up, and when I returned
here after the game, they were still on my desk, but I went to
the toilet and when I came back—"

"They were gone," Caprisi finished.

All three men stared at Field.

"The originals have disappeared from the lab, and Ellis
has gone on holiday to San Francisco until the autumn."

"You couldn't have mislaid them?" Macleod asked.

"No."

"No one left a note saying they'd taken them?"

"No."

Caprisi and Macleod stared at the floor. Their silence was,
Field thought, imbued with suspicion. A new wave of resentment prevented him from offering any further explanation.

An old woman came in, bent low, an apron around her

waist. She stopped in front of Chen and asked him, in English, whether anyone wanted tea. Field and Caprisi nodded. The other two shook their heads.

"What did you find out yesterday?" Caprisi asked.

Field took out his cigarettes, lit one, and offered them around. They all refused. Field recalled Caprisi telling him that all physical evidence should be given to him and kept outside the precinct and felt stupid again for not having acted upon this advice.

"There are two other similar cases," Field said. "Anna Simonov on May 1 and Irina Ignatiev at the end of March. Both women lived on Avenue Joffre, but I cannot find a house number for either. Irina was definitely one of Lu's girls, and Anna may also have been. I looked for the report card on Anna Simonov, but it was missing. I know one was filed, because the numbers skipped. So I checked the incident book and found it there. I worked backwards, until I found the Ignatiev case, but the book didn't go any further back than March."

There was a long silence.

"If we apply to the French, is there any chance they will share information on the latest murder, at least?"

Caprisi shook his head. "They'll say it was a domestic. And if we apply formally, we show our hand." He rubbed the bridge of his nose. "We've arranged to see Lu this morning and the manager of the Fraser's factory this afternoon."

"There is clearly a pattern," Field said. "If we can find out where these other girls lived, there may be evidence from their neighbors that would prove more conclusive."

"Lu is challenging us," Macleod said. "Whether he has intended it or not, this is a head-on confrontation. We all know the French police are entirely in his pocket, but the Orlov murder is a challenge to us. If he did not murder the girl himself, he is certainly protecting whoever did, and if we let him get away with it, we might as well hang up our boots and go home."

They were silent again as they contemplated Macleod's wisdom. To Field, it had seemed like a speech to a larger audience. Macleod was even more withdrawn today, and Field wondered if ambition, and the proximity of the decision on the new commissioner, were beginning to take their toll.

The Chinese woman brought in the mugs of tea on a battered metal tray. Field thought briefly of the fine, polished silver of the country club and the Donaldsons' house in Crane Road. Although it was too hot to drink comfortably, the smell of the tea alone made him feel a little better.

"It is Monday," Caprisi said. "The shipment mentioned in Lena's notes is on Saturday."

"And?" Macleod asked.

"We know Lena had a reason to make a note of this shipment, but after that's gone . . ." He shrugged. "The lead will then be lost."

The American looked at Field again.

"Sewing machines?" Macleod asked.

"Yes."

"I still don't see the bloody relevance."

"We can't see any, either." Chen took Field's cigarette, leaned over to the cubicle beside Caprisi's, and stubbed it out, half closing his eyes as the smoke twisted up into his face. "The captain of the ship is still lost down Blood Alley. The machines are made by an electrical company. I could see nothing unusual about them. They're just . . . sewing machines." He put his hands back in his pockets.

"The manager is British?" Macleod asked.

"Scottish."

Macleod scowled, not certain if this was a joke. "It's a Fraser's company?"

"Yes," Caprisi said.

"Field can arrange an audience with Charlie Lewis." Macleod looked at him, then smiled for the first time. "Lighten up, man. I'm pulling your leg."

Caprisi sipped his tea. "We should talk to Lewis."

"We should find out where these women lived," Field interjected.

They stared at him, frowning at the truculence in his voice.

"One step at a time, Field," Caprisi said.

"We could send some plainclothes officers down to do door-to-door."

"Avenue Joffre is at least three miles long. And you think the French won't get wind of a door-to-door?" He shook his head. "One step at a time."

Chen went ahead to get the car. Field walked to the toilet and confronted his bloodshot eyes and tired face in the mirror while he washed his hands.

Caprisi was waiting in the corridor outside, holding a large white box. He handed it to him. Field took off the top and pulled out the gray suit. He put the box down. The jacket was beautifully made and many times lighter than his current one. "My God."

"My Chinese tailor."

"Thank you."

"Put it on. You'll feel better." Caprisi bent down and took out two shirts wrapped in tissue paper. "Thought you might need these."

Field pulled back the wrapping and felt the quality of the cotton.

Caprisi bent down once more. "And a decent silk tie."

"I don't know what to say."

"Then don't say anything."

"If we can go down to the bank, I can pay you straight-away. I've got money now and—"

"It's on me."

"Don't be ridiculous."

Caprisi shook his head. "It's my pleasure."

"I can't allow—"

"Fortunately, you don't know how much it cost."

"But it's too generous."

"I can't watch you melting in this heat anymore, polar bear."

"But I have the money."

Caprisi was shaking his head and waving his hand.

Field sighed. "Thanks, Caprisi." He looked at him. "Thanks."

"Don't mention it." The American smiled. "Isn't that what you English say? Don't mention it."

Field smiled and looked down again at the jacket in his hand.

"Put it on, polar bear."

Field went back into the toilet to get changed, and emerged transformed.

Caprisi whistled. "Wait till they see you down at the Majestic, kid."

They got into the lift together. Field had begun to worry that the American would have got the wrong impression about the money. He suddenly wondered if it had been appallingly naive to imagine that any supplement could be legitimate and straightforward. "Who would put cash into my account without my knowledge? Is it—could it be an official thing?"

Caprisi shook his head. "Someone in the cabal."

"It couldn't be a special supplement unique to a department?"

Caprisi smiled. "Not that I've ever heard of."

"What should I do about it?"

"Nothing until someone approaches you. Then it's up to you. If you don't want a part of it, then say so and offer to pay the money back if they ask for it, which they won't."

"Who will approach me?"

Caprisi shrugged. "Sorenson, Prokopiev, take your pick. It is hierarchical, as far as we can tell. Even if you joined, it would probably be years before anyone told you who was in charge, if they ever did."

The lift jolted suddenly to a halt. They stepped out as a group of uniformed officers got in.

Inside the car, Field asked, "Who took the prints?"

"Someone in the cabal. It doesn't matter who."

"But Granger is the head?"

"That's a matter of speculation, Field."

"But—"

"I've told you what we think." He smiled. "You can draw your own conclusions."

Caprisi leaned toward the driver. "Rue Wagner, number 70."

Through the window, Field watched a young boy aggressively trying to sell newspapers to the passing crowd while a beggar lay sprawled by his feet, apparently unconscious.

"Do you think Macleod will be the new commissioner?" he asked.

Caprisi turned and was about to say something, then thought better of it and shook his head. "I don't know. It's a difficult time for him."

"He seemed distracted this morning."

"Lu is already our central suspect. We're going to see him this morning. If we upset him, then he will bend the ear of those council members who are indebted to him in some way, which probably means most of them." Caprisi looked at Field. "Macleod will be held responsible for our actions, and therefore he must be careful. But on the other hand, he says there are council members who feel Lu is out of control, so if he could check him, or better still, bring him down, then that might stand in his favor." Caprisi smiled again. "He wants to find a way to bring Lu down, but if he messes it up now, then he's finished."

Field had assumed they were going straight to see Lu, but had omitted to take into account the extent of interconcession bureaucracy. There were papers to be filled out, coffee to be drunk, and, since they were in the gendarmerie, croissants to be eaten.

The headquarters in Rue Wagner was an old colonial villa with an extension on the back only a few hundred yards from Lu's house. It had the same relaxed atmosphere as the station in Little Russia. The inspector sat behind his desk, long boots resting on a footstool. Above his head was a photograph of a café in Paris and another, alongside it, of a house that looked as if it was somewhere in Indochina.

The inspector had a thin, hawkish face, but a disarmingly genial manner. He'd already explained to them that he had come to Shanghai only after ten years in French Indochina, first in Saigon and then Hanoi. There was something weary about him, Field decided, not so much cynical as plain tired, as if the heat had finally got to him.

He couldn't imagine the heat not getting to everyone, in the end. Not even his new lightweight suit was enough to prevent him from sweating.

The inspector spoke English with a heavy French accent and moved his hand in slow circular motions as he talked, pausing as a Vietnamese officer came in to refresh their coffee.

"The girl," he said. "A prostitute."

Caprisi edged himself forward in his seat, cradling his cup. "Not Blood Alley."

"Classy."

"Well . . ."

"A Russian." The inspector waved his hand again, as if this were sufficient explanation. "I know." He put his feet down and looked at the paper on his desk, then returned to his previous position. "Lu . . ." He shrugged. "It's not his style, no?"

"The girl lived in his flat."

"She was his? He has so many."

"Yes. She was one of his women."

"He is greedy. Like a Chinese." He cleared his throat and looked briefly at Chen. "So you think that he . . . you know? She was stabbed. Many times . . . In the vagina you say?" He grimaced.

"Yes."

"And it was Lu, you think?"

"We certainly believe he knows who it was."

Caprisi had not touched his croissant, so Field pulled over his plate and began eating. He was suddenly ravenously hungry.

"There are no other cases . . . there has been nothing similar here?" Caprisi asked.

"Here?" The inspector shrugged, as if to say such things could not possibly happen on French territory. "No." He thought about it some more, head tilted to one side, before shaking his head. "No."

Twenty-five

hey pulled up outside a three-story house with an open balcony on the first floor, hidden behind ornate balustrades: number 3, Rue Wagner. Caprisi leaned forward and looked up at it. His expression reflected the nervousness Field felt. "Know how many men Lu has at his beck and call?" the American asked.

"Twenty thousand."

"Right. An army. A fucking army. What do you think, Chen? Leave our guns in the car?"

The Chinese detective turned around, his mouth tight. "Let them disarm us."

There was no one on the veranda, but as they climbed the stone steps to the entrance, one of the big wooden doors swung back to allow them to pass into a gloomy hallway with a black-and-white-checkered stone floor. At first, Field could not see who had opened the door, but as one man in a dark suit stepped forward, he saw another in the background, leaning against a glass-fronted gun cabinet that was well enough stocked for the outbreak of a war.

Both men were Russian, and the one closest, who was bald, indicated with his hand that he wished them to give up their weapons. Caprisi reached reluctantly into his pocket and handed over his revolver. Field followed suit. Chen hesitated, but once he, too, had obliged, they were ushered toward the stairs and left to climb them on their own.

Field wanted to look back but resisted the temptation. The

staircase was wide, the floor above gloomy, too. The place felt
like a funeral parlor.

They walked slowly toward a pair of doors that opened
into a large room with shutters closed and thick, dark red curtains half-drawn, the only light coming from a dull lamp in
one corner. Lu sat facing them, his legs resting on a footstool
while a Chinese girl in a silk dressing gown massaged his feet.
He dismissed her and beckoned them toward him, indicating
that they should sit on the two chairs that appeared to have
been placed opposite him specifically for their visit. He
showed no sign of recognizing Field from the altercation in
the Majestic.

Chen was left to stand.

Lu sat in a low leather armchair, between a Chinese cabinet
and a grand piano bedecked with framed photographs. It was a
moment or two before Field realized that they were pictures of
girls—his girls, Lena and Natasha Medvedev ostentatiously to
the fore. They were studio photographs, similar to those one
saw of film actresses like Bebe Daniels and Lillian Gish.

Field stared at them.

Lu opened and closed his right hand slowly, as if stretching
his fingers.

"Tea?"

"Yes," Caprisi said.

Lu hit a bell and within a second a houseboy appeared.

Lu coughed once. His lungs sounded heavy, and his com-
plexion, as Field had noticed the other night, was sickly, his
cheeks scarred. His expression was sour, his mouth turned down.
His eyes were small but piercing, and, if his body appeared weak,
his eyes revealed a quick mind and a soul consumed, Field
thought again, by burning anger and barely suppressed
aggression.

"You wish to speak to me?" he asked once the houseboy
had gone. He raised his hands and placed them together, two
sets of portly, manicured fingers resting against each other
beneath his chin. He spoke English well but quietly, with an

accent that clipped the ends of some words, but not others, so that "wish" was perfectly enunciated, but "speak" half-lost. His voice was cold.

"About Lena Orlov," Caprisi said.

"Lena, yes." He nodded.

"We're obviously sorry to trouble you about it."

Lu nodded again. "I spoke to your colleagues in the French police."

"But we're conducting the investigation. Excellent as our colleagues are, you would expect us to wish to speak to those involved."

"How am I involved?"

The houseboy came in with a tray and placed it on a table next to Lu's chair. Caprisi waited until he had withdrawn. "'Involved' is perhaps the wrong word. Connected."

"How am I connected?"

Caprisi shifted uneasily in his seat. "Lena Orlov was living in a flat which we have been led to believe belonged to you."

Lu frowned, tapping the bottom of his chin with his fingers. "Happy Times block?" he asked himself, as if trying to recall it. "Yes, I believe it is owned by one of my companies. That is all."

Field could see that, for the Chinese, this was a game. Recalling the hostility in evidence at the Majestic, he wondered how long it would last.

"You didn't allow Lena Orlov to live there for free?"

"Why would I wish to do that?"

"So she was paying rent?"

"I do not know. Perhaps she had a relationship with one of my men." He shrugged, to emphasize the extent of his disinterest. "I do not know. I have many companies, many men. I cannot know what is happening with them all."

"So you did not know her personally?" Caprisi asked, his eyes conspicuously drawn to the photograph of Lena on the grand piano.

"I know many people, Officer."

"So you knew Lena?"

"This city has many beautiful women to admire."

There was something in the way he said this—the grotesque satisfaction of a man of humble peasant origins who has risen far enough to buy the right to abuse women he could once never have dreamed of even meeting—that so outraged Field that he had to restrain himself from getting to his feet. He looked at Caprisi and saw a muscle twitching rapidly in the American's cheek. For the first time he felt naked without his revolver.

His aggression dissipated as he sensed the power of this Chinese man. Field could see how often and with what little consideration death was dispensed with a curt wave of one of those hands.

"So you did know Lena?" Caprisi asked.

"I knew the girl. I know many."

Caprisi was sweating now and he wiped his forehead and took out his notebook. "Do you mind if I take notes?"

Lu looked unsettled for the first time, waving his hand at them and frowning deeply. "Better not."

"We are detectives, Mr. Huang."

"You are police."

Caprisi left his notebook on his lap but didn't open it. "Lena Orlov was not, then ... You knew her, but she did not ... You had no arrangement with her?"

"Arrangement?"

"She was not a concubine?"

He wrinkled his nose in disgust at the idea of having such a formal relationship with a Russian woman.

"There was no relationship?"

"What do you mean relationship?"

Caprisi sighed, leaning forward in his chair. "Mr. Huang, we have no wish to be difficult, but you will appreciate that Lena Orlov was murdered with extraordinary brutality, even by the standards of Shanghai."

"You don't like Shanghai?"

Caprisi bent his head.

"We both find it an exciting city," Field said.

Lu shifted his eyes slowly, looking at Field for the first time. "Exciting, yes."

"Perhaps the greatest city on earth."

"Greater than London? Paris? New York?"

"Their equal. An example of harnessing the benefits and strengths of two cultures."

"Or their faults." Lu's face was impassive.

"And their faults."

"Lena was one of your girls," Caprisi said more bluntly.

"My girls?" Lu had raised his hand, an ivory bracelet on his wrist trailing down half the length of his forearm. "We spoke a couple of times. I did not know she was living in a flat we owned."

"You had no idea she lived in the Happy Times block?"

"Why should I know? I cannot know everything." He smiled at Field, as if now considering him an ally.

"Lena was paying rent?"

He shrugged again, as if this was becoming absurd. "How can I know?"

"But you had met her?"

"Met her? Yes, I'm sure." He gestured at the photographs. "There are many beautiful women in Shanghai, Officer. I meet many."

"It is not possible that you—or one of your men—owned her and gave her to someone else? Lent her."

Lu was still frowning. "My men . . ." He shrugged.

Field could see this was pointless. He edged forward in his seat and looked across at Caprisi, but the American didn't move, his face fixed on Lu's. Field wondered if Caprisi would produce the notes Lena had made but now considered that to do so would be a mistake.

"The doorman of that building . . . the block owned by your company. He was removed, taken to the Chinese city, and then beheaded."

"I had not heard it."

"It does not concern you?"

"Concern me, perhaps. He was a communist?"

"No."

"Some are too enthusiastic. Many are accused. These are dangerous times."

"But you had not heard that a doorman of your building was taken away and summarily—"

"I have explained, Officer." Lu sat up straighter, his tone and manner more menacing. "There are many interests. I believe you will find a company on Bubbling Well Road . . . the owner of this Happy Times block. I will instruct my men there to cooperate with you."

Caprisi hesitated, sipping his tea. Field sensed a new, stubborn determination in his colleague.

"So you barely knew Lena?" Caprisi asked.

"I have said. I will instruct my men to help you."

"I wasn't asking about your men."

Field cleared his throat. "Did you know Irina Ignatiev?"

Lu turned to him, his head tilted to one side, as if turning the name over in his mind. He shook his head, once.

"She was murdered two months ago. She was also one of your girls."

There was silence for a second, then Lu hit the bell twice and there was the sound of footsteps as his bodyguards arrived, two from downstairs, one through the door at the end, all with machine guns.

Field had stood, as had Caprisi. Lu pushed himself to his feet. The game was over. "You challenge me?" He took a pace toward them, his head pushed forward. "You come to my house and challenge me?" He was looking at Chen. His right hand was suspended in midair, and as he cut down with one swift motion, the bald-headed bodyguard stepped forward and swung his machine gun into Chen's stomach.

"Jesus." Caprisi stepped toward his colleague.

"Stay." It was Chen. He was bent double, kneeling, the instruction barked out through the pain.

"For Christ's sake."

"Silence," Chen said, his voice commanding. He slowly stood, straightening with difficulty. No one moved until the Chinese detective had recovered his composure. Once he had done so, he stared at his tormentor.

"Do not come to this house again," Lu said quietly. "I have tolerated your rudeness long enough."

Lu waved at his bodyguards to lower their weapons.

The weather had changed while they were inside. The wind had got up, bringing with it a thick bank of cloud, which was advancing on the city like a foreign army. A distant crack of lightning was followed by a loud rumble of thunder. "Typhoon coming," Chen said once they were back in the car and the first spots of rain were bursting on the windshield.

Caprisi had tried to assist Chen on the steps but had been waved away. Either the blow had not been as painful as it looked, or it was a matter of face that Chen leave the house unassisted.

Field looked out of the window at the clouds. He'd seen storms before, of course, but none that had looked quite as malevolent as they approached. It was the temperature, too, he thought, the heat that came with it, that made it feel different.

"The Master of Rain chooses his moment," Caprisi said.

Field turned to face him, frowning.

"According to legend," Caprisi explained, "affairs in the other world are governed by gods——"

"Officials," Chen corrected, from the front of the car.

"Officials, of whom the Master of Rain is probably the most powerful. He sits up there, controlling the city, its destiny."

Field nodded. "Have you ever had any dealings with Lu, Chen?"

The Chinese detective did not turn around.

"Chen grew up in Pudong," Caprisi said quietly. "They

grew up together. Lu hates him," he added with a finality that did not invite further discussion.

"Will that meeting create difficulties for Macleod?"

Caprisi waited for Chen to turn around and answer. "Not yet," the Chinese detective said. "But the girls are a problem."

"In what way?"

"Now he is aware that we know more than one girl has been murdered. The stakes are raised. He will wait to see what we do, and then we must see how he reacts."

"Why is he guarded by Russians?"

"He doesn't trust Chinese. The Russians are stupid. They know nothing, but their loyalty is absolute. Any threat, they shoot. He remembers how he destroyed the Red Gang and does not trust Chinese." Chen shook his head. "Lu is arrogant now. He has big head. He believes no one can touch him."

As they drove along the wide boulevards of the French Concession, Field watched the passersby hurrying to get out of the rain. The houses were all large here, most hidden behind ivy-clad walls. On the corner, as they turned right, a woman with a thin, pretty face held her raincoat around herself with one hand and a little boy in uniform with the other. As they passed, Field thought she looked forlorn and lost, her damp hair flattened across her forehead, her boy resting his head against her side as they waited to cross the road.

Field thought of Natasha.

And then he saw her. She was standing on the sidewalk, and he had to look up and down the street to ascertain that they were on the Nanking Road. The car had stopped and there was a crowd ahead, blocking the way, people shouting, some clapping, a firecracker going off in the air, dropped from the roof above. Field looked up to see a group leaning over the wall around the roof garden at the top of the Sun Sun store, dropping leaflets to the crowd below.

Natasha was now alongside him, half hidden by a group of

protestors, raincoat pulled tight, her hair whipped by the wind. She had a pile of leaflets and was giving them out to passersby.

"A protest," Chen said, pushing open his door.

The Chinese detective and Caprisi did not seem to have noticed Natasha, but as they got out and walked around to the front of the car, Field watched her.

She was smiling as she gave away each leaflet, but she did not look happy. A couple of police sirens wailed in the distance. She raised her head sharply, trying to make out where the sound was coming from.

The sirens closed in quickly. Field heard a whistle and saw a group of Sikh policemen charge past the car and begin to flail at the edge of the crowd with their batons. Protesters screamed as they were clubbed to the ground.

Natasha had frozen. She was staring at them.

Field pushed the door open, stepped onto the sidewalk and lunged for her, but her instinctive response was not submission but resistance. She pushed him away, punching him, then grabbing his hair as he tried to move her toward the car.

"Chen!" he yelled, but the effort distracted him and she bit his hand hard. The pain made him rougher than he'd intended, kicking her legs out and bundling her headfirst toward the rear of the car as the Chinese detective came up to help him, moving easily, as if the assault at Lu's house had had no discernible effect.

Caprisi climbed in the other side. "Let's go," Field said. Natasha was no longer struggling. Her hair hung limply over her face. She still clutched the leaflets. Caprisi took them from her and glanced through them before looking up at her. "Big mistake," he said. "Big mistake."

They reversed away from the crowd.

It took only a few minutes to get to the Central Police Station, and Natasha did not raise her head on the journey. As they pulled up outside, Caprisi told Chen to take her down to the cells. Field resisted the temptation to look at her as she was taken away.

Inside, Caprisi said, "I'm hungry. You want to get some lunch in the canteen?"

Field tried to think clearly about what he ought to do.

"If you want my advice," Caprisi said, "I would leave her to think it over."

ownstairs, there was a long line for lunch, and Field might have given up if his stomach had not been loudly protesting its hunger. He chose meat that he was assured was beef, potatoes, beans, and overboiled carrots. It was like being back at school.

On the way to their table, a big gray-haired Scotsman, who'd played lock forward against him two days before, slapped Field on the back. "Well played." He laughed. "Teach that fucking Yank a lesson."

Field smiled at Caprisi as they sat down. "Friend of yours?"

"Brits." He shook his head.

Field poured himself a glass of water and covered his food in salt and pepper in an attempt to instill some taste into it.

"Will you ever go back to America?" he asked, trying to focus his mind on something other than the woman in the basement.

Caprisi didn't react. His elbows rested on the table, his fork pointing down toward his plate as he chewed.

"It's hot in Chicago at this time of year?"

"It's hot."

"But not as hot as here?"

"Nowhere is as hot as here."

"The Gobi desert, possibly."

He gave Field a thin smile. "It doesn't rain in the Gobi."

"Did you meet Capone?"

"No."

"Did you like Chicago?"

"Yes."

"Do you ever answer questions with more than one syllable?"
He smiled again. "No."

Field put a potato into his mouth and spoke as he chewed.
"Okay, let's have a competition—see who can come up with a
topic of conversation that will take us further than three sen-
tences in a row."

"Where are you from?"

"Uh-uh. No. If your past is off-limits, then so is mine. I'm
from Yorkshire, you're from Chicago—that means we're quits."

Caprisi leaned back. He pushed away his plate, exchanging
it for a bowl of custard and some kind of cake pudding. "You
went to one of those smart schools, I know that."

"Not that smart. Where did you go to school?"

Caprisi shook his head, in the midst of another mouthful.
"Your uncle's one of the elite."

"He is, yes."

"And your aunt."

Field pushed his own plate away and started on his pudding. "You know, I could lose my sense of humor in a minute."

"Who'd notice?"

They were smiling at each other now. Field looked down
at his food and sighed. "God, this is disgusting."

"Leave it," Caprisi said. "I'd hate to see you poison yourself. I'm looking out for you, remember."

"You're just like my mother."

"She's got hairs on her chest?"

"That same look of anguished concern, as though I'm not
capable of looking after myself."

"Maybe it's not you she's thinking about."

Field frowned. "What do you mean?"

The American looked up from his food. "She's looking at
your face thinking that she's devoted her whole life to you and
now you're gone. So the anguish is for her, not for you."

"How do you know that?" Field said quietly.

Caprisi shook his head. "I've already said enough."

"You can't say one minute that we're friends and then leave us knowing nothing about each other."

"What I like about you, Field, is that you're the best of British—solid and uncomplicated—so don't—"

"You think I am, but you don't know. Solid maybe, I'd like to think so. Uncomplicated? I'm not so sure."

There was a long silence. Caprisi stared at his food as though it were suddenly the most interesting thing he'd ever seen. When he looked up, Field saw something in his eyes that spoke of a loss that was beyond words. Field knew that look.

"My wife's name was Jane and we were childhood sweethearts. My father owned a hardware store and Jane's family lived in the house opposite, just across the street. As kids, we used to wave at each other at night." Caprisi looked down again. "We started dating." He rubbed the bridge of his nose. "We got married and it always felt right. In a way nothing has since. We had a boy ..." He seemed about to say the name but was unable to manage it. "He was a good kid." Caprisi looked up, shaking his head slightly, his lips tight and his eyes narrowed as he fought to contain his emotions. "He was a great kid. Affectionate ... Jane wanted a big family, but we couldn't ... you know, we only had our one boy. It was okay, we had each other, we'd always said that, you know, even before we got married, we said if we couldn't have kids, that would be all right, because we were in it for each other." Caprisi shook his head again. "It's too cute. I should come up with a better story."

Field did not know what to say.

"Have you ever been in love, Field?"

"I don't know."

"Then you never have been." Caprisi sighed. "We had what both our parents had, and it was all we wanted and the boy was a blessing. He was a God-given extra. Do you believe in God, Field?"

"No."

"There's nothing out there, just darkness?"

"I don't know what's out there, but I don't think it's God."

"Jane would have tried to convince you. She was a believer. The little boy was so loving, it made everything all right, you know? It was okay that there would be no more. We'd come to accept it, that he would be enough, that that was it. We were a family."

Caprisi was gazing at a point over Field's shoulder. The silence stretched between them.

"We went to a party. A christening. It was bootlegged, of course, and I always went for the whiskey. Jane hated that, but I guess it helped me. I guess it helped me not to think too much about work, about what was going on in the city . . . It wasn't until I got *here* that I realized Chicago wasn't the only place justice and truth are in pretty short supply . . ." His voice trailed off. "She didn't want me to drive, but I insisted. We argued; she gave in. She didn't want to fight about it, she said. Not worth fighting about." He looked at Field, his face a mask of pain. "I got out without a scratch."

"I'm so sorry."

"Everyone's sorry."

"I know, but . . ."

"You're satisfied now?"

Field didn't answer and Caprisi sighed. "That was unfair. I'm the one who should be sorry." He leaned forward. "It seems to me that everyone I've trusted in has been taken away."

"You don't have to protect me, Caprisi."

The American looked at him for a long time and then smiled gently. "Yes I do." His expression hardened. "You need to be tough on her, Field."

Field didn't answer.

"I'm sure you will be." He pushed his tray away. "She's not a child and I should think she's experienced at manipulating people. She was caught doing something that could see her in prison for a long time. If she has information, make sure you get it out of her."

"I understand."

"Do you?"

Field stared at his hands. "It's not wrong to be searching for something better, is it?"

"What do you mean?"

Field looked up again. "I've never had what you had. I'm sorry you lost it—truly sorry—but I've never had anything like that. In all my childhood, I have to really struggle to remember one happy day or moment. Everything was so . . . pressurized. We existed under this cloud that was my father's anger, and the first moment I ever felt free of it—happy—was the day the liner that brought me here docked on the Bund. I got off, breathed that polluted air, saw the grand buildings of the waterfront, and, more than anything, I wanted to put *everything* I had ever known behind me and start again."

"It's all right to want something better, just don't look for it in the wrong place. Be patient. It will come."

Field stood.

"And you need to find out why she's Lu's girl. Don't take no for an answer."

The cells were like everything that was wrong with the worst parts of Shanghai. The smell of the sewers, damp, and decay, undiminished by any kind of flow of air, created a cocktail that assaulted his nostrils the moment Field opened the big steel door and began to walk down the stone steps.

Caprisi's remorse and guilt came with him. Field had wanted to talk about love, and about what he felt now, but he knew what he had to say would appear ludicrous to anyone but himself.

He hesitated. What would her reaction be, here?

"Natasha Medvedev," he told the duty sergeant. "Came in about forty minutes ago."

The Chinese officer took out his pen and looked up expectantly.

"Field. S.1."

"She was signed in as C.1. Chen." He pointed at Chen's name, detective number, and signature alongside Natasha's name.

"Correct. We arrested her together, but this is now an S.1 matter."

The man looked doubtful. Field thought how absurd it was that the mistrust between the two elite departments of the force had grown to the point at which ordinary uniformed officers were wary when there was any point of contention.

"It's a joint Crime and Special Branch investigation," Field said. "I'm working with Caprisi."

He signed in. He put the pen down and straightened his jacket as the door ahead of him was opened and he was handed the key to her cell. He stepped into the gloom, hesitating as the iron door was slammed shut behind him. It was a couple of degrees cooler down here, but he slipped his jacket off and loosened his tie.

A man in the cell to his right began to cough and didn't stop, his lungs racked by convulsions, before giving way to wheezy, uneven breathing.

Field's footsteps were noisy on the stone floor.

Natasha's cell was at the end of the corridor. She was sitting on her bed, with her feet pulled up and her head on her knees, face down. Field watched for a second through the grille and, when she didn't look up, put the key in the lock, opened the door, and stepped in.

He waited, hands in his pockets. There was an open drain in the corner, next to the tin bucket that was supposed to be used as a toilet. The smell here was much worse than outside.

She lifted her head, spinning her hair back and away from her face. Field saw fear, not defiance, in her eyes. He pulled over a chair. "Do you mind if I sit down?"

"I think you will do what you want."

Field put his jacket over the edge of the mattress. His polished shoes looked out of place.

Natasha was still wearing her raincoat, but she'd taken her shoes off and he found himself staring at her feet. Her toes were unusually long, their nails painted dark brown, or perhaps green.

"What are you going to do to me?"

"I don't know. What were you doing there?"

"You saw what I was doing."

"Why were you doing it?"

She didn't answer.

"Your father was a tsarist officer. A proud man, from the way he looked in the photograph I saw. How can it be that you're—"

She had begun to cry, her eyes closed and mouth screwed up tight.

"I'm sorry," he said quietly.

She wrapped an arm around each shoulder, as she had on the day he'd first seen her, until her body stopped shaking. She wiped her eyes with the back of her sleeve. "You English . . . so damned polite."

Field waited. "You're going to have to help us."

"Help you? How can I help you?" She was staring at him in disbelief. "Don't you know anything?"

"Then you'll go to prison."

He saw the anger in her face. "You think you can send me to prison?"

"You've committed a crime."

"And you think you'll find witnesses prepared to—"

"I am a witness. So are my colleagues. We're not impressed by Lu's intimidation."

As quickly as it had come, her defiance evaporated and she dropped her head.

"You will face a trial in the mixed courts, you'll be found guilty of spreading Bolshevik propaganda, and—I would guess you're looking at fifteen to twenty-five years. We can

ensure that you serve it in one of our prisons here so that Lu
cannot bribe the guards and get you out."

Natasha put her hands to her temples, as if trying to prevent this information from sinking in. She stared ahead, without answering, and then slowly crumpled. She rested her head
against the wall, closed her eyes, and cried with a pain that
Field had never seen in anyone before.

"Who was Lena seeing?"

She wiped her eyes again. "I don't know."

"Did Lu murder her, or one of his associates?"

"I don't know."

"What about Anna Simonov?"

There was terror in her eyes.

"Did you know Anna Simonov?"

She shook her head violently.

"Did you know Irina Ignatiev?"

"No, I . . ."

Natasha rested her head on her knees again.

"I'm going to ask you one more time," Field said, his voice
tight with frustration. "Did you know Anna Simonov?"

"No."

"Did you know Irina Ignatiev?"

She shook her head.

"For Christ's sake!" He was on his feet. "You're all from
Kazan. Do you think I'm an idiot?" He took a step closer.
"Aren't you frightened, Natasha?"

She began crying again. This time Field moved instinctively to her. He put his arms around her and she moved
against him, without resistance, placing her head on his chest.

He tightened his arms, hugging her.

He eased the pressure, lifted his right hand, and touched
her head, smoothing the hair back from her forehead, calming
her until the crying had lessened and then ceased, all the time
keeping his eyes on the iron grille in the door.

"It's all right," he said.

She was quiet and still, but he did not let go. She pressed

her head deeper into his chest and reached around to grip the sleeve of his shirt with her hand, as if clinging to a life raft.

"It's going to be all right," he said.

"No," she said. "It can never be all right."

He released her gently and stood. She was leaning forward now, still wiping her eyes periodically with the back of her hand. She looked frail, almost childlike in her vulnerability, a world away from the cynical sophisticate of his first acquaintance.

"What will you do with me?"

"I spoke to someone who knows you well," he said quietly. "And she said that, of all the Russian girls here, your circumstances were the most impaired."

"Mrs. Orlov, from the Majestic."

"What did she mean?"

Natasha lowered her eyes. "I don't know."

"If you don't help me, I cannot help you."

She looked up, the hurt deep. "No one can help me, Richard."

"You're wrong."

"No I'm not."

"In what way are your circumstances impaired?"

She shook her head. "Do what you want with me, but please don't ask me any more questions about it."

Field felt his mouth tightening. "How did you become one of Lu's girls?"

"I cannot talk about him." There was another long silence as Natasha wrestled with herself. "Lena . . ." She stopped.

"Go on."

"I . . . There was someone new. You asked if there was someone else, and it was true, there was. He . . . Lena did not talk about it, about him."

"For how long before her death?"

"About two months. She seemed happier, as if something good had finally happened to her."

"Lu asked her to see someone else?"

Natasha nodded.

"Do you have any idea who it might have been? Did she give you any clues? His nationality, for example, or the type of work he did? Or why Lu would be wishing her to do this?"

Natasha shook her head.

"Does he often ask his women to see other men?"

"He has many women, and many uses for them."

Field wanted to know, more than he had ever wanted to know anything in his life, whether Natasha had slept with Lu, whether she was forced to lie down and degrade herself beneath that sallow, scarred face, and before he could stop it, he was assaulted by an image of the two of them together, naked, Lu's portly manicured fingers on her dark smooth skin.

He stood up, stepped over to the door, and looked out of the grille before coming back and resuming his seat. She was sitting demurely, her arms wrapped around her legs, looking at him.

"Anna Simonov, Lena Orlov, Irina Ignatiev—stabbed so many times, crying out in pain, screaming in agony and terror, but nobody heard them." He looked at her. "And even now, nobody can hear them."

She lowered her head again, staring at the bed.

"All Lu's girls. Who is next, I wonder?"

She did not answer.

"Perhaps it's you?" he said at length.

She went on staring down.

"Do you have any cigarettes?" he asked.

Natasha straightened, fumbled in her raincoat pocket, and then threw the box toward him.

"Do you want one?"

She shook her head.

Field lit one and inhaled heavily, enjoying the smoke and the way it brought momentary relief from the smell. He looked at Natasha and then stood once more. "I want to get you out of here."

Caprisi was at the door, his face against the grille. Field

wondered how long he had been watching. "Macleod wants a word, polar bear."

Field stepped out of the cell and wiped the sweat from his forehead. Caprisi pulled him away from the door so that they could not be heard. "Macleod has heard she is in, and he wants her."

"What do you mean, wants her?" Field's heart was thumping again.

"He wants her to go down, as a warning to Lu. She'll get fifteen years and there will be fuck-all Lu can do about it. It would be a demonstration of who's in charge of the city."

"No."

"Steady, polar bear."

Field trailed the American, his mind whirring as he climbed the stairs.

Macleod was on the phone, standing by the window, but he put the receiver down as Field and Caprisi came in, and moved behind his desk so that he was no longer blocking the light. "Well done, Field . . . Take a seat."

"We can do better from this girl."

"I'm sure you can, but this is a decision—"

"Nobody informed me of any decision."

Macleod frowned. Field saw that Caprisi was imploring him to moderate his tone. "No one has to inform you of anything, Field." He sat down. "It's excellent work, though, very quick thinking. The commissioner is pleased."

"We can do better."

"If you want to take it up with Granger," Macleod said, his lips tight now, "then do so."

Field breathed in deeply, trying to calm himself. He sat down. "It's not my position to say, I know," he said, trying to buy himself time. "But this wouldn't hurt Lu, really, would it?"

"Depends how he feels about the girl. Depends how good a fuck she is."

Field breathed in heavily again to settle the pounding

urgency of his blood. Macleod was fiddling with a stone paper-weight on his desk. Field could see that his brusque and deci-sive manner hid a deep nervousness.

"Lu Huang remains our prime suspect." Field looked at Caprisi, who was standing between them, his back to the wall. "Shouldn't we still play for the main goal? This girl may be able to help us."

Macleod's face had softened a fraction.

"And if we cannot, in the end, prove that Lu murdered Lena Orlov, then perhaps we could find another way to bring him to court."

Macleod looked doubtful.

Field sighed, glancing at Caprisi once more. "Lu Huang keeps a ledger," he said in desperation, catapulting forward a plan that had barely started to form in the recesses of his mind.

Macleod looked at him as if he had gone mad.

"There's a clue in Lena Orlov's notes. She said the pay-ments were in the second ledger. Lu is a businessman. Every single transaction must be recorded in a ledger."

"I'm sure you will begin to make sense at some point," Macleod said.

"Every single transaction," Field went on. "Legitimate and otherwise. What are the shipments referred to in Lena Orlov's notes? If they are not legitimate, as we strongly sus-pect, then who is being paid, how, and where? A Fraser's com-pany is doing the shipping."

Macleod was alert now. "How do you know about this ledger? There's a file upstairs?"

Field hesitated. "Yes," he lied.

"Granger has opened a file? Have you got it?"

"No."

"Can you get it?"

"I doubt it."

"Why not?"

"It seems to have vanished."

"But you've seen it?"

"Yes."

"It talks about criminal transactions being recorded?"

"All transactions." Field considered the logic of what he was saying for a moment. "I'm sure they are not noted as criminal transactions, but we might be able to prove a link between a crime and the payoffs associated with it."

Macleod walked back to the window. He leaned against the dark wooden frame, fingering his chain.

"It would provide concrete evidence of—"

"I'm not stupid, Field." Macleod turned, staring out of the window at a thick cloud of black smoke that was drifting over the rooftops. "Would he really note down criminal transactions in black and white?"

"The majority of his transactions are criminal. Every business needs to keep a record of—"

"It's a hostage to fortune."

"He's safe in the French Concession and the house is a fortress."

"The woman should still go to jail." Macleod turned back. "Medvedev, whatever her name is. That would be a signal, not just to Lu but to his associates, that when we catch people, they go to prison and he cannot protect them."

"Natasha has access to his house. She is summoned down there."

Macleod thought about this. "Where is this ledger kept?"

"In his bedroom, we think."

"The murder inquiry is too important. If Lu remains the primary suspect, then—"

"It remains the focus of our efforts." Caprisi turned to his boss. "Field is saying that these ledgers serve a dual purpose. They could help us with the inquiry, by not only giving us an indication of what exactly these shipments are, and who else is in on the deal, but also providing a whole new avenue for prosecuting Lu." Caprisi paused. "If the girl is frightened enough of prison, and is willing to work for us, then she could prove useful in a number of ways."

Macleod snorted. "She's one of his women. She's not going to work for us."

"Field thinks she will." Caprisi looked at him.

Macleod tapped his fingers against the paperweight and then began to drum them on his desk, before getting up and looking out of the window again, sucking in his stomach and hitching up the waistband of his trousers. "All right," he said, "but make sure she understands. She should be in bloody prison."

Field stood, trying to hide his relief. He walked out ahead of Caprisi, but Macleod called him back. "I hope you don't think I'm being harsh," he said, closing the door behind the American. "I appreciate the work you're putting in."

Field nodded.

"I know it's difficult, this not being your department, but we do appreciate your efforts."

"Thank you, sir."

"Things are a bit difficult at the moment, but it will be worth it in the end. You understand?"

Field nodded.

"You're not offended?"

Field smiled. "No."

"Good. Good man." Macleod pulled the door open with one hand and rested the other briefly on Field's shoulder.

Twenty-seven

he process took longer than Field had thought. The Chinese sergeant refused to let Natasha go without someone from C.1 signing her out and wouldn't budge even when Field got angry. Caprisi was nowhere to be found, and in the end Field had to summon Macleod to the phone, to tell the desk officer to do as he was asked.

He didn't want to bother with arranging a car, so they got a rickshaw outside and crammed in together. He was conscious of the fact that their legs were touching. She made no attempt to move away.

Natasha let him into her flat. She slipped off her raincoat and stood in the middle of the room. She wore a simple, dark blue dress, cut close. Its hem rose above her knee as she ran her fingers through her hair.

"Do you want something to drink?" Her voice was an octave lower.

"No thanks."

"Tea?"

"No."

"You want something to eat?"

"No, I had lunch . . . of sorts."

"You don't think I can cook? Most Russian girls can't. Lena couldn't boil an egg when she came here. But my mother died when I was a little girl, and sometimes I used to cook for my father."

"Perhaps sometime . . . you could cook me something."

She smiled for the first time today and it lifted his spirits. "I'd like that."

"Perhaps tonight."

"Perhaps."

Field did not know if that was a yes or a no. "But *you* must be hungry. Please don't let me stop you."

"I can wait."

Natasha sat down, indicating that he should do the same, but the atmosphere had changed now.

"I hope you're not thinking that your freedom comes without cost."

She looked at her shoes. When she raised her head, Field saw that she was smiling.

"What's so funny?"

"You are funny. I'm watching you wrestle with yourself."

"I'm not sure I follow."

"Do you want me, Mr. Field, or will you reject me? Which of you will win?"

"I'm doing my job."

"Of course you are." She stood, walked to the mantelpiece, and took down a packet of cigarettes. She lit one and then sat back down, her dress riding up her thigh.

Field's throat felt dry.

"Is it because you think I belong to him? Does that disgust you?"

"You do have to help me." Field no longer trusted his voice, which sounded as if it belonged to someone else.

"I don't have to do anything."

He stared at her. "Have you ever seen the inside of a Shanghai prison?"

"No."

"I doubt you'd survive a month."

"Perhaps you'd be doing me a favor."

"If that's what you think, I might as well take you back right now."

"You cannot hide behind your badge."

"You don't believe we can protect you from Lu?"

"Half of you work for him."

"And you think——"

"No. That's why I'm talking to you." She shook her head in irritation. "Please. Do what you want with me, but don't talk about this anymore." She took a deep breath. "You ask me if I know who Lena was seeing, but I don't. She was secretive those last few months."

"She told you nothing about him?"

Natasha shook her head.

"And yet you lived next door."

Natasha shrugged. "It was always a desire to be private."

"So you never saw a man entering her apartment, never heard a voice, never saw a car parked outside?"

"No."

"It's hard to believe, isn't it? The two of you friends, knowing each other back in Kazan. You end up living next door to each other, and yet you know nothing whatsoever about her life?"

"Believe what you want."

"What about the notes she left on these shipments——the SS *Saratoga*, due to depart with a load of Fraser's Electrical Company sewing machines?"

She was still shaking her head.

"I would say the notes were left for someone who would be able to decipher them and would know what they meant. Were they left for you?"

Natasha stared at him without answering.

Field stood and crossed to the window. He looked down toward the racetrack and saw, to his surprise, that the large clock read almost five o'clock.

He turned around. "Do you ever go to Lu's house?"

"Sometimes."

"What do you do there?"

She dropped her head an inch, looking at her hands, and Field felt his face reddening again.

"Of course, you go into his bedroom."

"Of course."

The emotion was like a drug. His mind raced, his heart thumping in his chest.

"What do you . . ."

"Can we not talk about this now?"

"We don't have a choice."

"No." She was avoiding his eyes. "Of course, but I'm tired." She looked up. "Please, just not now."

He could see the pain in her eyes. "I have to go, anyway," he said. "We have to investigate this Fraser's factory."

He stopped at the door.

She had followed him over. "Thank you," she said.

"Tonight, then?"

"Yes, perhaps."

And then the door was closing, she was smiling, and reality, once again, was spinning away from him.

Caprisi was standing by his desk, his holster on. "I've been waiting," he said. "The manager finishes at six." He pointed upstairs. "Granger was looking for you."

"I'd better go and check in."

"Come on, Field."

"I'll be quick." He sprinted upstairs to his own office.

Yang was packing up to go and she eyed him without comment. Prokopiev was bent over a pile of newspapers, his jacket on the back of his chair, his thick suspenders off his shoulders. "Lucky bastard with that Medvedev woman," he said. "You get all the luck."

Field knocked on Granger's door and pushed it open.

Granger was on the phone, his feet on the desk. "Yes, sir," he said. "Yes, sir." He put down the receiver and raised his eyebrows as he turned toward Field. "Department is using too many paper clips; the commissioner's very worried." He lifted his hand and lowered his feet. "It's a joke, Field. You look anxious."

"No, just in a hurry."

"What's the rush?"

Field hesitated. "We're just going down to this factory."

"Which factory?"

"One of Fraser's . . . an electrical company."

"Where?"

Field hesitated again. "Yuen-Ming Road, I think."

Granger frowned.

"It's to do with this Orlov girl. She made some secret notes about a shipment—sewing machines. We don't know why it's significant."

"Well, be gone, man. Give me a shout later, tell me what you're up to."

Once they were in the car, Caprisi asked him what had happened.

Field explained, as far as he could. "She's frightened of Lu," he said.

And then, as if responding to the flick of a switch, there was the roar of thunder and the heavens opened again, the rain falling with such force that the driver had to slow to walking speed. Field watched people scurrying for cover.

It took them about thirty minutes to find the factory in Yuen-Ming Road, the driver frequently stopping and placing his face up against the windshield in an attempt to get his bearings.

There was a sign and then a blue iron gate, open just enough to allow a car through. The front wheels dipped into a large puddle as the car turned off the road.

"Stop," Chen said, and the driver did so instantly. The Chinese detective was suddenly agitated. "There's no security at the gate, why isn't anyone here?" He raised the machine gun and placed the tip of it against the window. Both Field and Caprisi pulled out their revolvers. Field's heart was pumping fast.

"Go on," Chen told the driver. The man looked around. He was much younger than Field had realized, and he was frightened.

They edged forward slowly.

"Come on," Chen said, his voice tense. The driver revved up and they shot through the gate. The entrance to the factory loomed ahead of them, its doors pulled back wide.

"Run," Chen said. They threw open the car doors and Field followed him. Caprisi was two paces behind.

Water was dribbling down Field's face, his feet and clothes soaking from the short sprint to the awning. He raised his hand, revolver pointing forward.

The roof was high; metal lamps hung down on long metal poles. In front of them, there were hundreds of wooden work-tops, to their right a line of heavy machines. In the far corner, an iron staircase led up to a glass box that Field assumed was the supervisor's office.

Chen's face was harsh, his mouth pursed with aggression as he walked forward, swinging his machine gun in a wide arc.

He stopped and looked at his watch. "Not yet six and no one here." He turned to his right and touched one of the big machines. "Still warm. They got out quick." He dropped to his knees, and as he did so, there was the sudden roar of an engine and a loud bang as a car smashed into the side of the factory door.

Field was blinded by headlights as the first bullets whipped into the metal behind him. He dropped to the floor, deafened by the sound of the ricochets, crawling away as Chen and Caprisi were doing, trying to find cover behind one of the big machines.

Chen got there first and rolled onto his side beneath it. Caprisi slid beyond him as the bullets pinged off the metal. The rest of the fire was indiscriminate, glass from the windows high on the wall showering them like confetti.

There was a momentary lull. Chen pulled his knees up underneath him, jumped to his feet, and returned fire. Field tried to follow, but Caprisi took hold of his sleeve and shouted over the noise for him to stay still.

Chen fell back, hitting one of the machines and landing on his side, his machine gun clattering on the floor in front of them. The Chinese detective clutched his arm, grimacing in pain. Caprisi lunged forward and tried to pull him to safety. "All right," Chen said through clenched teeth. "Arm. All right."

There was silence.

They heard footsteps.

Caprisi was gripping Chen's arm and trying to stop the bleeding, his face twisted with the effort. He pulled at Chen's raincoat, trying to get it off so that he could reach the pressure point on the inside of the arm, while holding his hand up in the air, above the level of his head.

Field looked over to the machine gun.

The footsteps grew louder. His hand was shaking.

He saw the corner of a fedora.

He lunged over Chen's legs, dropping his revolver, diving for the machine gun, kneeling, head down, trying to get his finger to the trigger, looking up to see the man in the hat swinging around.

The machine gun juddered in his hand, thumping back against him. The man was peppered with holes, and specks of blood floated above him in a fine mist as he fell, his face white with the shock of his own death.

Field got to his feet, turned toward the next man, and pulled the trigger. The gun flew up in the air, but the other two men behind turned and ran.

The car revved up and reversed as they sprinted toward the door, shouting.

Doors slammed, the car's engine roared, and then it was gone, leaving the factory eerily silent.

"Is he—"

"Check the others are dead," Caprisi said, still fighting to get Chen's raincoat off.

Field stood. His legs were shaking, the gun hanging down beside him.

He walked slowly, listening to the sound of his own foot-steps as he moved toward the bodies.

Both men were Chinese. The first wore a blue suit. His

chest was full of holes, a pool of blood beneath him. His fedora lay a few feet away.

Field had hit the second man in the head. There was less blood, but his face was contorted and ugly.

"Are they dead?"

"Yes."

"What?"

"Yes," Field shouted.

"Well then, come back."

Their voices seemed to echo.

Field returned and crouched beside the American. "It's an artery," Caprisi said. "Get his sleeve off that arm and rip it. Rip the coat or the shirt—anything."

Field handed him the strips of material.

"Now, while I keep my finger on the pressure point, get this off. Tear it. Don't worry about Chen."

Field grabbed Chen's raincoat underneath the arm and pulled it off. Caprisi gave him Chen's hand and indicated he should hold it up while he tried to get the makeshift bandages around the wound to stop the bleeding.

"It's all right, Chen," he said quietly. "It hurts, but it's not going to kill you." Caprisi stood. "All right, let's get you out of here."

They lifted Chen up. One arm was over Field's shoulder, and Caprisi still held the other above the level of his head. The front of Caprisi's shirt and his hands and face were covered in the Chinese detective's blood. As they walked past the line of machines, the American said, "They knew we were coming."

The rain was still like a wall beyond the entrance, pounding onto their heads and into their eyes as they stepped out, trying to spot the car. The lights were not on, and several seconds passed before they realized that it was full of holes, the windows broken, their young driver slumped forward over the wheel.

Twenty-eight

This is a declaration of war."

There was silence as Macleod looked around the room, waiting for someone to challenge him.

Field hadn't been in Commissioner Biers's office before and he was impressed. They were sitting at a round table, surrounded by tall windows which, on a clear day, would have afforded a panoramic view out over the rooftops, toward the Customs House and Hong Kong Shanghai Bank in one direction, and the race club in the other. Outside, the rain pounded on the glass. Behind him, a brass lamp on the commissioner's teak desk struggled to dispel the gloom of the gathering night.

If it was true that Biers was rarely sober, he was hiding it well tonight. He'd been solicitous and charming to both of them, gripping their shoulders, asking after Chen, before slipping into a discussion of the Dempsey-Carpentier fight at Jersey City some five years ago, clearly picking up on an earlier conversation, oblivious to the fact that Caprisi was not in the mood for small talk. The commissioner was softly spoken, with the hint of an accent that betrayed his Irish-immigrant background. He did not remember Field from their meeting the other night.

Biers began to fiddle with the pen and papers he'd brought from his desk. Field could see that he was nervous. "Yes," he said, clearing his throat.

"This is a direct attack on some of our most important men."

"Well, we've been attacked before." The commissioner cleared his throat again. "You chaps have been brave, of course."

"During a robbery, but that's different. This was premeditated. An ambush."

The door opened. Granger strode to the table and pulled back the leather-cushioned chair next to Field. He touched his shoulder in a gesture of support, or possibly consolation, as he sat down. "Sorry I'm late."

"Good evening, Patrick," Biers said warmly, as if greeting a favored son. Field noticed that both Macleod and Caprisi avoided Granger's eyes.

Granger loosened his tie, unbuttoned his collar, and stretched his long legs. He was smartly dressed in a dark three-piece suit, a gold watch at his waist.

"Perhaps you could give us your assessment, Caprisi," Biers said, "as the senior officer."

The American detective leaned forward, his elbows on the table. He glanced at Macleod, then Field. "Chen's all right. We've taken him to the Hôpital Ste.-Marie."

"I meant about the events tonight."

Granger lit a cigarette. He offered the silver case to Field, but no one else, then got up and brought back an ashtray.

"They were waiting for us. The machines were still hot. They'd left in a hurry."

"They knew you were coming?"

"Yes."

There was a long silence; the only sound was Granger sucking in smoke, then blowing it out into the air above them.

The commissioner appeared to be in a trance.

Macleod leaned forward. He seemed calmer. "The question is, what have we done to attract such a response? Is it the murder investigation, or the notes that implicate the factory? And who knew that we were going to the factory today?" He turned to Field. "Did you tell anyone?"

Field shook his head.

"After you left us in Crime, you went straight out?"

"No, I went up briefly to see Mr. Granger, but—"

"He certainly didn't mention the visit to me, or I'd have told him to be more careful." Granger looked around, reprimanding them for their naiveté. Macleod and Caprisi stared at Field, as if daring him to contradict his boss.

He said nothing, his jaw clenched.

Field recalled that he had also told Natasha they were going to the factory. He tried to remember the exact words he'd used.

He found it impossible to accept the idea that she could betray his confidence.

"So from this side, no one knew of the impending visit," the commissioner said.

"I knew of it," Macleod said. "And Caprisi. No one else."

There was another silence as Granger stubbed out his cigarette and pushed the ashtray toward the middle of the table. "There's Chen," he said.

"He would never tell anyone," Caprisi said. "He's smarter than that."

"How can you be so sure?" Granger asked.

Caprisi glared at him but made no attempt to respond. Granger had kicked this subject into the one guaranteed gray area—the true loyalties of the Chinese detectives on the force—and Field could see that it had infuriated the men opposite him. Upon reflection, it enraged him, too. Chen was a good man and he was in hospital.

Biers ran a hand over his head and smoothed the few hairs that remained there. Field met Macleod's steady gaze. It seemed, suddenly, vitally important that this man and not Granger become the next commissioner.

"The next question," Macleod said, "is what are we going to do about it?" He looked first at the commissioner, then Granger. "This man is no more than a gangster. He's murdered a girl in our jurisdiction, or covered up for the man who has; he's removed a perfectly innocent doorman and had him executed; and now he's made a brazen raid on our men as they went about their duty. And all in the space of five days."

The commissioner nodded, unconvincingly.

"We have to teach him a lesson. We cannot let this situation continue."

There was another long silence. Granger lit another cigarette; Biers fiddled with his pen. Field looked at his reflection in the tabletop.

"How do you propose to go about this?" Granger asked.

"We have to find evidence," Macleod said. "We do it the old-fashioned way. We build a case, we get evidence, we lure him into this part of the city and arrest him."

"Easy."

"We are making progress, but I think it's important that we acknowledge now that this is our aim."

Field looked up. Macleod was staring at him again.

"We must make sure information is tightly controlled, so that there are no further leaks." Macleod turned toward Granger.

Biers was twiddling his pen over the back of his hand, as Field had done in lessons at school, trying to spin and catch it in one movement.

"What is the Municipal Council going to think," Granger said. "I'm not sure if they've signed up for a war."

The commissioner did not answer, spinning his pen again and again, until he managed to catch it.

Field had no choice but to follow Granger after the meeting. The pair of them took the stairs while Caprisi and Macleod got into the lift.

The Special Branch office was dark. Granger did not bother to switch on a light until he got to his room. He kicked the door shut behind them with such force that the whole cubicle shook.

"You're wondering why I lied about tonight," Granger said, lighting Field's cigarette and then his own. "Fuck it."

Field didn't answer.

"Macleod was trying to catch us out. Make us look bad in front of the commissioner." Granger scowled and threw his cigarette in the bin. "He hasn't got you distrusting me, has he?"

"Of course not."

Granger looked at his watch. "Fuck. Caroline will kill me." He followed Field out of his office and locked the door after him. "We'll talk about this tomorrow," he said.

Field walked over to his desk and sat down, listening as Granger got into the lift and pulled the cage across, then slowly descended.

He leaned forward, glad to be surrounded by the darkness. The rain still thundered on the windows above him, like a stranger demanding entry. He remembered the days he'd spent inside the house in Yorkshire as a young boy, staring out at their small, waterlogged garden. The rain here unnerved him; it was relentless and angry. He ran his fingers back and forth along his temples and then rubbed his eyes, trying to relax. His head felt heavy.

There was someone behind him. He banged the light as he spun around, one hand reaching for the revolver inside his jacket.

"Caprisi." He breathed out. "What the fuck are you—"

"Keep your voice down."

Macleod was standing behind the American. "You told him about the factory. I thought Caprisi had told you not to give away—"

"I didn't think it would matter. He just asked why I was in a hurry." Field stood up, forcing them both to take a pace back. "Christ." He rubbed his forehead. He almost told them that he'd also mentioned the factory raid to Natasha, then thought better of it. "I don't understand . . . I mean why tonight, in response to what, specifically?"

"The cabal and Lu act as one," Caprisi said. "This was a warning. This case is obviously sensitive to them, either because of what is going on at the factory or because of who the murderer is, or both. We cannot be bought, therefore they have to warn us off. If we pursue it, things will be taken to the next stage."

Field sighed.

"We've got to be more careful, Richard. No leaks. Make sure no one is told what we are actually doing."

"What do you want me to do?"

"Try and stay close to Granger. Tell us if you see a move coming."

"We'll meet every morning down below," Macleod said. "At seven sharp, before anyone else gets in."

After they'd gone, Field switched off the light and sat there, finding the darkness briefly comforting.

He finally got up and walked down the stairs, intending to climb into a rickshaw and go to the Donaldsons' house, where he was sure of a warm reception, but that was not the address he gave. A hundred yards short of the Happy Times block, he shouted at the man to stop and got out. He thrust a generous note into his hand.

The rain was thundering down and Field had left his trilby in the office, so the water ran in rivulets down the back of his neck. The smell of Soochow Creek hung heavily in the air and a single gas lamp hissed beside him. Field wiped his face and walked, his feet squelching water with each step, like a primitive pump.

There was a light on in her apartment. Field stopped short and ducked into the doorway of a building opposite. He opened his raincoat and fumbled in his new coat pocket for his cigarettes, but his matches were damp.

He looked up as the light in her apartment went off.

He imagined the white gown falling from her shoulders. He could see it crumpled around her ankles. Natasha was walking toward Lu, he reaching forward, smiling, to take possession of her.

A dog barked loudly and a barge honked twice on the river. Field could hear the rasp of his own breathing.

A tram rattled past.

Field stepped out, unable to stop himself. He walked through the puddles in the road and stamped out the water on the steps into the Happy Times block, leaving a trail of dirty prints across the reassuringly clean stone floor. It looked as if no one had been in tonight.

The porter was a younger man, with short hair and a lean face. He was on his feet. He nodded a greeting, not willing to challenge Field's presence.

Field walked through the fire exit door and began to climb the darkened stairwell. The door into her hallway creaked as he opened it. He stopped to listen, but could only hear the sound of his own breathing.

Field wiped the palm of his hand across his hair to remove some of the rain.

He knocked on her door once, loudly, then stepped back.

Light spilled out beneath the door, across the puddle of water that had gathered around his feet.

The door opened, the light behind her as it had been on that first day, her dressing gown only half done up, her hair tousled.

"You have a guest."

She looked at him.

She stepped forward and curled her arms around his neck, her lips soft, her mouth warm, tasting as he had always imagined she would. The smell of her was intoxicating.

Field pulled at the back of her dressing gown. He kneaded, with strong hands, the soft flesh in the curve between her buttocks and thighs. She leaned back. Her hands rested gently on his neck, her eyes searching his.

Natasha was tall, but he lifted her easily. She wrapped her legs around him and rested her head on his shoulder as he kicked the door shut behind him.

She straightened by the entrance to her bedroom and

released herself, leaning momentarily against the door frame. Her face was dimly lit by the city's lights, her eyes, still searching his, betraying a combination of softness and deep loneliness. The rain rattled against the window.

He touched her, the flat of his hand against her cheek, and leaned forward to place his face beside her own. Her skin was smooth against his, warm and soft.

Field leaned back and her eyes once again searched his for something deep within.

She took his face in her hands and gently kissed him. She closed her eyes and tipped her head back against the frame. Field found that his own hands were shaking as he pushed the hair from her neck and ran his fingers down to her shoulder.

He bent his head to kiss her neck, breathing in the scent of her as though it were a drug. Her skin was soft as velvet and she inhaled sharply as he traced his fingers down between her breasts, slipping them inside her gown.

Field put his lips to her skin. He sank to his knees, feeling the curve of the breast with his hand, her nipple hard but supple as he took it gently into his mouth.

She breathed in again, arching her back. Her fingers massaged his scalp and pressed him closer.

Natasha pushed him lower, his lips brushing her ribs and then her smooth, flat stomach, her hands gripping him harder as his own ran up her thighs and over her hips. She guided him firmly, until his lips touched the soft hairs between her legs.

He kissed her harder and she leaned back, lowering her body, holding the frame behind her with one hand and his head with the other.

Each movement of his tongue within her was matched by the swaying of her hips, her breathing punctuated by almost inaudible gasps. Her fingers ran slowly through his hair, before again gripping his skull.

And then she was pushing him back and tearing at his clothes, pulling off his jacket and fumbling at the buttons of his shirt as he struggled to remove his trousers. She gave up and tore his shirt off as he tumbled onto the bed and she kissed him again, her lips on his cheek and his neck, his shoulder and the center of his chest, her warm, soft body flattened against him.

Natasha was slower now, more gentle, her lips on his, her long fingers caressing his face and neck and chest and arms.

She slipped off him, lay back, taking his right hand and inviting him to raise himself above her. She parted her legs, light from the racetrack illuminating the length of her, from the hair that spilled onto the white sheet beneath them to the round curve of her breasts to the darkness at the base of her belly. She brought him gently forward, guiding him, never taking her eyes from his as she let him slip silently inside her.

They were slow. Natasha shut her eyes, her arms above her head, her face tipped to the side, her mouth parted. She raised her legs and brushed them against his hips before opening her eyes and looking at him again. She touched his face.

She hardened her grip on his hips, clasped her legs behind him, then sat up, kissing him, passionately, on the mouth, then the cheek, breathing into his ear. His hand sought the contours of her ribs and her breast as they tumbled across the bed, parting for a moment, before she raised a leg to his waist and slipped him back inside her. She was laughing now, smiling at him, teasing him with her lips. "Richard Field," she said quietly, testing the sound of his name. She laughed again.

She rolled on top of him. He cupped the curve of her buttocks with his palms as she pressed down on him, her breathing low and rhythmic.

Natasha slipped off him, gliding onto his stomach. She pressed herself against his chest, then lay back and pulled him gently above her again, filling herself with him once more.

Twenty-nine

They lay entwined together in silence, their bodies covered in a thin sheen of sweat. Her head was in the crook of his neck, a hand on his chest, her face by his ear, so that he could listen to her breathing.

The rain still hammered against the window.

"It is so comforting, the rain," she said.

Field did not answer. Her hand caressed his chest and then found his, her fingers playing with his own. She hugged him, her leg over his waist and groin.

"When I was a child," she said, "we used to lie in bed and listen to the rain, all warm and safe."

"With your mother?"

"My sister." She lifted her head so that she could look at him. "Did you like to listen to the rain, Richard?"

"Yes."

"Did you have someone to listen with?"

"No."

"You have no sister, or brother?"

"I have a sister."

"What is her name?"

"Edith."

"You are not close?"

Field stared at the ceiling. "I think we were close."

Natasha hugged him again. She ran her hand through his hair, ruffled it. "Now you are always smiling!" She laughed.

"So are you."

She held his hand and they lay still. Natasha examined his fingers, running her own along each and then placing her hand over his. "How only think so?" she asked.

"Think so what?"

"How do you only think you were close to your sister?"

Field stared at the ceiling. He tried to pick out mosquitoes in the gloom but could not see any. Her nets worked. "It was a different life. It's confused. Everything back home is confused." Field tried to recall home clearly, but it was hard to think about anything while looking at her. She nodded, to encourage him. "It's almost as though I have only been alive since I've been here and everything that went before is . . ." He stopped. "Did your family come?"

She put a finger to his lips and rolled off the bed, her long hair hanging down her back as she moved toward the bathroom.

Natasha returned, unashamedly naked, and knelt on the end of the bed.

She slipped from her knees onto her hip, arching her back so that her hair hung back over his toes.

Field leaned forward and touched the flesh above her knee.

Natasha pushed him gently back onto the pillow, her lips warm, the smell of her still more intense, her nipples against his chest, the skin of her neck soft, her legs across his.

The urgency had gone, her touch now more deeply satisfying. She ran her fingers across his chin and through his hair, brushing it back from his forehead. Her tongue ran around his lips and then slipped between them, finding his own and withdrawing.

She smiled and leaned back onto her left leg, moving the other up beside his face. As he touched her ankle and ran his hand up her knee and then along her thigh, he watched her put the fingers of her right hand in her mouth.

She reached down between Field's legs, making a ring of her thumb and finger. She bent down to kiss him.

Field's muscles were tense, his arms straining.

She released him, straddling his waist, taking his hand and guiding it. Her breathing quickened as she pressed down onto him, and he groaned as he slid into her once more.

Natasha threw herself back, her breasts high in the half-light, her legs pressing against his thighs, her hands resting on his stomach. She pushed down harder, raising herself so that she was teasing the end of him, before forcing herself back down.

She closed her eyes and, just for a moment, unease at the contrast between her expertise and his inexperience crept into the corner of Field's mind, before she leaned forward once more, her hair tumbling into his face, her mouth warm, and he lost himself in the curve of her thighs.

Afterward, they lay in almost exactly the same position, Natasha's heart hammering against his chest.

Field listened to it, and his own, slowing.

"Have you always been a fighter, Richard?" she said, looking at him, resting on her elbow. "I think somebody once hurt you very badly."

He frowned.

"So determined and yet so vulnerable." Natasha stood and shook her head. "I can imagine you as a little boy." Without waiting for him to answer, she walked to the bathroom, her hands on her slim hips.

He listened as she ran the tap and brushed her teeth and then turned on the shower.

"*Tu arrives?*" she asked.

Field stood and walked into the bathroom. She was half-visible through a glass screen.

He opened the door of the shower. She put her arms around his middle and drew him in, her body slippery and cool.

Natasha looked younger with wet, straggled hair across her face, her nipples hardened by the water. She was smiling at him, as if she were enjoying a private joke.

She pushed him gently away and stepped out of the stream of water. She lathered the soap in her hands and began to wash him. She started with his neck, then worked under his arms, before pushing him back so that she could wash his chest and stomach.

She worked down his body to his feet, washing them as carefully as the rest of him, before pulling him forward into the stream of water.

Field took the soap from her. He began at her neck. She watched him as he washed under her armpits and across her breasts, teasing her nipples with a soapy hand.

"Washing."

Her stomach was flat, her belly button tiny and shallow.

He knelt down, working the soap into a lather again, washing around her hips and then into the mound of hair at the parting of her thighs.

He worked downward, placing his hand gently between her legs, feeling the response in her body.

He washed her feet but without conviction. She stepped forward, her body quivering and pressed hard against his, the water streaming over them. Natasha lifted herself against him, into his arms, her legs around him as she leaned back against the glass screen.

They dried each other afterward, and then she brought over his clothes and put them carefully on the bed. She placed the flat of her hand against his stomach, then began to dress him, her touch reassuring. His suit was crumpled and still damp from the rain.

"A new suit?"

"Yes."

"You should take better care of it."

Natasha placed her own clothes on the bed. She pulled the garter belt around her waist and then sat down. Field took the stockings and placed them over her toes, rolling them slowly up her legs and fastening them at the top as she watched him.

"You haven't done this before, have you, Richard?"

Field found it impossible to answer. It seemed to open up too many other questions. She stood and took his head to her stomach. When he straightened and put his big arms around her, he noticed, for the first time, a picture of the tsar and tsarina on the mantelpiece above the fireplace on the far wall. It was a formal picture, Nicholas in military uniform, his wife in a long white lace dress. Natasha followed his gaze.

She walked to the closet and turned. "I know a café in the Concession which will be open. It is early, we will not be seen."

She took a long red dress from the closet, more suitable for dinner than breakfast. She slipped it over her head and then turned her back to him, to allow him to do up the buttons. It was well made, elegant, and obviously expensive.

Natasha searched for her keys in the silver pot by the door and then stepped out into the dark hallway, her heels noisy on the stone floor. Field looked at his watch. It was five o'clock in the morning, but he had never felt less tired in his life.

In the lift she checked herself in the mirror, rearranging her hair. He touched the curve at the bottom of her back and she gripped his hand and smiled at him.

Outside, there were no rickshaws, so they walked beneath the streetlamps that still brought only a dim glow to the streets.

Field took her hand and she held his for a moment before letting it slip free. She did not smile at him, and now that they were in public, her mood seemed to have cooled.

"Did somebody hurt you?" she said.

"What do you mean?"

"Always so angry." She imitated him. "Shoulders hunched, fists bunched. Like a boxer!" Their footsteps kept a steady rhythm. "Tonight you are smiling and it is better."

Field didn't answer.

"Why did you come to Shanghai?" she asked.

"To escape. Like everyone."

"To escape what?"

"Just to escape."

"Your family?" She took his hand again briefly, glancing about her, a teasing smile at the corner of her lips. She seemed much younger suddenly. "Why do you care about Lena . . . about me?"

Field did not answer. The first glimmer of dawn was visible through the leaves of the trees. Thin shafts of light fell across their faces as they walked beside the gracious houses with their angular, corrugated tile roofs and small attic windows still lingering in semidarkness.

"You have family here?" he asked.

She shook her head.

"But you left—"

"My mother died when I was a little girl, my father before we left Russia, my sister of tuberculosis here."

"I'm sorry."

They turned into Avenue Joffre and stopped by a family sleeping together in a huddle against the window of a jewelery shop, two young children sandwiched between their parents. Natasha reached into her pocket and slipped a note under the father's hand. Field could see the man was an opium addict; his eyes were drawn and haunted, his skin pallid and yellow. The children and the mother were so thin that the bones in their faces seemed ready to break out of their skin. "Your uncle should do something for the poor of this city," she said.

Field looked at her. "My uncle?"

"Your uncle is the municipal secretary, no?"

"How did you know that?"

She laughed. "So *you* can find out about *me*, but not the other way around?" She shook her head. "They do nothing, the businessmen here, only pillage it, like . . . pigs. All for big business and their own pockets, while so many starve."

"Yes," he said, not wanting to argue.

"They live in their big houses and offices and clubs and they pretend this world does not exist."

"It's the same everywhere."

"But worse here. I do not believe anywhere is worse than here. So much wealth, so much suffering. Worse even than Russia."

"That's a surprising view, given—"

"Why surprising?"

"I thought your family was driven out by the Bolsheviks."

"That's ideology. Ideology is the enemy of humanity." She stopped and faced him. "You make a war with Lu, but for the Chinese, your leaders are worse than he is."

"I don't think—"

"He gives back. He is an animal, but for the Chinese a leader. The others give only back to Europe."

She turned away.

"You lived in Kazan?" he asked.

She shook her head dismissively and walked on. "It was a long time ago."

"In the picture—"

"I do not like to talk of it."

"You still feel—"

"It was all too long ago, another life."

"You came here with your sister."

"Yes."

"You were close to her."

Natasha smiled. "She was older, but she was shy and kind and a little timid. She always looked after me. Papa called her the little mouse." She frowned. "But it was an affectionate name."

"What was her real name?"

"Please. Enough." She smiled at him softly. "Tell me about your family."

Field stared at his feet. "My mother and sister live in Yorkshire. My sister is married, but they have no children."

"And your father?"

"He's dead."

"I'm sorry. It was long ago?"

"About a year."

"He was ill?"

"In a way, yes."

"In a way?"

Field hesitated. "He committed suicide."

There was a sharp intake of breath. "So sad."

"That's one way of looking at it."

She turned to him, confused. "You did not love him?"

"No."

She stopped again. "You sound so hard."

"Not as hard as he was."

"He hurt you?"

"Mostly my mother."

She looked at the ground, then moved on again. "Now I understand a little more."

"Understand what?"

"About you." She sighed, almost inaudibly. "Why so angry."

The café was opposite the Siberian Fur Shop and it had only just opened. Behind the counter, a grumpy, overweight Frenchman with a long gray mustache eyed Natasha in a manner that irritated Field.

They sat in the corner, at a small round wooden table, and watched the dawn gathering beyond the window, a red sky chasing away the remnants of yesterday's storm. Field ordered coffee and a croissant and Natasha borscht and black bread.

"What kind of man was he?" she asked.

"Does it matter?"

"To know you—" she shrugged—"it matters."

Field thought for a moment. He looked out of the window again. "He wanted me to be an accountant or a missionary and he was the worst combination of both."

"And you are neither."

"His father was a shoeshine boy, and for him, there was no margin of error." Field held up thumb and forefinger so that they were almost touching. "One mistake, no matter how tiny . . ."

"He was a missionary?"

"He acted like one. My mother came from a well-to-do family, and her parents believed she had married beneath herself. She grew up in a big house with plenty of servants, and they didn't think my father was worthy of her." Field sighed. "He was an accountant, but he was ambitious and he started a business selling hosiery. The shops always struggled and I don't remember . . ." She leaned forward to touch his hand. "Neither of them ever smiled. I don't recall them appearing to be anything other than miserable." Field withdrew his hand and leaned back, not wanting the intimacy of someone else's touch as he recalled the past. "Sometimes my father would come home in a terrible temper and we would be sent out of the room and then he would push Mother until they began to argue. He would shout louder and louder." Field could hear their raised voices as if they were in the next room, and he wanted to put his hands to his ears as he had done so often as a boy. "The next morning my mother would have bruises on her face."

Natasha looked at him with concern in her eyes.

"What about *your* father?" Field asked.

Natasha shrugged. "He died of a disease . . . something . . . we never quite knew." She waved her hand. "It was a long time ago."

"But it doesn't feel like it."

She shrugged. "Life is sometimes sad."

"And sometimes happy."

She smiled. "Sometimes."

Thirty

ow old were you when your mother died?" he asked.

"Seven."

"Do you remember her well?"

"Remember, but not so well."

"She was beautiful."

"I'm not beautiful."

Field did not dignify this with a response.

"Tell me more about your father," she said quickly, as if trying to move him away from her own past.

Field felt that there was something stilted about their conversation that was not present in their lovemaking, as if only in bed could they shed the thousands of barriers, seen and unseen, that separated them. And yet, he reflected, the purity of emotion was the same. Here he felt as he had all night. He wanted to know about her and perhaps she him, but their questions were oblique, their answers wary. He looked out of the window. "He's dead."

"Was he like you? Not the cruelty, I mean but—"

"Albert Field had a platitude for every occasion."

"Tell me one."

"Honesty is a cloak to keep out the chill of loneliness."

She frowned.

"In his eyes, if you're honest, you'll always have something to hold on to, no matter what the world chooses to strip from you. You will always have your integrity and a sense of self-worth and value."

As he watched the color draining from her cheeks and realized what he'd said, Field wondered if, subconsciously, he had chosen the quote deliberately.

"So part of him was a good man?"

Field did not answer.

"I think you are your father's son, Richard."

Natasha was suddenly subdued and withdrawn as the café owner brought their coffees on a round wooden tray.

"And you," he said. "Are you your father's daughter?"

"I am glad he did not live to see Shanghai." She sat up straight. "What will you do with me?"

"He was in the army."

"What will you do with me? You have discussed it with your colleagues?" She was nervous and suddenly uncertain at the intrusion of the real world.

"What do you do for him, Natasha? You go to his house?"

"I do not want to talk about it."

"I'm afraid you've got to tell me exactly what happens."

"It is my business." He thought the defiance he could see in her eyes was in fact fear.

"Has he ever shown any violence to you? Has he ever hit you or—"

"He does nothing."

"Nothing?"

"Sure."

"Why does he—"

"Why do you want to know?"

Field continued to stare at her.

"I go . . . Always the same. To his house. There is a telephone call and I go down. I am shown to the room on the first floor by his bodyguards, and there I wait. Then one of the housekeepers comes down. Sometimes it is a long time. One hour, two. More."

"You're alone in that room?"

"Yes."

"Then what?"

"Then I am taken upstairs, and the housekeeper—always the same, a Chinese woman wearing a uniform—she tells me to begin. At first, she explained, I must take my clothes off slowly and then, when he waves his hand, I can go."

"The housekeeper withdraws."

"Yes."

"And . . ." Field felt his stomach tense. He wanted to shut out the image of her and Lu, and yet he desperately needed to know.

"I begin. I take my clothes off."

"What do you wear?" he asked, no longer trusting his voice.

"Does it matter?" Her voice was sharp.

"It might." He swallowed hard. "Lena was handcuffed to the bed, wearing stockings and a garter belt. Has he ever used handcuffs, or asked you to wear anything in particular, anything like that?"

Natasha shook her head.

"And when you have done that?"

"It's all right, Richard."

Unconsciously, he was tensing up again. He fought the urge to stand and punch the window. "And when you are finished?" he asked with exaggerated care.

She shrugged. "I pick up my clothes, and there is a dressing room. I put on my clothes and leave by a side door, back into the hall and down the stairs, past the bodyguards."

"They are—"

"They think I'm a whore." She put her hand to her mouth and started to bite one of her fingernails. Visibly upset, she turned to face the window and crossed her arms protectively across her chest.

"And Lu—what does he do? Where is he when . . ." Field cleared his throat. "Where is he when you come into the bedroom?"

"He is lying on the bed in a silk dressing gown."

"Fully dressed?"

"He has a dressing gown on." She shrugged. "There is an opium pipe beside him and his eyes are glazed."

"But he is looking at you?"

"Please stop it, Richard."

"He watches?"

"Yes."

"But he never touches you? He never beckons you over to him?"

"I would never . . ." Her fist was bunched now, her face screwed up with pain. "Whatever you think, I would never . . ."

Field leaned back again, breathing out heavily.

"You think I have a choice," she said. "About him, about my life. You think I have a choice."

"And it hurts you that I think that?"

She did not answer.

Field fought to believe her. She only took her clothes off. There was nothing more involved. "Lena hid those notes for someone," he said. "The ones we showed you."

Natasha didn't react.

"Did she leave them for you?"

Natasha shook her head but without meeting his eyes. Field thought there was a hint of color in her cheek.

"She discussed the notes with you."

Natasha looked at him. "I don't know anything about it."

Field did not want to accuse her of lying, though he was certain that she was. "The notes refer to a second ledger," he said. "Lu keeps a complete record of all his accounts, including transactions, payments, and shipments, somewhere in the private quarters of his house."

"I do not know."

"Have you ever seen anything like a ledger—probably a series of them? Does he have a study? They must be somewhere Lena could get to them. Have you ever seen ledgers that could be accounting books anywhere near his bedroom?"

"No."

"Nowhere in the house?"

Natasha shook her head, but the more she denied knowledge of the ledgers, the more certain he was that she knew exactly what he was talking about.

"Did Lena ever talk about them?"

"No." Natasha stared at him. "When I go there, this is what you want?"

Field leaned closer. "I would like you to establish that these books exist and find out where they are kept."

Her face betrayed nothing. "This is what you want me to do?"

"Yes."

"When I go, this is what you want me to do?"

"Yes."

She tilted her head. "If I am seen, then I will be executed, of course."

Field didn't answer.

Natasha sighed. "So this is why you slept with me?"

"Natasha, I—"

"You are a hard man. Perhaps like your father."

"I don't have a choice. And nor do you. My superiors will send you to prison if you don't cooperate. It will be out of my hands."

She stared at him. "So when I am vulnerable, you seek to punish me."

Field shook his head.

"You have caught me in your net and you will watch me until I die."

"I—"

"I hope you enjoy it, Richard."

"It is not my decision."

"A coward blames others for the work that he does." Natasha shook her head. "I'm glad I was able to give you something before—"

"It's not for them."

"Not for who?"

Field stared at her. "What kind of life are you going to have?"

She frowned. "I do not understand."

"It has nothing to do with my superiors. I want to break you free of Lu and this is the only way I know how."

She shook her head, still frowning.

"He has overreached himself. He has the fatal weakness of a man who believes he cannot be touched. He has forgotten that the international powers still control this city. He can be broken."

Natasha gazed out the window, a look of utter hopelessness in her eyes.

"What life will you have if you do not try?" he asked.

"It's not about my life . . ."

"I'm asking you to trust me."

She snorted, quietly but with derision.

"Can you speak and read Chinese?" he asked.

"Of course." She looked at him. "Who knows about this?"

"A very small group of people."

"And you trust them?"

"Yes," Field said without hesitation. "Completely."

"You shouldn't. Everyone is corrupt here."

"I'm not."

"You're young."

"So are you."

She didn't answer.

"Parts of the force are corrupt, but not the unit that I'm dealing with," Field pulled up his chair and leaned onto the table. "We believe Lu has overreached himself. He has become complacent and Lena's murder was a challenge to the integrity of the force. We know we can break his hold on the city. I can take you away from here. When this is done."

"When it is done?"

"When this is done," he went on, "we will go away, somewhere better."

"To Venice, perhaps."

He hesitated, not sure whether she was mocking him. "If you like."

"As a little girl, I dreamed of Venice." She looked up at him. "Have you been to Venice, Richard?"

Field shook his head. "No."

"Would you like to go?"

"Yes. My . . ."

She waited for him to go on.

"My sister also. It was a dream."

"Then she is a romantic, too." Natasha's smile was fragile and hesitant. "What is it like, do you think?"

"My sister loved art. Florence, Venice. Even the thought of it was an escape. The idea of it." He stared out of the window. "It was how we imagined life if money was no object: long hot days and hazy, languid sunsets over still water and the shouts of the boatmen." When he turned back, Field saw the deep longing in her eyes.

"You would like to live in Venice?" she asked.

"I would like to live in Venice."

"We could live there together."

As she smiled at him, he tried to stop his stomach from somersaulting again.

"We could sleep in late and then have wine in the piazza— it is the right word?"

"It's the right word."

"And we could watch the sunset over the lagoon and then lie out and watch the stars."

Field didn't know what to say.

"Mama and Papa took their honeymoon in Venice. Papa was at military school in St. Petersburg and Mama only a schoolgirl; they met and married one month later and then went to Venice." She looked at him. "Papa always talked of it. He used to take out photographs of the lagoon, and one of Mama, and there would be tears in his eyes. He told me how they had planned to go back, one last time, even as she was dying." Natasha shook her head, tears in her own eyes.

Field reached for her hand, but she withdrew it.

"What do you dream of, Richard?"

He looked at her. "I dream of you."

She stared at the table in front of her. "Then it must remain a dream."

"Natasha . . ."

"My life is not my own."

"There must be—"

"An escape?" She stared at him. "Don't you think I have tried?"

"Dreams are what keep us alive."

"When I was a girl," she said, "my father took me to the circus. There was a hall of mirrors."

"Yes."

"There are no dreams here. Only illusions."

"Then we can go somewhere else."

"Where?" Her eyes narrowed. "Where do I belong now? Nowhere, and nowhere more than here. I have no passport, no money."

"I can help."

"No one can help."

Field stared at her. His heart was thumping again.

"No one can help me. There is nowhere we can go. But I will do what you ask. I will try to help you."

"Natasha . . ."

"Please. You may contact me by letter to tell me what you wish me to do. I will telephone when I am summoned to his house, but please do not come to the apartment again."

"What about last night?"

"Richard . . ." Her eyes pleaded with him. "Last night was . . . it was not just for you."

Natasha glanced across the road and suddenly stood. Field followed the direction of her gaze. Sergei was outside his apartment on the far side of the street, staring at them.

"Wait."

"No."

She walked away.

Field stood, then sat back down as she hurried past the window.

He lit another cigarette and smoked it. Sergei had gone.

Field left some money on the table and walked across the road. He climbed Sergei's gloomy stairwell. At the top he knocked and waited.

Sergei opened the door a few inches. He was in a long white nightgown.

"Just getting in from work, Sergei?"

"Yes."

"I've been talking to yet another of your compatriots who has told me nothing, but if you speak to Lu, Sergei, you can tell him I'll get to one of you in the end."

"I have nothing to do with Lu."

"I'm pleased to hear it."

Sergei shifted his weight from one foot to the other. "You looked very . . . close."

Field stepped forward. "Want to see how close I can get?"

Sergei tried to shut the door, but Field pushed it open and barged his way in, forcing the Russian back to the center of the room. "You're frightened of Lu, like the Medvedev woman and the rest of them."

Sergei's head drooped. "I've been working all night."

Field looked at him, relieved. He did not think Sergei had seen anything that could have compromised them.

Thirty-one

ield walked into the station slowly and stood in the center of the lobby on the ground floor. He looked about him, as if taking in his surroundings for the first time.

A dial above the lift swung to indicate it was descending. He glanced up at the clock. It was half past seven.

Field stepped forward and surveyed the curved dome of the ceiling with its gables and ornate stonework. This was a grand building, but it felt gloomy and neglected, designed for a greater purpose than it had achieved.

Field hesitated before hitting the button for his own office on the fourth floor.

The room was empty, the frosted glass grudgingly letting in the daylight. Field walked to his desk, his footsteps noisy on the parquet floor. Yang had left two notes: *Stirling Blackman called.* And: *Penelope Donaldson telephoned—three times.* Beside them, half hidden beneath a small mound of paperwork, Field noticed two envelopes. The first was addressed to him in neat, tiny handwriting. It was from the account monitoring manager at the Hong Kong Shanghai Bank, number 12 the Bund, Shanghai. The letter inside had been typed.

Dear Mr. Field, it read. *One of my senior clerks responsible for handling new clients has drawn my attention to the state of account. I enclose balance for your convenience.*

We aim to provide very best service for very best customer

*and I esteem an honor if you would in future contact me directly
if need assistance.*

Yours very respectfully,

Chen, C.W.

Field held up the thin sheet of paper attached. Under his
account number were two lines:

New credit: $600.

Account Balance: $1,012.

The other envelope was from Jessfield Properties Limited,
Jessfield Road. It advertised a property on Foochow Road, *close
to the racetrack, set back from the street, with elegant facilities.
Three reception rooms, charming, well-kept garden, tennis court,
and spacious veranda.*

Field folded it and slipped it into the bin. He picked up the
first letter and tucked it into his pocket. He got up and headed
back to the lift.

The sixth-floor corridor was dark. Maretsky was not yet in
his office, but Field did not have long to wait. Maretsky bus-
tled along a few minutes later, not noticing him until he had
the key in the lock. "You again," he said.

Field followed the Russian inside. He closed the door
behind him and waited until Maretsky had lifted himself onto
the high stool in front of his desk.

"I need a map," Field said.

"I believe stores—"

"One of Lu's women is caught red-handed distributing
Bolshevik propaganda."

"No pun intended, presumably."

"She faces a minimum fifteen-year sentence and may be
able to help with an investigation into a series of murders—"

"Natasha Medvedev. I have warned you, Field."

"At times she appears to be . . . coming over. But then we
lose her again. I think she's terrified that she may be the next
victim."

"Perhaps she isn't terrified only for herself."

"Who else?"

"Does she have a child?"

"No."

"Brother? Sister? Father? Mother?"

"No."

"Or so she says." Maretsky stared at him through dirty round glasses. "For a Russian, certainly, the penalty will be death, for all connected."

"So when they talk about impaired circumstances . . ."

"They mean points of influence. Loved ones. I would say she has a child."

"That's impossible."

"Nothing is impossible."

Field straightened. He paced to the other side of the tiny room and back again. He looked at the picture of Lu Huang presenting a check to the Sisters of Mercy Orphanage. "So if she appears," he said, "to want, somehow, to break away from him . . ."

"You are in love with her."

"No."

"Don't be a fool, Field. You can't say I haven't warned you."

"You misunderstand."

"She'll manipulate you, if she has not already."

"To what end?"

"To his end. She belongs to Lu, Field. Please listen to me. About this you don't yet understand as much as you should."

"And it's impossible to break this?"

"Yes."

"So his control is absolute?"

Maretsky sighed. "Not absolute, no. He does not control you. You are here without family—at least, only an uncle that even Lu might balk at challenging. If you do not give any hostages to fortune . . ." Maretsky cleared his throat. "He will try to buy you, of course, through his operatives in the force. Through the cabal. Perhaps he has already."

"I don't understand."

"You will when the time is right. And you probably do already, even if you won't admit it to yourself." He shrugged. "The woman, Medvedev, is trapped, so it is possible that she is not manipulating you; possible, of course, that in a wild moment she toys with the idea of escape, of romance, of being her own woman. But if that is the case, Field, then the dangers for you both are greater still."

Maretsky sighed deeply, reached over, and took a buff-colored folder from the top drawer of his desk. "Come on." He held the folder up. "Against my better judgment, I have helped you. Let's go downstairs to Crime."

Maretsky had set out the three pictures from the folder on the coffee table in front of Macleod's desk downstairs. Caprisi had his arm around Field's shoulder in a gesture of easy comradeship.

Field found the pictures difficult to look at.

The first woman was in a position strikingly similar to Lena Orlov's. She was handcuffed to a brass bed, the sheet rumpled, her body half-turned. She wore a black garter belt and stockings but was otherwise naked, her breasts and nipples small. Like Natasha, she had strong, well-toned arms, one of which was thrust across her stomach, as though in a last-ditch attempt to shield herself from the knife. There were perhaps ten or fifteen stab wounds in her breasts and belly. This girl's hair was long, like Natasha's, her face turned away from the camera.

Natasha. Natasha would look like this. For a moment Field had to fight to prevent himself from being sick.

The second woman had short, straight, black hair. She was completely naked. She wasn't handcuffed, and her body lay flat on the bed. The last photograph was of Lena Orlov.

"Which do you think was first?"

Neither of them answered, reluctant to turn this into a game.

Maretsky pointed to the one without handcuffs. "This woman. This is Irina. She was, I believe, a prostitute out-and-out, not a tea dancer." Maretsky paused, a chubby finger to his lips. "Murdered at home, not in the brothel, so an outside arrangement. Neighbors saw and heard nothing. Didn't know her, never spoke to her, rarely saw her. So they say. That is, so the French detectives say."

"One of your contacts?" Macleod asked.

Maretsky did not answer.

"The French did not try to solve the murder?" Macleod went on.

"It would appear not," Maretsky said.

"This girl, the first one, belonged to Lu also?" Caprisi asked.

Maretsky shrugged. "How can we know, when the French do not pursue these things? A grubby apartment—not one of his regular girls, I shouldn't think, but I'll talk about this in a minute." He looked at the photograph. "The second girl, the one with the long hair, was Anna Simonov, also a prostitute. Like Lena, she was handcuffed. There was more . . . scene setting. What's the point here?"

"Irina was not dressed up," Caprisi said. "Not handcuffed."

"Yes." He put his finger on Irina's picture. "Irina was the beginning, I think. It feels—to me, it feels rushed. There is no scene setting, no planning, it is just a sudden, violent act." Maretsky pointed at the other two photographs. "Afterwards, he gets to Anna and then Lena, and by now he knows what he wants. Now he is more confident, in control, more able to exactly dictate how he wants the evening to unfold."

"Why the . . ." Field looked at Maretsky. "Why the stockings and the handcuffs?"

He shook his head. "This is about sexual inadequacy, I think. This is what arouses him, or once did, but he has had a bad experience. He is immature or angry emotionally; he blames others for this inadequacy, which he feels deeply. It is not his fault, but that of the women, and . . ." He gestured at each of the three photographs in turn. "You see, these are not girls, these are women. All are in their twenties, at least, all fully grown, mature."

"So these are the women he blames?"

"Yes."

"Why?"

Maretsky hesitated. "We are outside the realms of modus operandi."

"So this stuff is a hobby," Caprisi said. "We know that."

"Perhaps such theories have no place in a police investigation."

"Get on with it, Maretsky," Macleod said with impatient affection.

Maretsky sighed. "I would have to be familiar with the precise nature of his sexual inadequacy to tell you why. All I can say here is that he feels this inadequacy deeply, and an accompanying sense of rage. The way the girls are asked to dress, the handcuffs, that is part of the picture."

"I think," Field said, "that Lu Huang may be impotent."

They all looked at him. Maretsky frowned.

"The Medvedev girl?" Macleod asked.

"Yes. She is summoned to his house in Rue Wagner, then made to wait for up to two hours in the living room on the first floor. Eventually, a housekeeper comes to fetch her and takes her to the bedroom on the second floor. She is required to stand in front of the bed and take off her clothes. Slowly." Field was trying not to show any emotion, but he could feel his cheeks reddening again. "Lu lies on the bed, an opium pipe next to him."

"And then what?"

"When she is naked, she stands there." Field hesitated, reluctant to share these intimacies. "He looks at her with glazed eyes and then she retrieves her clothes from the floor, goes to a dressing room, dresses again, and leaves by a separate door."

"That's it?"

"I think so, yes."

"That's what she told you?" Macleod smiled at him, benignly but with more than a hint of disbelief.

"Why would she lie about that?"

"He doesn't touch her, ask her to come over?" Maretsky asked.

Field hesitated. "I don't think so, no."

"She says not?"

"Yes."

"And you think she is telling you the truth?" Macleod said, daring him to be naive.

"I don't see why she would lie about it."

"To manipulate you, Field," Macleod said. "Which appears all too easy."

Maretsky was thinking, eyes narrowed behind his still-greasy glasses. "Has he ever asked her to wear anything in particular?"

"Not that I'm aware of."

"Not that you're aware of, or definitely not?"

"She says not."

Maretsky crossed his fat legs, his trousers only reaching two-thirds of the way to his feet. "The impotence would fit. He has become impotent, but does not blame himself and his addiction to the drug, but rather the women who once aroused him. He wants them to dress in the manner he once found so appealing, so that their punishment is more satisfying. It is one explanation." He looked around. "But only one."

Field leaned forward in his seat. "But why does he invite Natasha—the Medvedev woman—to his house at Rue Wagner? The others were all murdered in their own apartments."

"They were killed at home," Maretsky said, "but we do not know what occurred in the weeks or months preceding their deaths." He shook his head. "Whoever it is, he must wish to get to know his potential victims. There may have been previous occasions on which he asks them to strip for him—to attempt to arouse him. Perhaps he believes on each occasion that this girl is the one to excite him and to revive his performance, and his anger is therefore all the greater when it does not work. Perhaps he likes them to perform to stoke that anger, so that the murder is all the more satisfying." He uncrossed his legs.

They digested this. Field willed Maretsky to gather up the pictures and put them back in the folder.

Caprisi stood and leaned against the wall, beneath a shield from the New York Police Department. "The girl Irina was the first victim. The naked one."

"Yes. The first one took some savoring. It was exciting. Satisfying, but it probably took him time to bring himself to the point where he needed to do it again. Now he is into the habit of it. He is addicted. The intervals between are likely to get a little shorter; each one is not quite as thrilling as he anticipates. A law of diminishing returns."

"Unless there were others we don't know about," Caprisi said.

Maretsky turned toward him. "Yes."

"But why Russian girls?" Macleod asked. "He could kill any number of Chinese out there and no one would bat an eyelid. Why Russian girls in the Concession, and now the Settlement?"

"Testing the limits of his power. Perhaps also part of what excites him."

"But if it is Lu . . ." Field looked at each of them in turn. "Given his reputation for ruthlessness . . . I mean, why now? He could have been doing this for years."

"Dispensing death with an order to a subordinate is not the same as plunging the knife in them himself."

Macleod rubbed his chain between thumb and forefinger.

Caprisi took out his notebook. "You have an address for either of the girls?"

"My friend said this file and nothing further." Maretsky stood. "He is smart enough to know what will happen if he gives out addresses." He left without another word.

Field watched him walk to the lift. Then he reached over and put the photographs back into the file.

"If the French catch us asking about these girls in the Concession without permission, they'll create hell," Caprisi said.

"We've no choice," Macleod said. "But be discreet." He turned to Field. "What about the girl?"

"I'm still working on it."

"You have briefed her?"

"Yes."

"She knows what we require?"

"Yes."

"She has seen the ledgers?"

"No, but she will look."

"You really think she is reliable?"

Field hesitated.

"She'd better be, because if she isn't, I want her back inside."

"She is."

"It's Lu she fucks, no one else?"

"She doesn't—"

"She's not mentioned anyone else?"

"No. She goes down to his house."

"And does he ever come to her apartment?"

Field thought of the dressing gown she'd given him, with the short arms. He clenched his fist. "I guess sometimes, yes."

Macleod looked at him intently. "Lu doesn't know she was taken in?"

"No. I don't think so."

Macleod turned to Caprisi. "Are the handcuffs all the same make?"

The American took out the photographs again. He examined each one carefully. "Impossible to say," he said. When he put them back down on the table, the picture of Anna Simonov was on top.

"Are we missing something obvious?" Macleod asked. "What about Lena's other neighbors?"

"Chen talked to them all, but he got nothing."

Macleod turned to Field. "You're going back to the factory

this afternoon. You will travel with an armed escort. I have asked Charles Lewis to be present at three P.M.; it's his bloody factory. I might even come myself if I can get out of this damned budget meeting."

Field put the photographs away again. Then he folded the file and slipped it into his jacket pocket.

Thirty-two

ive minutes later Caprisi and Field were sitting alone in the canteen, drinking coffee.

"How's Chen?" Field asked.

"He's fine. We should go and see him this morning."

"We were lucky."

Caprisi didn't answer.

"Granger must have called Lu," Field said.

"We've been over that."

Field took out his letter from the bank and pushed it across the table.

Caprisi read it. "They certainly want you."

"This is the cabal paying money into my account to get me used to the idea, correct?"

"Correct."

"So they tempt me with the money before they make an approach."

"I don't know, but I'd say they want you badly, probably because of your social connections. That's why it's so much dough."

"What should I do?"

"Do nothing."

"Shouldn't I give it back?"

"To who?" Caprisi leaned his elbows on the table. "Field," he said, "tell me you don't really believe that this woman isn't fucking her boss."

Field looked at his partner and saw the warmth in his eyes.

"This isn't a great moment to be losing touch with reality."

"No. I understand that."

"There are thousands of good-looking Russian broads in this city, so don't do anything foolish, understand?"

"You don't think it's possible to free anyone from his clutches?"

"I doubt it."

They smoked in silence. Caprisi blew rings and watched them rise toward the ceiling.

Field suddenly felt dog-tired. He stubbed his cigarette out. "So are we going to do door-to-door inquiries on Avenue Joffre and try to find out where these women lived?"

"Probably."

"They have to be connected, don't they?"

Caprisi nodded. "I think so."

"I've asked Immigration to check their lists," Field said. "They must have a note of the girls' addresses. Even if they're not up-to-date, they'd provide a starting point. We could go down and speed things up."

"I was thinking of the Russian church," Caprisi said. "If nothing else, both women would have been buried there, right?"

Field nodded, feeling brighter.

"There would have to be some paperwork with a last residential address."

Field said, "Lena Orlov was from Kazan, so is Natasha. We know Irina was, too. They all attended the *New Shanghai Life* for at least one meeting. Is that coincidence? And why do we have no record of an Anna Simonov? Sergei claims not to have known any of them well, and yet I'm certain he knows exactly who they are. I think Natasha does, too."

"It may end up being my pleasure to beat it out of Sergei."

Field smiled. "I'm there first."

"Have you seen Granger this morning?"

"Not yet."

"From now on"—Caprisi smiled at his colleague again—

"try not to give him any idea of our movements." The American got up and patted him on the back. "I see the suit has taken a beating."

"Oh . . . yes. Got caught out in the rain. Sorry."

"It's *your* suit, Field."

Field led the way out of the canteen, the swinging doors banging shut behind them. Caprisi drew level with him on the stairs. "Make sure your girl plays ball."

"Why do you say that?"

"I say that because she'd better play ball."

"Or what?"

"Or I wouldn't want to be in her shoes."

"Why not?"

The American sighed. "Macleod wants to win this time. I wouldn't want to be the reason he doesn't."

They walked up the next flight, side by side, in silence.

Caprisi stopped. "I know what it's like, Field."

"What?"

"I told you, I once had it all. I can see a man in love. But please trust me: you've picked the wrong woman. You'll find someone else."

"Have you?"

Caprisi looked at him. "It's different for me," he said, and Field saw the aching loneliness in his eyes.

Only Yang was in the S.1 office and Field exchanged nods before retrieving the notebook from his desk. Perhaps it was his imagination, but the way she looked at him seemed to contain more than the usual hint of interest.

He heard Granger before he saw him. "Field." The tone was imperious. "Just the man. Come in."

The telephone rang, and Granger answered it, motioning to Field to take a seat. As Field watched the man's hand gripping the heavy black receiver, an idea took shape in his mind. He got up, indicating that he would be back. Prokopiev gave him an expression of mild surprise as he walked down the center of the office.

Field gathered speed down the stairs and almost punched through the swinging doors into the lobby, his footsteps echoing across the hallway beyond. If Granger had telephoned Lu before they'd been ambushed at the factory, then the switchboard would have logged the call.

There were two people in the switchboard room, a plump Chinese woman in a brown cardigan and a tiny man beyond her. The woman had her back to him. "Trying to connect you."

Field glanced down at the large notebook in front of her. The man was noting down the details of a call. The woman frowned and took her headphones off.

"All telephone calls placed through this exchange are logged, correct? I need to see the logbook for last night, please."

"I'm sorry, but—"

"Field, S.1." He showed her his card.

"But this is an internal matter. I would need permission."

"I'm afraid there is no time for that." Field reached over and pulled across the red book. He flicked through the pages. "This is new. Where's yesterday's?"

She was flustered. The man eyed them nervously as she pulled her chair back and opened the drawer.

Field took the new book. "Now I need a number for Lu Huang at 3 Rue Wagner. If you haven't got it, call the external operator, please."

She hesitated.

"Hurry, or I will have to get Granger down here and he won't like that."

While she put her headphones back on, Field flicked through the pages. During the day there had been hundreds of calls, but by teatime the volume had dwindled. He looked over as she wrote a number down on her pad, then scanned the entries between five and six.

He put the logbook in front of her, his finger marking the point, the blood pumping through his head. "Did you write this?"

She nodded. He could tell he was frightening her.

"It says Caprisi, correct?"

"Extension 2082. Detective Caprisi, yes."

"Caprisi?"

"Detective Caprisi, yes."

"It must be a mistake."

She didn't respond.

"It must be a mistake." He took a deep breath. "You put through his call to Lu Huang?"

She nodded.

"You recognized Caprisi's voice?"

She hesitated. "I think so, yes."

"You think so, or you did?"

"I did, yes."

"You recognize everyone's voice?"

"I've worked here ten years, sir. I do, yes."

"So it was Caprisi."

"That's what he said."

"You asked for his name and that is what he said."

"Yes, sir."

"Caprisi is English, right?"

"Yes, sir."

"No he's not. He's American."

She was flustered. "That's right."

"So it was or wasn't Caprisi?"

"He said it was."

"And his accent was American?"

"Yes, sir." She looked as if she would burst into tears.

"You must have made a mistake."

"No, sir . . . no. I listened to the first few seconds. A Russian gentleman answered the telephone and he said, 'Caprisi, yes.' I remember."

"All right," Field said quietly. "All right."

Thirty-three

utside, Field leaned against the wall by the stairwell, out of sight of the lobby, and sank down until he was sitting on the step.

He stared at his battered, scuffed shoes. He hated his damned shoes, hated the poverty of the past and the unexplained wealth of the present. He hated himself for wanting friendship and love and being weak enough to seek it in the wrong places.

He placed his head in his hands, his eyes closed.

"God," he whispered. He felt tired. He could not raise his head.

Field heard footsteps on the stairs and knew that he should move, but could not.

They stopped close by. "You all right, polar bear?"

With an effort, Field raised his head. Caprisi was looking at him, concerned.

"Had some bad news?"

Field sighed. "In a way."

"Want to tell me about it?"

"Not really."

Caprisi smiled. "Then we'd better get going."

Field watched him walk away, then stood, took off his jacket, and adjusted his holster. He followed the American out onto the stone steps. The dark cumulus had been replaced by a limitless azure sky and scalding heat.

They climbed into the back of the Buick.

Field assumed that they were going to the Russian church,

as Caprisi had suggested earlier, but the driver continued on past its distinctive spires to Route Père Robert and the imposing modern stone building that housed the Hôpital Ste.-Marie. He parked by the wide, circular veranda at the front. Field squinted as he stepped out into the sunlight.

"All right?" Caprisi said as they entered the cool hallway.

"Fine."

"You seem tense."

"I'm fine."

Caprisi shrugged, leaving it.

They stood before the reception desk. With its black-and-white-checkered floor and swaying tropical plants, the hospital reminded Field of the police stations they'd visited in the Concession.

The French receptionist directed them up the wide stone steps to the floor above. They passed two nurses in starched white uniforms helping a man in pajamas with a broken leg and then another lying on a makeshift bed, fast asleep. The landing was tall and airy, enormous windows on their right open to the barely perceptible breeze.

Chen's room was at the far end of the building. He was asleep. A tiny woman sat by his bed, her head bent. As soon as she saw Caprisi, she stood, bowed, and began to speak with machine-gun rapidity in Shanghainese. Field understood enough to know that she was thanking Caprisi and that he was trying to say it was nothing.

Chen suddenly awoke and spoke sharply to her, and she bowed once more, eyes down, and darted from the room, closing the door quietly behind her.

Chen pushed himself up. He pulled the pillows up behind him. The windows were large in here, too, the whiteness of the walls and sheets making Field squint again.

"I'm sorry for my wife," Chen said. "She is most grateful."

Field nodded, not understanding what she was grateful for.

In the silence that followed, Caprisi took out his cigarettes, lit one, and then tossed the packet to Chen.

"Better not," he said. "The nurses."

"French nurses," Caprisi said. "You lucky bastard."

Chen smiled.

"How is it?" Field asked.

Chen nodded.

Field wondered how much Chen knew of Lu Huang and what exactly Caprisi had meant about them growing up together. "I guess you'll need a long rest," he said.

"Not long."

"A long rest," Caprisi repeated.

"Not long."

"If you think we can't get along without you, you're wrong."

"I'm not wrong."

Caprisi smiled again. "You're an obstinate bastard."

"We must survive." Despite his determination, Chen was clearly still weak. He kept closing his eyes and letting his head rest against his pillow before remembering they were there and snapping them open again.

Eventually, he did drift off to sleep and they let themselves out.

Chen's wife was sitting on a bench in the corridor. Caprisi spoke to her briefly, but her gratitude began to embarrass him, so he touched her shoulder and they went down to the main hall.

"I guess," Field said as they emerged into the sunshine, "the commissioner does take care—"

Caprisi looked at him sharply.

"It's not the cheapest hospital," Field said.

"The commissioner doesn't pay for a thing."

Field frowned.

"Are you all right?" Caprisi asked again.

"You've asked me that already."

"You keep staring at me like I just fucked your sister or something."

Once inside the car, Field offered to pay half of Chen's medical costs, but Caprisi just shook his head curtly and continued to stare out of the window.

His mood seemed suddenly as somber as Field's.

"Do you know Lu?" Field asked.

"In what way?"

"Was our interview the other day the first time you've had any direct dealings with him?"

"More or less." Caprisi thought about it. "Yes it was. Why?"

"No reason," Field said.

They stepped through the gate of the Russian church a few minutes later and walked down a stone path, past the dark gravestones, with their extravagant gold lettering.

Inside, the church was dark, the air heavy with the smell of incense. Their footsteps on the flagstone floor echoed around the dome above them. The altar was covered in a white satin cloth, upon which a gold cross stood between two oil paintings. The first was of the Virgin Mary with her infant son; the second showed Christ on the cross. The atmosphere of the place was both opulent and forbidding, in stark contrast, Field thought, to the deprivation of a significant proportion of its congregation.

It made him think of his father. At least he had practiced what he preached. Generosity to others—outside the family—was, Field supposed, one of his few redeeming features.

A priest in a long black robe and beard appeared from behind a pillar and walked toward them. He wore square glasses.

"Good morning," Caprisi said.

The man nodded.

"You speak English?"

He shook his head.

"*Vous parlez français?*" Field asked.

"*Bien sûr.*"

Field glanced at his colleague. "*Nous sommes policiers, et nous enquetons sur les morts…non, les meurtres des femmes Russes. Deux femmes. Irina Ignatiev et Anna Simonov."* Field enunciated the names with exaggerated care. *"Nous pensons… nous croyons qu'elles sont…enterrées ici, les deux. Vraiment, oui?"*

The priest shrugged.

"Si elles habitaient ici, il suit, je crois qu'elles seraient enter-rées ici—oui?"

"Exactement—ou d'ailleurs?"

"Anna etait mouri le premier mai; Irina un mois avant. Nous avons besoin de leurs addresses—vous avez les papiers, je crois?"

"Bien sûr."

The priest studied them for a moment and then quietly turned away. Field felt unreasonably tense and thought that Caprisi was, too.

"You explained?" the American asked.

"He has the papers. He seems cooperative—he's just gone to look them up."

Field wanted to smoke but thought it would be inappropriate here.

After about ten minutes the priest returned, walking with his head down, as if deep in thought.

"Mais non—Irina, elle, je me souviens, je me souviens faire les papiers, mais ils n'existent plus. Pardon."

"Les papiers sont…disparus?"

"Il m'apparait que oui."

"Translate, please," Caprisi said.

"He remembers Irina, but her papers have gone."

"Mais, vous vous souvenez de l'écrire?"

"Oui."

"Vous vous rappelez l'addresse d'Irina?"

"Non."

"Et Anna?"

"Je ne me rappele pas. Peut-être un autre prêtre."

"Nous pouvons voir les papiers?"

The priest shrugged. *"Servez-vous."*

"Come on," Field said.

"What?"

"He says we can look at the papers."

They were led into a cramped office with a desk and three metal filing cabinets. It had a picturesque view of a garden through a mullioned window, and was much lighter than the church. The priest opened a drawer and gestured with his hand. Field stepped forward and began to flick through the papers. They were filed in alphabetical order. He looked through "I" and then "S," which was in another drawer. He pulled out the forms on either side of where "Ignatiev, Irina" and "Simonov, Anna" should have been and handed them to Caprisi. They were all the same, written in black ink, with the name at the top and an address next to the section that was headed *Residing at.* The names of close relatives were listed in the bottom right-hand corner. The next of kin for each of the deceased had signed at the foot of the page. For some, this section had been left blank.

Field took the forms from Caprisi, put them back into the cabinet, and pushed the drawer shut. He turned to face the priest. *"Nous vous remercions pour votre assistance—y-a-t'il un autre moyen des apprendre?"*

The priest shrugged again. *"Je suis désolé."*

Field and Caprisi walked slowly through the church, the priest following them noiselessly. As they stepped outside into the bright sunlight, he stood behind them and pointed toward the corner by the gate. *"Là-bas."*

"Irina?"

"Irina, oui. Là-bas."

They found her in the far corner, the earth newly turned around her grave. It was shorter than Field had imagined, with gravel scattered on top and a simple, black stone. *Irina Ignatiev,* the inscription read, *1899–1926.*

Only the year dates were given, and there were no homilies or expressions of affection, regret, or loss. It was as if she had never really existed. They looked at the grave in silence. In the center was a small stone flowerpot, but it was empty.

"Give me a minute, will you?" Caprisi asked.

Field hesitated.

"Alone."

Field walked to the gate, lit a cigarette, and smoked it. Caprisi had moved over to a grave, two or three rows in from the far wall. As Field watched, the American sank to his knees, his head bent in prayer.

Field felt like a voyeur and turned away. He finished his cigarette, smoked another, then waited with his hands in his pockets.

Caprisi walked back in silence.

As they got back into the car, they both saw the gray Citroën parked opposite. Two men in suits sat in the front seat, with the windows shut.

"French?" Field asked, looking over his shoulder as they drove off.

"Seems like it. The French police are in Lu's pocket. Maybe he has set them onto us."

"How did they find out we were here?"

Caprisi stared at him. "Perhaps there is a leak."

Field felt his face reddening again and turned back to face the road. The Frenchmen had not followed them.

"To save you having to go back to look," Caprisi said, "I did meet someone else here. Her name was Olga and she thought I wouldn't propose to her because she was a Russian tea dancer, but she never understood that it was about Jane, or rather that it was about me. I wanted to keep a sense of distance. I couldn't bear any more loss. She got pneumonia, but her friends say she died because I had said I would never marry her and she'd given up hope. Was that selfish of me?"

Field saw the hurt deep in his colleague's eyes. "I don't know."

"Her friends didn't tell me she was ill, and by the time I found out, she was dead." The American shook his head slowly. "That's why I say be careful. Sometimes, if you've suffered as much as they have, love can create an unbearable sense of expectation, of hope." Caprisi appeared almost to be pleading with him. "Do you understand, Field?"

Field cleared his throat and nodded in response, not trusting his voice.

"Guilt is a heavy burden."

"I know."

Field turned around once more, to check again that they were not being followed.

"Just so that we're clear, the papers were stolen," Caprisi said.

"From the church? Yes."

"The girls were buried there, but their papers have been removed."

"Irina was buried there, as you saw, but the priest didn't remember Anna Simonov."

"Someone is cleaning up," Caprisi said. He glanced again in the mirror.

Caprisi invited Field to join him for lunch in the canteen. It was now almost deserted, only a few dishes left in the big metal serving trays. Field again ordered beef. He wished, as he sat down, that he'd been able to think of a quick excuse for taking lunch somewhere else.

"Macleod has got two Chinese tecs in plain clothes doing door-to-door down Avenue Joffre," the American said. "They'll be less conspicuous and should turn up the Russian girls' addresses."

"Good."

They ate for a while in silence. Caprisi went to get two glasses from the side and a jug of purified water from the end of the table. Field nodded when he was offered some.

"You going to say anything?" the American asked.

Field shook his head. "Probably not."

"Get out of bed on the wrong side?"

"Something like that."

"You going to tell me what's bothering you?"

Field hesitated. He recalled the catch in Caprisi's voice as he'd talked of the dead Russian girl, and the compassion in his eyes. Then he thought of the telephone call. "Are we right to trust each other?" he asked.

"And what's that supposed to mean?"

"It's just a question."

Caprisi sighed. He shook his head and leaned back in his chair. "Jesus Christ, Field."

Field held his stare.

The American gestured with his glass, his dark eyes again intense. "I tell you what. I'm going to make a conscious effort not to be insulted by this, my friend, and, as an act of sentimental generosity, I'm going to put it down to the fact that you're new to all this."

Field shifted uneasily in his seat.

"You were making an accusation?"

Field closed his eyes for a moment, exhausted. "No."

"Just a sense of disillusionment?"

"Yes."

"It comes to us all." There was a long silence. Caprisi put his glass down. "You asked about Al Capone."

"Yes."

"Everybody knows about Capone, but he started as the lieutenant to someone else."

Field shook his head.

"John Torrio. After Prohibition, he began bootlegging in Chicago when Big Bill Thompson was mayor. He was clever. Sophisticated and diplomatic, not a thug like Capone. He believed in total control. All officers got bribed according to their rank. All elections were rigged." Caprisi paused. "They didn't throw you out if you weren't on the take, but you couldn't get anything done, and everyone thought you kind of strange. Prohibition was the enemy. Everyone in the city thought it was crazy, everyone drank. But you know what? That let the genie out of the bottle, and now it's out, no one will ever get it back in." Caprisi picked up a forkful of food. "John Torrio retired to Italy last year. Know how much he had in the bank?"

Field shook his head again.

"Thirty million U.S. dollars. Thirty million in five years. No one in organized crime ever made that much money before."

"Did you know Capone?"

Caprisi shook his head.

"Then why are you telling me about it?"

"I'm trying to explain."

"Explain what?"

"You don't understand the nature of this city. Every man who comes to serve here comes to escape or to enrich himself. No one belongs here, so I guess that makes it worse than Chicago. Men come out to make something for themselves and the choice is simple. They can be honest, save a little, go home with a pension and live a modest life. Or they can get rich in a way they never imagined, by turning a blind eye . . . turning their eyes toward home and dreaming of the house and the green fields they'll own."

"I don't understand what you're saying."

"What I'm saying is that the disease has already spread. Macleod has something that is priceless in this city. He's chosen to be honest when he could be rich. Don't ask me why he is the way he is, but he pathologically hates corruption." Caprisi pushed his food away. "He is the last chance—the last, Field—and we have no choice but to stand behind him and to trust each other."

Thirty—four

Charlie Lewis was not at the factory on Yuen-Ming Road at three o'clock.

Macleod had skipped his meeting and joined them, with the promise that the questioning would be left to Caprisi. Field was in the middle car, Caprisi in the front, and a total of seven armed officers stepped out inside the factory gate. This time, however, the factory was full, the machines in noisy operation.

An anxious security guard showed them up to the glass box above the workshop floor, where they were greeted by the Scottish factory manager. Field could see immediately that he was nervous. "A snifter?" the man asked.

Caprisi and Field shook their heads as he poured himself one. Field looked down at the police officers standing guard by the door. Macleod scowled at the man.

"Gordon Braine. I've not introduced myself."

Caprisi ignored his outstretched hand. Braine had a long nose with hairs poking out of it and hollow cheeks. He looked ill.

"What happened last night?" Caprisi asked.

"I'm sorry, dreadful thing to happen. Glad no one . . . you know . . ." He sat, taking a sip of his whiskey.

"No one except a driver whose family won't be quite as relaxed as you are today," Caprisi said. "What time do you normally shut up?"

"Seven. Normally seven. But, of course . . ."

"Go on."

"Last night our head of security received a call, saying that we should close early."

"And what was the reason?"

"No reason was given, but . . ."

"But what?"

Braine avoided their eyes. "These are difficult times, Detective. Our workforce is Chinese. Strikes, protests. I said we shouldn't give in and I didn't see why—but this is a man whom we trust to be in touch with . . . you know."

"The underworld."

"Yes. And with whatever intelligence there is—the Bolsheviks, the protests. Some factories have been damaged, of course, burned even, when they are the subject of intimidation and they—"

"So you were being brave?"

Braine took another sip of whiskey. "Our man was insistent that we must vacate the floor immediately and go home. I did not understand it, but as I said, he was sufficiently alarmed to make me feel there was no choice but to comply."

"You didn't think to tell the police?"

"I thought it would blow over—just one of those things that happen here, from time to time." He took another sip and gained confidence. "Doing business here—it's a far cry from Scotland."

Macleod fiddled with the cross around his neck. Field was glad that he had chosen to come along. Out of the office, he exuded a quiet confidence and strength.

"Where is this man?" Caprisi asked.

Braine looked confused.

"The head of security, where is he?"

"Oh, he is . . ." The confidence disappeared. "He is ill today, I believe."

"Ill?"

"I believe so, yes."

"How convenient."

"I'm sorry. I understand it must be frustrating and I can quite appreciate—"

"Where does he live?"

"I'm not sure we actually have an address. You see—"

"You employ a man as your head of security and you don't know where he lives?"

"In the Chinese city, I know that, but . . . He was employed before my time, and he is always here, in place when I arrive and still here when I go. I never thought to ask. He really controls the shop floor. He would have details of the employees, and he ensures—"

"He will be in tomorrow?"

Braine was embarrassed now. Field did not think that he was carrying this off at all well. He was coming to the conclusion—as he could see Caprisi was—that the man was frightened. "I do not think he will be in tomorrow. He said he was quite ill."

"You will contact us when he reports back to work?"

"Of course."

"There is a consignment of sewing machines to be shipped?"

"Yes," he said, eager to please. "They go on Saturday at midnight."

"From here at midnight?"

"N-no," Braine stammered, realizing he might have said something he shouldn't. "No. The ship sails at midnight."

"Why do you know what time the ship sails?"

There was silence. Braine was not a clever man, and Field could see he was trying hard to work out the direction of Caprisi's questioning.

"What time will it be loaded up?"

"I do not understand."

"What time will the goods be taken from here to the ship?"

"To the ship?"

"To the ship, yes. During the day or at night?"

"Before it sails, I suppose."

Caprisi took a step toward Braine, his expression quietly menacing. "Mr. Braine, I think we are in danger of misunderstanding each other here. You have just told me that your shipment—a major shipment of your factory's goods—leaves Shanghai at midnight on Saturday. You are the manager. There is a reason you know the exact time of the ship's departure, and I'm sure you will be wanting to see the goods get off from the factory in proper order, so you're now going to tell me when they will be taken from here. During the day or at night?"

"In the evening."

"After nightfall?"

"Yes. I mean, I don't know. In the evening, that is what I've been told."

"And is there something untoward about this shipment?"

"No." He said it convincingly, then made the mistake of repeating his denial. "No, absolutely not."

"Just sewing machines?"

"Yes, of course."

"Being loaded under the cover of night."

"No." Panic crossed his face at the realization of the extent of his mistake. "Not—I mean, in the evening, that's all."

"Just a coincidence that they're loaded a few hours before the ship sails."

"No. I mean, yes, it is not—"

"Is that when cargo is usually loaded?"

"Yes. It depends."

"I would have thought it more logical to load during the day, when you can see what you are doing."

They heard the sound of footsteps on the stairs, and a languid whistle. Charlie Lewis appeared, dressed in a white linen suit and white Panama hat. "Good day, chaps . . . Dickie?" He threw his hat onto one of the chairs and ran a hand over his slicked-back hair. "Macleod."

Field was embarrassed. "This is Detective Caprisi."

"Pleased to meet you, Caprisi." He offered his hand and

the American shook it, his eyes wary. Lewis shook hands with
Macleod with a formal nod, though Field could tell there was
no warmth between the two men.

"Sorry I'm late. Bit of a long meeting, which I should be
grateful to you boys for freeing me from." He turned around
and looked down at the factory floor. "Never been here before,"
he said, offering his hand to Gordon Braine as an afterthought.
"You must be the manager. Charles Lewis."

"Yes, sir, of course."

"What have you chaps been up to, then? Sorry about last
night. Dreadful business. The commissioner called me this
morning and I'm glad this Chinese lad is on the mend."

"The driver is not."

Lewis was not unsettled. "No, well, sorry to hear that." He
sat down and looked at Field. "I think you're right, old boy.
Whatever the hell is going on, this chap Lu needs a lesson."
He grinned at Field. "By the way, gather you're to sample
Mrs. Granger's legendary home cooking. Got a call asking if I
wished to join the merry throng on Friday."

Field smiled thinly, acutely aware that Caprisi and Macleod were staring at him.

"I think Penelope and Geoffrey will be coming along."

Field knew his face was reddening.

Lewis turned toward Caprisi and Macleod. "What can I do
for you? Sorted it out with Brandon here?"

"Braine," the American corrected him.

"Braine, yes."

"Did you know the factory had been evacuated last night?"

"No."

"No one informed you?"

Lewis picked up his hat and began to turn it in his hand.
"Fraser's is a pretty big company, as you know."

"I'm aware of that."

"I'm not informed of every last—not of much, actually, on
this kind of level. The taipan's role is really strategic. It would
be the same with all companies of this size. As I said, I've
never been here before, let alone met the good Mr. Brandon."

"Braine."

"Quite."

"So you know nothing of the shipment this Saturday night?"

"Shipment?"

"A consignment of sewing machines is leaving this Saturday, and they are, Mr. Braine here has informed us, being loaded at night, which is highly unusual."

"Are they? Is it?"

"You're not aware of anything untoward about the shipment?"

Lewis was showing signs of annoyance. "Untoward?"

"It's just sewing machines?"

"I've no idea." He turned to Braine. "Is it sewing machines?"

"Mostly, sir. There are a few other electrical goods, but it is mostly sewing machines."

Lewis turned back. "There you are."

Field could see that Caprisi was trying to control his temper. "Perhaps we could check the inventory?"

Braine did not hesitate, was almost nodding with enthusiasm. Field knew, before they left the office, that they would find nothing of interest.

The consignment to be shipped was being kept in a storage area to the rear, the machines themselves stacked in rows, close to a wall of wooden crates that stretched almost to the ceiling.

"Fortunate they've not been packed yet," Lewis said.

Caprisi crouched beside one of the machines.

"Could we get someone to take it apart?" Macleod asked.

"Take it apart?"

"Yes."

"Of course." Lewis looked bewildered, as if not understanding why they could possibly wish to do this.

Braine went back through to the shop floor and returned with an assistant carrying a toolbox.

They all watched in silence as the man started to take apart the machine next to Caprisi.

Field wondered if Lewis enjoyed putting on a performance for his social inferiors.

When it lay in pieces, Lewis looked at his watch. "Have you chaps got anything else?"

"No," Caprisi said curtly.

"Good. Then, if you don't mind, I shall leave you in the capable hands of . . . my colleague here."

"Good of you to come," Macleod said.

Lewis said, "It's been my pleasure. Always happy to help the force, as you know. Richard, do you have a moment?"

Field followed Lewis out through the factory floor, into the sunshine. He watched a flock of seagulls circling a chimney on the opposite side of the road.

"Word of warning, Richard, as a friend."

Field looked at him. Lewis's face was serious, his eyes apparently sincere.

"Be careful of Natasha Medvedev."

Field didn't respond.

"She's a great ride and a woman of skill."

Field's anger was like a storm, instantly whipped up; the image of she and Lewis lying together crashed through his mind.

"Don't go down with a sinking ship, or imagine to do so is a painful romantic tragedy."

"I think I've heard enough."

"Natasha has turned deceit into an art form." Lewis's face was almost earnest now; there was no sign of the indolent playboy leer Field had grown used to. "I've been here a long time, and I'm trying, again, to help. I saw your face the other night—"

"Perhaps you've been here too long."

"Perhaps."

"And I don't need any help."

"That's up to you, but set aside romantic notions for a moment and consider the possibility that Natasha is not the victim you imagine."

"What do you mean?"

"Lu is a powerful man. Through him, she wields power. Believe me. All the more so once rivals are eliminated. She's a woman of ambition."

Field thought of the way Natasha had sat, straight-backed, close to Lu in the nightclub—a possession.

"Perhaps they deserve each other," Lewis said.

"How do you know about—"

"Fraser's is the biggest company in Shanghai, Richard." His look was hard now. "It's my job to know."

"So . . ."

"You are playing with fire, and you will be burned."

"So I keep being advised."

"Then you have friends who know the city and care about you." Lewis shook his head. "It's part of being a policeman, I know. It's not a job for a man of breeding, and I'd like to bring you on board, but I can't do that if you're not going to exercise good judgment."

"I don't want to be on board."

Lewis put his hat back on. "That's your choice, Richard. But as things stand, I don't give much for your chances of staying afloat."

"What do you mean?"

"Your uncle's a good man, Field. But there is only so much I'll do for him." He lowered his voice. "For a man in his position, old Lu shows restraint on occasions, but not for much longer, I wouldn't think."

Thirty-five

he three of them waited in the middle car outside the factory. Macleod was beside the driver, Caprisi and Field in the back. The American had suggested they go on to see if the captain of the ship had returned from Blood Alley, but Macleod remained silent. It was hot, so Field wound down his window.

He knew what his colleagues were thinking.

"Does it go all the way to the top?" Caprisi asked. "Does Lewis know what is going on here?"

"It would fit," Macleod said. "Lewis in business with Lu on the shipments, a highly profitable arrangement. Lu gives Lewis the girls as a bit of entertainment. It gets a little rough, but Lu cleans up behind him."

Field watched a group of Chinese and Eurasian schoolgirls walking along the sidewalk. He turned back and took out his cigarettes. "Lewis must be the richest man in Shanghai. He doesn't need the money."

"Greed," Macleod said. "The rich can be greedy, too." He shook his head as Field offered him a cigarette. "But if the murders are down to Lewis, we will have to tread even more carefully."

Field saw his own puzzlement reflected in Caprisi's expression.

"He's the taipan of Fraser's, for Christ's sake," Macleod said.

"A few days ago," Field said, "Lewis took me to a club—a brothel."

"Which one?" Macleod asked.

"Delancey's." Field cleared his throat. "I extricated myself, but as I left I passed his room."

"He was fucking someone."

"There was a girl. A Chinese girl. She was handcuffed to the bed. She was screaming."

"We'll need more than that." Macleod opened his door. "I'll take the last car back to the office." He slammed it shut and stalked off. Caprisi tapped the driver on the shoulder. "The wharf."

As they moved away, Field said, "Why was he being so negative?"

"It's complicated."

"I thought we were all agreed."

"Lewis isn't one of his supporters, and putting him in the frame for murder . . ." Caprisi whistled quietly. "It's not the best time for that, is it? Unless the evidence is overwhelming, which it isn't. I'm not sure the Municipal Council is going to like one of its candidates for commissioner going after the most powerful businessman in Shanghai."

"So we wait until it happens again?"

Caprisi sighed. "Calm down, Field . . . or should I call you 'Dickie'?"

"He's nothing to do with me."

"Dickie? They call you 'Dickie'?"

"He was patronizing me."

"You've nice friends," Caprisi said. "Charming."

"He's not my friend."

"Of course he's not. He sure is an arrogant bastard, I'll say that. What did he want outside?"

Field sighed. "Nothing."

At the wharf the fat customs officer was not there—on the river, his assistant said—so they made their own way down to the SS *Saratoga*.

Caprisi had not dismissed their escort, and the effect was

exactly as he'd intended. As they walked up the gangplank, the Indian deckhand they had seen the other day got to his feet and scrambled into the cabin. Caprisi banged on the door, and a few moments later the captain appeared, hastily tucking a filthy vest into his trousers. He was an Indian, too, much older and fatter, with a few days' growth on his chin. He'd obviously been asleep.

"Enjoy Blood Alley?" Caprisi asked.

"What do you want?"

"We have some questions."

The captain studied them for a few moments, then led them through the doorway and up to the bridge. There was a rag over one of the brass instruments and he used it to wipe his forehead.

"You're leaving this Saturday," Caprisi said.

The captain nodded.

"What are you carrying?"

"I cannot remember without looking at the manifest."

"Sewing machines?"

"Perhaps. I don't know."

"What do you normally carry from this company?"

"Electrical goods." He yawned. "I don't know—whatever they ask us to carry."

"Why are you loading the goods at night? On Saturday night, after dark?"

"We load them when they bring them."

"Isn't that unusual? Doesn't it make you suspicious?"

He shook his head. "Why?"

"Wouldn't it be easier for you to load shipments during the day?"

"Easier for me, yes, but I am not paying. If they want to load at night, we load at night. They are the customer. What are their reasons? How can I know? Maybe they have a full shift on Saturday and want to wait until the last of the machines are done before beginning to load."

Field could see Caprisi thinking. This man was not going to be caught out.

Caprisi placed one hand on the wheel and looked out toward the deck. "All right, Captain . . ."

"Sendosa."

"All right, Captain Sendosa. Thank you for your time."

They retraced their steps. As he got into the car, Caprisi said, "He's in on it. Whatever is going on, he's in on it as well."

Field watched the American for a moment before turning to look out of the window at the activity on the wharf.

Field climbed the stairs to the Immigration Department quickly, arriving just as it was closing. The woman he'd spoken to before took a lot of persuading, but eventually she led him into the back, along a corridor, and up the stairs to a room on the floor above, where the dust hung in the air, illuminated by the rays of the dying sun. A small Westerner with thick glasses sat hunched over a ledger by the door. The rest of the room was filled from floor to ceiling with steel filing cabinets. There was barely enough room to squeeze between them.

"Mr. Pendelby, this is Mr. Field."

They shook hands. The man had a nervous smile.

"Mr. Pendelby has worked through 1918 and 1919, without success. If you wish to help, you can begin with 1921, but I must insist it is only one hour. I have to close then. Mr. Pendelby, you must go home now."

"I'm happy to do one more hour." He smiled at Field, who returned the compliment.

"Very well. I shall return in one hour. Otherwise, you may come back tomorrow, Mr. Field."

Field smiled and she turned to go.

"You're on 1920?" Field asked.

Pendelby nodded. He tugged awkwardly at his mustache.

"Thanks for your assistance. I appreciate it."

Pendelby nodded again, then, without speaking, got up and disappeared down one of the corridors between the files. He emerged a few moments later with four thick, leather-bound ledgers. "The first half of 1920," he said.

Field took the top book down, opened it, and began reading. All entries in the ledger were chronological. He soon realized that the best way to proceed was to run his finger over the names, so as to be certain he wasn't skimming, but even so, it was difficult. The book provided a record of information about nonresident country citizens: every arrival, every departure, every change of address. Resident country citizens had their passports examined upon arrival and did not have to attend Customs to register officially, but nonresidents—like Russians— had to wade through a mine of bureaucracy for years. Every time they moved, they were required to inform Customs, and failure to do so could result in heavy fines and even imprisonment. Some names appeared frequently as a result, and many, if not most, were Russian. It made it a tedious task.

Field kept on having to go back on himself. He told himself that all he needed was one address to begin a proper hunt for Irina Ignatiev or Anna Simonov.

After about half an hour—at a guess, since he did not have a watch—he stepped outside and had a cigarette.

When he returned to the room, Pendelby looked up and smiled at him again, before continuing with his own work.

Field glanced again at the columns in front of him: *Markov, Alexander,* he read, *residing at 47a Avenue Joffre, to Harbin by train. Julius, Anthony, residing at 27 Bubbling Well Road, to Cape Town, South African passport, no. 407681, on the SS Sarawak.* Beside this, at the end of the column, a clerk had written, *not intending to return.* The next entry was for a *Semtov, Vladimir, of 7c Bubbling Well Road.* The clerk had written, *to Harbin, return November, or before if business completed.*

Field had reached June 1920 by the time the woman returned, and he recognized that he was too tired to continue.

"I'm sorry, Mr. Field," she said gently. "You can come back tomorrow, but we must lock up."

"Of course. What time do you open?"

"At eight."

"I'll be here."

· · ·

Field dozed on his bed at Carter Road for two or three hours.

Swinging his legs off the bed when he awoke, he tried to rub the tiredness from his eyes. He washed his face in the basin at the other end of the corridor.

He nodded at the steward sitting nearby, then walked down the stairs and slipped out into the heat of the night. He wondered where Lewis had gone to school. Eton, almost certainly.

Field was carrying his jacket over his arm, no longer bothering to conceal his holster, which slapped against his chest as he walked. He put on the trilby Geoffrey had given him.

He thought he ought to go and see Geoffrey and Penelope. He wanted their wisdom and support and experience. But he no longer felt entirely in control of his own actions.

It was clear tonight, but close again, and there were damp patches under his arms by the time he reached Foochow Road.

The light was on in her apartment.

He stood in the shadows, away from the streetlamp on the far side, and lit a cigarette, rarely taking his eyes from the balcony above.

The door onto the balcony opened and she stepped out, a glass in her hand, the sound of jazz from the radio drifting out into the night. She bent over to water a plant, then straightened again. She was wearing a loose, bright yellow dress. She turned and looked down at the street.

His heart pounded.

Was she looking at him?

Natasha stood motionless. Then she turned swiftly away and stepped inside.

Field threw the cigarette into the drain. He took off his hat and wiped the sweat from his forehead.

He walked quickly across the street and into the lobby. In the lift he saw the heat in his face, the sweat on his chin and lips and forehead.

The sound of the radio was louder in the hall outside her flat, and Field stood in the semidarkness, listening to his breathing. He stepped forward and was about to knock when the door opened.

She seemed taller, fiercer, more beautiful, her dress split almost to the waist.

He took another pace forward, their noses touching, then their lips, her mouth warm, her hands running through the wetness of his hair and wiping the sweat from his forehead.

Her skin was cool to the touch.

"I'm—"

"I'm weak," she said.

Thirty-six

atasha rolled Field over onto his chest. The white cotton sheets were luxuriously cool on this side of the bed. She lay on top of him, her heart thumping in time with his, both of them covered in a thin sheen of sweat.

He closed his eyes and drifted off to sleep. Sometime later he became aware of the soft touch of her lips against his ear. "Wake up, Richard."

"I'm awake."

"You're sleeping."

"I'm . . . comfortable."

"Too comfortable." She rolled him onto his back and straddled him again. She smiled. Very slowly, her hair gathering around his neck and face, she lowered herself. Her fingers touched the side of his face gently as her lips met his.

Now Field did sleep, and when he awoke, she was looking at him, leaning on her elbow.

"What's the time?"

She shrugged. "Almost dawn."

"You've been watching all night?"

"No. You sleep peacefully."

He rolled over onto his back. "I slept deeply." He noticed a clock on the bedside table and leaned over to try to get a closer look. "Five," he said.

Field stared at the ceiling. A streetlamp lit the corner of the room nearest to the window, but the rest was lost in the darkness. She was kneeling in a pool of light on the side of the bed.

"Do you have any cigarettes?" he asked.

She took one from the packet on the bedside table and lit it. She threw another across to him and leaned over with the match still alight. She put a shell ashtray between them and they smoked in silence.

When they had finished, she said, "You will have to go soon." She took the ashtray and lay down, moving closer so that her back was alongside him. As he rolled over, she brought her knees up and took hold of his arm, wrapping it around her stomach and caressing his hand. "Hold me tight, Richard."

They lay still, her body warm.

"You're frightened," he said.

"Of course."

There was another long silence.

"Whatever anyone says," she said almost inaudibly, "I loved you."

"What do you mean 'loved'?"

"Perhaps the end will be a relief," she said.

"The end of what?"

She did not answer, so he spun her around roughly. Her eyes and face were wet with her tears. "What do you mean?"

Natasha looked into his eyes without answering.

"What do you mean?" Field rolled off the bed. "What do you mean 'the end will be a relief'? Will you stop talking like that?"

"I'm just tired, Richard."

Field breathed out heavily. "Me too. Want to know why?" he asked. "I've been looking for the lives of two more ghosts, Irina Ignatiev and Anna Simonov, and can we find any trace of them?"

She lay on her back, staring at the ceiling. He waited in vain for her to respond.

"And all the time," he went on, "you know exactly who they are."

She remained absolutely still.

Field moved around to her side of the bed and sat beside her. "You tell me you dream of a life in Venice or Paris. Well, we can do it. We can stop Lu. But not unless you start to tell me the truth."

She turned to face him, but he knew, from the distant look in her eyes, that he'd lost her again. "I want a drink of water," he said, and before she could answer, he stepped into the corridor.

There was a glass by the sink and he filled it with some purified water from a jug and drank greedily. He returned to the living room with a full glass for Natasha.

Field glanced toward the balcony and the clock tower above the race club. Then he noticed the bookcase.

In the bedroom he put the glass down beside her, but she didn't thank him. He lit another cigarette.

"You don't like Charlie, do you?" she said.

Field drew the smoke into his lungs. "Lewis?"

"How many others do you know?"

"One or two." Field imagined Natasha throwing her head back, arching her spine, and then looking down at Lewis as the two of them fucked. He sucked even harder on the cigarette, trying to eradicate the image, which was as vivid as if he'd been watching it happen.

"I can tell by the way you look at him."

"Tell what?"

"He's rich."

"Is that why you slept with him?"

"That's what you think?"

Field watched the smoke drifting from darkness to light.

"Charlie's not the man you think he is," she said.

Field did not answer.

"He's a little sad."

"I'm sure."

"You Englishmen."

"What about us?"

"Always like little boys, like someone hurt you."

Field cleared his throat. "I don't see Charles Lewis as a victim."

"Why? Don't they say money doesn't buy you happiness?" Natasha rolled over onto her back. "Charlie was angry when I asked him to leave," she said.

"What do you mean?"

"You don't think a Russian girl has a right to say no?"

Field stubbed his cigarette out in the ashtray in front of her. "What have you done with all the photographs?"

She looked at him, and even in this light he could see the depth of her annoyance. "I do not understand."

"The bookshelf in the living room. I just wondered what had happened to all your photographs."

"Which photographs?"

"When I came around the other day, your bookshelf was covered in photographs."

"I took them down."

"What did you do with them?"

"It is not your business."

"Can I see them again?"

"Why do you ask this?"

"Just . . . interest."

"No. You cannot."

She sat up, moved to the side of the bed, and picked up her gown. She slipped into it and tied the knot around her waist. "I'm sorry, this has been unfair of me. I said to you that I am weak."

"Stop."

She turned to him. "What do you mean?"

"I mean don't go down that road. I mean stop."

"Stop what?"

"I know what you are going to say and I don't want you to say it."

Natasha sighed, closing her eyes.

He knelt on the bed. "Everything has changed."

"Richard—"

"No. You said, 'Everyone needs to dream.' So let's dream. Longer. No more questions." He stood. "Let's ... do something. Let's get out of here. Now. We can go for a walk."

She was still looking at him, confused and uncertain, and for a moment he thought that she would reject him again.

She stood and began quietly to dress. She pulled on her stockings first, unselfconsciously, knowing his eyes were upon her. She indicated with the tap of a finger that he should button her dress, and as he did so, he wanted to kiss the curve of her back.

They did not speak as they walked down the stairs and, outside, she led the way, as if this had been her suggestion and she had a destination in mind. It was cooler this morning. A light breeze rustled the leaves of the sycamore trees.

A barge honked on the river, but the street was quiet save for the hiss of the gas lamps and their footsteps on the pavement. She wore a simple blue dress, a string of pearls around her neck, her hair untidy. She looked as if she had just got out of bed, and for some reason this pleased him.

Natasha took his hand, her own warm in his. She squeezed harder and he responded and then, as he was becoming used to this public display of affection, she let go.

She clasped her other hand around her waist.

"Where are we going?" he asked.

"We're walking."

"Anywhere in particular?"

"I thought perhaps a coffee at the French Club, then I want you to meet a friend."

"You're a member?"

She looked at him, without emotion. "They tolerate me."

"Tell me about your house," he said after a moment. "In Russia."

"Why?"

"Because I'm interested."

"So long ago."

"Not so long ago." Field tried to take her hand again. "Natasha, tell me about your home."

She held his hand briefly, then let it slip away. She sighed. "It was not a grand house. Not like Lena's."

"In Kazan itself?"

"It was a farm. Quite far from Kazan. Closer to Chistopol, on the other side of the river." Natasha smiled. "It was a beautiful place."

"Your father was a farmer?"

"For many years, we . . ." She hesitated. "Papa was an officer in the army, like Lena's father. He was away so much, and when Mama died, we had to run the farm."

"You and your sister?"

"Yes."

"She was older or younger?"

"Older. Four years. I told you. She looked after me after Mama died."

"What was her name?"

Natasha hesitated. "It is not important."

"You had help on the farm?"

"Of course." She smiled again, gently. "But the workers were happy. Papa was always generous. It was a simple life."

They had reached the French Club, the Cercle Sportif, and Natasha led him through the wrought-iron gates and across the neatly clipped lawn, past the cedar trees and crafted bushes. Light spray from the fountains settled onto their faces. Field thought this the most elegant building in Shanghai— long and low, with a curved awning in the middle, beneath which a liveried doorman was stamping his feet, as though trying to keep out the cold. He nodded at Natasha as she led Field through the hall to the terrace. They took a table close to the garden and looked down toward the pavilion, now fringed by the dawn light. They were the only customers.

"They open early," Field said.

"They never close."

"I thought you said you were not a member."

"I'm not, but they tolerate me."

A waiter stood before them, smiling, his white linen coat so starched it looked as if it could walk on its own.

"*Café, s'il vous plaît,*" she said quietly.

"*Moi aussi,*" Field added.

"*A manger?*"

They both shook their heads.

"You speak French?" she asked after the waiter had gone.

"A little." He leaned forward. "Your father must have fought in the Great War."

"Do not hold my hand here, Richard."

"I—"

"It is early, so it is safe, and, whatever you think, I don't want to live in fear. You have encouraged me. But if we were seen, it would be dangerous."

Field nodded. He swallowed, his throat dry.

"What I have to do, I do, but he does not control me. He does not own me."

Field nodded again, not trusting his voice.

"But we must be careful," she said, her expression a mixture of defiance and fear.

He let the silence stretch between them.

"It must have been hellish. The war, I mean," Field said.

Natasha smiled again. "Papa sometimes seemed so stiff to others. So formal. But he was just a bear. That's what we called him."

"He came home as soon as the war was finished?"

"He was in St. Petersburg with his regiment during the revolution. He escaped home and told people what he had seen, but no one believed him. Everyone thought he was exaggerating. He was frightened and silent and we did not know what to think or do. You know?"

"I understand."

"When the Bolsheviks arrived, the killings began in Kazan. They rounded up people of consequence—many friends. Landowners, army officers, university teachers—they put them into basements and shot them, or forced them onto barges on the river and blew them up."

Her face had gone white. "Papa did not want to go, but he knew there was no choice." Natasha closed her eyes. "So far.

You have no idea. No one can ever imagine. By camel, across the Steppes, for months. Huddled up as we crossed Lake Baikal by sledge, the air so cold. No money, no food, no kindness. And after all that he had seen, Papa so . . ." Her voice trailed off, her eyes tight shut.

"You reached Vladivostok?"

"It had fallen to our side, but we knew it could not last. There were so many rumors. We had to force father to leave. We had to convince him it was hopeless and we must flee while we still could." She shut her eyes again.

The waiter came with two cups and a jug of coffee on a silver tray. As Natasha opened her eyes, Field examined the figure on the bill and pulled some money from his pocket.

"I'm sorry," she said, "it is expensive."

"It is no matter. I'm no longer poor."

"You don't have to apologize, Richard. I do not—"

"Yes, but—"

"It is not important."

The coffee was in a silver jug and Field poured it, spilling some on the white linen tablecloth. He handed a cup to her. "Did you leave with Lena? You were friends?"

"We were at school together in Kazan and then St. Petersburg, but I had come home to help on the farm."

"They say St. Petersburg is beautiful."

"Of course, it was . . ."

"What kind of girl was Lena?"

She did not answer immediately. "Lena liked to laugh. At school she was very funny. She always tried to make a joke of everything. She was popular, quite forward with boys. Not intimidated, but . . ." Natasha stopped again in midsentence.

"You traveled here together?"

"No." Her voice was firmer now. "I said people thought Papa was stiff, but he was the kindest man I knew, gentle, and he left for us. He did not want to go, could not imagine a life without Russia, but he could see that there was no future for us—so many friends being killed, so brutal. What could we do? But it was so hard for him to leave. Lena's father was prouder and more stubborn. He was really a stiff man, inflexible, and he would not leave until the last moment. They had a big house, very beautiful, with gardens that had taken so many years to build and a long lawn that ran along the banks of the river. They were quite rich and the father would not go. Papa went to see him. On our way, after we'd left, we went to the house, but Lena was playing in the woods and Papa would not let us come in. I remember Papa walking out, across the snow, back to the sledge, still in his uniform boots, shaking his head. Lena's father was standing on the steps of the veranda and I could see all the way down to the frozen river and it was a clear day, blue sky, sharp and beautiful. I saw Lena's mother in the window, looking out at us. She was so frightened and I felt afraid all over again."

There was another long silence. "But they left?" Field asked. "In the end."

"Only just in time. They were warned by a friend from Kazan that a mob was coming, and we later heard that the Bolsheviks burned the house down an hour after they had gone. But they left in such a hurry, and the father would not believe it would be for long. He did not want to escape, just hide for a few days, he thought, because the White Army was coming. And it was true: the Whites were close and the city was freed by General Kappel a week later. We knew about this and asked Papa, but he wouldn't turn back. He understood. He did not want to go, could not bear to leave, but he understood. It was finished. He knew that it was all finished and our life was gone forever.

"Lena's family lost everything. They came back to the house, but there was nothing left. The Bolsheviks had stolen so much and burned, and they had attacked some of the servants who tried to defend the house. Lena and her family were left with nothing, and then they had to go. The journey was even harder for them. Her father . . . he killed himself on the Steppes. Her mother died also on the journey, and the brothers turned back. She had to fend for herself and her sister. She was a brave woman."

"And it—"

"When she got here—a long time after us—she was different, as though a light had gone out, do you understand?"

Field nodded.

"She was never the same. There was no laughter." Natasha stared at him. Field wasn't sure what she expected him to say.

"I won't be like that, Richard. I won't lie down and die."

"Lena believed she could escape."

Natasha sighed. "The last few weeks, she was more like her old self, just a little. It is hard to say what I mean, because there was so much we did not—could not—talk about. The past—you think it binds us, but it's not like that. It seems black, do you see? It all seems black. What we have lost—it is so terrible, and the present so bleak, that we can never talk about it. Sometimes with others, if they had lived in Moscow or somewhere else, then it is possible to discuss the past or talk about the revolution. But not to Lena, because we had known each other too well."

"Because there is no escape?"

"Of course. But Lena believed. And—"

"You think it was a mistake?"

Natasha didn't answer. She was staring out of the window.

"Your father died in Russia?"

For a split second he saw the uncertainty in her eyes as she turned to face him and tried to recall what she had previously said. He wished immediately that he had not spoken. "On the ship," she said.

"You buried him at sea."

"No, in Harbin."

Field wanted to ask if she ever went up to see the grave but thought it a subject best left alone.

She smiled at him. "You are a good listener."

He shrugged.

"Few men know how to listen." She paused. "It is strange.

Once, I would have been your equal. Now, if you took me to one of your clubs, you would be thrown out in disgrace."

"I'm not a member of any clubs."

"No, but——"

"And I doubt I was ever your equal."

Natasha did not respond.

"I don't think running hosiery stores matches up to being a tsarist officer."

"I told you, Richard, there is no shame in being poor."

"There is when it matters more than life itself to be rich." Field shook his head. "My father sank so deep into debt that his only escape was to blow his brains out."

"But you admired him."

"No."

"But you loved——"

"I hated him. I hated what he did to my mother, to us, to himself." Field stared at his hands, trying to contain his anger.

"How can this be so?"

"If your relationship with your father was different, then you can count yourself fortunate in that, at least. Mine was incapable of valuing what he had, or of not overvaluing what doesn't matter, and the result was that he carried his anger within him. You say your father was soft; well, mine was hard. He would come home from work and the atmosphere in the house changed, as though someone had flicked a switch. We had to be quiet or we would be beaten, my sister and I. If we didn't put our toys away, we were beaten. If he caught us talking after our lights had been put out, then we would be beaten. I say we, but it was usually me, and all the time, my mother did nothing."

Field realized he'd said more than he'd intended but now could not stop himself. "She would never say a single word. She would come in and soothe us, put her hand on my brow as I was crying and say that she was sorry, and the more she did that, the more I hated her, too." Field was staring at her. "You don't want to hear this."

"I do." Her face was white. She put her hand on his and he tried to withdraw it, but she gripped it fiercely. "No."

"You said——"

"I don't care."

Field ripped his hand free and glanced around the empty room. He bent his head. "I don't know why I'm telling you this." He lit a cigarette, his hand shaking. He leaned back.

"They're your family, Richard."

"It's extraordinary how anger can sustain you. My whole life, until I came here, was like a shirt that didn't fit. I didn't come here to escape, I came here to begin again——to forget, to discard everything that had gone before." He looked at her. "You cannot go back. I don't want to. We're a perfect match."

Field sighed. "He always used to say, 'Don't be fortune's fool, Richard. Whatever you do, don't be fortune's fool.' "

Thirty-seven

Ten minutes after leaving the French Club, she led him through a pair of wrought-iron gates and down a stone path that ran along the edge of an enormous, well-tended garden. It was so peaceful here that they could have been miles from the city. The house was tall, with a dark roof and narrow windows, and covered in ivy.

The woman who opened the door was small and rotund, perhaps about fifty—though it was hard to tell—her graying hair held back by a red peasant scarf. Without saying a word, she took Natasha in her arms and hugged her hard and long.

"This is Richard," she said quietly. The woman smiled at him, her face flushed. He stepped forward to offer his hand, but she took him, too, into her arms, with such vigor he thought his ribs would crack. She stepped back into the kitchen. "Ivan," she shouted.

There was a grunt from within.

"Look who has come to see us." Her English was heavily accented.

Ivan was thin and angular, with a hook nose and a chin thick with stubble. "Natasha," he said, transformed by her presence and repeating his wife's greeting, suddenly boyish in the way he walked and smiled. He offered his hand stiffly to Field as they were introduced and gave him the stern look of a prospective father-in-law.

"Come, come," the woman said. She took his arm and led him to a large table in the middle of the darkened kitchen.

Ivan glanced anxiously at the clock on the wall. "There is time," his wife scolded him. "It is Natasha." She looked at Field and smiled.

Field smiled back.

"I wish to know all about you. Some tea?"

"Tea, yes, that would be wonderful."

"All."

"There's not much to tell . . ."

"You are shy. Natasha has never . . ." She looked at Natasha, whose face burned red.

"You are from a good family?"

"Katya . . ."

"You have a good education?"

"His uncle is the municipal secretary," Natasha said. Katya looked at her husband and garbled at him in Russian. They both nodded with satisfaction and Field knew that he'd passed some kind of test.

He eased himself back in his chair and caught sight of a picture on the shelf behind them. It was a recent formal photograph of Natasha, taken with the clock of the Customs House in the background. She was standing next to, and had her arms around, a young boy of five or six. They looked happy.

She followed his eyes, then stood suddenly and moved in front of the picture so as to block his view. "We really should go," she said, her head bowed. Field saw the shock in the old couple's faces as they realized their mistake, the easy familiarity of a moment ago evaporating in an instant.

He stood, mumbled a good-bye, and slipped through the house before following her retreat back down the stone path.

"I must be mad." She turned to him once they'd reached the street, a new determination in the set of her chin. "For me, it is—"

"He's your son."

"No." She shook her head forcefully.

"For God's sake."

"On my mother's life, I swear it." She stared at him. "I made a mistake," she said. "I started to dream again."

"I don't think you understand . . ."

"It is you who do not understand." Her expression darkened. "Why will you not believe me when I say that I am not free to love you? What I have done I had no right to do."

He stepped toward her.

"No," she said firmly. "Go now. I have some things I need to tell them."

Field took a step back, but still hesitated.

"Good-bye, Richard," she said, and went back inside, shutting the wrought-iron gate behind her.

Field watched her go, willing her to look around, but she did not.

Thirty-eight

ield set about the record books in the Immigration Department with renewed energy, burying himself in his work, frustration and anger driving him until lack of sleep began to overtake him.

The sweat settled on his brow and it was as much as he could do not to lower his head onto the book in front of him.

He took numerous cigarette breaks and, all through them, Pendelby plowed on, never seeming to lose concentration, until he stood and announced he would be breaking for lunch. Field was suddenly alone in the room, listening to Pendelby's retreating footsteps on the stairs.

He leaned back in his seat, wiped his brow again, and cursed the heat silently. He stood and walked along the corridor and down the stairs to the back of the immigration counter, where he asked the woman politely if he might be able to borrow a telephone. She took him through to her office.

Field called Yang and asked if he had any messages. There was one from Caprisi, asking him to ring back. Field stared at the phone, then picked up the receiver and asked the operator if she would again put him through. The taste of betrayal was in his mouth. He thought himself a fool to have trusted anyone here.

"Caprisi, it's Field."

"Polar bear."

There was an awkward silence.

"You called me," Field said.

"Yes, where are you?"

Field hesitated. "The Immigration Department."

"Hunting for addresses?"

"Yes."

"Well, keep hunting. Macleod has called it off; the door-to-door boys were being tailed."

"By whom?"

"The French."

Field could hear the sound of his own breathing.

"Still there, polar bear?"

"Yes."

"You're very quiet again."

"Am I?"

"Are you all right?"

"I'm fine."

"Call me when you get back to the office."

"Sure."

"And polar bear . . ."

"Yes."

"Be careful with that woman."

"Which woman?"

"You know who I'm talking about."

Field felt his anger flaring.

"You were around there last night, so don't kid me you don't know who I'm talking about."

Field could feel his heart beating hard in his chest. "How do you know?"

"I have my sources."

"I've noticed."

"What's that supposed to mean?"

"It's funny how they always seem to know what we're doing."

There was another silence.

"What are you saying, polar bear?"

"I'm not saying anything."

"Doesn't sound that way to me."

Field didn't answer.

"You need to wise up. I know where you were, because I can see it coming. It's impossible, Field. Trust me. And dangerous for both of you." Caprisi breathed in sharply. "If you won't believe me, then there is nothing I can do."

"Then do nothing."

"The possibilities are not endless, Field."

"So I'm told."

"Told by whom?"

"Never mind."

"If she is loyal to him, then you are being manipulated. If she is seeking a bit of fun, or if she really loves you and seeks an escape, then you are playing a dangerous game."

Field sighed quietly.

"You may be free, Field, but she is not. By association with her, you come into his orbit. He does not allow his assets to escape, or behave as they please. She may not be a concubine, but there is no way she is leaving this city if he doesn't want her to. Please tell me you understand that."

"I think I understand perfectly."

"It is too easy to die here, Field. If you anger him, if you make him lose face, he dispenses death with the flick of a finger. Your death, her death, those of anyone connected to you."

"I'll see you later."

Field put the phone down before Caprisi could say anything more. The desk in front of him was neatly ordered, with two wire trays—one IN, one OUT in the center, next to a mug full of pens and a stapler.

Field returned to the files. He was still working through the latter half of 1921: *21st November, Ivanov, Dr. Oleg. Change of address: 21c Boulevard des Deux Républiques. Now conducting business from 78a Avenue Joffre.* Alongside this entry, a clerk had written: *Information passed to SMP S.1 dept upon request.* Field looked at the name again. He had never heard of Oleg Ivanov.

He continued with dwindling concentration for another

half an hour or so, until he felt himself awash with meaning-less names. Eventually, he stood and walked through the still-packed immigration room and then down the stairs to the Bund.

Field crossed the road and strolled under the trees by the wharf, watching the sampans and steamers on the choppy waters of the river. He passed a cargo boat that was unloading. It was small, so must have come from upstream, carrying goods from the Chinese hinterland. The coolies and deckhands were shouting at each other, all stripped to the waist, their bodies glistening with sweat. Field put on his hat and squinted against the sunlight. He was not wearing his jacket, and his holster was visible, so he attracted a few curious glances as he passed. A fresh breeze from the sea was pushing the pollution inland, and the air here was relatively fresh, save for the ever-present aroma of dead fish.

He ended up in the public gardens, opposite the British consulate. He sat down on a bench facing the sun.

Ahead of him, two young expatriate children—a boy and an older girl—were feeding the birds in the midst of an arrange-ment of wooden flower boxes and triangular lawns ringed by low iron fences, while their uniformed nanny stood by, hold-ing a packet of seeds. When they had finished, she produced a metal flask from inside her blue pinafore and poured each of them some water in a green mug.

Field was grateful that Chinese were banned from the park. It was a peaceful haven in the heart of the city.

He stood and retraced his steps along the wharf to the Cus-toms House. He glanced up at Big Ching to see that it was already almost two o'clock.

Pendelby was at his desk but did not raise his head as Field came in.

Field returned to his books, soon lost in the rhythm of his quest as his finger progressed down the page.

They did not take another break. They sat like assiduous students, Field almost nodding off in the afternoon heat, wiping his forehead periodically with the back of his hand before returning his finger to the page. It was soon black, so he had to continue the task with the tip of it an inch or so above the paper. Frequently, he would realize that he'd not been concentrating and be forced to retrace his steps.

As a result, he missed the entries the first time and only spotted them at the second sweep. Perhaps he'd become too focused on his search for Simonov and Ignatiev.

He stared at the page.

January 21st, 1922, it read. *Medvedev, General Feodor. From Kazan on the Volga, via Vladivostok. Temp address: 71 Avenue Joffre, Hostel Margarite.*

Field's heart started to thump.

Medvedev, Anna Federovna. As above.

Medvedev, Natasha Federovna. As above.

He felt as though he had been punched in the stomach. Natasha had arrived here with her father in 1922. He had not died at sea, nor been buried in Harbin. Was Anna Simonov really Anna Medvedev? Had Natasha's sister changed her name?

Field swung around. "Pendelby?"

The man looked up, startled by the sound of a human voice. "Russians have to inform Immigration of a change of address, but only for a few years?"

"Three years."

"So, after three years, if they haven't informed you of a change of address in the meantime, they have to come and tell you and that's it?"

"Yes."

"So if I find the entry of an arrival, then go forward three years and work back, I should find a recent address."

"In theory. Did you find something?"

"Not what we were looking for; something else."

Pendelby looked disappointed and Field turned back to his ledgers. He went forward three years and then began to work backward.

He did this for about twenty minutes, then stood. "I'll be back," he said.

"It's almost time."

"Tomorrow, then."

The immigration room was closing, a clerk waiting by the door to lock it after the last of the people inside had left. Field slipped through and then ran quickly down the steps outside, into the slightly cooler air of the Bund. He beckoned a rickshaw puller brusquely and climbed in. "Avenue Joffre," he said. "Church, Russian. Ruski."

The light was fading when they reached the churchyard, leaving a crimson stain tinting the horizon. He had to look closely at the lettering on the headstones that were not engraved in gold.

Field completed his task methodically. He started in the corner closest to the church and walked slowly down each row. As the light faded, he had to lean closer to each stone.

It was almost dark by the time he found them.

He stood stock-still.

The two graves were alongside each other. The inscriptions were in Russian, but Field could make out the name and date on the first:

General Feodor Medvedev.

1.4.1871—7.6.1923.

The second was newer, the inscription free of moss, the gold lettering still bright:

Anna Federovna Medvedev.

1.7.1896—1.5.1926.

This was the woman he knew as Anna Simonov. She had died on the 1st of May.

Field could not understand the rest of the inscriptions, but on both he recognized another name: *Natasha Federovna Medvedev.*

Field squatted down. He stared at the graves until his knees and thighs ached.

He put his head in his hands.

At length, he straightened, ran his hand slowly through his hair, then smoked a cigarette in the darkness.

Field had not known her father was a general. He imagined an old man, in fading uniform, trying to cling to his respect in a city that must have damned him at every turn.

Field walked away fast, then broke into a run. He did not know if his haste was driven more by the need to get to her, or to get away from the graves behind him.

Thirty-nine

ield went to the office first to check whether Natasha had left a message. He tried to gather his thoughts.

He told himself that he'd known she was a liar. And he realized it made no difference to him at all.

It was seven o'clock by the time he got to the Special Branch room and it was dark but for his own desk light. Yang had written him a note: *Patrick called. You are invited to dinner tomorrow night. Penelope rang, please call back. Stirling Blackman telephoned from the* New York Times. *He said you'd know what it is about.*

Field pushed the paper aside and saw that there was another page underneath. *Natasha telephoned. She said it is tonight at seven at the usual place.*

Field sprinted to the end of the room and bounced against the wall as he careered down the stairs.

"Rue Wagner. Number 3. Hurry," he said as he climbed into the rickshaw.

He thought of her curling up beside him in the bed, cradling her fear.

He put his hand on the gun and watched the man's sinewy back as he pulled, his feet slapping against the road.

Field closed his eyes and tried to think clearly.

As they rounded the corner and he caught sight of the ornate balustrades of Lu's house, Field shouted at the rickshaw man to stop. "Wait," he said. The man was confused. Field pulled out a ten-dollar bill and shoved it into his hand, waving to indicate that he wanted him to stay where he was.

There was a light on in the first floor, but Field could not see through the windows because of the protruding balcony. He wiped the sweat from his forehead with the flat of his hand, then got out. "Wait," he said again.

He was at the junction of the street opposite, shielded by the shadow of a sycamore tree. He stepped in closer to the wall and pushed his hat more firmly down onto his head. He looked at the red door at the top of the steps.

Did they keep a watch on the street?

Field took out a packet of cigarettes. He removed one with difficulty, his hands shaking. He lit it, inhaled, then threw it into the gutter in disgust.

Field's eyes flitted from the door to the window and back again. He could see, in his mind's eye, the white gown slipping from her shoulders and gathering around her feet.

He could see her slipping out of her underwear, coming forward to allow Lu to run his portly fingers over the smooth, warm skin of her flat belly.

Field could see her beneath him, her mouth tightly shut, her body frozen . . .

Or was her pleasure real?

Field turned to the wall and then back again, his mind grappling with dramatic, confusing images of duplicity and debasement. Was this the end? Was this what she had anticipated? Was he beating her now, a prelude to a far more violent death?

Field lit another cigarette and forced himself to smoke it.

The door opened and she came down the steps to the sidewalk, her head bent, so that he could not see her face.

He moved quickly, the blood pounding through his head. He took hold of her roughly, pulled her across the road.

"Get in," he said.

She resisted.

"Get in. Foochow Road," he told the man. "Hurry."

"He will have seen," she said as they pulled away.

Natasha was watching the rickshaw man's back, her face impassive and cold. She did not speak until she had opened the door of her apartment. "Please go," she said, once she had moved inside.

"What happened?"

"Please leave."

"What happened?"

In an instant she crumpled and he caught her. He lifted her and carried her to a chair by the window. He gripped her tightly, with stretched fingers, so that her head was on his shoulder, her hair once again in his face. He closed his eyes.

And then, just as quickly, she was struggling to be free and pushing him away. She got to her feet again. "No," she said. "No."

"What happened?"

"He knows."

Field stood. "Knows what?"

"He knows." She shook violently. "Something was different."

"What was different?"

"In his eyes. He was less . . . not so far away with the drugs and he made me stand there such a long time, just staring."

"Did he say anything?"

"Normally, he is hardly looking at me. Just so drugged and—"

"How long?"

"An hour, I don't know. And he did not say I could go. I could not stand it anymore and I went and picked up my clothes and left and—"

"He just looked at you?"

She did not answer.

"He didn't talk? He didn't say anything?"

Slowly, she raised her head. "He asked me if I liked to wear stockings. Why did I not wear them?"

"What did you say?"

"I said I would wear them the next time."

"He didn't touch you?"

Natasha stared at the floor.

"Did he touch you?"

"It is not your business."

"Did he touch you?"

"In the dressing room there were two ledgers." She looked up. "A chest was open. They were on top."

"And you looked?"

"I was frightened."

"But you looked?"

"There were many figures. All the writing was in Chinese."

"But you could read it."

"No, I—"

"I can see it in your face." She stared at the floor again. "And you saw something." Field took a step closer. "You knew what to look for."

Natasha did not respond.

Field frowned. "You have seen them before? Whatever it was that Lena knew, you know, too. She told you. She was like a sister to you."

Her face was hostile, a brittle anger in her eyes, her mouth tight. She held her arms protectively across her chest. "You have brought me fear again."

"I have brought you nothing you haven't brought upon yourself." He was inches away from her now. "Lena was like a sister to you, Natasha. How does that feel? She lived the life your sister lived, and she died the death your sister died." He reached out and put his hand under her chin, forcing her to look at him. "Anna Simonov was your sister, Natasha. I've seen her grave. And your father's."

Her eyes filled with pain, but the anger burned within him. "All the time I've been chasing around trying to find the truth," he said, "you have just been playing me along." Field's teeth clenched and he tightened his grip. "If your father died in Russia, Natasha, or on the ship from Vladivostok, how is it that he's buried here?"

"What is it to you?"

"That's why the photograph of Anna is no longer on your bookshelf, isn't it? You thought I'd recognize her." He let her go. "Do you know what I felt when I saw the picture of her body? For Christ's sake, I thought it was you." Field walked to the window, then turned. "What purpose have I served?"

Her eyes had followed him. "What do you mean?"

"I mean what purpose have I really served? Tell me where I fit in."

"I don't understand."

"Well, it can't be love, can it?" He spread his hands. "Or even sex. Did you feel anything? Or are you so practiced in the art of deception that—"

"Stop it, Richard."

"Stop it?" He took a pace toward her again. "Stop it?"

"Why are you being—"

"She was your *sister!* Do you think I am so fucking stupid?" He thrust his face close to hers. "Do you?" There were tears in her eyes. "Anna Federovna Medvedev. What made her change her name? Was it shame, Natasha? She was buried in Little Russia, beside General Feodor Medvedev, beloved father to Natasha Federovna Medvedev."

"Please stop, Richard."

"Is this causing you pain, Natasha? Is this hurting you?"

"Stop it."

"She was your sister."

"Please."

"She was your fucking sister."

"I knew that you would find out."

"Did you really?" Field breathed in heavily in an attempt to try to control himself. "I'm a policeman, for God's sake. Of course I would find out. It happens, even in Shanghai, occasionally. So where did she live? Which number on Avenue Joffre?"

"I could not tell you."

"Which number?"

"Number 73. On the ground floor."

"Who was she seeing?"

"I don't know."

"She was your sister."

"We did not talk of it."

"What about Lena?"

"I don't know." Natasha shook her head. "I just do not know. It was sensitive for both of us, for all of us, so we did not talk of it. It is dangerous to know these things."

"But Lena told you about the shipments?"

Natasha didn't answer.

"So what about me, Natasha? Where do I fit in? Can you tell me that, at least?"

"I could not tell you."

"This man either killed your sister or was involved in her murder, and still you go down there and take off your clothes and let him—"

"Stop it!" Her eyes were wild.

"Did you see Anna's body, Natasha? Did you see what he did to her? The photograph is in my desk. Do you want me to get—"

She launched herself at him and she was strong. Her arms flailed, her fingers scratching at his eyes. He felt a scalding pain on his cheek as he instinctively kicked her legs out from under her. He fell with her. He pinned her legs and arms.

She spat, her face twisted with fury. "You like this. You like to hurt."

He got to his feet.

"You are just the same as the others," she said, scrambling up and retreating across the room. "You think you're different, but you're just the same."

"You lied to me," he said quietly.

"I could not tell you."

Field put his hand to his cheek. "I don't understand . . ."

"She did it so I wouldn't have to. That was what she did, Richard. Is that what you want to hear? She was a prostitute. A whore. So we could survive, so that her beloved little sister wouldn't have to do the things that I now do. Do you think I would be there if I had a choice? Do you think I have not dreamed of escape?"

"How did your father die?"

"I'll tell you," she said, defeated. "I'll tell you, Richard. One day Papa found out. We had said we were teaching French to rich English children, and to begin with, that was true. But then the family that we taught most left for New York, and there were more and more Russian girls looking to teach English or French or music, or anything at all. We started to get hungry, Richard. It would pick up soon, we told Papa. We sold everything that we had of value, trying to shield our poverty from him, but he knew.

"We went on telling him that we were teaching, and he knew that we were poor but believed that we were honest. But our hunger grew. And then Papa was ill and needed medicine and we had no money for that. At first, Anna did not tell me. Then she said she could keep it from me no longer. She had done it so that I didn't have to, she said. So that I would only have to dance. My poor, sweet, gentle Anna. There were no tears in her eyes when she told me. I think she had no tears left to cry. So I cried for her, and I thought I would never stop."

Natasha wiped her eyes. "There was a little more money then. The teaching was getting better, we told Papa, but a friend, a friend, told him it was not true." She stared at him. "Papa was a very proud man, Richard." She nodded. "Like your father, he was so proud. He did not believe his friend. How could he believe that his two beautiful daughters would do such a thing? It was impossible. Impossible. So he came to see for himself. He was ill, shuffling. He had lost everything, but came to be certain that that which was priceless could not have been sold. It was impossible. He knew Shanghai, of course, and he had never chosen to come here. By the time we

left Russia, flight to the West was too risky, and we had no
family there, so we went east, like Lena, hoping that, by some
miracle, the White generals in Vladivostok would turn the
tide. And once it was clear Vladivostok would fall, where
could we go? We were poor then, living by selling the last of
our possessions. Where could we go? Shanghai...like so
many others. It was better than nothing. Papa knew nothing
of commerce, but he was proud and believed we could begin
again. He believed we could be poor and honest and he knew
his friend's vicious slander must be a mistake. Then he saw
her. She was on a raised platform inside the door of this place,
and in front were men queuing to fuck her—his precious,
beloved elder daughter, whom he raised himself after Mama
died and whom he loved more than life itself. She was in red,
she told me. Her best outfit. Red garters, with a corset and fur
lining on the collar. That was what Papa saw. And the men
were watching her dance, then they—just so, with a flick of
the finger, they ordered her. Upstairs to a tiny room with a
mattress. And for a few dollars, they could do what they
wished, Richard. Anything they wished. They could beat her.
They could humiliate her. What could she do? A Russian girl.
Once proud and beautiful, the daughter of a general of high
breeding, with a farm on the Volga. But now—"

"Stop."

"You want to know—you must know." She wiped her eyes
again as she sat. "You must know the end of the story, because
it is the story of Natasha. She was Papa's favorite daughter.
She would never, never be dancing for money—with anyone
who wanted her. General Medvedev would never believe this.
It was absolutely impossible. Perhaps Anna . . . he loved her, of
course, she was his firstborn, but perhaps...the death of
Mama...she had been the most affected. Perhaps she was
weak, too easily influenced. But Natasha? She was a daughter to adore, to be proud of. One day, he dreamed, she would
marry an officer of the regiment. Or perhaps another land-
owner in Kazan, so that she could be close to home. His heart

is so soft that it melts for her. Always. And even here in Shanghai, she is supporting him, looking after him as he gets older."
She shook her head. "No. Not Natasha. Please, Lord, if you have any mercy, then not Natasha. It could not be. Not with any man who wants to grab her breasts for money. It is not possible. A whore and a tea dancer, his two darling girls, keeping him alive by selling themselves." There were tears in her eyes now. "But it was true. It was all true. Everything his friend had said. He saw it with his own eyes. So Papa put on his uniform. A general again in the tsar's army, with everything in its proper place. The crops were almost ready to be harvested. A few weeks in St. Petersburg for the winter. Perhaps he would take us along. We could stay at the Rivoski on Nevsky Prospekt and he would take us shopping. There would be balls and dinners and perhaps we would even find a husband, Anna and I. We would be so excited."

"I'm so sorry."

"But we are not in Kazan anymore, Richard, we are in Shanghai." She looked up at him. She was starting to cry. "He put the cold barrel of his army revolver in his mouth, and then he pulled the trigger. Gone. With Mama. To a better, better world. Shanghai killed him. And we did."

The fight went out of her. Her shoulders sagged and she wept, her body racked with pain.

Field took a step toward her. "No," she said firmly, raising a hand. "I haven't deceived you, Richard."

Field didn't answer.

"If you love me, then you must leave." Her face softened. "If you love me as you say, then please go now and don't come back."

"I cannot."

She looked at him, tears flooding her eyes. "He killed himself three years ago. I have mourned him every single day since."

He nodded. "When I saw that photograph of you all together, I envied you." He knelt beside her chair. "All I wanted, all I ever wanted, was for my father to say just once, 'I love you, Richard. I love you, my boy. Well done. You played really well, you tried really hard, you did your best.' Just once. Just once. Your father loved you, Natasha. I saw it in his eyes. I hear it in your voice. However it ended, you did what you had to do. You had no choice, but my father . . . Just once, that was all I wanted, just once, and even if he couldn't bring himself to say it, at least to have felt it, to have shown it. A hand on the shoulder, my hair ruffled. It's so meaningless unless you don't have it, and then it's the most important thing in the world." Field thought he was going to cry himself. "My anger is because he blew his brains out as well and I never had the chance to say all the things I wanted to."

She stared at the floor.

"Please go now," she said quietly.

"I won't go."

"You don't understand, do you? This is what I did to my father, Richard. And this is what I will do to you. It is what I am."

"No, you don't understand. Everything has changed for me now. It's like I woke up and the world is a different place and everything has moved and the view is so bleak in one direction, and so filled with possibility in the other, and without you—without you, there's nothing."

"There's already nothing. You can't change anything." Her voice caught. "You . . . you must accept that."

"Who was the boy, Natasha?"

She shook her head. "It is not important. He was not mine."

"I won't give up."

She looked at him and he could not tell what he saw in her eyes: sorrow, or anger, or fear. They were windows to a lost soul. "Richard, I have taken risks to be with you that I had no right to take."

"I cannot accept that there is not a way to escape, and I will go on until I can make you believe that we can find one."

She sighed, her head bent. Then she turned to him, her expression that of a woman he didn't know. "Very well," she said. "I will tell you the truth."

Field felt his breath quicken.

"Why do you think I go down to Lu's?"

"Don't do this."

"I do it because I'm a whore. I don't like him touching me, Richard, no, I don't like that, it's not like it is with you. But what can you give me? I had a home. I had a family, but where are they now? I have no one. No one. So I go down to Rue Wagner and I take off my clothes for him—"

"Stop it."

"You don't want to hear it?"

"You're lying to me again."

"I'm telling you, Richard, what you need to hear. You've pushed me, and now you will hear it. You were a momentary escape. A handsome boy, naive, a little foolish, perhaps brave. But the reality does not change. So I go down there because I like to live here. Look around you. How else could a Russian girl afford all of this? Do you understand? This is what I want."

"This is not the truth."

Her face was a mask. "What is *wrong* with you?"

"I know what is true. I know it here." He touched his chest.

"You know it, so it must be true?" She shook her head, incredulous. "Do I have to spell it out to you? Do you want me to tell you that I *enjoy* the power? You saw me in the night-club, you know how it is."

"I saw fear in your eyes, not power."

"Do you want me to tell you that I enjoy him touching me, watching the power I wield over him? Do you want to see the lust in his eyes, the things he dreams of doing to me?"

"Enough."

"Do you want to know that I enjoy it when he reaches out with his fingers—"

"Enough." Field lunged forward, grabbed her arms, and shook her. He got to his feet, raised his hand, fist clenched.

She looked up at him, her lip curled. "Go on, Richard, hit me. Isn't that what you want—to hurt me? Isn't that it? Go on, be a man."

Field turned and left, slamming the door. His feet pounded on the stairs as he tried to stamp out the image of Lu's stubby fingers running slowly along the length of her body, caressing the soft skin of her breast, moving inexorably toward the patch of dark hair at the top of her thighs.

He ran out into the warm, fetid air of the street and bent over as he tried to catch his breath. A thick fog had descended and a tram rattled past, ahead of him, unseen.

Field straightened, thrust his hands deep into his pockets, and forced himself away.

He took ten paces and then turned, convincing himself for a moment that this was just a test, that she must be following him.

The doorway was half-hidden by the gloom, but he could see that there was no one there.

Forty

umber 73 Avenue Joffre was an ugly three-story building, close to the border with the Chinese city, built with deliberate disregard for the attractiveness of most of the buildings in the Concession. Field felt barely under control—unwanted, uncontrollable images of Lu and Natasha together still tearing through his mind.

It had been another long, sleepless night. For much of it, he had walked through the darkened streets.

Both ground-floor flats had tiny yards beside them, behind a wrought-iron fence, next to the road. In both, lines of laundry swayed in the breeze. Anna had lived in 1A, and the woman who lived there now also looked like a prostitute—heavily made-up, with high leather boots and a tight top. She must have been fifty, and looking at her made Field feel queasy. The door was slammed in their face.

"Silent again today, polar bear," Caprisi said as they turned away.

Field didn't answer.

"But I'm glad you called."

Field still didn't respond. He wasn't certain whether he had been right to give Caprisi Anna Simonov's address. He hadn't told him that she and Natasha had been sisters.

"You've done well, polar bear."

In the flat opposite, they found an elderly couple named Schmidt who, shaking their heads sadly, said they had known Anna and invited them in.

The sitting room was even smaller than Field had expected, and nothing about it suggested any connection at all with Shanghai. Neither of them was allowed to refuse Mrs. Schmidt's offer of chocolate torte and coffee, and as they listened to her— she was a talker, he could see, too often devoid of company— Field studied her husband and the photograph of a young boy in uniform on the sideboard.

"Our son," Mr. Schmidt said proudly.

"Otto," his wife said, handing each of them a plate with a large slice of cake. "He is the butcher now."

They both spoke with broad German accents, and Mrs. Schmidt had said this without a hint of irony.

"Your son is a butcher?" Caprisi asked.

"It was Hans's business when we married and we build it up. Now we give it to our son."

"He fought in the war?" Field asked.

She looked at him, trying to gauge if there was any hostility in his eyes. "He wished to. For his country."

"We understood," Hans said in a manner that indicated they had not.

Hans was a small man, with a face permanently set in a smile, a long nose and forehead, and an almost oval skull, with a few hairs straying in different directions across its crown. His wife was plump, neat, and ordered, her dress pressed, her hands placed carefully in her lap.

They were poor but honest, Field thought.

"Anna," Caprisi said.

"You were friends?" Mrs. Schmidt asked him.

"In a manner of speaking."

She leaned forward. "Do not worry. You are police, I can tell, but we will not . . ." She looked at her husband conspiratorially, then back again. "The French police . . ."

"Yes." Caprisi cleared his throat. "You knew her?"

"Of course! We are neighbors. I know it is the way of some in the big city to . . . But we are from a small town in Bavaria. It is not our tradition." She looked at her husband again. "We have lived here so many years."

"So you knew her well?"

"We would look after her cat sometimes. And her little boy, of course." She shook her head sorrowfully.

"Her little boy?" Caprisi said.

"Yes. Alexei."

"How old was he?"

"Her little boy?" Field asked, finally taking in what she'd said.

"Alexei, yes. He is six."

"She had a son?" Field said.

"Yes."

"Anna Simonov had a son?" he repeated.

"Yes."

"It was her own?"

"*Ja.* Of course."

"Anna Simonov had a boy?" he said once again. They were all frowning at him now. "What has become of him?" he added quickly.

The Schmidts looked at him, as if he were stupid. "The orphanage, of course." Mrs. Schmidt turned to her husband. "What could we do? We could not have him. Could we, Hans?"

"No." He shook his head firmly.

"Where else could he go?" she said.

Field felt a sense of despair creeping over him. "The boy, Alexei, went to an orphanage?"

"*Ja.*"

"What about his family?"

The Schmidts looked at each other, shaking their heads.

"Anna had no family?" Field said. "No one who came to see her, no one the boy could have gone to?"

They shook their heads again.

"Which orphanage?"

Mrs. Schmidt exchanged glances with her husband. "They came in a car . . . there was a nun. I do not know her name. In Shanghai they are all the same."

"Did he want to come here?" Caprisi asked.

"How could we?"

"We are old," Hans said. "We are old!"

"It was Otto. He should never have had . . . She was no good for him. Afterwards he could not bear to see the boy."

"The boy . . . Alexei was his?"

"No!" She shook her head vigorously. "Of course not. My Otto is not like this. He is an honorable man, but the boy reminded him of his love for her and the family they could have had. He could not shake her from his silly head, even before she died." Mrs. Schmidt looked at her husband, then back at Caprisi. "She was pleasant to us, always friendly. I must say that. But she was——"

"I know."

"How could our boy be interested in a woman like that?"

"Of course."

"It was a foolish thing. He had forgotten her, but then . . ."

"Yes." Caprisi nodded.

She sighed heavily.

"Did Anna ever . . . entertain . . . people at home?" Caprisi asked.

"Sometimes. Not often, because of the boy. She would go to . . . it is not work. Prostitution is not work."

"No." Caprisi cleared his throat. "But men would sometimes come here?"

"Sometimes."

"During the day? At night?"

"When the boy was at school. Sometimes at night."

"Was there anyone in particular the last few months before her death?"

Mrs. Schmidt turned to her husband again, seeking his approval. He nodded. "The last month—no, more, two months—there was a change."

"In her, or the pattern of her behavior?"

"In both. In the day there were no more visitors, but at night I think one man came."

"You think?"

"She would let him in the side gate, to the yard."

"Did you see him?"

She shook her head. "From here, we could not see."

"Never heard his voice?"

"It is too far away." She clicked her tongue to indicate her frustration.

"And did she talk about him?"

"Yes," she said, punching the air with her forefinger. "Yes. She was happy, she said, things would get better. She had met a man, a rich man, powerful, and she would be able to get away with Alexei, start again, somewhere new . . . Europe. She asked us where she should go if she were to visit Germany, and what kind of country it was, and if we had ever been to France and England." She looked at them, suddenly suspicious. "Otto was upset, but it was not serious. He would have got over it, and I said, *Liebchen*, she is . . . you know. Leave her to her powerful man."

"So you never saw this man?"

"No."

"And you never heard his voice or found out his name?"

"*Nein, nein.*"

"Was he Chinese?"

Mrs. Schmidt shrugged extravagantly. "How could I know? It is possible, likely, given her . . . type. It would be like her type to go with a Chinese." She wrinkled her nose in disgust.

"So you have no idea who he was?"

"Rich. Powerful. So she said. Good. He makes her happy. Good. *Ja.* She finds a man willing to consort with her . . . type. He gives the boy presents, so—"

"What kind of presents?" Field asked.

She shrugged again. "A model airplane. Wooden. Nothing special."

As her good-neighbor act fell away, Field was beginning to find this woman vexatious in the extreme.

"Otto has given her a silk scarf, but she does not like it. She does not like it! She asks him if she can take it back to the shop!"

Somehow Field knew it had not been Otto who had picked out the scarf.

"Do you think he murdered her?" Caprisi asked.

For a moment Mrs. Schmidt's face went white, until she realized that Caprisi was referring to the mysterious nocturnal visitor and not her son, whereupon she looked as if she would faint with relief.

"*Ja,*" she said. "We do not know."

"It is possible," her husband added. "It is possible."

"Coming like a thief," she went on, getting into her stride, "in the middle of the night." She shook her head, as if desperate now to clear her son beyond doubt. "Otto is not here, of course. The whore drove him away. He has gone to Manila and we have not heard from him. Not a letter . . . With this new man, the thief in the night . . ."

Caprisi stood abruptly, as if unable to contain himself any longer. He thanked them unconvincingly and strode out into the hallway.

Outside, they squinted in the glare of the sun.

In deference to their position in the French Concession, they had left their pistols and holsters beneath the seat of the car and so they were just in shirts and ties. Field rolled up his sleeves. Caprisi had moved along to the end of the wrought-iron fence, to the gate into the yard, and looked through the bars. Field could see that he was checking whether or not it was possible to see the gate from the Schmidts' house. He shook his head.

"He wanted to get in and out without being seen," Field said.

"Yes." The American detective turned on his heel.

"Why?"

"A rich and powerful man."

"Lewis?"

"It certainly sounds like a big fish."

"The boy," Field said.

Caprisi straightened. "Yes, perhaps the boy saw him. The present may have been given in person." Field caught sight of a black Buick parked opposite, its engine running. "Prokopiev and Sorenson," Caprisi said. "They've been with us since we left the station this morning."

They watched the car. It didn't move off.

"They're in the back?" Field asked.

"You're the Special Branch expert."

Field turned. "You saw them coming out of the lobby, or they were already in the car?"

"They were leaning against it."

"So they were happy to be seen?"

"I think they thought they were out of sight."

"So they knew we were coming out this morning?"

Caprisi shrugged. "Do you think the boy is still alive?" he asked.

"I've no idea."

"Which orphanage would they have taken him to?"

Field shook his head, though he had a fairly good idea he knew the answer.

Field waited until he was sure that Sorenson and Prokopiev had chosen to follow the American. Then he headed back to the International Settlement and the Happy Times block.

He took the stairs three at a time and was covered in sweat when he reached the top floor. He wiped his forehead with the sleeve of his jacket and then knocked once, hard.

There was no answer. He looked at his watch.

Field stepped back to press the button for the lift, then knocked once more.

He waited. He cursed, stepped into the lift, and pulled the iron cage violently across.

He hailed a rickshaw and gave the man Katya's address. He knocked on the back door and waited.

Katya opened it, but only enough to catch sight of his face. "She's not here," she said before Field had had a chance to speak.

Katya tried to shut the door again, but Field jammed his foot in it.

"Please, Katya."

"She's not here."

"Then tell me where she is."

"She doesn't want to see you."

"I know the boy was Anna's."

Katya faltered, easing the pressure on Field's foot.

Ivan said something in Russian behind her. Katya opened the door further, without answering.

"Can I come in?"

"Not here," Ivan said. He sounded nervous and frail, and his eyes anxiously scanned the garden over Field's shoulder.

"The boy," Field said. "She and the boy are in danger. The boy can probably identify Anna's killer. The . . ." Field sighed in frustration. Their English wasn't up to an explanation of the threat posed by the police investigation. If Lu felt they were close to identifying the killer, he wouldn't hesitate to liquidate the boy. "They are in danger. I have to find them. I have to take them to a safe place."

They both looked at him with pained disbelief.

"Does she know what happens in that orphanage?" Field cleared his throat, thinking of the picture of the handsome little boy inside. "Boys are taken for Lu to abuse, and then they're disposed of."

"Not here," Ivan said. Field didn't know if he'd understood any of it.

"Please go," Katya pleaded.

"I must see her."

"Not here," Ivan said, more firmly this time.

"Please get a message to her."

"She left here," Katya said, "and told us she would be back to see us soon. We do not know where she is."

"Is she inside?"

"No," they said in unison. "No," Katya added for emphasis.

"She said that she would come here if she was ever in trouble," Field lied.

"We do not know where she is. Please leave us."

Field hesitated, then turned away and walked slowly down the path toward the gate, willing them to call him back.

He stepped out into the street, leaned against the railings, and then sat down, his head in his hands, trying to think.

He pushed himself to his feet again and dusted himself down. He lit a cigarette, threw the rest of the pack to a beggar, along with his matches, and strode down toward Avenue Joffre, where he hailed another rickshaw.

He allowed himself to look back once, but there was no one at the gate.

Forty-one

ergei Stanislevich wasn't in his apartment, but Field found him in the café opposite. He pulled up a chair. The Russian was reading a copy of the *New Shanghai Life*.

"Coffee," Field told the waiter. "White, no sugar."

"Black," Sergei said.

The man retreated behind the bar.

"Well, well," Sergei said, blowing cigarette smoke into the air, "this is becoming one of your favorite places." He smiled to himself. "I saw you here only yesterday, I think."

"I need to find Natasha."

"Who doesn't?"

Field stared at him.

"Everyone is looking for Natasha." He sighed theatrically, well aware of the impact of his words. "So beautiful, so dangerous."

The waiter brought their coffee and waited, notepad poised, to see if they would order anything else. Field shook his head as Sergei lit another cigarette from the stub of his first.

"Yes, everyone longs for Natasha," Sergei continued. "Everyone is in love with her. That is her skill. But only the richest can afford her."

"Natasha is not for sale."

Sergei leaned back in his chair and laughed, harshly and without mirth. "If you say so, Detective. Have you seen her apartment? Of course you have. I'm sure she will be content with a life of poverty, an honest cop by her side."

"We need to know where she is, Sergei."

"I've no idea."

"Is there anywhere—"

"How can I know?" He raised his hands, palms up. "These girls . . . they . . ." He breathed out smoke. "Sometimes they like a Russian man inside them again—I told you—maybe just to hear the language and feel their betrayal, so I do them." He smirked. "Lena—sometimes Natasha—they all want to be done." Sergei ground out his cigarette and leaned forward, conspiratorially. "They want to be done, so I make them pay. I make them scream!"

"You've slept with Natasha Medvedev?"

"Only when she begs me to."

Field had grabbed the Russian by the collar of his jacket before he had even thought to control himself. The table careered into the side of the bar, their coffee cups smashing on the stone floor.

Field had the Russian up against the window, his feet off the ground and flailing vainly, then kicked his upturned chair to one side and dragged him by the scruff of his neck past the astonished owner and into the street. He waited for a tram to pass, then crossed over to and climbed the narrow set of stairs beside the Siberian Fur Shop. Sergei no longer struggled or made a sound.

When they got to Sergei's rooms, Field kicked the door down, then picked the Russian up by his collar again and hurled him onto the unmade bed.

"Now," he breathed in deeply. "Sit up!"

Field heard the sound of footsteps pounding up the stairs and turned. He drew his revolver, only to see Caprisi appear in the doorway. They looked at each other for a moment and then Field replaced his gun and turned back to face Sergei.

He reached for a spindly wooden chair and sat down in it. He took out a cigarette, but neglected to offer one to the pathetic figure who now perched on the edge of the bed, his head bent. Caprisi didn't move from the doorway.

"Now, let's start again," Field said. "Where would I find Natasha Medvedev?"

Sergei shook his head, his face twisted in contempt. "How should I know?"

Field stood and took a step forward, his fist raised.

"All right." Sergei recoiled. "What do you want?"

Field was aware of Caprisi's eyes on him but could not stop himself.

"Who are her friends?"

"I only saw her at the Majestic and with Lena."

"Did you see her with anyone else?"

"No."

"You've never seen her outside the Majestic?"

Sergei hesitated. "I don't think so."

"You don't think so, or definitely not?"

Sergei shook his head again. "I don't really know her," he said plaintively.

Field took a deep breath and rubbed his hand across his chin. He sat down again, not looking at Caprisi. "Who was Lena Orlov seeing during the two months before she died?"

"I don't know."

"Let's try again, Sergei. Who was—"

"*I don't know!*"

"I thought you were her boyfriend?"

"I told you, only sometimes. It's what I said. Sometimes she wanted a Russian boy." He looked up. "Lena," he added warily, "that's what she said—to hear her own language."

"So who was the other man?"

He shook his head again. "She wouldn't say. English. Wealthy. Powerful." For the first time, he managed a look of something approaching sincerity. "That's why she was happy at the end."

Field straightened. "He was English?"

"Yes."

"The man who came to see her?"

"Yes."

"He was certainly English?"

"That's what I said, yes."

"He wasn't Chinese? There was no way she could have been covering up for——"

"Why should she cover up that? Everyone knew Lu owned her. Owned her apartment, her clothes, her——"

"So it wasn't Lu?"

"You're not listening. Englishman."

"There is no chance that you are mistaken?"

"She was drunk, I not so much. She did not intend to tell me and knew, once she had done so, that she should not have. But she did not worry. She trusted me."

"Did she give any clue as to this man's identity? Did she mention the company he worked for? Did she mention Fraser's?"

He shook his head. "No. Rich, powerful. Decent. That's what she said. He had promised her a new life. A passport—a British passport—money, a new life somewhere outside Shanghai." Sergei looked at Field soberly. "She believed him. She wrote to her sister in Harbin, to get her——"

"That's what Lu had on Lena?"

Sergei looked puzzled.

"Anything Lena did wrong would be taken out on the sister?"

Sergei nodded slowly. "She sent the girl to Harbin, but she knew Lu could find her if he wanted. She said he believed in insurance policies."

"The Englishman," Field said. "He was a businessman, a taipan?"

"I should think so. Even when she was drunk, she would not say."

"Tell me about the shipments."

"What shipments?" Sergei began to get up.

"Sit down."

"I want some water."

"In a minute." Field stood. "Hidden in Lena's apartment was a list of shipments—consignments of sewing machines bound for various European cities. There's one leaving this weekend. The *Saratoga*."

Sergei's eyes darted left and right. "I don't know."

"Yes you do."

"I know nothing about them."

The Russian was looking down at the floor again, and Field moved swiftly, taking a pace toward him and smacking him across the side of the face before Sergei had had a chance to protect himself.

He lay whimpering on the bed, curled up in a ball. Caprisi still didn't move.

"Jesus . . . Jesus . . . ," Sergei groaned.

"Quickly."

"I don't know." Sergei was crying now. "Drugs. That's what she said. The best opium."

Field pulled him upright. "We've worked that out, but what's the deal?"

"What do you mean?"

"I mean what's the deal, Sergei? How does it work?"

"It's a syndicate. It's about connections. Lu provides the opium and then they stack it into the machines and import huge quantities of it into Europe. The authorities here, the police . . ."

"Who?"

"I don't know. She just said it was cast iron, that they knew they would never be caught, because they had everyone at every level tied down, all the way through to the destinations."

"Why was Lena making these notes?"

"What do you mean?"

"What I said, Sergei. Why was Lena taking notes? How was she finding this stuff out, and why was she keeping a note of it?"

The Russian was shaking now. "I don't know. Her lover told her, or she overheard. I don't know. It was her attempt at an insurance policy. She would go to the press, she said, if they didn't give her what she wanted, but I said . . . you know, I told her, these people are dangerous, maybe they even control the press."

Field heard the siren of a French police car in the distance, getting rapidly closer. "Fuck," he said, feeling for his holster and checking that he still had his revolver.

"That's the——"

"Shut up," Field said. "Is there a back way out?"

Sergei shook his head.

"A window?"

"From the bathroom you can jump onto the roof of the store below."

"Did Lena say that she'd seen some records of these shipments?"

Sergei looked frightened.

"Did she ever say that she'd seen a record of it in Lu's house? Is that how she was making the notes?"

Sergei started to shake again.

Field walked to the window overlooking the street. A green Citroën sedan pulled up outside the café. He turned back to Sergei. "We did not give you our names, and you do not know who we were."

Sergei nodded. He looked utterly wretched.

Field went into the bathroom, opened the window, and dropped down onto the flat roof. Caprisi came down behind him. He did not look at the American until they had clambered down to the street and walked clear.

Field stopped to light himself a cigarette. "So now you're following me, too."

"I don't trust you on your own, polar bear."

"Cut the polar bear crap," Field said.

"You're going down and I don't want to see it."

"Well then, close your eyes." Caprisi was looking at him with concern, possibly even affection, but Field couldn't tell which. He felt he'd lost the ability to distinguish between what was real and what was imagined. "I'm a grown man,

Caprisi, and I'd be grateful if you could refrain from following me. I don't want to shoot you by mistake."

Caprisi's eyes were steady, his face hardening. "I can't force you to help yourself, Richard, but we had an understanding—that we needed to exercise extreme caution—and you're breaking the rules."

"Whose rules are they?"

"You're supposed to be running the girl, remember? Using her for us. How long do you think you can go on flailing around like this before her owner discovers what is going on?"

"I've discovered there are no rules."

"You're behaving like this is a game."

"I can assure you, it's not a game to me."

"You were the one who wanted to take him on, Field. We are trying to catch a killer, and in the process bring down the man who protects him."

"I thought Macleod wanted to clean up the city."

"Macleod knows what he is dealing with."

Field sighed. "And so do we. A powerful Englishman. The most powerful in the city."

Caprisi looked at him. "I hope that is what your mind is on, polar bear. I really do."

"Charles Lewis?"

"It fits. It more than fits. Lena talked about a powerful English taipan. She finds out and makes notes about drug shipments that are being moved through one of his factories. Lu cleans up after him in order to keep the syndicate operating. It must be Lewis. It all points to him."

"But . . ." Field's brow furrowed. "I mean, he's an arrogant bastard, and I know he likes to hurt women, but why would he risk everything?"

"Rich people don't like to kill anyone?"

Field pictured the Chinese girl at the club, handcuffed and whimpering. Then he thought of Natasha and Lewis. "I've got to go."

"Go where?"

"Just something I need to do."

"I've said my piece, Field."

"Yes, I heard it."

Caprisi stared at him.

"You won't follow me this time, will you?"

"Just make sure no one else does. They're interested now."

"What's got them interested?"

"At a guess, the other girls. Ignatiev and Simonov. Lu must know we know about them. Perhaps the killer is beginning to get nervous. Perhaps, beneath his customary air of cool, Lewis is getting worried."

Field looked at Caprisi for a few moments, then turned away.

Forty-two

The Sisters of Mercy Orphanage was situated half-way down Avenue Joffre, a solid, white building set back from the road behind a tall iron gate, which squeaked as Field opened it. He walked down two steps and through a colonnade of stone pillars to a cavernous entry hall, which was cool after the heat of the street. It smelled of damp, paint peeling off its walls.

Field had wanted to work alone, so he had not told Caprisi he was coming to the orphanage, though perhaps he'd guessed.

If he could find the boy, Field believed, then he would be able to ascertain beyond doubt that Lewis was the killer.

A corkboard in one of the alcoves was covered with notices, including the same newspaper article on Lu Huang that had been pinned to Maretsky's wall. Above it a printed sheet announced:

Our benefactor will grace us with a visit at ten p.m. on Wednesday. Bedtime will be delayed accordingly. All dormitories must shower before nine. Songs in the hall will be followed by a dormitory inspection. All children will stand by their beds. Mr. Lu has promised to find homes for at least two more children.

Field stared at the last line.

The notice was signed, *Sister Margaret.*

Field turned around. The orphanage must be only a minute or two by car from Lu's house.

He thought of the young orphans standing by their beds,

waiting to see if they would be the lucky ones. Would they have an inkling of their fate—or would their hearts be bursting with joy that they had been chosen for "adoption"?

Field felt physically sick, his pulse quickening. He wondered why Natasha had not taken Alexei in.

There were three wooden chairs in the hallway. Beside each was a pile of pamphlets and Field picked one up. It was a list of prayers.

He replaced it and walked into the gloomy corridor beyond, his loud footsteps, the damp, and the stifling odor of sanctity providing uncomfortable echoes of his own past.

A man in a dark suit was walking toward him. He carried a Thompson machine gun, and the incongruity of his presence suggested to Field that he was one of Lu's men.

The man looked at him as he passed, before turning toward the front gate.

Field reached a central hallway, encircled by thin shards of light from the glass dome above. He could hear the sound of children playing. He approached an open door in the corridor to his left, where a light was on, and knocked once.

The woman who looked up was pretty, her white habit not quite denying her femininity. She was startled and then flustered.

"My name is Richard Field, from the Shanghai police," he said. "I'd be grateful if I could speak to Sister Margaret."

She stood, nodding, and disappeared into the room behind.

Field retreated to the hallway again and looked up. A shard of light fought its way through the filthy windows set in the roof and fell directly on his face.

He moved to the corner and sat in one of the straight-backed chairs. He picked up a copy of the newsletter from a long altar table beside it and fanned his face. He waited a long time. The sound of the children seemed to have grown fainter.

Field heard movement at the other end of the corridor and looked up to see the nun he'd spoken to leading a smaller, older woman quickly toward him.

"I'm Sister Margaret," the woman said. She spoke with a Scottish accent. Her skin was pale and her handshake cool. The light caught the top of her wimple, illuminating the few strands of red hair that poked out from beneath it.

"Richard Field, Special Branch."

Sister Margaret nodded once and then led Field into her office. Through the window he could see the children playing in the courtyard. They were all in clean, pressed white uniforms, their hair neat. Most seemed to be Chinese or Eurasian. A small group of boys was playing football. Field searched their faces for one he might recognize.

"Would you like some tea, Mr. Field?"

"Thank you. Milk, no sugar, please."

She indicated the seat behind him, a small, tall-backed wooden pew, before leaving to arrange for the tea. Field went back to scanning the playground. He could see only one Caucasian boy, but he had blond hair, was older than Alexei had been in the photograph, and bore no resemblance to either Anna or Natasha.

Sister Margaret appeared again so silently that Field did not realize for a few moments that she had returned. She sat down behind her desk, beneath a picture of the Virgin Mary holding the infant Jesus. She moved a pile of papers to the edge of the desk, brushing off the dust that had gathered beneath it. "How can I help you, Mr. Field?"

Field returned to his seat. "You have been here long, Sister?"

"Some years, yes."

"It's a long way from Scotland."

"Most places are."

"I'm from Yorkshire." Field smiled.

"Then you had a shorter journey."

She was impervious to small talk. Field cleared his throat. "You are . . . Mr. Lu Huang is one of your donors."

He saw the wariness in her face immediately. She gave an almost inaudible sigh. "He is a most generous benefactor."

"I'm sure."

They were silent.

Sister Margaret's clothes rustled. "I am aware of what people say, Mr. Field, but in my situation, I believe beggars cannot be choosers."

"Of course."

Sister Margaret searched his eyes for signs of insincerity, her own expression defensive. She placed her hands in her lap, entwining her fingers.

The younger nun came in with a tray. As she placed a cup in front of Field, she smiled shyly at him.

"Thank you, Sister Jane," the older woman said sharply.

Field waited until she had gone. "I see that Lu—Mr. Lu— is coming to visit the children."

"We are grateful that he finds the time."

"Of course. I assume—well, he was an orphan, so he must like to see children being better cared for than he was."

Sister Margaret did not answer. Her eyes rested steadily upon Field's face, her expression still guarded, before it slipped far enough to betray a blend of resignation and something else—moral compromise perhaps. Field felt a cloud of depression begin to envelop him. He had hoped Maretsky was wrong and that the situation here was not as debased as he had suggested.

"Lu sometimes finds children a home?" Field asked.

"Sometimes, yes. He very kindly found two of the young boys homes earlier this year."

"Expatriate parents?"

"Chinese, I believe. They were Eurasian boys."

Field looked down. He wanted to relieve his frustration and anger by shouting at her.

"Are you all right, Mr. Field?"

He sipped his tea. "Yes, thank you." He cleared his throat again. "Lu—Mr. Lu—picks out the children himself on these visits?"

Sister Margaret hesitated. She dropped her gaze. "Yes."

Field swallowed hard. He could not be certain how much she knew beyond doubt, how much she suspected and tried to block out.

"The parents are happy? They have worked well—the adoptions, I mean?"

"We do our best here, Mr. Field, but, of course, the boys were excited to leave." She shrugged. "Mr. Lu kindly made the arrangements and the boys were thrilled—of course, they were."

Field hesitated. He imagined two young boys darting down the corridor outside, bursting with happiness at the thought of the better life they believed awaited them beyond the gate on Avenue Joffre. He could see Lu Huang's portly fingers as he habitually opened and closed his right hand. "They're happier now?"

"I believe so, yes. Mr. Lu kindly keeps us in touch with their progress."

"Yes, I can see that."

"You're a policeman, Mr. Field, so perhaps you can appreciate the true nature of this city."

"I believe so, yes."

"Without the orphanage these children would have perished long ago. All of them. Without our benefactor there would be no orphanage."

Field looked at her. For a moment, believing that she was completely aware of the extent and scope of her Faustian pact, he felt like throwing up.

"Alexei Simonov." Field saw immediately that Sister Margaret knew the boy. "Mr. Lu—or his men—brought him here and asked you to give him shelter?"

Sister Margaret did not answer.

"The mother . . ."

"It is a tragedy," she said.

"Of course." He allowed himself a mournful pause.

Sister Margaret raised her hand. "We have had five Russian children in one year," she said, spreading her fingers.

"Five."

"Suicide is against God's will."

"Yes."

"But it is still a tragedy, of course."

"Of course, yes."

Field reached into the inside pocket of his jacket and pulled out the photograph he'd kept in his desk. He stood and handed it to Sister Margaret. "This is how Anna Simonov committed suicide, Sister."

Her face went white. After a few moments she handed it back. She did not catch his eye.

"Would it be possible for me to speak to the boy?"

"Out of the question." She shook her head.

"It's just that—"

"Out of the question." She shook her head again, in case she had not sufficiently emphasized this point. "He has been traumatized."

Field looked out of the window at the boys still playing football in the yard.

"He is not here, Mr. Field."

"Supposing that the boy did turn out to have family, after all, then he would—"

"We are past that point, Mr. Field. Alexei must be allowed to begin his life again. Mr. Lu has his best interests at heart and he was most clear on this point. No one is to see the boy."

"It is touching to hear that Mr. Lu takes so much time to consider the welfare of individual orphans when he must be such a busy man."

She glared at him.

"Sister, Anna Simonov was stabbed about fifteen times in the vulva and the lower part of her stomach." He looked her in the eye.

Sister Margaret's face was sheet-white again.

"We think Alexei saw his mother's killer. We believe he is the only person who can positively identify him before he does this"—Field held up the photograph—"to another woman."

Sister Margaret's lips tightened. "I cannot allow it," she said. "I cannot."

The children had stopped playing football on the far side of the yard. They were drinking water and splashing it on their faces. Their hair was damp with sweat. Their uniforms seemed to sparkle in the sunlight, a green cross at the center of each shirt. They sat down against the far wall, talking among themselves.

Field reached for a notepad and took out his father's pen. "This is my number. I leave it up to you." He handed her the piece of paper and left the office.

Field stopped when he reached the central hallway. He could hear the sound of his breathing. A door opened behind him and he turned to see Sister Margaret walking in the oppo-site direction. He watched her until she reached the far end of the corridor. She did not look round.

The hallway was silent again.

Field half turned and saw that some of the children were watching him silently. There were four of them, all young Chi-nese or Eurasian boys. They did not move, their gazes solemn.

Field walked out through the entrance hall and into the bright sunshine.

There was a car waiting on the far side of the street, about fifty yards to his left. He watched it for a few moments before setting off, but the car didn't follow him.

Once he'd turned the corner, he stopped beneath the shade of a sycamore tree and leaned back against the iron railings of a large house. He shut his eyes. He'd never felt so tired.

When he opened them again, he looked at his watch, then fumbled in his jacket pocket for Prokopiev's old surveillance notes. He glanced over them, then put them away and began to walk.

It took him only a few minutes to reach Lu's house, but he looked at his watch again to be sure of the time. It was twelve-thirty. If Lu's routine had not changed, he would leave at one o'clock.

Field stood beneath the trees opposite the house before deciding that he was too conspicuous and retreating a few yards.

He took out a cigarette, but then put it back in the packet.

He looked up at the bedroom window. He fought against the idea that she was a willing—even an enthusiastic—prisoner. He thought of her apartment and her elegant clothes and the look that had crept across her face as she had forced him away.

The door opened. Lu's bodyguards came down the steps and surrounded the car. As the blond one, Grigoriev, scanned the street, Field turned quickly and walked away. He kept on going until he was round the next corner, then spun around and came back, keeping in the shadow of the trees.

Field watched as Lu came down the steps with a girl of about thirteen or fourteen. He had a brief glimpse of her frightened face before she was pushed into the back of the car. Lu moved slowly, Grigoriev supporting him as he came down the last step.

Natasha was not with him. Field felt his shoulders sag with relief.

The bodyguards climbed into the car or onto the running boards, and the car moved off in the direction of the Bund. Field looked at his watch again. It was one o'clock exactly.

He stepped farther into the shadow of the trees and lit a cigarette. He glanced up at the bedroom window but saw no movement. Every so often he wiped the sweat from his forehead.

Lu returned at five minutes past two. All four bodyguards were on the running boards now. They jumped off before the car had come to a halt, taking up the same positions as they had done earlier. After about thirty seconds Field saw Grigoriev tap the driver's window and another of the men stepped forward to open Lu's door. He went slowly up the steps to the house. The bodyguards followed him and the car drove off. There was still no sign of Natasha.

Field lit another cigarette.

He was about to leave when a rickshaw pulled up outside the house.

Before Field had even had time to retreat farther into the shadows, Lu's door had opened and Field caught a glimpse of the man who had arrived. It was Caprisi. He stepped inside.

For a moment Field stared at the door and the empty street. Then he leaned back against the tree. His shoulders sagged; hope drained from him. Natasha had been right. Everyone and everything was corrupt; nothing here was left untainted.

He could feel his father mocking him, and he realized that to have believed in any kind of purity, to have sought any kind of victory, moral or practical, had been doomed from the beginning.

It made him fortune's fool.

Forty-three

aprisi stepped out of Lu's doorway. He lit a cigarette and glanced deliberately up and down the street, as if assuming he was being watched. He looked deflated; the meeting had not gone well. By Field's watch he had been in there exactly half an hour.

The American beckoned to his rickshaw driver, walked down the steps, and climbed in.

Field watched for a few moments before following on foot, occasionally having to break into a run to ensure he did not lose the rickshaw as it turned off toward the Chinese city.

The streets were narrower now, swift progress no longer possible against the oncoming wall of humanity.

They did a series of turns, and Field was soon lost, a stranger still in the dusty, teeming sprawl beyond the European boulevards.

The rickshaw pulled up at an intersection and he ducked back into a doorway as Caprisi got out and put a note into his driver's hand. Field was bent low, beneath a lamp, a baby crying in the open courtyard of the tiny house behind him. He listened to its mother trying to soothe it.

The American began walking, and for fifty yards they were the only two people in sight, then Caprisi turned right into a busier street. Field bumped into a woman herding a group of pigs, and when he looked up, the American was gone.

Field stopped, then turned off to the left.

This alley was dark and much narrower. The dust rose

around him as he walked, the only sound that of distant voices. There was no sunlight to penetrate the gloom. He heard the tinkle of a bicycle bell.

A figure came at him from a doorway and knocked him down. The man was onto him as he regained his feet, pushing him back hard against the wall, a revolver pressing against Field's nose.

"What the fuck are you doing?" Caprisi growled.

Field waited until he'd regained his breath. "Following you."

"Why?"

"I saw you go into Lu's house."

Caprisi held him still, then relaxed his grip and took a step back, without lowering his gun. "You're lucky I didn't kill you."

"So you're on the take, like everyone else?"

The American raised the revolver again so that it was pointing at Field's face. "You holier-than-thou Brits are getting on my nerves."

Suddenly, Caprisi's expression changed. He lowered his gun and put it back in its holster. "All right," he said. "You want to know? I'll show you."

He walked away fast, so that Field had to struggle to keep up. They were in another warren of narrow alleys, where still almost no light penetrated and the smell of sewage and human excrement was overwhelming. A group of children played in an open drain to their right as they turned into a narrow path and ducked through a doorway.

Inside, it took a few seconds for Field's eyes to adjust to the darkness. He heard a hacking cough and followed Caprisi over to the corner, where he was greeting a young woman and holding both her hands. He had crouched down and was taking something out of his satchel—bread and a metal flask of clean water.

"This is a"—he hesitated, looking at Field—"a friend."

Field knelt down and smiled at the girl. She was pretty. In

another world, without the dirt on her face and the rags on her back and without the stench in this place, she might even have been beautiful.

There were three children behind her. They stared at him, their eyes hollow with suffering. One, a girl, must have been six or seven; another, four or five; the youngest was a boy of, he guessed, two or three. Behind them a man lay flat on a thin straw mat, shirtless, his head on a small pile of clothes. When he coughed, it shook his entire body, shook the glistening sweat from its place.

Caprisi spoke quickly in Chinese, with his back to Field.

Field looked around the room. The five of them had only a small corner to themselves, and he estimated that there must be six or seven different families living in here, each with no more than a few square feet of floor space. They were all watching Caprisi and the woman, though most were trying to pretend they were busy with something else.

Field looked back to see the American take something else from his satchel—a bottle that looked like medicine and what could have been a roll of money. He placed the items in the woman's hand and closed his own over it.

Caprisi stood. He touched each of the children on the head, as if blessing them, and then marched out. Field saw, as he passed, that he was upset and angry.

The American did not slow down until they were back at the rickshaw. "Do you see now?" he asked.

Field didn't know how to answer.

"You see the great city we're building? We're always fucking congratulating ourselves on how marvelous it is . . ."

"Would it be any better if we weren't here?"

"Don't hide behind false moral choices, Field. At least it would be their city." Caprisi sighed. "She was begging outside my apartment with all her children, looking even worse than tonight. Her husband is an addict and he stole some opium from one of Lu's men, so if he's found he'll be executed. His family probably will, too, as a warning to others."

"So you went to see Lu."

"They're small-fry, nothing to him. I said I would pay for what he had stolen."

"But he said no?"

Caprisi nodded.

Field looked at his colleague, relief and regret threatening to swamp him. "I'm sorry."

"After all that we've said, you doubted me."

"I'm so sorry."

"Why?"

Field crossed his arms defensively. "I was watching Granger on the telephone a couple days ago, after our first visit to the factory, and it suddenly occurred to me that if someone had called Lu to warn him that we were going to the factory—I mean if Granger had—then the operator would have made a record of it."

"And?"

"The call came from your telephone."

"And you think I made it?"

"Not anymore."

"But you have thought that?"

Field said nothing for a moment, then nodded slowly. "You've been a friend to me—the only one who has—and I'm just so sorry."

There was another uneasy silence. Then Caprisi took hold of Field's hand, shaking it hard. "Okay," he said. "Okay, Field. That's it now, all right?"

Field felt his heart flooding with relief and warmth. "That's it." They clasped each other in a bear hug, then stepped apart, awkward in their newly rediscovered affection.

"You know . . ." Caprisi stopped as a trolley full of night soil was wheeled past and they were both forced to take a step back. The smell, which caught at the back of their throats, hung in the air long after the cart had passed.

Whatever he had been going to say, the American thought better of it.

"What will become of them?" Field asked.

"Of who?"

"That family."

"Does it matter?"

"To you."

Caprisi said, "But does it *matter*? I'm not changing a thing, am I? There are thousands like them. The parents die, the children are sold or starve to death or, if they're lucky, wind up in an orphanage."

"If they're lucky." Field hesitated, his throat dry. "Lu says he has found homes for some of the children from the Sisters of Mercy Orphanage and takes them away . . ."

"And?"

"He must have found homes for them, mustn't he? It's not possible that he just . . . disposes of them?"

"Field, this city is run by big business for big business. They pretend it's part of the empire when it suits them, and if you're American or British, then fine, but anyone else . . . Look around you." Caprisi shook his head. "You think they care what Lu does with his own kind? You think your uncle or the French actually care how many little boys Lu takes away and abuses and dumps in the canals? You think what he does with them would make them pause over their breakfast served on silver salvers for a single fucking second? What do you think would be happening to ten times that number if Lu didn't fund the orphanages in the first place? You've seen people dying in the streets. What do you think happens to the children once they've gone?"

Caprisi's voice had become hoarse with bitterness. He climbed into his rickshaw.

"Caprisi."

"It is all right, Field."

"No it's not."

Caprisi put his hand up to tell the rickshaw driver not to pull away. "So who did make that call?"

Field didn't have an answer.

"Macleod left the office with me; we were the last to go. I switched the lights out."

Field was about to ask the American who he thought it had been, when Caprisi said, "Is there anything to tie Lewis directly to the murders? Do we have anything approaching evidence?"

"We've just got Lena's notes. The fact that the shipments are coming from his factory." Field paused. "What I saw at Delancey's."

"What about the boy? We believe he can identify Lewis, correct?"

"I've found the orphanage where the boy was taken, but he's been moved and the sister is going to need to be persuaded."

Caprisi flicked the dust from his trousers with the back of his hand. "What if we went to talk to Lewis? Said we had a witness who'd watched him go into Anna Simonov's house on the night of her murder. See how he reacts."

"Anna?"

"Her or Irina. He won't be as prepared for questions about them. He knows we've got nothing to link him with Lena Orlov's murder, but the others he may be less confident about."

"What about Macleod?"

Caprisi had a stubborn set to his chin. "He can say he didn't know we were doing it. As you've said, there may not be much time."

"I thought you said we should be careful."

"We can wait until another girl is killed, if you like."

Field shook his head.

"Tough questioning," Caprisi said, "might at least make him more cautious. He'll surely be in less of a hurry to kill again if he thinks we are close to him."

"And what about Delancey's?"

"What about it?"

"Perhaps we should begin by finding out exactly how cruel Lewis really is."

Caprisi thought about this. "Yes," he said.

. . .

The iron-framed door of Delancey's was shut and no one answered the bell, so they had to walk down a dark side alley beneath a huge metal water tank in order to gain access.

The Chinese secretary sitting at an untidy desk in the back office looked as if she would scream when they walked in. The door through to the stage was open, the smell of alcohol and cigarettes pervasive even in here. Two girls were sitting on the edge of the stage and turned nervously in their direction. Field was about to ask where the manager was when a short Chinese man appeared behind them. He had greasy black hair and sallow, pockmarked skin. He wore a dark pinstripe suit and two-tone shoes.

"Help you?" His voice was higher-pitched than Field had expected, and "help" sounded more like "hep."

Caprisi looked at him as though he were a piece of excrement. "Detective Caprisi," he said. "And this is Detective Field from Special Branch."

The man looked even more frightened than his secretary.

"Charles Lewis is one of your clients."

The man looked nervously from Caprisi to Field and back again.

"I'd like to speak to some of your girls." Caprisi walked toward the door and out onto the stage.

The manager was rooted to the spot for a moment, but then fluttered around Caprisi like an anxious bird. "You cannot," he kept saying, but Caprisi ignored him.

The American came down the stage and stood in front of two girls. If this club exuded a certain seedy glamour at night, it now appeared merely sad. The girls looked dirty and tired.

"You both know Charles Lewis." Caprisi spoke in English. Field knew it was for his benefit.

The girls gave no sign of any acknowledgment. Field did not recognize their faces.

"Have either of you been with him?"

They stared at the floor.

"We are investigating a series of murders of young women, and we need to know whether Mr. Lewis has ever shown violence to any of you." Caprisi repeated himself in Shanghainese. "We know he likes to tie girls up. To use handcuffs. We know he likes to beat girls."

"You canno, must no," the manager repeated in English, the *t*s at the end of the words lost.

"Mr. Field," Caprisi said.

Field took a pace forward. "I'm afraid we believe that this establishment has been employed for the purpose of distributing Bolshevik propaganda." Field repeated the last part of this sentence in halting Shanghainese. Caprisi corrected him. Field took out his revolver. "You will be handed over to the Chinese authorities; they are waiting for you."

Field stepped to the side and pushed the manager roughly toward the door. Caprisi tugged the two girls to their feet by the necks of their dresses. It took a moment for the message to sink in, and then both girls screamed. The manager shook his head but was unable to utter a word. "Taipan," he managed to say. "Taipan."

Field pointed the revolver at his chest. "Have any of the girls here disappeared?" Caprisi asked. "Or has he ever met any of them outside of this club?"

The manager shook his head so violently Field thought it might fall off. He looked at the girls, but they didn't add anything.

"He likes to handcuff the girls?"

The manager nodded. Both the girls looked down.

"Sometimes he hits them?"

The manager nodded again.

"Always," the girl on the right said.

Caprisi turned to her. "What does he do exactly?"

"He uses handcuffs to the bed," she said in Shanghainese, clearly enough for Field to understand. "Then he likes to hurt."

"Does he require you to wear certain clothes?"

"He likes underclothes." She lifted her dress to reveal a stained stocking.

"What form does the violence take?"

She didn't understand this question and looked at the other girl, who indicated, with the flat of her hand against her face, that he liked to slap them.

"But he has never taken it further than that? He has never asked to meet any of the girls outside of the club?"

She shook her head.

"There have been no unexplained disappearances?"

She shook her head again.

"Have any of the girls died this year in any circumstances?"

"No," she said.

"How much violence does he like to inflict?"

The girl looked down again and Caprisi glanced over toward Field, shaking his head.

The Fraser's headquarters was on the Bund. A uniformed security guard took them from the reception desk, across the wide marble lobby, to the lifts.

Lewis's office on the top floor reminded Field of the private room at the Hong Kong Shanghai Bank, except that the windows were bigger here, affording a still more panoramic view of the bend in the river. Lewis's desk faced the water and he sat in a leather chair, invisible save for his feet on the desk.

Field looked out beyond him at a line of junks on the far side of the river that appeared to be sailing tied together. They bobbed up and down violently, their patchwork sails tilting to and fro like fans. A thick plume of smoke from another steamer cut a jagged line through the sky. Field could see the passengers on deck and sticking their heads through dirty portholes. New arrivals, he thought, feeling that his own seemed like years, rather than months, ago.

When Lewis finally replaced the receiver, he swung round, dropping his legs to the floor. He stood and walked over to the sideboard. He was in a vest and shirtsleeves, and he moved aggressively. "This had better be good. Drink, gentlemen?"

"No," Caprisi said. "Thank you."

"Never drink on duty?"

"Something like that. The shipments go the day after tomorrow. Will you be monitoring them?"

Lewis looked at Caprisi, and then at Field, as if they were insane. "I'm sorry, but—"

"We have a witness," Caprisi said. He looked as if he were going to step forward and thump him. "A witness who saw you entering Anna Simonov's house on the night of her murder."

Lewis poured himself a whiskey. A muscle in his cheek was twitching, and he scratched the end of his long nose with an elegantly manicured fingernail. "I haven't the faintest idea what you're talking about."

"You claim you've never heard of an Anna Simonov?" Caprisi pulled out his notebook.

Lewis was still being icily polite. "If you would care to explain, Officer, then perhaps I could help you."

"I'm sure you know that Anna Simonov was the Orlov killer's previous victim. We know you were seeing her, and have an eyewitness account of you going into her apartment on the night of her murder."

"Should I call a lawyer?"

"It is your prerogative."

"That was a joke, Officer." Lewis took out his cigarettes, lit one, and then threw the case to Field. "I'm afraid I have no idea who your Anna is."

"She's Natasha Medvedev's sister," Field said, without having intended to.

"Poor old her."

"So you knew her?" Caprisi asked.

"No."

"But you know Natasha Medvedev?"

Lewis smiled. "There are a lot of fish in the sea, Officer."

Caprisi turned toward the wall. Like all the others, it was covered in pictures of previous taipans of the company.

"Do you have family here?" Caprisi asked.

"If you're asking if I'm married, then the answer is no."

"Other family?"

"Why is that relevant?"

"I'd be grateful if you would answer the question, sir."

"Well, Officer, my father is, of course, dead, which is why I am taipan. My mother chose to return to Scotland. My first cousin Hamish and his wife are therefore my only close family here, though I have a number of other cousins involved at different levels of the company."

"Did you know Lena Orlov?"

"As I have previously said, we may have met a couple of times at the Majestic."

"But you never went to her apartment?"

"No." Lewis had his arm draped over the leather chair. His eyes were steady as they moved between the two of them.

"You've never been to the Happy Times block?"

"I didn't say that, Officer."

Field felt his face reddening.

"You've been to Miss Medvedev's apartment?"

"Once or twice."

"Only once or twice?"

"Generally speaking, Officer, I like to avoid associating with Russians. They're too much trouble."

Caprisi moved toward the window. "Lena Orlov kept detailed notes about illegal shipments from one of your factories. We understand from Delancey's that you have certain proclivities that would fit the profile of this case."

Lewis looked at Field, unperturbed. "Really, Officer."

"Lena Orlov believed she was going to escape Shanghai. She told friends that she'd been promised a passport and passage to a new life in Europe. She kept the details of these shipments as an insurance policy."

"Influential as I am, Officer, even I don't have the right, I'm afraid, to hand out passports on behalf of Her Majesty's Government."

The more Caprisi said, Field thought, the more languid and arrogant Lewis appeared to become. If, at first, he'd been irritated, he was now laughing at them. "Is there anything else?" he asked.

"We have a witness who saw you going into Anna Simonov's apartment on the night of her murder. When we approached your factory on the first occasion, your men attempted to kill us."

"So what do you want from me, Officer, exactly?"

"An explanation, before we move to bring charges."

"I keep thinking to myself that this must be April Fools' Day."

"You can think what you like, Mr. Lewis."

"Gentlemen, I could go on all day. Really, I could. It's been most amusing, but I have work to do." His expression hardened. "I'm afraid to say that running the biggest company in Shanghai doesn't give me much time for listening to this kind of fanciful nonsense."

"Very well."

"If you wish to bring charges, then please be my guest. But I suggest you run your so-called evidence past your superiors before you do so. I wouldn't want to be in your shoes if you don't." He narrowed his eyes. "I may say that I've always been a great supporter of the work of our police force, but I am beginning to wonder why." He looked from one to the other. "I'm sure you can show yourselves out. Do give my regards to Mr. Macleod."

Forty-four

utside, the sun was still shimmering on the choppy waters of the river, but it had begun to lose some of its heat.

They watched a steamer tied up on the wharf, belching black smoke from its funnel. It hooted twice and was greeted by a cheer from a crowd of people waiting on the dock.

Field leaned against the car.

"You didn't tell me the two women were sisters," Caprisi said.

"No. I'm sorry."

"Tell me more."

Field turned around and looked up toward the top floor of the Fraser's building. "Anna Simonov was Natasha Medvedev's older sister. She changed her name once she started work as a prostitute, but their father found out anyway and shot himself. He'd been a general of the tsar and couldn't cope."

"So Anna was also one of Lu's girls?"

"I think so, yes." Field realized that he had never asked Natasha.

"Why doesn't the boy go live with his aunt?"

"I don't know."

"He kidnaps the boy so that he has a hold over Natasha."

Field thought of his last exchange with her.

"Can she help us find him?"

"She seems to have gone to ground. I can't find her. I—I thought she might have gone to Lu, or perhaps been taken by him. I've tried her apartment, her friends. Where could someone like Natasha hide in this city?"

"Perhaps she is not hiding."

Field frowned.

"I hope she is, Dickie, and that she turns up alive. For your sake, I hope so."

Field walked the short distance to the Majestic. He climbed the stairs and scanned the stage and the dance floor. They were almost deserted this early in the evening.

He made his way to Mrs. Orlov's office and knocked once before he heard her sharp command to enter. She was still sitting at her desk, as though she'd not moved since his last visit.

Examining her more closely, he thought she seemed older, more tired and frayed. She looked weary and cynical, her eyes hooded. Field wondered if this was just a reflection of his own disillusionment.

"I'm looking for Natasha Medvedev."

Mrs. Orlov shook her head.

"Will she be in later?"

The woman maintained her studied disinterest. "I haven't seen her—not for at least the last few nights."

"Do you have any idea where she might be?"

"You know where she lives."

"She's not there."

"You know where she might be found."

Field felt his face reddening. He took a step back, into the doorway. "Do you know of any associates or friends she has in the city?"

Mrs. Orlov shook her head, her manner still frosty.

"Did Anna Simonov ever dance here?"

She shook her head again.

"Anna Medvedev?"

Her frown deepened.

"Irina Ignatiev?"

"I do not know these girls."

Field looked at her for a moment. "Thank you." He moved to close the door.

"Would you like me to give her a message?"

"No."

"Shall I say you called?"

"No, it's . . . No."

Field ran down the steps, the old anger starting to burn within him.

At Crane Road, Penelope opened the door. "Soldier," she said as she stepped back, very slightly unsteady on her feet. "How nice."

Penelope gently coaxed him over the threshold, leading him through to the drawing room, an arm draped over his. She pushed him onto the long sofa in front of the Chinese dresser. It was uncomfortable and, like the room as a whole, felt unlived in. "Geoffrey is out at meetings, but you must relax. You look like you've been working too hard."

Field had told himself he'd come to see Geoffrey and he was therefore, he assured himself, disappointed.

The Chinese servant came in carrying a silver tray with two empty glasses. "This will do," she said. She took a full bottle of whiskey from the sideboard and poured two drinks.

Penelope was wearing a low-cut silver dress, a long string of pearls hanging around her neck. She looked as if she was about to go out.

She handed him a glass before collapsing onto the sofa next to him. "Chin up."

Penelope knocked back her drink in one and Field found himself doing the same. It burned his stomach and he groaned quietly, then leaned his head back.

"Tired soldier," Penelope said.

She moved to her knees in front of him and tugged at the laces on his shoes.

"No, I'm . . ."

"Come on," she said. "Don't be silly. It's about time you relaxed. That's why you came here, isn't it? The comfort of family." She took off both shoes, then whipped off his socks, tickling the bottom of his right foot as he withdrew it.

Penelope refilled the glass and handed it back to him. "Geoffrey is just like this. Doesn't like to talk about things."

Field took the glass, looked at it for a moment, then downed it in one again. Penelope followed suit, smiling at him. She held up the empty glass. "To the comfort of family," she said. "Look at your shoulders." She put her glass down and moved around behind the sofa. She massaged his neck and back expertly.

"You're hurt." She came around to the front. "What happened to you, Richard? Your girl let you down?"

Field didn't answer. "Do you know Charles Lewis well?" he asked.

"Charlie?"

"Yes."

"One knows him."

"Would you say he is the most powerful man in Shanghai?"

There was a mirror opposite, and Field watched Penelope tilt her head to one side, frowning slightly. "I suppose so. I've never really thought about it."

Field's mind was now so overrun by questions that he shut his eyes again.

"Do you know who killed the Russian girl?" she asked him.

"We're getting close."

"Tell me. Who is it?"

Field didn't answer. He didn't want to think about it and he knew she was only making small talk.

Penelope released him. She took his glass and refilled it again. She placed a hand against his cheek. "Drink up, soldier." She poured herself another, too, and they faced each other and drank. "Ooh . . . I feel quite drunk now. Geoffrey hates me drinking whiskey."

Penelope bent down, her breath warm against his ears. "Relax, Richard. Let it go."

Field closed his eyes.

"Has she hurt you, Richard? Is that what it is? Has the Russian princess betrayed you? They always do, you know." He felt the glass against his lips. "Drink, Richard."

Field stood. "I just need to excuse . . ."

"Upstairs, I'll show you." She held his hand.

"Actually, I should . . ."

"Geoffrey will want to see you. You can talk to him about it."

She was still holding his hand, leading him up the stairs, and then they were in her room and she was turning, slipping the dress from her shoulders, so that she was naked from the waist up, wearing nothing but a garter belt and stockings below.

Her mouth was warm and sweet, despite the whiskey, her skin soft. She reached down and took hold of him through his trousers, releasing her grip only to brush against him, moving her hips from side to side.

He staggered, trying to pull away, but her grip was strong. "I know you came for this," she hissed. She kissed him with sudden ferocity as she unbuttoned his fly.

Penelope sank to her knees and took him into her mouth. He could feel her tugging at his trousers, taking her lips from him only long enough to free them, the wetness soothing as she took him to the base of her throat. She stood again, unbearably close as she took off his holster and unbuttoned his shirt.

She led him back toward the bed and lay down, legs slightly apart, so that he could see the pink lips glistening beneath the dark hair. She took his head and guided it there, the smell of her filling his nostrils. He tried to pull away, but she grabbed his hair savagely and pulled his face toward her own, taking hold of him and forcing him into her.

Penelope suddenly pushed him over again, onto his back. Her nipples were erect and she put a hand over his and pulled it to her breast. She pressed down against him, so that he found himself grunting, half in pain, half in anger.

. . .

His remorse was instant. Field waited perhaps ten seconds, but as soon as she was off him, some of his semen dripping back onto his stomach, he stood up and wiped it away with his shirt.

He put his shirt on, not caring how squalid that felt.

Penelope sat up, clutching her knees, resting her head on them and looking at him, her hair across her face. "Everything is not as it seems."

"Isn't it?" he said as he tried to pull his trousers on. "I suppose you're going to tell me your husband doesn't make you happy."

"The world isn't always simple."

"Well, it is to me."

"You don't have to blame yourself."

He stopped and looked at her. "One of the things my father—my lower-middle-class father, the disgrace to the family—one of the things he always said was that you should take responsibility for your own actions."

Field thought about the way Penelope had draped her arm affectionately over her husband's shoulder on the first night they'd all met up.

"You don't have to be chippy, you know. I don't care about all that."

"All what?"

"The family."

"Great. Fine." He did up the buttons on his shirt.

"Don't blame yourself, Richard," she said, sitting up on her elbow and looking at him, the sheet falling away from her breasts. "No one will know."

"No one will know," he repeated. "I will know." He stood. "It was a mistake."

She glared at him. "A mistake?"

"A mistake, yes." He gave a hollow laugh. "Don't tell me you think it wasn't."

"Just a mistake, that's it?"

Field sighed.

"This is why you came here, and don't you deny it."

"Fine."

Her face was small and angry as she thrust it toward him. "You were intent on fucking me the moment you came through that door."

"It wasn't a mistake, then."

"You were trying to get even, is that it?"

"I'm going to go."

"Determined to get back at the family because——"

"Oh please . . ."

"Well, you've succeeded. Are you happy now?"

"It has nothing to do with——"

"Your girl. Is that it?"

"Look . . ."

"I can see it in your face: it's the Russian princess. Another bloody Russian princess."

Field frowned.

"Oh, don't worry, Richard, she'll find out. I'll make sure of that and then your love will wither on the vine." Her eyes flashed. "You're all the same: you think you can get away with it, but you can't."

Field raised his hand, suddenly tired and wanting to leave with the minimum possible rancor. "I'm sorry," he said quietly.

"What will she think when she knows?"

"I'm sorry if I upset you."

Her anger disappeared in an instant. Her smile was sickly sweet. "Do you want me to get Chang for you?"

"I'll get a rickshaw."

"Will you give me a kiss, Richard?"

"Penelope, please . . ."

"You just fucked me, Richard. Be polite, if nothing else."

He walked forward and leaned over. She kissed him with an open mouth, briefly grasping the back of his neck. "I'm sorry if I've hurt you," she said.

Field hesitated. He looked at the gold Buddha beside her, then walked away.

"Richard?"

He didn't stop.

Field went to the Happy Times block and stood beneath the line of trees, but there were no lights on the top floor.

He tried to walk away, but got only a few paces before he turned back.

He moved quickly through the light and shadow, the heat of the night bringing sweat to his brow as he climbed the stairs again to the darkened hall. He knocked, quietly calling her name, but there was no answer.

Forty-five

he first glimmer of dawn awoke him and Field lay still, every muscle in his body screaming at the discomfort of the night. It took him a few seconds to remember where he was. He lifted his cheek from the cold marble floor and rubbed his eyes. His shoulder was cramped against her door.

Natasha had not been home.

He turned and paced from one side of the hall to the other.

Field took the notepad from his pocket and his father's fountain pen. For a moment, as he tried to think what to say, he wondered if this is what his father had felt for his mother. Was it love that ruined you?

Field wrote: *Please call. I will be in the office. Central 26522, extension 79.* He almost added, *I know about the boy,* but thought better of it. He did not sign it.

Slowly, he opened the door to the stairwell and began to descend to the street. It was still early, a hint of color on the rooftops, the air heavy and close. He felt the stubble on his chin. He thought he could still taste Penelope in his mouth and it disgusted him. His clothes were a mess.

Field passed a line of bodies huddled against the wall of the race club and then stopped by its entrance and turned back one last time. As he swung around, a short Chinese in a pinstripe suit and black trilby stopped about twenty yards behind him.

Field looked at him, but the man made no attempt to hide,

or to pretend that he was doing anything other than following him.

Field began walking again, listening to his own footsteps and the echo behind him. He felt for his revolver.

He kept a steady pace, skirting the race club and waiting for a solitary tram to pass before crossing the road. His pursuer maintained his distance.

In Carter Road, Field had thought to try and lose him, but as he walked past the church, the graveyard of which he would have used to shake off his pursuer, he saw another man reading a newspaper on the far side, and a third standing at the intersection ahead.

He slipped his hand inside his jacket and took hold of his revolver, then stopped. The footsteps halted behind him, but neither of the men ahead moved. He was ten yards beyond the church. He could feel his heart thumping in his chest.

His brain was clear. They would have shot him by now if that had been their intention.

He started walking again. The man on the far side of the road continued to read his newspaper; the one at the intersection ambled away down the street.

Field kept going until he reached his quarters, standing silently in the hallway beyond the porter. He took out his revolver and checked that all the chambers were full before turning into the common room and forcing himself to breathe more normally.

He poured himself a cup of coffee from the jug on the sideboard, took the copy of the *North China Daily News* next to it, and sat at one end of the dining room table in the middle of the room.

One of the boys came through the white swinging doors, but Field shook his head. "No cook."

"Bacon?"

Field shook his head.

"Eggs? Very good. Build you up."

"No thanks."

The boy wiped a corner of the table that had not looked

dirty with his tea towel and withdrew. Field sipped his coffee, then picked the mug up and went and sat in one of the leather chairs at the far end of the room. Pulling open his newspaper, fighting to concentrate, his eyes strayed to a picture of Bebe Daniels advertising her latest picture, *Miss Bluebeard*. He thought her mouth and nose were like Natasha's.

He put the newspaper down and went upstairs to change. In the corridor Prokopiev was pulling up his suspenders.

"Good morning, Field," he said, his accent thick and sarcastic.

"Good morning."

"Getting up early."

"Yes."

"And getting out of bed on the wrong side."

Field stopped. He looked at the Russian's bald head and sallow eyes. "Been busy, Prokopiev?"

He shrugged.

"What are you working on?"

"Working hard, my friend."

"Granger's orders?"

Prokopiev looked at him intently. "Not everything is Granger's orders."

Field held the Russian's stare, then unlocked his own room and slammed the door shut. He took his revolver out of its holster, placed it on the bed, within easy reach, then took some fresh clothes from the closet and put them on. His shirt had been neatly ironed by the hall steward, but was still musty and slightly damp.

He sat down, smoked a cigarette, and wondered if he should stay put. He decided that Natasha would not know where he was. He stood again and told himself that, if their intention had been to kill him, they would have done so earlier, when fewer people were around.

Field came out of the Carter Road quarters confidently, his hand tucked into the pocket of his jacket, gripping the butt of

his revolver hard. He saw them immediately. Two were leaning against the iron railings opposite, a third waiting farther
up toward the top of the road.

Field walked briskly, ignoring them. The man ahead drifted
forward and allowed him the space to do what he'd intended,
which was to turn into the churchyard.

He moved with less haste through the graveyard, as
though he had come to visit a dead relative. He entered the
front of the church.

Field had only been to one service here, but it was enough
for him to be familiar with the layout. He sprinted down the
center aisle, past the pulpit, and out into the vestry. The door
was locked, but he opened a narrow window next to it and
squeezed through. He climbed the wall behind and dropped
down into the street.

He was about to run when he noticed another man standing on the opposite side of the road. He was wearing a white
trilby and was not one of the three Field had seen before.

An expatriate woman walking her dog shot Field a curious
and concerned glance, surprised at his sudden emergence, perhaps sensing his unease. Field brushed down his suit and
began to walk again. The man followed and Field turned back
once to see two of the others swiftly rounding the corner, the
third climbing over the wall behind him.

Field waited for a black Buick to pass before he crossed the
road. He thought there were four or five of them, if not more.

Inside the lobby at Central, a group of uniformed Chinese officers was waiting by the stairs, their Thompson machine guns
propped up against the wall. Field passed them and climbed up
to the S.1 office.

As he entered, he could see Granger standing by the window in his glass office, the telephone to his ear, almost hidden
in a cloud of smoke. Prokopiev was at his desk, leaning back in
his chair, the suspenders of his trousers hanging down beside

his knees, his scuffed boots against one cubicle wall, his head against the other. He was reading a newspaper, a blue censorship pencil in his hand. He looked at Field steadily.

Yang stood from behind her desk. She had a note in her hand, and Field's spirits surged until he read, *Penelope called.* It was timed ten minutes ago.

"Richard?" Field looked up. Granger was half out of his door. "Have you got a minute?"

Field folded up the sheet of paper and slipped it into his pocket. He noticed Yang was avoiding his eyes.

He shut the glass door behind him, banging the blind.

"I'll take you up in a minute," Granger said as he sat behind his desk.

"Take me up where?"

"I don't blame you, Richard, but I would have expected to be informed."

Field frowned.

"This is not a cowboy operation. We are entirely reliant on the council for funding, and to go in riding shotgun, accusing someone like Charles Lewis . . ." Granger shook his head. "We'll go up in a minute. I'll come and find you." Granger pointed Field toward his desk. "You're still coming tonight?"

"Dinner. Yes, of course."

"Are you all right, Richard?"

"I'm fine, yes."

"You look distressed."

"No . . . I'm fine."

"We need to talk about this supplement."

There was a long silence. Granger looked at the smoke hanging in the air between them.

"I've a meeting of the budgetary committee this afternoon. I was thinking of around two hundred a month?"

Field realized he was expected to answer. He was about to say that he had already received two payments into his account, when he realized that this had nothing to do with what Granger was telling him. "That's generous."

"It will be paid directly into your account at the same time as your salary."

"So this will be the first payment?"

"Yes. To be honest, at the moment I don't feel especially like rewarding you, but I've got to put it in front of the committee and I promised we would discuss it, so we are. You don't seem terribly pleased."

"No . . . I mean yes."

"It is paid to all members of my department here and rises as you become more senior. It's an insurance payment."

"An insurance payment?"

"This is an expensive city and I want the members of my department to be immune from its temptations, do you see?"

"Yes."

"Nothing extra is expected of you; it is designed to reflect the special nature of the work in this department and the sensitivity of it. I hope you appreciate it, Richard. Most others do and it was a bloody nightmare getting it past the budget committee."

"This is definitely the first payment?"

"Richard, are you all right?"

"Yes, of course."

Granger stood. "Lewis will be there tonight, so try to restrain yourself." He took a step toward Field and glanced over his shoulder. "Don't be put off by the Eton and Oxford nonsense. Or any of that rubbish Macleod has fed you. Lewis is surprisingly straightforward."

"An honorable man."

Granger regarded him critically.

Field opened the door, wondering how anyone else had gained his bank account details.

"I'll come and get you in a minute."

Field closed the door quietly and walked straight through the office and down the stairs to C.1. Caprisi took hold of Field's arm and led him back to the stairwell.

"Macleod is fucking furious that we didn't warn him. But I said time was short and other girls will be murdered and he'll back us. I think he's on the phone to some of the other members of the council. We're up in front of the commissioner in a few minutes."

"I can't find her," Field said.

Caprisi looked at him. He touched his arm again. "It's all right, Field."

"Do you think they've——"

"I think she's gone to ground to avoid you. She's no fool."

He felt close to despair.

"Field."

"I had a tail this morning. From last night, I think."

"So did I."

"I tried to shake them, but there were four, maybe five."

"They can move in packs of ten or more." Caprisi smiled ruefully. "There's no shortage of manpower. And they don't mind if you see them."

"Lu's men this time."

"It seems so." Caprisi moved toward the stairs. "Let's go up. He's in a foul mood."

"I'd better come with Granger."

Caprisi nodded and Field went back upstairs. Granger was still on the phone, but he only had to wait a few minutes. They walked up to the sixth floor together. Macleod and Caprisi were already sitting on the other side of the table, beside the commissioner.

Granger lit up again. Field considered how even-tempered he was. He never seemed to get angry.

"Macleod," the commissioner said. "We all know why we are here: an official complaint from Charles Lewis. I've had Geoffrey Donaldson on the telephone this morning seeking an explanation, and Granger wanted all this thrashed out, so ... please."

"We've acted within the bounds that one could reasonably expect of this investigation," Macleod said, his elbows on the table. "There are members of the council who share our misgivings about Charles Lewis."

"Your misgivings," Granger said.

"We are not here simply to protect the rich and powerful."

"Though they pay our wages."

Macleod glowered. "Let us not forget that Lena Orlov was stabbed almost twenty times." He looked around the room and waited for someone to challenge him. "The notes left in Orlov's flat refer to a series of shipments, all of which have originated from Fraser's factories. We know they're smuggling opium and that the next shipment goes tomorrow. It defies belief that this could be going on without Lewis's express knowledge."

"I doubt he even knows where most of his factories are," Granger said.

The commissioner looked at Granger, flipping his pencil over the back of his hand.

"Lewis is tied to this murder," Macleod went on, "whether we like it or not. We have Orlov's notes; we have the fact of the shipments. It's inconceivable he's not in it up to his neck, and tough questioning was an entirely legitimate tactic. If nothing else, it might make him hesitate before killing any more girls. His response indicates guilt. I propose we have a watch on this shipment tomorrow night and on Lewis as well."

Granger leaned forward. "Tell me you're not serious."

The commissioner indicated that Granger should present his case, but he simply shook his head. "There's no evidence here that would stand up for a second in a court of law. Even if you are right about the shipments, there is no evidence whatever to suggest that Lewis knows anything about them. It could have been one of the factory managers who was fucking the Russian girl and shooting off his big mouth in an attempt to impress her. And the rest of it is so circumstantial as to be preposterous."

"His response has been swift," Macleod said.

"Of course it fucking has. His company taxes account for about twenty-five percent of our annual budget." Granger looked exasperated. "We're cutting our throats. As for the increase in the budget, we've spent months trying to persuade Geoffrey Donaldson." He sighed again. "You can kiss that good-bye, Macleod."

"Money doesn't buy innocence."

"But it pays our wages." Granger bristled. "You're wrong about Lewis, anyway. I know he's a little rougher on the inside than we expect in someone of his standing, but I don't believe he's behind these . . . girls."

"They were murdered."

"They were Russian."

"So they don't count?"

"Of course they do, but get a sense of proportion. If it was a society woman of his acquaintance, then it would be intolerable, but they were Russian prostitutes, for Christ's sake. If you have the evidence, then it's a different matter; but so far, you've not got a row of beans and you're acting like a bunch of cowboys."

"Perhaps that is what is required."

Granger rolled his eyes. He looked at the commissioner. "Are you going to say anything?"

"It does seem a little premature."

"Thank you."

The commissioner turned back to Macleod. "What explanation do you want me to offer Geoffrey Donaldson?"

Both Caprisi and Macleod were looking at Field. "We acted within bounds we thought were reasonable in a very unpleasant case," the Scot said. "No offense was intended and we apologize if any was caused. Clearly, the involvement of one of his factories and his association with some of these girls, and with that side of the city's life in general, may have led us to act in haste, but we will continue to pursue the matter vigorously." Macleod tugged at his nose. "I'm still going to watch that factory tomorrow."

"Then they'll move it through somewhere else," Granger said.

"Is that so?"

Granger and Macleod glowered at each other.

"That's enough, gentlemen," the commissioner said. "I think we've progressed as far as we're going to."

Forty-six

few minutes later, after watching Granger walk into his office and shut the door, Field went down to C.1. Caprisi was standing by the door, talking to one of the secretaries, and Field waited until she had gone back to her desk.

The American went to get himself some water.

"Where do you think she's gone?" Field asked.

"I've no idea."

"Do you think they know she is working for us?"

"*I* didn't even know. Is she?"

Field realized he was making a fool of himself. "We need to find the boy and we won't without her."

"If she's chosen to be lost, then we're wasting our time. People disappear here, if you haven't noticed. If she's been taken, we'll never find her."

Field contemplated for the first time the possibility that Natasha might be dead already.

"You've left a note?" Caprisi asked.

Field's throat was dry. He wondered now if even leaving the note was dangerous. "Yes."

"Caprisi!" Macleod shouted.

Both of them walked down to his office and shut the door behind them. Macleod retreated behind his desk, shaking his head. He was half-angry and, Field thought, half-amused, in the way that a father is with a troublesome but spirited child.

"So you're being tailed as well," Macleod said.

"Lu's men."

"Then I want you in the office, unless otherwise agreed. In fact, in the office, period. We'll arrange an escort back to your quarters tonight."

Caprisi looked at Field. "We believe Anna Simonov's son can positively identify the killer," the American said. "We need to look for him."

"Not today, gentlemen. If you're being tailed, then you're at risk, and I can't afford the manpower to move you around with an escort all day." Macleod leaned across and pushed his paperweight from side to side. "I'm going to fix a watch on the factory tomorrow, so we'll see what transpires. Perhaps that will be your evidence." Macleod stood. "Is Chen fit?"

"No."

"Fit enough to supervise a watch?"

"I doubt it."

Macleod looked annoyed by this. "Don't cause me any more trouble, will you, boys." It was not a question.

Field felt caged in the office, so, after lunch, he resolved to return to Katya's house.

He tried to get out of the station the back way. He walked through the canteen and the kitchen and emerged into a small side alley by the rubbish bins. He could see no sign of anyone, so stepped out into the street. He kept close to the wall and ducked under the steam that was pouring from an open kitchen window.

He had only walked ten yards when he saw them leaning against the wall at the far end of the alley: two on each side of the street. They straightened and Field stopped. For a moment he felt like testing them out, the adrenaline pumping through him, but his instincts told him the risk of inadvertently leading them to Katya's house was too great. He turned back. There was no choice but to sit by the phone and wait.

.   .   .

That night Lu's men were still out front, but Granger shoved Field roughly into the back of his Chevrolet and then turned to check that they were not being followed.

Granger had dismissed Macleod's suggestion that they would need an escort.

The house was close to Penelope and Geoffrey's, just behind the Bund, and of similar design and size, with a veranda and high-ceilinged, airy rooms. "Good man, Field," Granger said as he guided him into the hall. "You can lose your jacket. Wu!"

Granger went on through to the back while his number one boy took Field's jacket and revolver, then sprayed his ankles awkwardly with paraffin.

"Many bites . . . buzz . . ."

Field smiled. The man had not a single tooth, so "buzz" sounded like his father breaking wind. He paused, gathering himself.

Caroline Granger rose swiftly as he came onto the veranda at the back, offering her hand. She wore a simple, short black dress with a gold and diamond necklace, her dark hair shiny and her smile warm. "We meet properly at last." She turned. "You know Penelope Donaldson."

"We're related," Penelope said without standing. "I'm his auntie."

Penelope was also dressed in black. She looked at him as he sat down, dark eyes resting upon his face. He tried to smile back.

"Some champagne, Richard?" Granger held a bottle in one hand, a glass in the other.

Field hesitated.

"Hesitation means consent." He poured the glass and handed it to him.

Field took out his cigarettes and offered them around, but Granger shook his head and reached for his own as he sat on the wicker sofa beside his wife.

"I've been getting a hard time," Granger said, leaning

back in his chair and placing both feet on the glass table in front of him. "The ladies here believe their kind are in the process of proving themselves our equals in some ways, and our superiors in most."

"That woman who is planning to swim the Channel," Caroline explained. "Patrick doesn't believe she'll be able to do it and certainly does not find it a cause for celebration."

"I'd like to see her bloody dance."

"What's that supposed to mean?" Penelope asked.

"That she's probably not very feminine," Caroline went on. "Patrick likes his women strapped to the bed."

Penelope giggled.

Field took a sip of the champagne and a drag of his cigarette. He looked out, through the smoke, across the startlingly green lawn. They were surrounded by bigger buildings, but the garden felt private; the city was a distant hum above the noise of the gaslights.

The doorbell rang and Granger stood to go to the front door. Penelope stared at him as they heard Charles Lewis and Geoffrey in the hallway.

"The lovely Mrs. Granger," Lewis greeted his hostess as he came onto the veranda. "What a pleasure. Dickie . . . how nice." Field stood and Lewis gripped his hand hard, his manner icily polite, his glare piercing. He stared at Field for a moment, then moved along to Penelope. "Here's my girl . . ." He kissed her, too warmly.

Geoffrey came through the door. "Evening, nephew," he said, his face split by a smile of genuine warmth. Field felt a stab of guilt in his belly. "Sorry we're late. The Empire Day preparations are killing me, and then Charlie and I were yapping in the club about the cricket."

They shook hands. Geoffrey kissed first his wife and then Caroline. He sat on the wicker sofa beside Penelope. Granger opened another bottle of champagne and poured both men a glass, before refilling the others, ignoring Field's gesture of refusal.

"We almost got mown down outside," Geoffrey said. "Some moron absolutely hammering along."

"Drunk," Lewis said.

"You know they have white lines in the middle of the road in England now, and even lights—red and green to slow everyone down."

"Traffic lights," Lewis added.

"Yes. That's what we need."

Granger returned to his seat and put his feet back on the glass table. "Breaches of traffic protocol are," he said, "the very least of our problems."

They were silent for a moment. Field wondered whether they all knew about the interview with Lewis. Granger lit another cigarette.

"They've still got these bloody strikes in England," Geoffrey said.

"At least it's not just us," Granger said.

"Bolshevism is never going to take hold in England," Lewis said. "Not a chance, you mark my words. It's a nonissue."

"They're still on strike," Geoffrey said.

"The English worker's too damned sensible."

"The war hasn't helped."

"The war hasn't helped anything," Lewis went on. "But if they weren't so obsessed with their own problems—the government, I'm talking about—then they might pull their heads out of their backsides for long enough to get a glimpse of what we're actually up against here."

"They do know," Geoffrey said.

"No they don't. They've no idea. You might as well call this the battle for Western civilization, because that's what it is."

"That's a bit melodramatic, Charlie," Penelope said.

"No it's not. We don't fly under the flag of the colony and they never let us forget it, but that makes our struggle all the more important."

"You sound like a politician," Penelope said. "When you go home, you can stand for Parliament."

"Who says I'm going to go home?"

"What, never?"

"What is there to home? A long, fruitless struggle to find a decent bloody servant."

"But you're so young, Charlie," Caroline said.

"America beckons, if anywhere. I'd like to hear Louis in concert—now, that's something that would be worth a journey. Are we going to have some music, Patrick?"

Granger stubbed out his cigarette and put down his glass. He disappeared inside but left the doors open, so that the sound of Louis Armstrong's band soon filled the veranda.

"Keeping you up, old man . . ." Granger was at Field's shoulder. He ruffled his hair with a throaty laugh. "Fine rugby player, girls," he said approvingly, pointing at Field's head. "Strength, ability, speed, aggression, tactical awareness."

He was looking at Caroline and she nodded. "You'll go far," she said. "One day Patrick will start deciding promotions and pay according to what happens off the pitch." She looked up at him, smiling. "Though, of course, if he becomes commissioner, he will have to change."

"If," Geoffrey said quietly. "There's no 'if' about it."

"We cannot have that bloody Scot," Lewis said. "Not under any circumstances."

"What do you think, Richard?" Granger asked.

Field frowned. "About what?"

"This is a time for testing loyalties, don't you think?"

Field nodded. "Yes."

They were all staring at him.

"The commissioner formally announced today he is to retire," Geoffrey said.

There was another silence.

"I think," Lewis said, "that the police force is the ethical arbiter of a city, don't you?"

Field stared at Granger, then at Lewis, whose eyes were fixed upon him, his face taut. Geoffrey was smiling at Field encouragingly. "I think," Field said slowly, "that a police force reflects the ethics of the city but does not necessarily generate them."

"Well said, Richard," Geoffrey inserted. "Well said indeed."

A Chinese servant appeared at the door and Granger stood. "Dinner, I believe."

The women left the room first, followed by Granger and Geoffrey. Field was last, and as he came toward the door, Lewis suddenly spun around in front of him. "All right, Richard?"

Field didn't answer.

"Don't take this the wrong way, but I think you and your American friend need to be very careful."

"What do you mean?"

"I hear rumors, old man."

Field waited for him to go on.

"Take my word for it: be careful when you are out and about."

Field felt the tension and aggression in his back and neck.

"I'm warning, not threatening."

"You're always warning."

"And you're not listening." Lewis's voice was still icily polite, his glare piercing. "I'm warning you and you're *not* listening. I don't want to see you go down, but I'm not going to say it again."

Lewis turned around, leaving Field confused and angry.

He breathed in deeply and walked through to the dining room. He was ushered to a seat between Penelope and Caroline Granger.

Field watched Granger as he leaned across to talk to Geoffrey. He thought of the questions that cluttered his mind.

"How are you enjoying Shanghai?" Caroline asked. She was leaning toward him, smiling warmly.

"It has its moments."

"Only moments?"

He shrugged. "It's different."

"Charlie is an evangelist," she said quietly, glancing across the table at Lewis. "We're not all blind to the city's faults."

Field was not certain what she meant, so picked up a spoon and began to eat the avocado on the side of his plate, which was extremely ripe.

"Most of us went through phases . . . excitement, disillusion . . . realistic tolerance."

"Of what?"

"Of the poverty, of the inequality. Rome wasn't built in a day."

"But it was built nonetheless."

She frowned. "So much better that we are here than the alternative. We have to lead by example. That's what Patrick believes."

"Of course."

"And if we can't set an example, then we shouldn't be here. Otherwise what's the point?"

Field took a last mouthful of avocado, then put his spoon down, noticing that it was silver. He was thinking about Lewis's words and the sense of urgency in his voice. "Where did you meet Patrick?" he asked.

"In Ireland."

"You don't sound Irish."

"School in England." She smiled again. "My father should have been loyal to the English, but he was a believer and we hid Patrick in the house." She touched Field's arm. "That's what I love about Shanghai. You may have a past, but even if everyone knows about it, they don't hold it against you." She glanced at her husband, a look of deep, measured affection. "Anyone can be anyone." She got up, still smiling, to supervise the preparation of the main course, and Field took the opportunity to go down the corridor to the lavatory. He washed his hands and then his face in the big enamel basin. He looked at his bloodshot eyes in the mirror and wondered what was happening to him.

He thought of Patrick and Caroline and how easy they were together, and the wealth on display—the silver and the servants and the big airy rooms. Was that what he wanted in life? To scramble to the top, to accumulate?

He wondered if he could stay in this city, if he could accumulate wealth under Patrick and take possession of Natasha. If he cooperated, wouldn't they give him that?

Is that what Patrick was always doing—subtly offering him a chance to join the club? Was he just missing the opening?

He still didn't understand the question of the supplement. Were the previous payments from someone else, not Granger, or was Granger just being disingenuous?

Field wondered what in his father's upbringing had made him so hostile toward the idea of pleasure and ease. Honor wasn't going to feed anyone, and it had certainly never fed them. Perhaps integrity was a luxury of the rich.

The door opened behind him and she stepped in. "Jesus, Penelope . . ."

"Keep your voice down."

"For Christ's sake, they're only in the next room."

He saw immediately that she was drunk. She was fumbling for something in a long thin silver and black handbag. "Everyone gossips, Richard. Everyone in this city. Everyone will soon know."

"Is that what you want? Why me, all of a sudden?"

"Why not?" She looked up. "Are you ashamed, Richard? Of what we did?"

Field didn't answer.

"Just an easy fuck, is that it?" she asked, her face twisted. She shook her head. "I can see what you think—see it in your eyes. It is the same with the others: just an easy fuck. Well, you don't get off that lightly."

"I'm not ashamed."

"But you still think it was a mistake?"

Field saw no point in provoking her.

She looked down. "Geoffrey will go back to work tonight. You can drop me home."

He moved toward the door.

"You'll be mine now, when I want you."

"You're drunk."

"All of a sudden, you don't like the idea of fucking me when I'm drunk."

Field looked at her, his disgust no longer disguised.

"I'm an easy lay when I'm drunk, aren't I, Richard?"

"I don't like the idea of fucking you under any circumstances."

She yanked her dress up and took a step toward him. "Don't you want to stick it in, Richard? Or have you had enough already? Want to go back to that Russian bitch, is that it?"

She lunged for him, her dress still raised, thrusting her crotch against his and trying to kiss him, her tongue on his lips before he could take hold of her arms and force her back.

"Penelope?"

They both heard the soft shuffle in the corridor outside. She stepped back, straightening her dress and checking her hair in the mirror. She was suddenly cool and calm. "Yes," she said.

"You all right?"

"Yes, I'm fine."

"Where is Richard?"

"I don't know. I think he must have gone upstairs."

They waited, heard a shuffle as Geoffrey moved away again. Field leaned back against the wall, catching sight of himself in the mirror and shutting his eyes in despair. Penelope let herself out quietly, without saying another word.

Field slipped up the stairs to cover himself. When he returned to the dining room, he squeezed between Patrick's back and the Chinese sideboard, avoiding Geoffrey's eye and looking as if he had just been sick.

"Are you all right?" Caroline asked.

"I'm fine," he said, sitting down. "Just been feeling a bit off-color all day."

"Working the boy too hard, Patrick," Lewis said sourly. "You should take a break, Dickie, go down to the coast."

"He's working on a murder," Geoffrey said sharply. "He's hardly got time for that." Field looked up and saw the hurt in his uncle's eyes and knew that he had heard.

That he knew exactly.

The meal dragged after that, like nothing Field had ever experienced. It was even worse once the women had retired and the four men were left to their port. Geoffrey and Charles Lewis returned to a discussion of British politics, a conversation that neither Patrick nor Field contributed to.

As soon as Field could reasonably get away with it, he announced his intention to leave, explaining that he still did not feel at his best. He managed to avoid meeting Geoffrey's eyes as they shook hands, and then Patrick was on his feet to show him to the door. Patrick finished his cigarette as Field put on his holster and jacket. Lewis came into the corridor and leaned against the wall, glaring at him.

Field went back to the veranda, walking past Lewis without comment. He said good night to Caroline and Penelope and then came back to shake Patrick's hand.

"Good luck, old man," Lewis said, still watching him.

Field stepped out into the street.

The road was deserted save for a black sedan parked outside a house twenty yards away. As he looked at it, its lights came on and it pulled out into the middle of the road. For a moment Field wondered if it was someone he knew—Caprisi perhaps—and then he heard the rattle of the machine gun and felt a stinging pain in his shoulder.

He was over, on the ground, his head on the sidewalk staring at the night sky, the car's tires screeching as it stopped, the bullets punching into Granger's car in front of him and into the sidewalk beside his head.

There was pain, blinding, in his arm—his left arm. He reached into the holster with his right, the gun in his hand now, pointing toward the sky, his finger on the trigger, squeezing off a shot, into the air.

He moved. He swung himself around as the door above him opened and he saw Patrick Granger charging out, as if in slow motion, his gun in his hand. He fired. He was shouting. Field turned his head once more to see a man towering above him, a machine gun in his hand, his face exploding.

Forty-seven

amn it, man." Granger was kneeling beside him, tugging at his coat, trying to pull it from his shoulder. "You're all right."

Field winced with pain, recoiling from Granger's rough embrace.

"Stay still. You're all right." He had the coat off Field's shoulder now and tore at his shirt. He exposed the wound, then stuck his fingers in it to stop the bleeding.

Caroline was at the top of the steps, her face ghostly. Penelope, Geoffrey, and Lewis swam into view behind her.

"Get a bandage or a shirt," Granger shouted. "Anything clean."

Caroline disappeared. Penelope looked as if she was about to cry as Geoffrey and Lewis came down the steps. Geoffrey stood beside him. Lewis took off his shirt and began tearing it.

"Are you all right?" Geoffrey asked; his face was etched with concern.

"He's fine," Granger said. "Hold his arm up, Geoffrey. Higher. It's not an artery."

Granger took the strips of shirt from Lewis and began to bind them tightly around Field's upper arm. He pulled hard so that there was maximum pressure on the wound. "It's all right," he said again. "Only flesh—glancing blow. You're lucky. Bloody fortunate."

"Who was it?" Lewis asked, but both Geoffrey and Granger were concentrating on Field, so the question went unanswered.

"Geoffrey, call an ambulance, will you?"

Granger stood. He moved around behind Field, put his hands beneath his arms, and pulled him to his feet. Charlie Lewis was waiting on the steps, shirtless, next to Penelope. Caroline came through the door, holding a bandage, which she could see her husband no longer needed. The body of the gunman lay in front of them, the back of his head blown across the edge of the sidewalk, his hand resting against one of the wheels of Granger's car.

There was a screech of tires, and, as if in slow motion, they all watched the black sedan tearing back down the street toward them. A fraction of a second before he heard the sound of the bullets, Field felt the force of Granger's push. Caught off balance, he careered to the ground once more, smashing against Granger's car. He fell back against the sidewalk, the pain in his head intense as he hit the body of the dead gunman and rolled across him.

The car roared away and then there was an ear-piercing scream.

Field raised his head. Patrick Granger was lying behind him, spread-eagle across the sidewalk, his head resting against the bottom step. Caroline was upon him, whispering, "Patrick, Patrick," but Field could hear only a low groan.

Charlie Lewis moved her aside roughly, dragged Granger flat, and tried to take his pulse. Geoffrey hobbled down the steps and bent over him on the other side, his ear to Granger's mouth, listening for the sound of breathing.

Field pushed himself to his feet, ignoring the pain in his shoulder. He stood unsteadily. He could see that Patrick had been shot six or seven times in the chest, bloody holes in the whiteness of his shirt.

Geoffrey straightened, and put his hand on Caroline's shoulder to indicate that it was no use, but she did not let go. She clutched his head to her chest, sobbing, whispering his name, her mouth quivering and her eyes shut. And then she convulsed, emitting a single howl of anguish more tortured than any Field had ever heard.

He closed his eyes. Caroline sobbed quietly and slowly,

each breath deep and wrenching. She mumbled her husband's name, over and over again, until Field could not bear to listen to it anymore. He opened his eyes, tried to step forward, and was vaguely aware of pavement rushing up to meet him.

When he came to, he was inside, on a sofa in the front room, Geoffrey's concerned face above him.

"How long?" he asked.

Geoffrey looked puzzled.

"How long have I been out?"

"You fainted. About two minutes, three . . . I don't know."

Field tried to sit up.

"Steady on. You must take it easy."

"No." Field pushed away his uncle's hand and sat up. He swung his legs onto the floor. "Where is the telephone?"

"You need rest."

"I need a telephone."

Field stood, feeling immediately unsteady. He forced himself to overcome it as he crossed the hall. His arm and shoulder burned with pain. He passed Penelope, who sat clenched in a ball on the floor, close to the door. Caroline was still clutching her husband on the sidewalk outside, Charlie Lewis above her, trying to get her to stand.

Field found the phone and had to struggle for a moment to recall the number of the Central Police Station.

The operator took a long time to answer. "It's Field here. I need to have the telephone number for Detective Caprisi, from C.1."

The man on the other end of the line hesitated. "I'm sorry, sir, but we're unable—"

"It's Richard Field from S.1. I'm at the house of Patrick Granger, head of S.1. He's just been assassinated, and I urgently need the number and address of Detective Caprisi from C.1."

"I'm sorry, sir, but I'm not empowered—"

"For Christ's sake!"

"I'm sorry, sir."

"Listen." Field tried to calm himself. "Listen to me. Let me repeat. This is Richard Field, S.1, at the house of Patrick Granger, who has just been shot seven times in the chest. I urgently need a number for Detective Caprisi."

There was another hesitation. "Do you have Detective Caprisi's Christian name, sir?"

Field tried to think. "No, I don't, but just look it up." He waited. "Come on," he said.

"I'm sorry, sir, I'm looking."

Field turned to see the number one boy emerging from the kitchen area.

"All right, sir, I have it. Detective Caprisi, Lane 1522, 6 Bubbling Well Road. Telephone number, Central 36278."

Field cut the connection and dialed Caprisi's number. It was busy. He tried again but got the same signal. "Come on, Caprisi," he muttered, but every time he dialed, he got the same response.

The number one boy was looking at the scene in the doorway and turned with a start as he sensed Field behind him. "Car," Field said. "Keys."

The man looked confused and frightened.

Field tried to imitate the action of someone putting a key in an ignition and starting a car. The man eventually understood and reached up to the shelf above him on which his master's hats were stored.

Geoffrey came out of the living room as the servant handed Field the keys. "Christ, man, you're wounded." He tried for a moment to prevent him from leaving, but Field pushed roughly past, catching his uncle off balance.

"For God's sake," he heard Lewis say, but he shut the door and reached over to set the spark and throttle levers, then turned the self-starter. He switched the levers again, released the emergency hand brake, and shoved his left foot against the low speed pedal. He eased it off and slipped into high gear as the car gathered speed.

He was going too fast as he came to the end of the street

and almost crashed into another dark sedan as he pulled out onto Peking Road.

A few spots of rain splattered against the windshield and he leaned forward, nursing his bad arm, swinging left into Yu Ya Ching Road and then right into Bubbling Well Road.

There was a small crowd outside Caprisi's apartment. Field sprinted up the iron steps outside the building to the first floor.

He stopped.

For a moment he could not move.

"No," he whispered.

Field took a step closer.

He fell to the floor, ignoring the searing pain in his arm. He touched Caprisi's cold neck, fumbling for a pulse. The glass in the door had shattered and Caprisi was lying flat on his back in the corridor, his revolver in one hand. He was wearing white shorts and T-shirt and, like Granger, he'd been hit repeatedly in the chest.

"No," Field said again.

He shut his eyes and tried to concentrate. He pushed his fingers into the skin and tried to locate some sign of life. He gripped the American's wrist.

Field put his head on Caprisi's chest, his hands on his shoulders.

He touched Caprisi's cheeks and stared into his eyes. He shook him. "Come on," he said. "Come on." He shook him harder. He took hold of the American's shoulders and moved him roughly from side to side. "Come on, for pity's sake."

Field ran his hands through Caprisi's hair. He took some between his fingers and pulled. "Come on."

He waited for a response.

"Come on!"

Caprisi's mouth was tightly shut, his eyes staring at a fixed point in the ceiling, his slicked-back hair ruffled where Field had held it. His head was tilted to one side, his left hand open, stretching toward the door.

Field sat back against the wall.

He did not move.

Field reached out and touched Caprisi's cheek with shaking fingers. "Sleep well, my friend," he said. In his eyes, silent tears were forming. A drop fell on his hand as he withdrew it from Caprisi's face.

He stood unsteadily. "Fuck it," he said, wiping his eyes with his sleeve. He took a step back.

He picked up a chair, lifted it, with difficulty, above his head, and hurled it through the broken window.

He took another step back.

Field took a thin yellow raincoat from one of the pegs above him and placed it over Caprisi's chest.

He leaned back against the wall and breathed in as deeply as his lungs would allow, his eyes shut in an attempt to close his mind to the guilt that threatened to engulf him.

Footsteps clattered up the iron stairs. Field did not move, no longer caring if they were coming for him.

The footsteps stopped. There was no sound. He opened his eyes and straightened slowly, turning to see Chen standing in the doorway, his arm in a sling, his face white from the exertion of the climb. He stepped in, leaned against the far wall, and slid down it, too, so that they faced each other across Caprisi's body.

Field sat back. "I never even got to thank him," he said.

Chen looked at him steadily.

"Why Caprisi?"

Chen sighed. "Caprisi did not fit into their world."

"Why tonight?"

"Your investigation. And the drugs. The *Saratoga* sails tomorrow. The shipment must go ahead."

"Lewis."

Chen did not answer.

Field straightened once more. He put his hands in his pockets and stepped into the tiny kitchen. Postcards were taped to the fridge, most from Chicago but some from other cities in America: Miami, Boston, New York, Los Angeles.

Field took them all off carefully and turned them over. They were nearly all from "Mom and Dad," though the one with the Hollywood banner on the front was from "Carol" and gleefully announced that Caprisi's little sister was going to make it big in the movies.

Field walked down the corridor to the bedroom—which was completely bare—and the living room.

There were two photographs on the mantelpiece: one of Caprisi with what looked like his sister and his parents, a handsome white-haired man and a large dark-haired woman, and one of the girl and the baby that Field had seen in the American's wallet. Field picked it up to take a closer look. Beneath it was a small, leather-bound album. He opened it and stared at the picture on the first page. It was of a boy of about three or four, wearing a baseball outfit and gripping a bat, a huge smile on his face. On the other side of the page was a more formal picture, and Field could see the family resemblance. The boy had straight, short, dark hair and solemn eyes, just like his father.

There was a shot of Caprisi standing next to his son, an arm on his shoulder, and another of all three of them in a studio. Caprisi and the boy wore serious expressions, but the woman had a warm, easy smile. She was pretty, with a small nose, dark hair, and a steady gaze.

The rest of the photographs had been taken in a backyard. There was one of Caprisi kneeling with his arm around his son, both of them again in baseball attire. There was another of the boy as a baby, in his mother's arms.

The last picture in the album was of the boy sitting on his mother's lap. She had the same serene smile.

Field stared at the photograph until the tears in his eyes made the figures blur. "Well, you're with them now," Field said. "Maybe what you wanted."

He closed the album, put it carefully back on the mantelpiece. Chen was still sitting on the floor close to the door, head bent.

For the first time in his life, Field wanted to believe in a God. He groped for something good beyond this, but found only icy despair.

He felt paralyzed, powerless to save himself.

The woman in the photograph seemed to be watching him.

He forced himself to walk back down the corridor. He knelt by Caprisi's body and after a moment's hesitation, ran his hand over Caprisi's hair, the way he'd done with Edith when they were children. Chen did not move.

Field leaned back. "Granger is dead, Chen."

Chen stood. "The cabal has guarded its secrets well. You must go, Field, before it is too late." He took out a piece of paper and wrote down a number. "If you need help . . ."

For a moment Field didn't respond.

Chen glanced down at Caprisi's body. "You can show your gratitude to him by staying alive."

Forty-eight

n hour later Field walked into the deserted lobby of the Central Police Station. He nodded to the doorman, Albert, and headed for the lift. He pressed the button and watched the dial as it descended. He looked about him, then stepped in and pulled the cage across with his good arm.

He hit the button for the fourth floor and it cranked into action. It stopped with a jolt when it reached its destination. Field pulled back the door and hesitated before stepping out into the darkness of the S.1 office.

He walked through the patchwork of streetlight and shadow, realizing that he should have asked Albert if anyone was in.

Field reached Granger's office. The glass door was ajar and he hesitated again, then pushed it open.

He rounded the desk and sat in Granger's leather chair, in the darkness.

As he flicked on the light, the picture of Caroline on the corner of the desk leaped out at him. He reached forward and placed it facedown.

Field looked up sharply and turned the light off again, thinking he'd heard some movement at the far end of the main office. It was several minutes before he was satisfied no one was there.

The desk appeared to have been cleared out. The middle and right-hand drawers were empty. The drawer on his left was full of expense forms, meticulously filled out in Yang's handwriting and signed by Patrick. Beneath them, he found a series of Hong Kong Shanghai Bank statements stapled together.

Field glanced through them. He was surprised to find that the Grangers appeared to have lived reasonably frugally, with few withdrawals, except for a large amount taken out on the first of each month. There were only two deposits, one of which was Granger's salary, a generous two thousand dollars a month; the other, for two hundred dollars, was apparently a transfer from London.

Field pulled out the last sheet of paper in the drawer, a letter from the secretary of the Municipal Council, Geoffrey Donaldson, dated today, acknowledging, in formal language, Patrick Granger's *interest in the post of police commissioner* and assuring him that it *will be taken very seriously at the appropriate time.* There was no personal flourish to the letter and it was signed, simply, *Yours, Geoffrey.*

The two cabinets in the desk were also empty.

Field stood, turned off the light, and pulled the door to Granger's office gently shut. He walked downstairs to the C.1 office and stopped by the door, listening carefully.

He edged forward, then walked briskly through the darkness to Caprisi's desk. He flicked on the light. There was a sheaf of paper in the American's in-tray, a typed report from Maretsky summarizing the details they'd discussed in person. The Russian had typed ORLOV MURDER in capitals at the top of the page.

Field glanced through it. On the third page, beneath Maretsky's signature, Caprisi had written, *Tackle the boy-friend, Sergei; why was Lena Orlov so happy in the final weeks?*

As with Granger's desk, the left-hand drawer was full of expense forms, the right-hand one empty. Field could see that the lock on it had been forced. He heard the lift moving and waited to see which floor it would come to. He turned off the light.

The lift stopped and the cage was slammed back.

Macleod walked briskly toward him. Field expected Macleod to see him, but he headed straight to his office and shut the door.

Field heard a drawer being unlocked, opened, and then shut again. A few seconds later Macleod emerged with a file in his hands.

Field flicked on Caprisi's desk light.

"Bugger—" Macleod recovered himself quickly. "You gave me a shock. Did you not see me come in?"

Field was looking at the file. It was the same color as the one containing the fingerprints. "I was thinking."

Macleod shook his head. "How's your shoulder?"

"Painful."

"It's a bad business."

Field stared at him. "I suppose any war has casualties."

"It doesn't need to."

"There's not many of us left now."

Macleod was avoiding his eyes. "You must be careful."

"I intend to be."

Macleod shifted his weight from one foot to the other. Field thought about the way in which he'd so easily assumed that, because the phone call to Lu before the attack at the factory had come from Caprisi's phone, Caprisi himself must have made it.

"What's in the file?" Field asked.

Macleod shook his head. "Nothing of importance."

"Nothing to do with the case?"

"No . . . something else."

Field stared at him. "Caprisi left some notes."

"Notes on what?"

"Retirement funds," Field lied. "Dirty secrets."

"Better keep hold of them, then."

"Yes, I'd better."

"You'll never know when you might need them."

"Quite."

Macleod put the file under his arm. "I'll see you tomor-row."

Field switched off the light and stood, so that they faced each other across the darkened room. "A good night for you, in one sense," he said.

Macleod hesitated, fingering his chain.

"You'll certainly be commissioner now. You get your chance to clean up the city."

"Caprisi was a good man, Field."

"Yes. The best."

"Brave but stupid."

"He wouldn't join your club?"

Macleod's chain snapped. There was a *chink* as his gold crucifix hit the floor. He bent down slowly to pick it up. "In deference to your uncle, Field," he said, "I'm going to let you leave. You have until noon tomorrow."

Field watched as Macleod turned, walked calmly to the end of the room and into the lift.

He sat down again, remaining still as it descended.

Forty-nine

ield saw the light of a candle flare briefly in Katya's kitchen window. He waited for the door to open. The moon was brighter now, leaving only the fringes of the garden in shadow. A dog barked and was swiftly answered by others nearby.

Field knocked again.

"Ivan, Katya, it's me. Please, I must speak to her."

Ivan opened the door. He had put the candle out, his face ghostly in the moonlight.

"I must find her."

"She has gone."

"Gone where?"

He shook his head.

"I've been given an ultimatum. I must find her quickly."

"She has gone."

"Gone home?"

"Not home."

"Then where?"

Ivan shook his head.

"Is Katya here?" Field heard a rustle and saw movement behind him. "Katya. For God's sake, please help me."

"She has gone," Katya said, her voice firm. "We do not know where she is."

Field pushed the door suddenly, forcing both of them back. Ivan stumbled. Katya was by the stove, beneath a row of saucepans, and Field could see the fear in their faces. "I know she's here," he said, but could tell immediately that this was not true. "Where is she?"

"We do not know." Katya was tired.

"Where can I find the boy?"

Katya shook her head.

"Please, there is no time."

Katya clasped her hands across her chest, and Field recognized the fatigue of people who have known fear too often and for too long.

"I must leave the city by noon tomorrow. There is a chance for her . . . *tell* her. The last chance. For her and the boy. Otherwise, they will both die here—you know it and she must, too. Tell her I will meet her in the cemetery at dawn. If the answer is no, then I will accept it."

Field took a step back. They closed the door slowly, without answering him, their eyes fixed on his. For a few moments he stood in the darkness, praying that she would come.

There were no lights on above the front veranda of the house in Crane Road, but Field did not know where else to go. He rang the bell.

He was about to turn away when he heard the familiar shuffle inside, and a sober, tired-looking Geoffrey opened the door. "I thought it would be you," he said.

"I'm sorry. It's late, I know."

"Come in." Geoffrey beckoned him over the threshold, placing a paternal hand on Field's shoulder. "We hoped you'd come back. Penelope is still up. We've had to sedate Caroline. Out of the question for her to stay at home. Come on through." Geoffrey caught sight of the wound on his arm. "Christ, man, have you not been to the hospital?"

Field said, "I think it's all right."

"Of course it's not."

Geoffrey took hold of him and led him through the house. He eased him onto the sofa opposite Penelope. She looked up, her eyes red, a glass of whiskey in her hand.

"The boy's not been to hospital," Geoffrey said quietly.
"Tell Chang we need antiseptic, clean water, and bandages."

Penelope got up. She did not acknowledge Field or meet
his eye and seemed to be moving as if in a dream. Geoffrey followed her, unsure she was even capable of such a simple task,
and he came back in alone, a bowl in one hand and some dress-
ings in the other.

Field tried hard not to wince as the wound was cleaned.

"It's a good thing you came here," Geoffrey said as he
pushed a swab into the wound. "It's only a nick, but would
have turned nasty. Infections set in fast in this heat."

When he'd finished, Geoffrey wound a bandage slowly
around the top of Field's arm and secured it with a safety pin.
Field watched his face, which was a study in concentration.

"You did this in the war," he said quietly.

"Many times." Geoffrey stood. "You'll be fine," he said,
misinterpreting him. "I've dealt with a thousand worse."

Field nodded. "Macleod is behind it all."

Geoffrey frowned. "You'll need a drink."

Field didn't answer, but watched his uncle shuffle to the
walnut sideboard and take out two glasses.

"The group of officers in the force who work for Lu is
called the cabal, and Macleod is its head," Field said.

"Macleod?"

"Yes."

"Impossible. He's as straight as a die."

"He's told me I have until noon tomorrow to leave Shanghai."

"I'm sorry, I don't understand."

"Macleod is in Lu's pocket. Caprisi and I were coming close
to unraveling the connection between the Orlov murder and
the drug shipments—shipments that go through Fraser's factories."

"Fraser's?"

"We think Charles Lewis has been operating a massive
opium smuggling operation. Lu provides the opium, Lewis the

transport. The opium is hidden in sewing machines or other mechanical products and shipped into Europe. Lewis was being given some of the girls Lu keeps as a favor, and Lu's men would clean up after Lewis had . . . finished with them."

Geoffrey's face had gone white. "Charles Lewis?"

"Yes."

"You have evidence of this?"

"We are very close."

"That's what tonight was about?"

"Yes."

"What about Granger?"

"Eliminating a rival."

Geoffrey drew on his cigarette, then looked out toward the veranda, deep in thought. "It's preposterous. Do you have any idea how rich Charlie Lewis is?"

Field nodded.

"His grandfather founded Fraser's, and he is certainly the richest man in Shanghai. He presides over a huge empire. The idea is absurd. He has less need of any illegal scheme than anyone I've ever met."

"We know he likes to abuse girls. He likes to be violent to the women he sleeps with."

"What evidence do you have?"

"We are very close to finding a relative of one of the dead girls whom we believe will be able to positively identify Lewis as her killer."

"Who is this?"

Field didn't answer.

"Is there any direct evidence of Macleod's corruption or of the activities of what you call the cabal?"

Field sighed.

"Then you must go."

"I'm not going to run away."

"This is not London, Richard, or New York or Paris. We cannot always win the battle, but we must win the war. I cannot go to the council about Lewis or even Macleod without

cast-iron evidence, and you have none. Macleod will certainly
be the new commissioner now, whatever I say, unless we have
something concrete to block his promotion." Geoffrey sighed.
"Your investigation has rattled cages clearly, but if Granger
and your colleague have been killed, then I'm afraid there can
be no further discussion. Go to Hong Kong. Get on a ship. We
can arrange for you to join the police there for a time." Geoffrey shook his head slowly and sat down wearily on the sofa
opposite. Field noticed, as he bent down, that his uncle had a
small bald patch on the dome of his sandy head.

"Can't Macleod be arrested?"

"On what evidence?" Geoffrey arched his hands, then
raised them to his chin. "You're the policeman, Richard. You
tell me what evidence you have."

Field looked at his reflection in the polished top of the coffee table. "I have responsibilities."

"Nonsense."

"A girl."

"A Russian?"

"Yes."

"Natasha Medvedev."

Field felt his heart thumping again. "How did you know?"

"Penelope said you'd formed an attachment. I've seen her
sing at the Majestic." Geoffrey's face was hard. "You have no
responsibilities to her or anyone else, Richard. Don't be a fool.
You must go. If you involve yourself with this woman any further, then none of us will be able to help you."

Field's mind was spinning. Geoffrey stood and went and
got the decanter of whiskey from the walnut sideboard. He
refilled both glasses and then lit another cigarette. He sat
heavily. "Russian girls have a habit, Richard, of not being
everything that they seem."

"I know that."

"You wouldn't be the first to be deceived."

Field nodded, without meeting his uncle's eye.

"Natasha Medvedev is a beautiful girl. So many are."

Geoffrey inhaled deeply on his cigarette. "I'm sure her story is tragic. They all are." Field looked at his uncle. "The fact is, you will not be able to save her from herself."

"I have no choice."

"It's love, I suppose."

Field didn't answer, staring at the light dancing in the golden liquid in his glass. He looked up. "I've no right to ask this, but could you get her a passport and the correct papers?"

Geoffrey stared down at his hands. Field became convinced that he would say no. "Do you have her full name?" he asked.

"Natasha Federovna Medvedev."

Geoffrey pushed himself to his feet and shuffled over to the sideboard, searching for a pen and paper.

"Date of birth?"

"April 1, 1900," Field said, inventing it.

Geoffrey turned toward him, suddenly smiling. "I'll see what I can do, but on one condition. There can be no debate about this. You must clearly understand the nature of this city and your predicament. You must leave tomorrow on the first ship available. I will do what I can for the girl, but I now wish you to put her out of your mind. Is that clear?"

Field did not respond.

"There must be no misunderstanding, Richard. You can do nothing further for this girl. You must leave at once."

Fifty

ield walked to the race club and squatted in the shadows beneath the clock tower. He did not know where else to go, and from here he could watch her apartment. There were no lights on up there. A family was sleeping alongside him, huddled together. The father, who was awake, watched him solemnly as the hours ticked past. Field thought of the family Caprisi had been helping and wondered what would become of them.

He remembered the ball at the race club he had attended with Penelope.

At about four o'clock a newspaper seller began to set up on the street corner, and Field stepped out of the shadows and bought a copy of the *North China Daily News.* The headline screamed "Bloody Friday." He walked down to a gas street-lamp away from the Happy Times block and held the paper up to the light. Most of the articles were devoted to Patrick Granger—*one of the finest public servants Shanghai has ever seen.* There was a short report on Caprisi, alongside his police ID photograph. The article described him as a detective from Chicago, who'd come to Shanghai *after killing his wife and young son in a drunken road accident.* Field wondered where they'd got such detailed information. From Macleod, presumably, twisting the knife even after the American's death.

Field folded the newspaper and checked how much money he had with him. He managed to scrape together twenty dollars.

He stepped back into the shadows, turned away from the family, took out his revolver, and checked that all the chambers were loaded. He had no further ammunition. He did not believe it was safe to go back to Carter Road.

He wondered if Macleod really would let him leave. He looked at his watch once more and then nodded to the father of the family, who was still staring at him, and began to walk in the direction of the French Concession.

The Russian church stood in darkness, the gravestones ghostly in the dim glow of the streetlamps.

Field stood just inside the entrance. He looked at his feet. His shoes were scuffed and dirty. He ran his hand over his stubble and through his hair.

It had only been nine days, but he found it hard to recall a world in which his every thought had not been defined by this woman, or to imagine one in which it might not be.

He thought he saw the first light of dawn creeping over the rooftops. He scanned the graveyard again. He imagined that she, too, might be waiting in the shadows.

Field thought he now understood what it was to await a sentence of death.

He waited, motionless, movement no longer releasing him from his agitation.

Field watched the gate as the dawn peeled away the darkness.

He took a step toward the gate and then another and then, on instinct, spun around.

She stood by the far wall, a black raincoat draped over her shoulders, her hair tied to one side. She was watching him, and although every fiber of his being screamed at his legs to run with all the force they could muster, he moved slowly, listening to his footsteps on the gravel path.

Her hands were in front of her, clasped together. "Hello, Richard."

Field waited, hardly trusting himself to speak. "I didn't think you would come."

"You didn't leave me much choice."

"I know he's your sister's boy."

Neither of them moved.

"When Anna was killed," Natasha said, "I tried to go. I took Alexei and got us onto a ship to Manila." She stared at the ground by his feet. "For a few moments I felt . . . I believed in the impossible: that by acting swiftly I had got him out of this terrible place." A look of inconsolable misery crossed her face. "But I turned around," she said, "and he was gone." She put her hand to her cheek, then let it fall. "A man came up to me to say that Alexei had been taken to an orphanage. Once a week, I go to Lu's house and one of his men takes me in a car somewhere—not always the same place—and I am allowed to go to a room where I can look through a window and see Alexei playing. I cannot speak to him or contact him, but I can watch him for just a few moments, and then they take me away. If I ever fail to do what they say, then I know what will happen."

Field waited for her to continue, but she stood before him, almost in a trance. He became aware that the silence was being broken by the sound of cars behind them on Avenue Joffre, as the day gathered pace. He took a step toward her. "I cannot force you to trust me, but I believe I can get us out of here. You, the boy, all of us."

Natasha did not lift her eyes. She shook her head.

"And if we do nothing, then we will all be dead. All of us. Macleod has given me until noon."

"Why you?"

"They killed my partner. Last night. And they tried to kill me." Field cleared his throat. "Even if you do not believe me, what kind of life do you think awaits Alexei in the orphanage and afterwards?"

She did not answer.

"Do you know what Lu likes to do with young boys from the orphanages?"

Suddenly, she lunged for him, her head thumping against

his chest, long, bony fingers digging into his shoulder blades, the smell of her skin flooding his senses, her hair in his mouth and eyes.

He held her to him, then tried to release her, but she would not yield.

He took hold of her shoulders and prized her away. He looked into her eyes, which spoke of her confusion and her relief and her uncertainty. "You must do exactly as I say."

"I'm not a child."

"We have only one chance. Where is Alexei?"

She shook her head.

"You must have some idea."

Natasha stared at him, and seeing only fear in her eyes, he tried to conceal what lurked behind his own.

Fifty-one

ield drove them straight to the orphanage. It was light now, the streets bustling with life as the city geared up for a new day.

He killed the engine, and for a few moments Natasha stared at the white building in silence. She did not move until Field went around to open her door.

Inside, the sound of the children having breakfast drifted down from the far end of the cavernous hallway. Natasha was moving slowly and he took hold of her arm.

There was no one behind the glass window, but a doorman appeared from a room to the side. He looked at Field and Natasha and then disappeared without a word. He returned a few minutes later with Sister Margaret.

She was not pleased to see him. Today there was no sunshine in the hallway and her hair seemed darker. "How can I help you, Mr. Field?"

"This is Natasha Medvedev. She is Alexei's aunt."

Sister Margaret's face hardened. "Alexei has been very lucky. Mr. Lu's men came around only half an hour ago to say that they had found a home for him."

Field stared at Sister Margaret and saw that he had misjudged her a moment ago. The hardness in her face was an attempt to stop herself from cracking. "Who came?" he asked more gently.

"They were Mr. Lu's men."

"There is no home for any of these boys, Sister."

She lowered her eyes, deep creases across her forehead.

"They are abused and then disposed of."

"Mr. Field, if you have come here to make accusations—"

"If we don't get to him immediately, that is what will happen to Alexei."

"Mr. Field, I'm afraid you will have to go."

"Is it worth it, Sister?"

Sister Margaret stared at the floor in silence.

"Please, Sister," Natasha said quietly. Field watched the muscles twitching in the nun's cheeks.

He turned and strode down the corridor to the source of the noise. The children were having breakfast. They faced each other across four long oak tables. The chattering died as he walked in.

"Does anyone here know Alexei Simonov?"

The children, with big eyes and subdued faces, stared at him in silence.

"Please, Mr. Field." Sister Margaret was tugging at his sleeve. "Please." He stepped back into the corridor. "There was no need for that," she said.

"Where is the boy, Sister?"

"I do not know."

"Sister . . ."

"I will find him." Sister Margaret looked from Field to Natasha and back again. "I will need a little time."

She was gone for almost an hour, and Field and Natasha did not speak. Natasha was frightened, but he knew that nothing he could now say would reassure her. He had to force himself to remain in his seat by the entrance hall. His eyes were repeatedly drawn to the article about Lu and the note saying he would be inspecting the orphanage on the coming Wednesday.

He tried to think clearly, to shape the plan that was forming in his mind.

Sister Margaret returned, her footfall soft on the stone floor. "Do you have a car?" she asked.

· · ·

Field drove slowly, following Sister Margaret's directions. They turned onto the Bund and continued over Garden Bridge onto Broadway East, and then through Hongkew past Wayside Park.

She indicated that he should stop as they came up to what looked like a school. Field parked alongside a rugby pitch where a small group of children was playing tag. They were close to the Settlement boundary.

As she got out of the car, Sister Margaret's face was pale and drawn, but there was a determined set to her mouth.

The sign on the facade said, *The Christian Brothers Orphanage,* and the entrance hall was as gloomy as Sister Margaret's own. She told Field and Natasha to wait and disappeared down a corridor to their left. Natasha had her head down, her knuckles white as she tugged at the fabric of her skirt.

Field heard voices and saw a small group of boys emerging from swinging doors at the far end of the corridor Sister Margaret had taken, talking quietly among themselves. As they turned away into one of the rooms, they stopped and eyed him curiously. The light was dim, but he could see they were all Asian boys, dressed in simple white uniforms, each with a blue cross on his chest.

"This way."

Field turned with a start, then followed Sister Margaret.

They headed through the swinging doors and turned into an even darker corridor.

The classroom, when they reached it, was strikingly bare; it had tables and chairs, but there was nothing on the walls save for a large, battered blackboard.

Alexei sat in one corner, a tall priest in brown robes towering over him.

The boy didn't move, and for a moment he and Natasha stared at each other.

Then Alexei broke free and ran, and Natasha swept him

into her arms, where she held him tight, her face transformed by joy and relief, her hands clasped around the back of his head, tears in her eyes. She stroked his hair haltingly with her fingers. The boy shook and she picked him up. "I'm sorry," she whispered, her eyes tightly shut. "I'm so sorry."

Like the other boys, Alexei was dressed in a white uniform. His short black hair was damp and combed neatly across his forehead. His eyes were closed now, too, his face still betraying his anxiety and uncertainty and fear.

The priest came forward and parted them roughly, yanking the boy back to the other side of the room. Natasha appealed to Field with tears in her eyes. Alexei was crying. "Stop it!" the man hissed.

Field said, "I'm sorry, I didn't catch your name."

"Father Brown."

"Father Brown, would you step outside for a moment, please?"

The man followed Field reluctantly with Sister Margaret. Field shut the door behind them. "I think it would be better if we were alone with Alexei for a minute. Then we can talk about what happens next."

"That's out of the question."

"The woman is the boy's aunt, as I think you are well aware."

"It's out of the question."

Field felt his temper flaring. "Sister—"

"No." Father Brown was intransigent.

"All right, let me make this clear," Field said. "This is not a debate. A crime has been committed, I'm an officer of the law, and I'm going to go and speak to this boy alone. Please wait at the other end of the hall."

Field could see the fury in the man's face. He pointed with his finger, and Father Brown retreated. Sister Margaret looked at Field with new respect as she followed the priest.

When Field came back into the classroom, Natasha was on her knees, whispering urgently to the boy. With his somber face, neat black hair, and hollow eyes, Alexei suddenly, force-fully, reminded Field of himself at the same age: sad, lonely, vulnerable, damaged.

"I've explained who you are," she said.

Field crouched down and offered the boy his hand. "I'm Richard." Alexei was shaking. Natasha took him in her arms again. "It's all right now, my darling. It's all going to be all right."

"I think we should leave," Field said quietly. He noticed that his own hand was shaking.

"They will not let him go."

"They'll do as they're told."

Natasha looked at him. He knew that she wanted desper-ately to believe him.

Field moved to the other side of the room and stepped out into the corridor. Father Brown and Sister Margaret were hud-dled by the doorway. Field tried to smile. "I'm sorry to have to do this without the appropriate paperwork, but we are going to have to take Alexei away now."

Father Brown looked as if he would explode. "You can't do that."

Field stared at Father Brown's bearded face and solemn eyes. "I'm not sure you clearly understand me."

"That boy is not to leave this orphanage under any cir-cumstances."

"Is that Lu speaking, or you?"

Father Brown gathered himself to his full height. "If you think I'm going to apologize for the unpleasant rumors that surround one of our most generous—"

"Rumors?"

"I know your type, Mr. Field."

"And I know yours, Father."

Field turned on his heel and Father Brown lunged for him. Field easily shrugged him off, then slammed him up against the wall.

Sister Margaret flailed at Field's back, screaming for him

to stop, as if the sudden act of violence had finally pushed her over the edge. He picked Father Brown up and threw him onto the floor, then kicked him once, hard, in the stomach. The priest let out a groan and Sister Margaret a shriek. Another priest appeared in the corridor, a group of children behind him. Natasha was in the doorway.

Field took his revolver from its holster and walked as calmly as he could to the classroom. "Come on," he said.

Fifty-two

hey drove away in silence. Natasha was in the back, her arms wrapped tightly around Alexei. The little boy's feet were draped over the edge of the seat, his eyes fixed uncertainly upon Field. Field concentrated on trying to project a confidence he did not feel.

They sped over Garden Bridge and onto the Bund. Field glanced briefly across at a steamer coming into dock. The sails of the sampans were like tiny pinpricks of light against its dirty steel hull.

Field checked the rearview mirror, then looked around to see if they were being followed. They passed the Hong Kong Shanghai Bank and the Fraser's building and the Customs House, and then he took a right into Foochow Road and a left almost immediately. It was quiet here, and he pulled up in the shade of the sycamore trees.

Natasha came forward and kissed him on the neck, holding him so hard that her fingers dug into his chest.

She did not let go.

He closed his eyes. He reached around and stroked her hair, then gently released himself from her arms. "It's all right," he said. "It's all right. Alexei, you're safe now."

Natasha slumped back and drew the boy to her. His body was limp.

Field glanced at his watch. It was much later than he'd thought. He tried to ease the tightness in his chest. "Tell me what Lu's ledgers look like."

She shook her head, not understanding.

"Describe the room."

"Please, Richard . . ."

He turned and looked at her. "We have only a few hours."

"Please."

"If we wait until he leaves the house, then there is a chance."

"I do not—"

"We have to have something to bargain with, Natasha. We have to buy your freedom. If we can get hold of the ledger and threaten to give it to a paper like the *New York Times* or get it to Washington or London, then we will have a chance. Without it, we don't have one at all."

She stared miserably at the floor.

"You have taken so many risks already, I know that, but this can buy your freedom. I'm getting you a passport and papers. We'll begin a new life. We'll go to Venice."

She slowly raised her eyes to his. "I do not understand."

"Yes you do. So did Lena. It was what she was trying to get."

Field felt the sweat prickle at his armpits.

"Lu's routine during the day is always the same. He leaves the house at one o'clock and returns at between five and ten minutes past two."

Field waited.

"You want me to go in there?"

"I want you to save yourself."

"You want me to do it?"

"I want a life for us."

Natasha stared at him, her eyes shining with loss and loneliness, with love and betrayal and insecurity and doubt.

She pulled Alexei's head gently to her shoulder and stroked his hair with her fingers as she looked out of the window.

Field did not take his eyes from her face.

"It is big," she said. "A dressing room, but also a study."

"And that is on the floor above the place where you are told to wait?"

"Yes."

"If you went in and said that he was expecting you, they would eventually send you up there?"

"Yes."

"Are you alone? Are there servants about? Would they stop you? Could you get up to the second floor if you were there alone?"

She didn't answer.

"Tell me about the room where the ledgers are kept."

"Clothes. Cupboards, always closed, with long mirrors. To the right, drawers, more clothes. Beyond that, a leather-topped desk . . . a light. Beneath, there is a silk curtain and behind that a safe." Her voice seemed to come from somewhere far away.

"You saw the ledgers?"

"Two, yes, both open. Big." She indicated their size with her hands. "Leather-bound. Many entries. Very, very small writing. And a pair of reading glasses beside them."

"They are always there?"

"Yes. Lena also saw them. She began to take notes. The man she had been seeing told her about the shipments. The man told her that Lu paid off many people, in the police, in the council; that many were involved, many important people. You are right. She thought it would help her."

"You saw names?"

"I think so."

"Western names?"

"Yes."

"Lewis?"

"I can't be sure."

Field swung around and rested his hands on the steering wheel. He looked at his watch, then pressed his foot on the low speed pedal and pulled out into the road. In the mirror he saw her continue to gaze sightlessly out of her window. Then she sat back, drawing her terrified nephew toward her once more.

Field drove back onto the Bund and brought the car to a halt outside the Cathay Hotel. He told them to wait and dashed inside. "Where's the manager?" he asked brusquely, and as a Chinese man in a neat suit emerged from a room at the back, Field produced his identification. "I need to make a telephone call in private, urgently."

The man looked around nervously before ushering him through a side door to the back office. Field pulled out the crumpled piece of paper that Chen had given him, and asked the operator to ring the number. It rang and a woman answered. Field asked for Chen and waited. He could hear the sound of children in the background.

"Who is it?"

"Chen, this is Field."

There was a pause. "You should not be here."

"I need you to tell me something. I pulled Lu's surveillance notes from Registry. They said that he goes out to Nantao every day at one o'clock and returns an hour later. That's what happened the other day, but I need to know whether his routine ever changes for any reason. Does he come back earlier? What does he do there? The notes say he conducts business from some tea—"

"Don't do it, Field. Don't risk it."

"I have no choice."

"You're right. Get on a boat. Go home. Survive."

Field paused. "I want more than just my own survival."

"Sometimes there is no more."

Fifty-three

ield parked in the street opposite Lu's house, about fifty yards from the intersection. It was already past noon.

On the far side of the street, a Chinese servant was sweeping the path to the back gate of his employer's house. Field could see the lush expanse of green lawn beyond. Otherwise, the road was deserted. Natasha and Alexei were huddled together in the backseat.

Field checked his watch impatiently until it was ten to one. Then he eased his foot down on the low speed pedal. "Try to come to the window," he said. He turned, but she did not look up. "Natasha, as soon as you are in the room, please try and come to the window so that I know you're all right."

He slowed the car to a halt ten yards from the Rue Wagner.

Two young children—a boy and a girl—emerged from the house opposite Lu's and began to play with a hoop, spinning it to each other, then keeping it rolling with a stick.

Field looked at his watch again. It was six minutes to one.

The door opened. One of the bodyguards came out and took up his position at the bottom of the steps. Grigoriev emerged, checked up and down the street, then went back inside.

The first man waited for a few moments, then walked down the road until he was out of sight.

The car pulled up. Grigoriev and three others moved swiftly down the steps and surrounded it.

The children had stopped playing and were watching the car's exhaust fumes billow into the still air.

Field's eyes were fixed on the front door. He could feel the adrenaline pumping through his veins. Grigoriev pointed in their direction, and the two men closest took a couple of paces toward them, raising their machine guns.

Field fingered his revolver but knew there was nothing he could do if they came any nearer.

Lu came out, moving slowly. Grigoriev barked an order in Russian. Lu ducked down into the backseat, and the car slid away from the curb.

"Now," Field said.

Natasha kissed Alexei on the forehead and touched his face with the palm of her hand. He gripped her arm and wouldn't let go. She released his fingers gently, without taking her eyes from his face, then kissed his forehead. She said something in Russian that Field could not understand.

Field felt his vision blurring.

Natasha opened the door and stepped out onto the sidewalk.

She walked toward the house, pulling her raincoat tight around her waist.

She reached the steps and knocked on the door. She turned back once, then stepped out of sight as it was opened.

Field unclenched his fists. He checked his watch. It was just past one.

Alexei clambered over into the seat beside him.

"It's all right," Field said, wishing he believed it.

The boy didn't respond.

Field scanned the windows of the house and then up and down the street. He lit a cigarette, gripping the handle of his revolver as he smoked, the metal cold against his palm.

The boy was still watching him.

Field leaned forward and looked up at the second-floor windows. They were dark, the curtains drawn. He lowered his gaze to the first floor, where he and Caprisi had had their audience with Lu, and where Natasha had told him she was always instructed to wait.

Why didn't she show herself?

The cigarette burned his fingers. He threw it out of the window, wishing the American detective were with him now.

Field looked up toward Lu's bedroom again.

Had he killed her today, as surely as if he'd pulled the trigger himself? He thought of Caprisi's warnings and was haunted by the look of pain that he'd seen so often in the American's eyes.

He looked at his watch. It was ten past one. *"Shit,"* he whispered. He wiped his forehead. "Shit."

Alexei had not taken his eyes from Field's face, but a creeping sense of hopelessness prevented Field from meeting the boy's eye.

The two children crossed over and spun their hoop along the sidewalk outside Lu's front door. They were both well dressed, the girl's blond hair in a pigtail, the hem of her white dress twirling as she turned to chase the hoop. The boy shouted something and ran after her. The Chinese servant who had been sweeping leaves through the back gate of his master's house stopped to watch them.

Field checked the windows again, but there was no movement. He could almost hear the minutes tick by.

Then he saw her. She had pulled the curtain back. She raised her hand, let it fall, and was gone.

Field stared at the curtains, willing her to reappear.

A Chinese woman in the uniform of a nanny or cook walked up to the front entrance and knocked. She was carrying a wicker basket filled with groceries. The door was opened. The children moved off down the road with their hoop in the direction of a well-dressed Frenchwoman who was leading a tiny dog, a large hat shielding her face from the midday sun.

The curtains did not move again.

Field expected to see her now. If she had got to the room and reached the ledgers, then it should be only a few minutes at most before she would leave.

It was half past one.

He tried not to think of what they would do with her if she was caught. Would they kill her in the house or take her somewhere else?

The full magnitude of what he had set in motion threatened to overwhelm him. She had always been a survivor, but he had forced her to risk her life for him, for what he wanted. *He* had forced her.

Field gripped the revolver still harder. He wound down the window a fraction, but there was not a hint of wind. The street was deserted, save for the Chinese servant who had returned to sweeping the back entrance to his master's house with the slow, methodical action of one who has no leaves left to sweep.

Field wiped his forehead with his sleeve and looked at his watch again. One-forty. He could feel the tension in his neck and back and legs as he looked up at the windows again. There was no sign of her.

Should he go in himself?

He glanced at Alexei. The boy was staring at him, desperation in his eyes.

"I had a wooden airplane," Alexei said.

Field turned back to the house.

"When I went to the orphanage, they took it away."

Field didn't want Alexei to talk. He could feel a muscle at the corner of his eye start to twitch.

"I asked if I could see his car. He always said 'soon.' I would still like to see it. I think it is a big one. He is very rich and has many airplanes. Mama said one day soon we will go away from Shanghai, to a better place, and then we will be rich and be able to go on airplanes and have our own car and everything will be very good."

"Come *on*," Field said to himself, willing the door to open.

He realized that he had no idea how she would get the ledger out of the house. It would be too big to conceal.

"Mama said he is very rich and can go on an airplane anytime he wants and he gave me one. A big one. I wish Father Brown had not taken it away."

The car was starting to feel like a furnace.

"What did they do with it, do you think, sir?"

Field tried to smile. "It's 'Richard.'"

"What do you think they did with it?"

It was one-fifty.

"I wish I had gone in his car. I think it was a big one."

"Come on, come on, come *on*," Field said under his breath, his eyes fixed on the door. He was cursing her now.

"I do not understand how he could have driven the car, though. He was not like you."

The children had returned and were playing with their hoop right outside Lu's front door.

"He only had one leg."

Field felt the rush of blood in his head.

"What? What did you say?"

Alexei did not answer.

"He only had one leg?"

"Yes."

"The man who gave you the airplane?"

Alexei nodded.

"He had one real leg and one wooden leg?"

"Yes. He was funny about it. I liked to knock it."

"He had sandy hair, with some gray. Flecks . . . little bits of gray?"

"Gray hair, yes."

"And he shuffled . . . with a wooden leg?"

"Yes."

Lu's car pulled up and the bodyguards jumped off the running board. Before Field could move, Lu got out and went inside, his men following him. Field began to push open his car door, then checked himself.

His every nerve end screamed at him to *do* something.

He forced himself to wait. The door opened.

Grigoriev led Natasha down the steps, a hand gripping her arm. She did not look up before she was shoved into the back of the car.

They drove off.

Field registered that there were two bodyguards left behind as he put his foot on the low speed pedal and pulled away from the curb. As he reached the turn, one of the men stepped out into his path, his machine gun leveled at the windshield.

Field stopped and the man came around and tapped his gun against the window. Field wound it down and tried to smile. The sweat was stinging his eyes. "Taking my boy to school. *Mon fils à l'école.*"

The man glowered, his machine gun inches from Field's face. The second bodyguard had moved to the front of the car, his Thompson aimed through the windshield directly at Alexei.

"I must—"

"Attends, attends," the Russian said sharply.

Field could see Lu's car disappearing, and his brain was screaming at him to do something. "My boy. *L'école est ici, là-bas.*"

"Attends!" the Russian barked.

"Mon fils, là-bas."

"Attends!"

Field took a deep breath. "May I go up and turn?" He forced his revolver between his knees and pointed to a side street.

The man shook his head. "Wait."

"I must—"

"Nyet!" The man hit Field in the face with his fist, then stepped back, his gun raised. Without lowering the barrel, he turned toward his colleague. They began speaking in Russian.

"What are they saying?" Field whispered.

Alexei was white with shock.

"What are they saying?"

The boy did not answer. Field gripped the handle of his revolver.

The Russians laughed, but the one standing in front of the car was alert, the barrel of his machine gun still pointing at Alexei's head.

" 'Another one for the Happy Times block,' they said,"
Alexei whispered.

"What do they mean?"

"The man has been waiting for his appointment. I do not
understand."

"They have taken her to the Happy Times block?"

"Silence." The man closest to the window stepped forward.
He pointed the muzzle of his gun at Field's head. *"Tais toi."*

They continued speaking to each other in Russian. Field
understood the word "Grigoriev," but nothing else.

"They are talking about when Grigoriev will be back,"
Alexei whispered, his head down.

Field's throat was dry. Bright pinpricks of light swam
before his eyes. A kaleidoscope of images: white sheets, red
blood, the glint of light on handcuffs, the downward arc of a
knife's blade. He tried to sweep them from his mind. Anna.
Irina. Lena. Natasha.

Natasha. He would force her to dress in the underwear he
liked. He would clamp her ankles and wrists to the brass bed.
He would look at her. He would take his time. He would hurt
her. She would be frightened. She would be wondering where
Field was and would not know that he was unable to help her.

He thought of the deep gashes in Lena's stomach.

He thought of Anna's body, twisted in a last, futile attempt
to protect herself.

Natasha would be able to do nothing.

She had been a victim ever since leaving Kazan and would
die like the others, abandoned and alone.

Geoffrey. How blind Field had been. Truly a fool, imagining as his investigation progressed that he was achieving some
mastery of a city where each truth only hid a deeper deceit.

The Russian in the front of the car turned away, and without thinking, Field began to raise his revolver.

The bodyguard beside him took a step closer. "The girl—
she was with you?"

Field shook his head. "Waiting for the boy's mother.

Always late!" Field forced himself to smile. The man did not respond.

"Is it a traffic problem?" Field asked.

"Not traffic."

"Do you mind if I get out and smoke?"

The man shrugged. Field pushed the revolver beneath his seat, then forced himself to get out. He took the packet of cigarettes from his pocket and offered it to both men. The one closest accepted and Field struck a match.

"It's a traffic problem?"

"Not traffic. You were with the girl?"

Field raised his hands, palms up. *"Mon fils est à l'école. Tard. Toujours en retard."*

The man shook his head. His French was clearly little better than his English.

The minutes crawled by. A light wind had got up and was creating small circles of dust along the edge of the sidewalk. Field pictured the deep craters in Lena's vagina and the thin strands of white skin strung across the top of them. He thought of the marks around her wrists and ankles where the handcuffs had rubbed as she'd struggled to break free.

In his mind's eye, he could see Natasha writhing and turning away to protect herself. He could hear her screaming in his head.

The men spoke in Russian again. Field could see Alexei's small, frightened face through the windshield.

He turned to face Lu's door, squinting against the sunlight and watching the burning ash as he sucked deeply on the cigarette.

He closed his mouth and exhaled, pushing the smoke through his nostrils.

Geoffrey couldn't kill Natasha.

Even as he tried to cling to the thought, he wondered at his own naiveté. He had placed Natasha's fate in the hands of a man he thought he had grown to understand, and yet did not know at all.

He could see Geoffrey's warm smile as he swept a hand calmly through his hair, the quiet confidence and authority he projected with every movement. He could feel the warmth of his handshake and the reassuring calmness and affection of his fatherly demeanor, the promise of a home away from home.

As the anger swelled within him, Field tried to conjure up an image of Natasha's face, but suddenly could not. He could see the wound on her chest, blood welling and flowing across her skin, but not her face.

He turned.

The Russians had not moved.

Field took a pace toward them, then forced himself to adopt an air of studied indifference. A man in a long khaki raincoat emerged from the street behind them. It was a moment before Field realized that it was Chen.

When he came level with the Russians, the Chinese detective affected to notice Field for the first time. He crossed in front of the two bodyguards as though they were not there. "Richard."

Field shook his hand and tried to smile.

"What are you doing here?" Chen asked, staring at him intently.

"Just taking my son to school. I'm . . . we're late. I'm not quite sure what the problem is."

Chen turned toward the Russians, speaking to them in their own language.

"They say you were with a woman." Chen was frowning, as if not having any idea what the men were talking about.

"No, no. I'm just . . ." Field cleared his throat and pointed at the car. "Taking my son to his school." He exhaled. "We're very late."

"Some woman, big trouble," Chen said. "They are worried you have something to do with her."

Field shook his head emphatically.

One of the men spoke directly to Field, in Russian. Chen translated. "He wants to know why you are taking your boy to school at lunchtime."

"Doctor. Doctor's appointment."

This time the conversation took several minutes, the Chinese detective no longer bothering to relay what the Russians were saying. Eventually, he turned back to Field. "A big problem, they say." Chen changed tack. "How was Allenby when you saw him last night?"

Field looked at him, confused, until he saw Chen's mouth tighten. "Oh, he was fine. You know. Just fine."

Chen's tone with the bodyguards became more forceful. He pointed repeatedly to both Field and the boy in the exchange that followed. "I've said you're a good friend of some very important people in the Settlement," he explained without turning around.

The Russians seemed unsure. They could no longer talk to each other without being understood, so stood in sullen silence, glancing up from time to time at the bright sun, as if the solution to their problem might suddenly reveal itself.

At length, the one closest to Chen stepped aside and waved his gun to indicate they could continue.

Field walked forward.

"Where are you going?" Chen asked. His manner was calm, his words unhurried.

"To the school."

"You're going on to the office?"

Field hesitated. "Yes, probably."

"I'll ride with you."

Field got behind the wheel and Chen moved around to the far side, nodding at the Russians as he passed. He slipped into the passenger seat, patting the boy on the head. He raised his hand at the men and smiled. Field moved off.

"They went towards Foochow Road," Chen said.

"The boy says they took her to the Happy Times block."

As he turned left, Field put his foot down on the accelerator.

"Not too fast."

The blood was pounding through Field's head.

"Slower," Chen barked.

"For Christ's sake."

"Be careful."

A tram had stopped ahead of them, a small group of people waiting to climb on board. Field began to pull out. "Wait," Chen said. He turned around. As Field was about to explode, he gestured with his hand. "Go on."

Chen looked back over his shoulder again. Field drove mechanically, the images around him disjointed and unreal, his gaze fixed on a yellow Chevrolet in front as they drove down toward the racecourse. "Slow," Chen said, exhaling. "Pull up before Happy Times."

Field drew up a hundred yards short, behind an old-model Ford that was disgorging a young family, the mother trying to prevent her two young children from running off down the street. Beyond them, Field could see Lu's men standing by the entrance. Grigoriev was smoking.

Field took the revolver from under his seat and put it back in its holster. "Stay here, Alexei. Don't leave the car." He got out and walked swiftly after Chen. He looked back once, but the men had not moved.

Chen led the way round to the back of the building and down a narrow alley. The service entrance was a black steel door, beyond a large bin overflowing with refuse. Chen took out his revolver and gestured to Field to pull the door toward him. They stepped inside.

The stairs led down to a basement and their footsteps echoed. Field fumbled for a light switch.

There were four or five buckets at the foot of the steps, a pile of paintbrushes, and a broom. Field could hear the low rumble of a boiler.

He held up the revolver, his palm slippery against the metal.

Chen raised his hand, his head tilted to one side. Field could feel the sweat gathering on his forehead.

They found the stairwell and emerged slowly into the light of the main hallway. As he opened the swinging door, Field could see Grigoriev standing outside with his back to him. They moved silently across the hall, Field's eyes never leaving the Russian. The front desk was empty.

They reached the entrance to the staircase.

Once beyond it, they sprinted up the stairs. As he neared the top landing, Field heard her scream.

Fifty-four

ield braced himself and kicked her door, hard, just beneath the handle. "Natasha!" He took aim and kicked once more.

He kicked again and again, until the frame started to splinter.

"Natasha!"

There was silence within.

The door gave with a crack like a pistol shot. Field crashed through it, raising his gun, Chen behind him. The curtains had been partially drawn. He blinked, trying to adjust his eyes to the patchwork of daylight and shadow.

The flat was silent.

There was the flickering glow of a candle in the bedroom doorway, and Field walked slowly toward it.

He saw her arms first, handcuffed above her head. She was almost naked. Geoffrey half sat, half knelt above her, his knife at her throat.

"Don't move, Richard."

He stepped into the room.

"Do not move." Geoffrey's voice shook with barely controlled anger.

Field stopped. He raised his hands slowly in the air, transfixed by the fear in Natasha's eyes.

"Put the gun down," Geoffrey ordered.

Field took a pace toward them.

"Both of you."

Field leaned over and placed his gun beside the bed. Chen,

standing directly behind him, bent down slowly and slid his weapon along the floor.

Field's heart was beating so hard he could hear it. He took another step forward.

Without a word, Geoffrey moved the knife from Natasha's throat and cut swiftly across the top of her right breast. She recoiled, giving a strangled cry. Field watched, frozen, as a rivulet of blood ran down the side of her breast and blossomed where it touched her camisole.

Natasha closed her eyes and, very softly, began to cry, her mouth shut tight, her teeth grating against the pain.

Geoffrey pressed the blade against the soft skin of Natasha's neck. "She is as good as dead, Richard," he said.

"I saw you as a father," Field said quietly. "I saw you as a hero."

"There *are* no more heroes, Richard. Did your father's suicide teach you nothing?"

"I don't think he felt he had a choice."

"His much-lauded integrity didn't take *him* to the front, though, did it?"

"He wanted to go. He failed the medical."

"Is that what he told you?"

Field didn't answer.

"You and your father are so alike it makes my skin crawl. That same insufferably sanctimonious sense of moral probity that you seek to impose upon the world."

"I grew up with the story of your sacrifice. It was your example that taught me there were things worth fighting for." Field searched for some humanity in his uncle's eyes but saw only the accumulated bitterness of the years.

"There's nothing left worth fighting for," Geoffrey said. "Open your eyes, Richard. Take a look around you."

Field moved closer, and Geoffrey sliced the blade once more across Natasha's chest. This time he did not even glance at her as she whimpered and writhed, the tears running down her cheeks.

"Don't do that again," Geoffrey said.

Field tried not to look at her, either. "This is because of what happened to you in the war?" he said.

Geoffrey went completely still. "Do you know how many men marched into Delville Wood that day?"

"Yes I do."

"And how many of us came back?"

"I understand."

"No you don't. You can't possibly understand. Nobody survived that day. We all died in Delville Wood."

"I'm sorry."

"Life goes on, of course. It goes on and on and bloody *on*. But people forget, Richard; they confuse meaningless sacrifice with nobility. The Great War? Oh yes. That was the war to end all wars. But Delville Wood? It's just a place on the map."

"I said I'm sorry."

"Spare me your pity. I've seen the look in your eyes when you watch me dragging myself through another roomful of bloody beautiful people. It's the same way Penelope looks when she's just been with someone who can fuck her—"

"What harm have these girls done you?"

Geoffrey's face twisted. "They despise me. They judge me. You all *dare* to judge me."

Field shook his head. "You've got it wrong, Geoffrey. My father destroyed himself by trying to prove himself worthy of you, of your family. So did Mother. She couldn't bear to incur your disapproval. They felt they couldn't measure up. The fact that you came back a hero was just . . . It made my father even more haunted by the mess he thought he'd made of our lives. He hated me for admiring you."

"So I've let *you* down as well?" The anger burned deep within Geoffrey's eyes. "You're disappointed, like your mother, that I'm not the man I was, that I am somehow diminished by my journey through seven versions of *hell? Damn you, Richard.* Your arrogance disgusts me. You've been in this city for little more than a heartbeat, and yet you believe you can lord it over us all."

"I've never believed——"

"Get out of my sight. And just see how long you last. This is *my* city, Field. It dances to *my* tune."

"Let me take the girl——"

A look of complete incredulity crossed Geoffrey's face. "She's a *Russian.*"

"She's got a little boy to look after. Anna's son."

"Get out, Field."

"It's not too late."

"Don't insult me further."

"It's not——"

"Get *out.* I'm damned if you'll lecture me. You cannot save the girl."

"*Why?*"

"*Because of the look in her eyes,*" Geoffrey exploded. "*Because of the promises she makes but cannot keep.*"

Natasha twisted suddenly, unbalancing Geoffrey, and Field lunged across the bed, grabbing hold of his knife arm. His momentum took them both crashing onto the floor.

Geoffrey managed to wrench himself round as they fell, forcing Field onto his back. The pain burned through Field's shoulder as he tried to keep his grip; Geoffrey was astonishingly strong. He looked up at the long blade closing on his neck and felt Geoffrey's free hand scrabbling at his face, fingers searching for his eyes.

Field let go with his right hand and hit him as hard as he could on the underside of the jaw. As Geoffrey's head snapped back, Field grabbed and twisted the knife, watching the blade disappear into Geoffrey's stomach as the bullet from Chen's revolver thumped into his uncle's chest.

Geoffrey's body went slack, his eyes widening in surprise, the knowledge of his own imminent death creeping across his face.

Field pushed Geoffrey off him and got to his feet. As he did so, Geoffrey began to convulse, at first violently, and then with diminishing force as the life drained out of him.

Field knelt and watched his uncle slip away, watched the cold anger disappear from his eyes, to be replaced by a sadness more profound than he had known.

The man who had sacrificed himself at Delville Wood searched Field's face, then fumbled for his hand. "Don't remember this," he said.

He tightened his grip, his hand slippery with his own blood. It was as though the Geoffrey that Field had once known was trying to summon himself back from the past, before it was too late. He struggled to speak, his mouth opening and shutting, but could not enunciate the words.

Field leaned nearer. Geoffrey closed his eyes. Field felt the dying man's breath on his cheek as he finally managed to whisper, "Don't—remember—this."

The pain ebbed from Geoffrey's face and his grip on Field's hand weakened. He did not open his eyes again. His breathing was now almost inaudible, the room suddenly quiet.

The silence was broken by the sound of footsteps pounding up the stairs. Chen was on one knee in the doorway. For a split second, Lu's bodyguards did not see them. Chen fired twice at Grigoriev, who fell back into the man behind him.

Chen stood, firing at the second man as he was still trying to scramble clear. The first shot punched a hole in his forehead, the second buried itself in his neck, spinning him back into the corridor.

Chen moved forward to check that they were dead, his shoes scuffing the wooden floor.

Field looked for a moment more at his uncle's face, then got slowly to his feet.

The keys to Natasha's handcuffs were on the table, next to the candle. Field wiped the blood from his hands on her sheet, then picked them up and sat on the bed beside her. When he had released her, she clung to him, her head on his chest, her fingers digging deep into his back. She sobbed quietly as he held her, her blood seeping through the front of his shirt.

Field gently prized her away and bent to examine the

gashes across her breasts. He stood and looked about him, then moved to the closet and pulled it open, ran his hands through the clothes that hung there, and pulled out a white cotton shirt and dress. He tore the material into strips and gently raised her chin. Her mouth was swollen and the skin around her right eye was already discolored.

Field folded a strip of the shirt. "Put your head back."

She did as she was told, closing her eyes as he placed the makeshift bandage across the first of the gashes and pulled it over one shoulder and under her arm, kneeling on the bed as he tied the two ends tightly behind her back. She caught sight of the blood seeping from the bullet hole in his shoulder. She touched his cheek with her fingers, her eyes on his, but he lowered her hand and continued to dress her wounds as best he could.

As he finished, she tipped back against him. His arms were around her, her hair in his face and mouth. "It's all right," Field said. He closed his eyes and breathed in the scent of her. "It's all right."

He held her tight, until her breathing began to ease. He ran his fingers through her hair, wiped the tears from her cheek.

Chen stood in the doorway. It was a few moments before Natasha seemed aware of his presence. She pulled away and walked to the corner of the room, where her raincoat was draped across a chair. She drew it around her, then reached into the pocket and threw a thick sheaf of paper onto the bed beside him.

"They said they had been looking for me. They made a telephone call. I only had a few minutes . . . less. I took as much as I could." She paused, the fear returning to her eyes. "Where is Alexei?"

"He's hiding in the car." Field stood. "We must go."

He leafed through the pages until he found the most recent entry: SS *Saratoga*, then today's date and the sum of $750,000 Shanghai.

Beneath it was a list of names and opposite each, a figure. Field ran his finger over the characters as he tried to decipher them.

She moved alongside him.

"Macleod," he said.

"Yes."

"Five thousand dollars."

"Yes."

"Geoffrey Donaldson, twenty-five thousand."

"Yes."

"Commissioner Biers, ten thousand."

She nodded.

"There is no mention of Lewis." Field handed Chen the pages and watched as the Chinese detective cast his eyes over them.

"Lu will not sleep until he gets these back," he said. "We must go *now*."

Field did not move.

"His men will turn the city upside down."

They heard a vehicle screech to a halt outside, followed by the sound of shouting and running feet. Chen ran to the window, Field half a step behind him. He saw Sorenson getting out of the front of a truck, in full protective gear, helmet on and a Thompson machine gun by his side.

A black Buick pulled up behind him, and Macleod stepped out onto the sidewalk. Another car stopped in the middle of the street, disgorging four of Lu's men, each also armed with a machine gun.

Chen opened the door to the balcony, stepped out, and fired twice in Macleod's direction, scattering the men below as they darted for cover. Then he walked past Natasha and out into the hall, letting off two more shots in the stairwell, before reloading his revolver with one hand. "The roof?"

Natasha looked puzzled.

"Up to the roof?" he barked. "How?"

"From . . . in the hallway."

There was a closet in the corner of the landing. Chen rattled the padlock briefly before stepping back, taking aim with his revolver, and shooting it off.

Inside, a bamboo ladder was stacked alongside a brush, a bucket, and a selection of cloths. Chen took hold of the ladder and pushed it at Field. "You must go."

"I can't."

"Otherwise, none of us will stand a chance. No one, Field." There were more shouts from below. Chen ran to the door and fired twice more into the stairwell. "If we are caught here, we will all be killed. You get out, and Lu cannot be sure what you have done with the ledger pages. That way, we all have a chance."

"The boy. I can't—"

"We have no *time.*"

They could hear voices again, coming up the stairwell.

Field pushed his revolver into the waistband of his trousers, took the ladder, placed it against the edge of the hatch, and began to climb. Natasha was staring upward, her face expressionless.

The stairwell was silent.

Field climbed out onto the roof and spun around. "The ladder," Chen whispered. "*Take* it."

It was almost weightless. Field hauled it up and threw it to his right. He took hold of the hatch cover. For a moment Natasha's eyes were fixed upon his.

Field hesitated. He could see she was certain that she would not see him again. He shook his head slowly.

"Go," Chen hissed.

Natasha turned away. Chen began firing again and Field heard a scream. He dropped the hatch cover and straightened.

The roof was flat and covered in gravel. Smoke from three tall brick chimneys drifted toward the tower above the race club. He could see the dome of the Hong Kong Shanghai Bank in the distance.

Field turned. The breeze tugged at his shirt as he made his

way to the side of the building, climbing over a series of telegraph wires. There was no wall or parapet. He stepped onto
the edge of the roof, making a conscious effort not to look
down. The building opposite was a foot or two lower, but it
was a long jump. He thought the gap was about ten feet, perhaps a little less.

The roof he was aiming for had no ledge around it, either.
A line of steel chimneys along its center billowed smoke in his
direction.

Field looked down. It was a long, straight drop to the alley
through which he and Chen had entered the building. Three
armed police officers crouched down by the service entrance,
next to the refuse bin. Another two were flattened against the
wall behind them.

Field turned before they had a chance to look up. The telegraph wires left him with only five or six feet of roof. It wasn't
enough to make the jump.

He heard more shots below and then a volley of machine-
gun fire.

Field focused on the roof opposite. He moved back as far as
he could go, until the telegraph wires were stretched taut
against the back of his legs. He closed his eyes for a moment.
He felt dizzy.

There was more shouting below. Field took his revolver
from his belt, opened his eyes, and ran, his feet thumping
against the gravel, the leap, the glimpse of the alley beneath
him, frozen in his mind before his feet smacked down on the
roof opposite and he tumbled onto his good shoulder, trying to
protect the gun and stop himself from screaming with the
pain.

He stood, unsteady, bits of gravel stuck to his shirt. There
was more gunfire from inside the building behind him, followed by the steady thump of machine-gun bullets.

A rusty iron ladder led up to a raised platform on the far
side of this roof. Field climbed onto it, the tower above the race
club still visible to his right.

He clambered over another line of telegraph wires and walked to the edge.

The next building was taller, beyond his reach, except for one small section directly ahead of him around a pair of chimney stacks. There was a ledge on this side where he would need to launch himself, making it impossible to get a running start, and only a foot or two of space where he could land, but he had no choice.

Field stared at the gap between the chimneys opposite him and the edge of the roof. There was a small rim along the edge, not more than the height of a single layer of bricks, but enough to grip hold of.

Field stood on the ledge, bent his knees, and then hesitated. His stomach lurched in the way it did when he was about to launch himself from a high diving board.

It was too far.

He looked around him. A window was open in the top-floor apartment of the building opposite, its lace curtain fluttering gently in the breeze. The alley beneath him was blocked at one end by a wall, so that there was no entry from Foochow Road. Lines of brightly colored washing were strung across it.

He could no longer hear gunfire.

Field closed his eyes briefly, then opened them, bent his knees and jumped, hurtling toward the ledge.

He hit it with the top half of his body, his hands scrabbling in the gravel and slipping, before catching the parapet. His legs dangled in space; one arm and shoulder fought to stay on the roof while the rest of him hung down the side of the building.

Field gradually pulled himself up, but then slipped farther, his shoulder on fire.

He tried not to look down but couldn't help himself. He saw only his feet and then the long drop to the alley below.

He managed to raise himself again, tearing his fingernails on the gravel, scrabbling for some kind of purchase with his feet, managing finally to get the inside edge of the sole of his right shoe into a small crack in the mortar. He put some weight on it, but a piece of the brick gave way and he fell farther, so that he was now hanging down vertically.

Field closed his eyes and pulled, willing the strength into his arms.

It was slow, and infinitely painful. He grunted, pushing his feet against the wall to relieve some of the pressure on his arms and shoulder, trying not to lose his grip on the ledge.

He got his good arm onto the roof and searched again for somewhere to put his feet. He found another tiny hole with the tip of his shoe and this time put less weight on it, pulling himself up slowly until both elbows, then shoulders, and finally his entire upper body were over the ledge.

He swung his legs around and then rolled over onto his back, staring up at the sky.

Field got to his feet. He waited until he had regained his balance, then climbed onto the chimney stack and rolled over onto the roof.

There was a hatch directly ahead of him, but before touching it, Field walked to each side of the building to get his bearings. The front of this building was directly opposite the racecourse, and he could see the truck and cars still parked in the street below.

A small group of uniformed officers stood behind a wall beyond the entrance to the Happy Times block, but Field couldn't see any sign of them on the other side or at the back.

He returned to the hatch, lifted the edge with his foot, and then tipped it off. He ducked down.

He could hear a baby crying but couldn't see anyone. He waited for a few moments, then climbed down a metal ladder bolted to the wall. The baby's wails echoed around the circular stairwell.

Field stepped onto the stone landing and waited again, breathing deeply. A mother or nanny was trying to soothe the child, but it cried still louder.

He put his back against the wall and began to walk down

the stairs, the revolver in his good hand, his eyes straining in the gloom. He saw a Chinese woman sitting with the baby, soothing it, caressing its forehead, rocking it from side to side. Field kept his revolver up, the sound of his footsteps echoing on the stone steps as he came down toward her.

The child's crying lessened. The woman caught sight of him but did not move or recoil, her eyes steadily on his. Field saw something in her look, compassion perhaps, then realized it was a warning.

"Stay where you are, Field. Lower your gun."

Prokopiev emerged from the shadows, the barrel of his revolver pointing at Field's forehead.

"*Lower your gun.*"

Field hesitated. The Russian's expression was hard and cold. Field imagined that this was the way he looked when he hurt the girls he brought back to the station house.

"Your gun."

Field slowly lowered his arm. They stared at each other. He thought fleetingly about turning and trying to run.

Prokopiev shook his head. "Shot in the back while trying to escape."

"I'm not escaping."

"Not yet." The Russian smiled.

"You've done this before."

Prokopiev nodded. "I have done this before. Do you still believe an officer of the law can afford to be an idealist in this town?"

"Someone has to try."

"Well, now is your chance." The Russian looked down. "I'm the only one here."

Field shook his head, not clear what the Russian meant. The adrenaline still pumped through him.

"You're a fool, Richard Field."

Field didn't answer.

"But a fool is better than a liar." Prokopiev gestured with his revolver. "Put the gun in your belt. You will need it."

Field frowned.

"This city makes liars of us all, Field. Liars and cheats." Prokopiev straightened, putting his gun back in its holster. His face was suddenly weary. "What good would it do me to kill you?" he said. "Perhaps you still have a chance to do something useful with your life. Just don't throw it away making bad choices." He turned and led Field down the steps. "Through here is a side entrance. All the buildings are being watched front and back, but I alone watch this alley, so go quickly."

"So Granger was right," Field said, almost to himself, "about everything."

"Granger was a man to follow, but now he is gone. And all you can do is run while you have the chance."

The Russian put a hand on Field's shoulder and then pushed him out into the sunlight, the steel door banging shut behind him.

Field walked away in a daze, his eyes half-closed against the sudden glare. He expected to hear a volley of shots and feel the sudden, devastating pain of their impact, but the alley was silent.

Fifty-five

he number one boy recoiled at the sight of him in the doorway at Crane Road. Field entered the house without further invitation and walked through to the living room at the back.

A record was playing. The mournful sound of a jazz band drifted through the open door to the veranda. Penelope was curled up in a ball in the corner of a wicker sofa, like a small child, staring at the lush green of her near-perfect lawn.

Field sat opposite her. He took out his cigarettes and put one in his mouth, his hand shaking violently as he tried to light it.

"I always know when he is going to meet one of his girls," she said. "It's the only time he allows himself to get excited." She spoke slowly. "It doesn't last, of course. They just remind him of everything he has lost."

"He's dead, Penelope."

"I always told myself," she went on, as if he had not spoken, "that it did not matter because they were *Russian* girls."

He didn't know if she was trying to provoke him, or if she didn't even realize he was there.

He stood and moved to the gramophone. He lifted the needle, then, in a fit of anger, swept the whole contraption onto the floor.

He turned, unsteady.

Penelope was sitting up. "Is it too late for me, Richard?"

"I'm not a priest."

Her eyes pleaded with him. "Please?"

"For God's sake . . ."

"He killed that girl, didn't he?"

Field stared at her. "Which one?"

Penelope frowned, her confusion genuine. Then her face collapsed as the truth finally rose up to swamp her.

"Do you *know* how these women died?" Field asked, taking a step toward her. "He stabbed them so many times, bits of skin were left strung across craters in their bodies the size of a bloody fist."

Penelope bowed her head.

"No one can give you absolution for that."

Field sat back down. He watched her shaking with her grief, but made no move to comfort her.

When Penelope looked up, her eyes were dark hollows, her face streaked with makeup. "I used to tell him he was the bravest man I'd ever met," she said. "But when he looked in the mirror, that wasn't what he saw."

"Everything changed at Delville Wood," Field said.

She nodded.

"And he took his anger out first on you, then on the Russian girls."

"He blamed me because I could not arouse him. At first it didn't seem to matter." She smiled sadly at him. "I thought love would provide the answer." She started to cry. "I thought it would be temporary. The impotence and the anger." She looked up. "His temper was so terrible, Richard. He would become furious with himself, with me. And then with the world."

"We know about Irina, Anna, Lena. Were there others?"

"When we came to Shanghai . . ." She sighed. "Oh, six years ago, it was to be a new start. For a time, I thought it had worked. At least he stopped hurting me. He didn't touch me anymore."

"But you knew he was hurting others?"

She looked down again. "I couldn't face going back, Richard. Please understand. I couldn't bear to go back."

"You knew he'd killed Lena."

A sad smile played at the corner of her lips. "Everything changed when you came, Richard."

"What do you mean?"

She sighed again. "Everything suddenly seemed so obvious. I—I don't know why I hadn't seen it before, but sitting opposite you on that first night, talking about that poor girl. I knew. I knew it must have been him. And, of course, I realized I had known since the beginning." She smiled again. "And he was always so on edge around you. He hated having you here."

"Why?"

She looked at him, amazed. "You really don't know?"

Field shook his head.

"You reminded him of who he was, Richard. You're the man he was and the man he could have been."

Field stared at her. "What are you talking about?"

Her expression grew more serious. "When the demons faded, you know, he could still be so kind and decent. He *was* the man you saw, the man you liked and admired. Once, he was like that all the time. He hated what he had become, hated the fact that he could not control himself. And he looked at you and saw the man he used to be and he hated you for it. For all that you have been through, you have kept your honesty. And he couldn't forgive you for that."

Field put his head in his hands.

Penelope leaned forward. "You need shelter. I can give you that. You will need money, and I can give you that, too."

"I don't want your money."

"It's not my money, Richard."

"They will turn the city upside down looking for me."

"They will never think to look for you here."

Field stared at the wall at the far end of the garden. He could hear a brass band on the Bund, practicing for tomorrow's Empire Day celebrations. He stood, walked to the end of the veranda, and looked out across the lawn. A servant was watering flowers. "Geoffrey was involved in a syndicate to smuggle vast quantities of opium into Europe. Did you know about that?"

"I knew he was getting the money from somewhere. He thought that I didn't know where he kept the key to his safe."

Field moved back toward her. "The opium was being shipped through one of Charles Lewis's factories, but Lewis's name doesn't appear on the list of payoffs that I have."

"Geoffrey always wanted to be rich like Charlie."

"The absence of Lewis's name on the list doesn't necessarily mean he wasn't involved."

"Charlie has more money than anyone could ever need." She shook her head. "Anyway, he doesn't think like that."

"How does he think?"

She looked at him, her gaze level. "He's more like you than you might imagine." She raised her hand. "Oh, I know you wouldn't accept that, and in an everyday sense you're right. He's unorthodox, even a little cruel at times. But he's honorable in his own way. Consistent, anyway."

"He's close to Lu."

She shook her head. "No, they tolerate each other. They have to."

"Lewis doesn't have to tolerate anyone."

Penelope shook her head. "You're wrong. He once told me that he viewed China as a great river. Sometimes you can divert it a little, but mostly you have to swim in the direction it flows. If Lu didn't exist, someone else would take his place. He, or his kind, cannot be eradicated, and Charlie likes stability. Rather the devil, you know. That is how he keeps himself and Fraser's where it is."

Field found himself thinking not of Lewis, but of Granger, using similar words on the sidewalk outside the Cathay Hotel in a world that seemed light-years away. Granger had understood.

He had the uncomfortable sense that he had been responsible in some way for Granger's death. He wondered if Lu and Geoffrey and Macleod had always intended to dispose of the Irishman, or whether his death had been an accidental by-product of their attempt to eliminate him and Caprisi.

"What will you do, Richard?"

Field looked down at the floor, trying to clear his mind. "I will contact Lewis and ask him to arrange a meeting with Lu.

Somewhere safe. Somewhere public. I'll offer them both exactly what they want, a continuation of the status quo."

"And what do you want in return?"

"Something that is of no importance to either of them."

"The girl?"

"The girl, yes. The *Russian* girl." Field heard the bitterness and reproach in his voice.

"Will you forgive me, Richard?"

He looked at her. She was biting her lip, on the verge of tears again, her face twitching nervously, and he understood her now. "You don't need me to forgive you," he said. "You need to forgive yourself."

Penelope looked down and began to cry again, but he still did not move.

She stood, shaking her head, and went inside. Field lit another cigarette, but barely raised it to his lips, watching the smoke drifting up beneath the eaves and melting into the sky, its blue now flecked with thin shards of gray.

Penelope returned and placed a brown envelope on his lap. "If you're to stand any chance at all, you will need this."

Field opened it up reluctantly, then spilled its contents onto the table in front of him.

"I haven't counted it, but I think there's more than ten thousand American dollars."

Field looked up at her.

"It's for you, Richard, and your Russian girl. I don't want it now."

"I cannot accept this."

"Then take it for her."

He shook his head. "No."

"Don't be stubborn, Richard. You have nothing left to prove here. You need to accept help." Her face softened. "I don't want the money. If you don't take it, I'll throw it away."

Field stared at the pile of cash spilling across the table in front of him. It was more money than he had seen in his entire life. It was enough money to live an entire life.

"I will take a thousand," he said, "if you agree to take the rest of the money to an orphanage. I'll give you the address."

She knelt in front of him. Her face was serious—soft and sane. "I'm not a bad person, am I, Richard?"

He didn't know what to say.

"Please." Her eyes implored him. She placed her head on his lap, like a child. After a few moments Field reached forward and placed the palm of his hand gently on top of her head.

The bedroom window was open, and Field could still hear the sound of the band on the Bund, but the garden was strangely quiet, shielded on all sides by new office buildings that had sprung up in the boom years since the end of the Great War.

There was a light wind up here, just enough to tug at the curtains.

He turned, realizing Penelope had been watching him from the doorway.

"Are you ready?" she asked.

"Yes."

Penelope breathed in deeply. "Forgive me if I don't come to the door."

"Of course."

"Good luck, Richard."

Field walked across the room, his footsteps loud on the wooden floorboards as he passed the foot of the iron-framed bed. He could not help glancing at the section next to the fireplace beneath which he had concealed the pages from Lu's ledger the previous night. He wondered if she had heard him pulling up the floorboards and understood.

He stood in front of her, their faces close. "What will you do?" he asked.

"Where will I go, do you mean?" Her eyes were peaceful now, her demeanor calm and unhurried. "I'll stay here, Richard. Unlike you, I have nowhere else to go. Or perhaps I should say, no reason to go anywhere else." She smiled.

Field pressed the knuckles of one hand with the fingers of the other.

She touched his shoulder. "Good luck."

Field bent to kiss her, but she took him into her arms, her grip tight as she held him. Then she released him and stepped back.

Field hesitated and then walked along the corridor. He stopped by the stairs and looked back.

She wore a fragile smile.

"Do you think," he said, "they will give me what I want?"

"I don't know," she said quietly, "but you are right to try."

Field looked at her. She stood with her legs together and her hands by her side, in a position of studied composure.

He put a foot on the stairs.

"Richard?"

Field stopped. He could tell it was taking every fragment of her strength to hold back the tears.

"He was a good man, you know. And that part of him was always there; it just got smaller and smaller."

She had begun to cry now, and Field stepped back toward her.

"No." She raised her hand. "Please." Penelope wiped her eyes. "Just tell me I was not completely wrong."

Field thought of the gaping wound in Lena Orlov's stomach, of Alexei's frightened face and the photograph that Maretsky had given him of Anna's mutilated body. He thought of Natasha's bruised lip and the fate that had so nearly befallen her. He hesitated, then looked up again at the diminutive figure in the shadows.

"You weren't wrong, Penelope." He shook his head. "You weren't wrong."

He began to walk down the stairs.

"Good luck," she said again.

Fifty-six

s the national anthem started, a great cheer went up. The crowd in front of him was a sea of red, white, and blue. They had gathered in their thousands, in front of the consulate. Field shifted to the right to get a better view.

He did not believe he had been followed from Crane Road, but there were so many people about that anyone who wished to tail him without being observed could easily have done so.

The sergeant, mounted on his horse in front of the guard of honor, shouted, "Three cheers for the king and emperor," and the crowd around Field erupted. "Hip, hip, *hooray!*"

Field helped a man who was struggling to get his young boy on his shoulders and rescued his Union Jack from the ground.

The nearest troops were the Sikhs, dressed in white, their buckles and bayonets gleaming in the midday sun.

A portly, middle-aged woman, with a tiny flag tucked into the band of her hat, turned to him with tears in her eyes. "Look at the marines," the woman exhorted him and whoever else was listening, gripping his arm. "Aren't they absolutely *marvelous?*"

The crowd began to sing the national anthem. Field watched the marines, who were ramrod straight and completely aware of the splendid, heartening spectacle they were creating, a reminder to every inhabitant of this city of the power of the empire, upon which their fortunes rested.

He checked the revolver in his pocket as a group of drunken young men surged forward, crushing those at the front as they attempted to drown out everyone around them with the noise of their singing.

Field edged forward, pushed himself closer to an elderly couple. They were talking to each other excitedly in German, the woman's face shielded behind an old-fashioned broad-brimmed blue hat. They were a wealthier version of the Schmidts and he excused himself as he shoved past them, fingering his revolver once more.

The crowd was thicker at the front, made up mostly of parents who'd fought to give their children the best view of the Bund. The white rope was ten yards from the line of Sikhs and only about a hundred from the gate of the consulate itself.

A gun went off as the national anthem came to an end—the midday salute.

He could see the sweat on the faces of the Sikhs as they stood to attention, their rifles now by their sides, the tips of the bayonets just above their ears.

There was another shout from the sergeant and they began to cheer, their turbans raised aloft on their bayonets. *"Sat Sri Akal!"*

Field pushed through the crowd again. He almost tripped over two young boys kneeling beneath the rope barrier.

As he walked toward the consulate building, a Sikh policeman, also dressed in white, hurried toward him. Field was sweating violently. "Richard Field, S.1," he said, holding open his wallet to display his identity card.

The man examined it more thoroughly than he needed to, perhaps for the benefit of the onlookers. Then he stepped away from the rope to let him pass. Field breathed a little more easily. He crossed the road and looked back at the crowd, which stretched to the line of masts and funnels on the quay behind and for as much as a mile in each direction.

He passed the line of marines and reached another group of Sikh guards outside the front gate.

"Field, S.1," he said, holding out his wallet once more.

The man he had approached was a sergeant, with a mature, confident face and a long, bushy white mustache. "I'm sorry, sir," he said, shaking his head. "But I'm afraid we have strict orders not to allow anyone through today."

"Charles Lewis is expecting me," Field said, his voice taut, sweat breaking out on his forehead again.

The Sikh continued to shake his head. "No one in here, sir, I'm sorry. C in C's orders."

"The C in C?"

The Sikh pointed to the man standing in the center of the dais overlooking the gardens, an extension of the terrace to the side of the consulate. He was dressed in white, with a large triangular, feathered hat. "Admiral Sir Edward Alexander Gordon Brewer, Commander in Chief, China Station."

"I'm from S.1, Sergeant. I'd appreciate it if you could send someone to find Charles Lewis and get him to come down here to collect me."

The Sikh was still shaking his head.

"I'm from S.1, Sergeant," Field repeated slowly, as if the man was hard of hearing. "If you don't want to be going home without your pension, I would get off your backside and go and find Charles Lewis. Now!"

Field had barked the order so loudly that a couple of women on the near end of the dais turned. The C in C was giving his address, but the wind was in the wrong direction. Field could not hear a word he was saying.

The Sikh was angry, but after a brief hesitation, he turned away and spoke urgently in his own language to one of his subordinates, who ran up the gravel path and through the big door at the top of the steps.

He was gone only a few minutes and returned to whisper in the ear of his superior, who then stood aside and opened the gate.

"Thank you, Sergeant."

Lewis was waiting in the hallway beneath a portrait of Disraeli.

"Good afternoon," Field said.

Lewis didn't reply. He led Field up a black and white stone staircase, past a series of oil portraits of previous commanders in chief of the China Station.

He stopped to allow Field through two enormous gold and blue doors and into a ballroom that was a more magnificent version of the Majestic, the wooden floor polished, huge mirrors interspersed with more portraits. He shut the doors quietly behind him.

Field walked to the end of the room and looked down over the head of the commander in chief at the dignitaries gathered on the lawn. The junks and sampans bobbed up and down on the wakes of the big metal steamers. The epaulets on the commander in chief's white uniform sparkled in the sunlight.

Field turned and it was a moment before he made out Lu standing behind Lewis, close to a small door in the far wall.

The Chinese approached, his eyes never leaving Field's face, his anger evident in every slow, deliberate step.

"One day, Mr. Field," Lu said, "none of you will be here. The . . . greed will hasten the end of the Europeans. But who can blame Mr. Geoffrey and his friends for wishing to use to the full the opportunities while they may?" For the first time, Field saw the hatred that burned in those small eyes, not just for him but for all of them, Lewis included. "You dare to summon me here?"

"I didn't summon you."

Lu tilted his head to one side. "You believe you will leave Shanghai alive?"

"That is for you to decide."

Lu sighed. "And what of the girl, the boy?"

Field did not answer.

"You come to my house. You steal my possessions. Mine. *Mine*. In my city. In Shanghai." Lu shook his head, then gave a cough that racked his body, making him seem momentarily vulnerable.

Field waited. "Natasha and the boy are all I want."

"You're insane," Lewis said.

"Insane," Lu repeated, alongside him. "Yes."

"I want—"

"You dare to bargain with me, in *this* city? I have many thousand men, and you believe you can *escape*?"

"I want the woman and the boy, that is all."

Lu stared at him, and this time Field held his gaze. "Yes," the Chinese said. "The girl is perhaps too old already, but the young boy . . . so vulnerable." Field felt the tautness in his throat.

"The boy . . . so much life ahead and yet, yes, still so vulnerable." Lu raised his hand to his cheek and scratched it idly, portly fingers against poor skin.

"I have the proof that you have been running an opium smuggling ring generating unimaginable profits, some of which you use to bribe almost every public official of importance in this city."

"Where do you have this proof?"

"Hidden."

"You have stolen *my* property."

"If anything befalls me, or the girl, *or* the boy, then you'll have a front-page article in the *New York Times* all to yourself. And that will just be the beginning of your problems."

Field watched the realization of the significance of what he was saying creeping across Lewis's face.

"This is China," Lu said.

"Washington and London would be forced to take some form of action, as Mr. Lewis will attest. Even if there were no prosecutions, the facts would be in the public domain, the ring would be broken, and untold damage would be done to your business interests. Even the everyday corruption in the Settlement police force could no longer be taken for granted."

Lewis took out his cigarette case, lit one, and walked to the window. Lu's eyes followed him, distractedly.

"You wish to have money?" Lu asked.

"No."

Lu smiled. "An idealist."

"The girl and the boy need a passport, papers. Mr. Lewis will arrange it. Once we have reached safety, I will tell you where to find the material that I have stolen. Your activities can continue uninterrupted."

Lu raised his eyebrows. "I see."

"I've told you what I want."

"Such a low bargain." Lu shook his head. "I am almost tempted." He raised his chin and scratched it again with his long fingernails. "You see, Mr. Field, the difficulty is, this is Shanghai. Not a foreigner's city. You steal my property and then you tell me what I must do. You... *threaten* me, yes? But how can this be? This is *Shanghai.* Who can say if you will leave this city? Who can say if the girl and boy are still alive?"

Field felt the blood draining from his face.

"You *demand* of me? No." He shook his head again. "No, no. It cannot be. An article in the newspaper you speak of? So far away. This is China. *China.* We can change so much before news travels so far. We can find the pages from my ledger. We can do anything, of course."

"My price is low, Mr. Lu."

"Your price is low? By whose... Who can say such a thing?"

Field felt the blood pounding in his head. He asked himself how he could have made such a terrible miscalculation, but his mouth continued to speak, as if no longer connected to his brain. "You will control China one day, I don't doubt it, but that day is not as close as you think. I offer you an arrangement that ought to disgust me; that *nothing changes.* All I ask is that two people who do not matter to you are released from your net. That is all. And one more thing: that Detective Chen is not harmed."

"He is Chinese."

"Yes."

"Out of the question."

"I insist."

"He is Chinese. This is not possible."

Field saw the fury in Lu's face as he struggled to remain calm himself.

"Of course, we do not wish to see our business interests disturbed." Lu looked down, taking a gold pocket watch from his silk gown. "You are correct to say that international attention would be inconvenient for all of us. I believe there is a sailing in three hours."

Lewis stepped forward. They had obviously discussed the details beforehand. "The *Martínez*, bound initially for Lisbon," Lewis said. "You will be on this ship. Provided that you are, and that there is no interference with the *Saratoga*, or sharing of the information you now possess, then Mr. Lu will dispatch the girl and the boy on another sailing two weeks from today. They will disembark at a port of your choosing."

"Venice."

"Very well. When they arrive in Venice, you will send Mr. Lu a telegram. It will contain the exact whereabouts of the stolen material and of any other documents that may be embarrassing to him. Providing that you do not mislead him, you and the girl may then live out your lives in peace. He has no interest in either of you, as long as you never return here. Is that clear?"

Field nodded. "Yes. But I must have a guarantee that Chen will not be harmed."

Lewis shook his head. There was steel in his eyes. "You will get no such thing, Field," he said, speaking as if Lu were not present. "Believe me."

There was a long silence. Lu said, "Good-bye, Mr. Field."

The Chinese turned and walked very slowly to the door.

Lewis turned his hat in his hand. He moved around the room, waving it at the grand ceilings and the portraits of administrators, admirals, and generals that adorned the walls. "This is China, Richard, though in here you wouldn't know it." He stopped and turned to Field. "We can never tame the tiger. Only ride it for a time."

"I know."

"You won."

"It doesn't feel like winning."

Lewis turned away.

"Will he send the girl?" Field asked, unable to contain the question.

Lewis faced him again, his expression serious. "I don't know, Richard. Only he can answer that. You will leave safely, in deference to me, but the girl is his possession." Lewis exhaled. "I cannot say, nor am I in the business of trying to save Russian girls through some foolish romantic notion. But you've done all you can. You must leave now."

Lewis spun his hat in his hand once more and then turned and walked to the door. "Good luck, Richard," he said. "Begin again. That's my advice. And be less ambitious in what you strive for next time. We must temper ourselves. Too grand and unrealistic a set of expectations can only lead to heartbreak. And not just your own."

Field felt the tightness in his throat again.

"Don't you want to know where she is?" Lewis asked.

Field found it impossible to reply.

"She's at her friend's house, Field. At Katya's." Lewis put on his hat. "Good-bye. I doubt we'll meet again."

Field listened to the sound of Lewis's footsteps disappear, then walked to the window and watched him emerging into the gardens, his white suit and hat brilliant in the sunshine. He stopped in the middle of the lawn, his stance casual, his hands in his pockets. A young woman in a flowing white dress approached him, her face flushed with the heat and the excitement. Lewis took off his hat and bent to kiss her, a hand resting easily upon her shoulder.

Katya's face looked older through the window of the house in the French Concession, her eyes framing questions that Field could not answer. She led him through the kitchen to Chen, who was leaning against the wall at the bottom of a winding staircase.

Field wiped the sweat from his brow and tried to calm himself. "I couldn't——"

"I know."

"No, I asked that you be protected——"

"Don't worry, Field."

Chen's calmness helped still Field's nerves and the guilt that had been consuming him since he'd left the consulate.

"Come with us, with me. Get your wife and family and come with me, on the boat."

Chen shook his head.

"If you stay, you know they will kill you."

"I was born here. I will die here if necessary."

"They'll hunt you down. You know it better than anyone."

"They will try."

Field looked down at the floor. "I could have used Lu's notes to change things. I could still do as I threatened and send them to the right people in London and Washington, to the *New York Times,* newspapers in England, Tokyo, Paris."

Chen laughed, tipping back his head, his smile only fading when he realized that Field had been serious. "There will be change here, Field, have no fear." Chen shook his head, smiling again. "No, no." He pointed up the stairs. "She is there. The boy was tired."

"Where will you go, Chen?"

"I have friends."

"In the city or elsewhere?"

"In all places."

Field suddenly understood. "You're a communist . . ."

"Whisper it quietly." Chen smiled.

Field shook his head.

"One day, you may come back to China, Richard. Then you will find no Lu Huangs, no Macleods, no taipans, and foreigners will be welcomed as honored guests."

Field stared at him. "Who else? There are many—in the force, I mean."

"They will have their time." Chen nodded. "The girl waits for you."

"There are three men at the gate. They followed me from the consulate."

"Of course."

"Will you go now?"

"When it is time."

Field hesitated. "Will Lu keep his word?"

Chen shook his head solemnly. "I do not know."

Field offered his hand, but Chen waved it away to indicate that it was not the end. Field held his stare until he rounded the corner and was climbing the last few steps to her room.

Natasha was asleep on the bed, in her dressing gown, her head resting on her arm. She was curled up, her hair spilling across the white sheet.

She awoke and pushed herself upright, her eyes bleary. "Richard?"

He sat down beside her.

"You must leave." Her voice was sleepy. "They will come for me now."

"It will be all right, Natasha."

"No, you must—"

"Natasha." He took hold of her arms fiercely. "It will work. Trust me."

She pushed herself onto her knees and stared at the empty bed between them. "Alexei is asleep in the next room. I . . ." She fell toward him, her arms around his neck.

When she released him, she took his face gently between her hands, her mouth close to his. "You have risked everything for me," she said.

"I have reached an agreement," he said. "I must leave today, now, but you and Alexei will follow in two weeks, and we will meet in Venice." He lifted her chin. "Together in Venice, the two—three—of us."

Hope flared briefly in her eyes, then she lowered her head.

"You're free, Natasha. Both of you are free."

"I cannot come to the wharf."

"I understand."

She looked at him, tears in her eyes. He moved toward her, but she raised her hand. "You must go."

Field stood and she came to him, her arms around him, her tears wet on his face. "My love," he said as he caressed the back of her head.

And then she released him again and turned away, so as not to look at his face. "Good-bye, Richard," she said with a finality that suggested she was certain she would never see him again.

He waited for her to turn around.

"Please go, Richard."

His throat was dry. "I cannot."

"You must."

Field felt the tears welling in his own eyes and he turned back down the stairs. Chen had gone and Katya was sitting at the kitchen table. He stopped in front of her. "It will be all right," he said, but as he moved beyond her and stepped onto the path outside, he felt as if he were drowning.

When he calculated that he had gone far enough to be seen from her attic window, he stopped and turned around.

She was not there.

Fifty-seven

he quayside was busier than Field had seen it, streams of coolies running up and down the gangplanks, loaded with leather trunks, cranes above them swinging cargo onto a steamer moored astern of the *Martínez*. The sudden hoot of a horn made Field jump.

A coolie bent down to take a hold of his bag.

"No," Field said, trying to prevent him, before realizing it was hopeless and showing the man his ticket with the cabin number listed above the second-class stamp.

Field followed the man up the gangplank.

Once on deck, they ducked through a door and down a steep companionway to the base of the ship.

Field was sharing a cabin above the engine room, which was all that had been available, and his companion had not yet come aboard. He watched the porter lift his bag onto the lower bunk—it would be cooler below—before turning expectantly. Field shoved a note into the man's hand; he looked at it but did not move.

Field reached into his pocket and gave the man all the small change he had left, which was not much. After the porter had reluctantly withdrawn, Field shut the door and locked it, then took out and checked his revolver.

He sat down on the bunk and faced the door, then looked around the small cabin, trying to ignore the smell of diesel and oil and remembering how sick he had been in the tiny third-class cabin on the way out. It would, he thought, be simplest for Lu's men to kill him now. His body wouldn't be discovered until they were well out to sea.

He stood.

He took out his key, locked the door after him, and climbed quickly up the steps to the deck. He walked to the rail overlooking the quayside, where he was in full view of a hundred people or more.

Field scanned the crowd.

Every face was a disappointment, though he told himself he had not expected her to come.

The sun was sinking slowly over the city, but was still bright enough to make him squint as he watched the plumes of smoke blowing across the rooftops in the gentle, late-afternoon breeze.

The horn on one of the funnels above him let out a series of loud blasts, and Field turned back to the quayside to watch the last of the passengers saying their farewells. His eye was drawn to a smartly dressed woman in a yellow dress and small, fashionable, matching hat, who was saying an emotional farewell to her husband and teenage children.

There was another, longer series of blasts, and the coolies assembled by the gangplanks. They pulled them back, then caught the ropes from the bow and stern as the *Martínez* drifted slowly out into the current, its engines surging as the propellers began to churn the muddy waters of the river.

And then he saw Penelope, a small, frail figure amid the crowd. She raised her hand to him and he acknowledged it.

She stepped forward, coming to the very edge of the quay, her eyes fixed on his, her hand suspended in midair. He could see that she was crying.

Field raised his own hand as the liner gathered steam and the propellers turned faster and the quayside began to recede, then he walked slowly down to the stern, flicking his cigarette far out into the river. He watched the sampans bobbing up and down in their wake.

"Mr. Field?"

He turned to see a man in uniform, with a gray mustache and a pleasant smile.

"I'm Captain Ferguson."

They shook hands.

"Mr. Lewis asked me to make sure your voyage is comfortable, so if there is anything I can do, please don't hesitate to ask. You are down below?"

Field nodded. "Yes."

"We'd be happy to move you up into a first-class cabin on deck here. We have one available."

Field hesitated. "Thank you," he said. "I'll be fine where I am."

The captain looked disappointed. "If you change your mind, please let me know. In the meantime, I hope you will at least do me the honor of dining at my table tonight."

"Yes, of course."

Field turned back toward the river. The buildings around them were dwindling in number and size, obscured gradually by the black smoke drifting across the sky from the factories in Pudong.

As they moved around the bend in the river, he watched the Union Jack high above the dome of the Hong Kong Shanghai Bank flapping idly in the breeze and faintly heard the clock on the tower of the Customs House striking the hour.

Field watched until they were gone.

Depression settled upon him. It was as though, with his last glimpse of the city, Natasha had slipped away from him, too.

The passengers melted away back to their cabins, and soon the buildings gave way to a patchwork of green paddy fields and small villages, close enough for him to see the children running along the banks of the river, waving.

Field walked to the bow and looked dead ahead as the *Martínez* left the river and began to pitch heavily as they struck out for the open sea.

The wind had strengthened, whipping the spray into his face.

He closed his eyes. He held on to the rail and tasted the salt in his mouth. He could hear his father's voice. "Whatever happens, Richard, don't be fortune's fool."

He suddenly felt terribly tired.

Epilogue

t was another of the perfect days Field had already grown accustomed to. He sat on the cobbled edge of the quay, the sinking sun still sparkling across the still waters of the lagoon.

He kicked his heels against the wall and watched the sea lapping beneath his feet. He looked at his watch for perhaps the hundredth time.

He examined the telegram. The *Aurora*, it said. September 1.

The lagoon seemed to Field to be surprisingly deserted. In the distance, two or three gondolas plied their trade off St. Mark's Square, and, beyond them, there was only the steamer that he'd spotted a few minutes ago.

He stood and walked across to the man who still leaned against the door of his office, his blue cap pushed back off his forehead and his tie and collar loose. "The *Aurora*?" Field asked, pointing toward the ship in the distance.

The man shrugged and Field smiled. He offered him a cigarette. "Perhaps," he said encouragingly, as Field lit it for him.

"A girl?" the man asked.

"Perhaps," Field replied.

Field wandered back to the water's edge. The liner was approaching fast, her white hull catching the sunlight as she steamed toward them.

He took his hat off, wanting to make sure that he was conspicuous, and tapped it against the side of his leg.

He did not move. He ran his fingers through his short hair,

trying not to let his mind run ahead of events once again. During the long nights here, hope had been his enemy, his imagination turning over a thousand times what her reaction would be to this city, to a life of freedom.

He could see her laughing—that was how her face always appeared to him now—her hand cool in his as they walked together.

Sometimes he even thought about what he was going to do with the boy. He'd need to be educated, of course. Field wondered what his mother and Edith would make of what he'd done, and how they would take to Natasha.

They would love her, of course.

If she came.

He put his hands in his pockets.

"The *Aurora, si,*" the man said behind him.

"Shit," Field whispered.

She was slowing, turning, and Field could see now that some of the passengers were gathered on deck.

He scanned their faces, trying to hold his nerves in check, but unable to see Natasha or the boy.

The *Aurora* came closer and closer. He found himself replacing his hat and staring down at the waters below as the ship edged toward the quay.

Field took a few paces back and waited.

He watched as the ropes were thrown down and secured, and a gangplank raised.

The passengers began to disembark, his eyes fixed upon each face. He saw no sign of her.

The last vestiges of hope drained slowly away, until there were no more faces. The passengers who had disembarked were now talking to the relatives who had greeted them, leaving the liner empty, save for the crew.

She had not come.

Field bent his head. He had known it was impossible.

He took another step back and looked up once more.

A Chinese in a dark suit and fedora stood at the top of the

gangplank, his eyes upon him. He stared at Field for a long moment, then moved back.

And then Natasha was coming down toward him, Alexei behind her, holding up a small brown suitcase and waving.

The Chinese disappeared.

For a moment Field stood motionless.

A gust of wind caught his hat and sent it spinning toward the water, and he was running toward her outstretched arms.